DROWNING TIDES

Also available from *New York Times* bestselling author

Karen Harper

South Shores

CHASING SHADOWS

Cold Creek

BROKEN BONDS
FORBIDDEN GROUND
SHATTERED SECRETS

Home Valley Amish

UPON A WINTER'S NIGHT
DARK CROSSINGS (featuring "The Covered Bridge")
FINDING MERCY
RETURN TO GRACE
FALL FROM PRIDE

Novels

DOWN RIVER
DEEP DOWN
THE HIDING PLACE
BELOW THE SURFACE
INFERNO
HURRICANE
DARK ANGEL
DARK HARVEST
DARK ROAD HOME

Visit karenharperauthor.com for more titles.

Look for Karen Harper's next South Shores novel

FALLING DARKNESS

available soon from MIRA Books.

KAREN HARPER

DROWNING TIDES

ISBN-13: 978-0-7783-3057-8

Drowning Tides

For questions and comments about the quality of this book, please contact us at CustomerService@Harlequin.com.

www.MIRABooks.com

Printed in U.S.A.

To our Boca Ciega friends Jim and Lee Ann Parsons
and my Naples, Florida, readers.

DROWNING TIDES

CHAPTER ONE

2014

"I'll get her back, Claire. I swear to you, I'll get your daughter back."

"*We'll* get her back together," she insisted, turning toward Nick as he drove the rental car across I-75 to Miami where they would catch their plane.

Thank God, Claire thought, Florida was narrow west to east, but the drive across the state on what Floridians called Alligator Alley seemed endless. Claire's four-year-old daughter, Lexi, had been kidnapped, taken to the Caribbean island of Grand Cayman. They had round-trip Cayman Airways tickets, leaving this morning from Miami and getting in to Grand Cayman early afternoon. They also had reservations for a place to stay on the island—all provided by the kidnapper who wanted much more than Lexi.

Claire clenched her hands so tightly in her lap that her fingers went numb. She frowned at the canal where alligators basked like logs in the early morning sun, and white herons and ibis fluttered in the tops of mangrove trees. Early October was just past the rainy season, and the air seemed crystal clear. But nothing looked beautiful to her anymore.

How could she ever have imagined when she went to work for criminal lawyer Nick Markwood that it would come to this? The two of them had been through hell enough already, but this horror was so much worse.

"Let's go over some things again," Nick said.

Ever clever, seemingly calm, even in the chaos of his own life, and now hers and Lexi's too, Claire thought. But she clung to that. She needed that—and him.

"Yes. Yes, all right," she agreed. "I know we have to go along with him, play by his rules. But we have to find his weakness, a way to save Lexi and you too—if he lets any of us go."

"Clayton Ames controls people the way he does his international business empire," Nick said of the sixty-four-year-old billionaire business mogul.

"Except for you. He found he couldn't control you, that you would pursue him for your father's murder, even if he had it staged to look like a suicide. You'd think by now he'd ignore your attempts to prove that, since he always just slips out of reach. Nick, that's what terrifies me about him having Lexi—and soon having us. He can make people disappear."

A noisy semi went around their car with a deep honk of its horn. They passed the exit to the Miccosukee Seminole Indian reservation on the edge of Everglades National Park. The lush foliage merged with the saw grass prairie of the Glades with its tree-filled raised mounds called hammocks. At last a scattering of West Coast buildings appeared along with green-and-white highway signs to Fort Lauderdale and Miami.

She stared at Nick's profile, which was seemingly set in stone. She was grateful he was as obsessed with saving Lexi as she was, and she loved him all the more for it. It seemed the long night they'd spent planning and packing had etched deeper lines on his chiseled face. The silver streaks along the temples of his dark hair seemed more pronounced and his gray eyes more intense than even during the days they'd struggled to get answers and stay alive on the St. Augustine murder/suicide case. He suddenly looked older than thirty-nine, but then, she felt far beyond thirty-two today.

How ironic she'd decided she would not work as his forensic psychologist again if an assignment took her away from Lexi, and now her daughter had been taken away from her—from her own front yard. Claire had vowed she'd stay home in Naples and stick to more mundane investigations through her Clear Path fraud-fighting website, but here they were, more desperate than ever.

"As I said, expect the worst from Clayton Ames," Nick told her, his voice hard as it always was when he spoke of his archenemy. "We have to watch what we say at all times, in the airport, on the plane, even once we get to our Grand Cayman hotel, because he could have places bugged or his lackeys hovering. Expect to be under invisible surveillance day and night. We'll walk on the beach away from others if we want to be sure we're not overheard. Nothing about Jace, especially. He's risking his neck to fly down on his own in case we need him."

It went unspoken between them that they couldn't have stopped Jace Britten anyway. Her ex-husband had arrived at Claire's house just after Lexi was taken and saw the threatening note the drone had delivered. Lexi's abductor had evidently driven a car like Jace's and even resembled him to a degree, to get the child close enough to grab. But Claire had to agree with Nick that Jace could be a loose cannon in all this.

"Jace and I may be divorced, but he'd do anything for Lexi."

"And for you," he said, turning to shoot her a sudden stare before looking back to the road. "He still cares for you a lot."

"I'll never forgive myself if his plan to fly down there on his own blows up. He's a skilled pilot and used to jets, so it's not that. But rather if he's harmed once he's there or ruins our chances of getting Lexi back."

"At least he knows the stakes. But as I said, Ames likes to know exactly what his competitors, even in business, are saying and thinking, what's going on. I wouldn't have rented this car at the last minute if I didn't think he'd manage to bug my other one."

"I know," she said, her voice shaky. She looked at the narrow, deep waterways that ran along this four-lane highway. "I'll be careful what I say and when." She turned toward him, tugging her seat belt out to give herself room to sit sideways. "Nick, I can't thank you enough for risking yourself to get Lexi back. I know Ames means to harm you."

"He does, but I'm banking on the fact he likes to exert his power, make his enemies twist and turn, control and ruin them, torment them. I'm hoping he means to make me toe his line somehow, not just trade my life for hers."

Claire broke into tears again when she'd tried since yesterday to keep calm. But she felt she was spiraling down into a dark hole. At least she didn't have a horrible dream last night from her narcolepsy in the half hour she'd gone to sleep. Right now, she didn't need her so-called "sleeping disease" or her powerful meds that controlled it. Despite her deep exhaustion, for once, she couldn't sleep.

"Sorry. I'm okay. I mean, not okay, but holding up. Really," she tried to assure him as she grabbed for a tissue in her purse on the car floor and swiped under her eyes.

"I'm sorry too, sweetheart," Nick said, reaching over the console to grip her knee with one hand. "But, despite all this, I can't be sorry we met, that we—we care for each other.

Again, I swear to you on my life, we will get Lexi back and get through this. Then I'll leave your life so that bastard doesn't try to use you and those you love to get to me again."

A tear trickled down Nick's cheek from under his sunglasses, but, focused on the road again, he ignored it. She loved him desperately despite hating him too over this—didn't she?

Claire made herself look away from him. Fear was on his face but fury too. Did he know her heart was broken not only over Lexi but over what he'd just said—that once they got her back, Nick would leave their lives?

As Nick took the turn south toward Miami International Airport through a maze of curved and elevated ramps and overhead signs, the horrible day he'd found his father dead came back to him. That waking nightmare crashed in on him sometimes when he least expected it. His attorney dad whom he adored and had later patterned himself after, dead. His head partly gone. Pistol in hand. Blood spatter and brain matter on the wall behind his desk.

He heard again his own shrill, young voice. "Dad! Dad! Dad!"

Obviously a suicide, the coroner ruled: late at night, wife out of town, son supposedly asleep upstairs, trajectory of the bullet, spatter pattern, only the deceased's fingerprints on the gun. And the fact his father had recently lost huge real estate investments, ones he'd made on the advice of his trusted friend, Clayton Ames, Nick's "Uncle Clay." Later, in his teens, Nick had found papers stashed in a metal box that showed his father had meant to expose Ames as a cheat and fraud.

But Nick had known even then, his mother did too, that Dad would not have killed himself and left them broke and bereft like that. The only good thing that had come from their public family tragedy was Nick's dedication to become a criminal lawyer and eventually to found two entities to help distraught people: Markwood, Benton and Chase, LLP, the law firm in which he was a senior partner; and South Shores, a secret, separate enterprise that sought out and defended those who were wrongly accused of or ruined by murder or suicide.

Once he'd seen forensic psychologist Claire Britten testify in court about interviewing witnesses and suspects, he'd known he needed her on his South Shores team. The problem was, it hadn't taken him long to learn he needed her in other ways too, though he'd tried not to mix purpose with pleasure. They had not yet made love, but he wanted her desperately. Before this chaos, he'd had hopes he could convince her they should be seriously looking at a life together. Now, he might even lose his life, but he was not going to forfeit hers—or Lexi's.

"You need to try to sleep or at least rest, now, on the plane too," he told Claire. "We're going to need, as they say, our wits about us."

"I can not only do my best, but what is necessary. My mother used to say that. I suppose she got it from one of her books she always had her nose in. My sister and I say it sometimes to get through tough times. Nick, I wish I could have told Darcy what happened. She's going to think I'm nuts, that I've taken Lexi and run off with you, like I stupidly eloped with Jace. But I had to leave her that note about us taking time away so she wouldn't call the cops. No cops, Ames's note said."

"She'll understand when you get Lexi back, when you can explain the truth, or some of it. We'll be there soon. Trust me, Claire. Again, on my life, I swear we'll get her back. Close your eyes. I've got to keep mine on this heavier traffic."

Out of the corner of his vision, he saw her settle back in her seat. But a big 747 jet taking off overhead from the Miami airport made her open her eyes again, sit forward and look up. Her ex was an international airline pilot, so what was she thinking in that beautiful head of hers? He was afraid to ask because he knew in his gut that she and Jace still cared for each other and not just because of the endangered child they shared.

Besides, unfortunately, Jace was blond and rawboned handsome, a real take-charge guy. Emotional, even volatile for a former navy pilot, Nick thought, so that could spell more trouble if the guy was frustrated or cornered in Grand Cayman. Still, even when Jace Britten was angry, he radiated that top gun charisma women probably went for. Evidently, Claire had fallen for him and hard. She'd said she'd eloped with the guy.

After she settled herself again in her seat, Nick stole one more glance at her. Her body stayed tense. Here in South Florida, she always seemed slightly unworldly, out of place with her porcelain complexion and stunning red hair—natural red hair, the color of a sunset over the Gulf. Most tourists and Floridians were tanned like he was, and her hue of hair was so—so Irish, or like a painting of an angel.

But her delicate appearance was deceptive. She was strong, great at psyching out people's lies and deceits and patching together the truth. She performed what lawyers called forensic autopsies, where a person, living or dead, was dissected through their statements and deeds to ferret out guilt. When he'd hired her, Claire already had a small consulting firm she called Clear Path. He wished he could find a clear path for her and Lexi—and himself—out of this looming catastrophe.

He felt guilty that he'd caused this crisis and at how much he still wanted her. He figured she knew that. And he was scared, not at how finding someone he could trust and love had finally come his way, but that, even if he saved Lexi, he had to lose Claire so Ames couldn't hurt her like this again.

Jace cruised over Cuba in the Cirrus SR22 turbocharged plane he'd borrowed from an old buddy who was a lot richer than he was. It was legal to pass over the embargoed island in a small plane. Several of his hotshot pilot friends had faked engine problems and asked for an emergency landing there just to look around in off-limits Havana. This was one heck of an emergency, but no way he was stopping anywhere but Grand Cayman.

He planned to get there in slightly under the three-hour flight plan he'd filed back at the Marco Island Executive Airport. He'd picked that smaller facility instead of Naples Municipal Airport, hoping the spying eyes of that damned Clayton Ames would have more trouble finding him there. Jace had obviously been researched and watched. He'd been sent photos of Nick and Claire together at an address no average outsider should have, but Ames's long arms seemed to pull a lot of strings. He felt really guilty that the guy who had snatched Lexi had resembled and pretended to be him.

The distance was just under 400 nautical miles, and he was pushing the Cirrus near its top speed of 180 knots, hovering just under its ceiling of 17,500 feet since the plane was not pressurized and he didn't want to mess with supplemental oxygen. He wanted to land at MWCR in the Cayman Islands as if he was a tourist. He'd case the area where Nick and Claire would be staying and, no doubt, where they would be contacted. Just as when he'd flown jumbo jets to Singapore and back or when he'd gone on Middle East combat missions, he wanted to be prepared and ready.

He didn't really have a specific plan after he landed, but he'd recon and get one. Anything he had to do to find this Clayton Ames who held his daughter's life in his dirty hands. So what if Nick Markwood said he'd been trying to get the goods on him, even locate him for years because he moved around so much? The guy might be rich, powerful and slippery, but he was going to pay for this, even if Jace had to take orders from Markwood for a while. Even if Claire was staying with the rich lawyer in what were probably luxurious digs on a gorgeous beach on a tropical island. Even if—this really scared him too—she seemed to trust Markwood, to look at him as if...

Damn, why hadn't Claire been content to just run Clear Path from her home office and steer clear of criminal investigations? She put her life—all their lives—in danger. This whole mess really got to Jace. It would be so easy to just end things up here over this vast blue-green water, to just disappear. Maybe Claire would talk to people he knew to try to find out if he'd been suicidal, why he'd kept changing his work flight schedule, why he'd considered giving up the international flying career he'd worked so hard for. She could use her forensic autopsy skills on him even if they never found his body.

He shook himself loose from that sick daydream. He was going to not only survive, but live. Really live. And with Claire and Lexi by his side.

CHAPTER TWO

As Claire and Nick's Cayman Airlines jet dropped toward the island's airport, Claire pressed her forehead to the window. Her beloved little Lexi was down there somewhere. Terrified? Tied up? Locked up? Drugged? Claire's mind could not let her go further. She prayed for her daughter's safety again, trying to send her silent reassurance and love.

"Those two cruise ships anchored there look like toys in a bright blue bathtub," she told Nick as he leaned closer to look out too. "Amazing, long, white beaches, even compared to those in Naples."

"That one is Seven Mile Beach. Look how close George Town is to it. Did you learn much when you checked out the islands online last night?"

"Until my eyes crossed. Like a lot of resort areas, it seems a mix of rich and poor, good and bad. For us, I'm hoping for the good."

She bit her lower lip and blinked back tears. Except when they'd had ginger ale to calm their nervous stomachs, she and Nick had held hands for most of the flight. They pretended to sleep at times so the lady with the British accent in the aisle seat would stop being so chatty. They couldn't put it past Ames that she was a plant. After all, he'd sent the tickets with the ransom note, so he could have bought three seats instead of two.

"And, of course, it's a tax haven," Claire went on, keeping her voice low. "Grand Cayman's offshore investment reputation means a lot of those pretty pastel-and-glass buildings down there are just fronts for companies that aren't really located here but want to escape taxes." She whispered even lower, "I read that big firms like Apple, Walmart and Exxon do business here. No wonder..." She checked what she was going to say about Clayton Ames and finished lamely, "I read too that Osama bin Laden was a genius at stashing money offshore." Clayton Ames was in good company here, hiding his assets, she thought. At least his Grand Cayman home must be luxurious. So Lexi might—must—be in a good, safe place.

After their aircraft taxied to the gate, they took their two carry-ons from the overhead bins and walked out through people waiting for friends and family. Claire kept scanning the crowd in case someone had a sign with her or Nick's name on it, to take them to Lexi. They assumed they'd be contacted at their hotel, but she had hopes of something sooner.

But nothing—no one for them.

They stood in line to take a brightly colored taxi, painted with a green turtle like the one on the Cayman Islands flag. Inside, as they'd decided earlier, they kept their conversation to tourist talk again. Claire was so physically and emotionally exhausted that scenery blurred by as the driver took them in heavy traffic—a lot of ritzy cars like BMWs, even Rolls-Royces—toward their hotel, the Sand and Sea Club, at the north end of Seven Mile Beach. Their cabbie spoke in a unique drawl and pronounced Cayman with the emphasis on the *man* part.

"Oh, look at that sign!" Claire blurted when the cab came

to a sudden stop. It read Iguanas Have Right Of Way. Drive Slowly. "I read the iguanas here are blue, the only place in the world," she added.

"They only blue when they mating," their cabbie said. "April, May, not now. They endangered, nuh."

Claire wasn't sure what *nuh* meant, but it got tacked on the end of sentences here, maybe like an exclamation point.

Again, sights seemed to rotate past: a pile of conch shells for sale, several pirate mannequins advertising Pirates Week Festival next month. The mannequins reminded her of Cecilia and Lola Moran, women she'd interviewed for Nick's St. Augustine murder/suicide case just last week. How far away that all seemed now.

She tried to convince herself that this warm, breezy location could pass for Naples, but it was far different, a mix of British and Caribbean, an exotic place all its own. Jerk chicken stands stood next to bars and pubs; she saw signs to squash clubs and cricket fields. Duty-free shops and banks were everywhere. She had read some of the workers were from Jamaica, the Philippines or Honduras, so, with the tourists, it was a real mix of people on the streets of George Town.

The American influence was here too. Signs advertised a Wendy's and a Kentucky Fried Chicken, but there were ones that read Sting Ray City and This Way To Hell. She heard Nick grunt at that. She'd read Hell was a tourist stop where strange seaweed had turned the coral rock shaped like flames black. She didn't need a place like that; she was so sick at heart about Lexi she felt she was in hell already.

Jace paid for a ridiculously pricey room over a row of shops on West Bay Road that ran along Seven Mile Beach. He'd told Nick he knew someone who lived on the island, but that wasn't true. He figured this dive overlooking the front street above a noisy area was at least several miles from the tonier place Nick and Claire would be. Close but not too close.

He ditched his gear, except for his camera and the pistol he'd managed to sneak in. He rented a motorbike, ignoring street hawkers trying to get him to windsurf, Jet Ski or take a jitney bus tour. He bought a really loud shirt with parrots on it and wore it with his worst-looking cutoff shorts and a ratty sailor's cap to hide his recent haircut. He hated flip-flops, but they looked like the shoe of choice around here, so he bought a pair of those. If he had to run fast, he'd kick them off.

He hadn't shaved for a couple of days and hoped he looked like a beach bum instead of former navy man. And he hoped that someone that rich and powerful felt secure enough that he didn't hire guards on his property, though Jace would have to locate it before he could case it. He tried to slouch and lose the military bearing and pilot pose. Top gun, heck. He just wanted to be top dad, that's all—top husband too.

He rode his motorbike north along West Bay past a loud, brass street band as he headed for the Sand and Sea Club where Claire and Nick would stay. Two massive cruise ships, which had disgorged passengers to shop or hit the tourist sites, were visible through gaps in the tinted glass, pastel-colored office buildings. He'd learned the ritzy places where Ames probably lived were a little ways out of town, but he needed to be where he could keep an eye on Claire and Nick, then follow them when the sick bastard who held Lexi contacted or summoned them.

He found the Sand and Sea Club a six-mile ride away at the north end of Seven Mile Beach in a cluster of similar rentals and "club" apartments, most really nice-looking if a bit dated. The Sand and Sea Club offered oceanfront suites and a restaurant with a menu posted outside that he stopped to glare at. It offered turtle stew, jerk chicken, coconut bread, conch fritters and panfried fish like snapper, grouper and marlin.

His stomach rumbled but not from hunger. He was as tense as when he used to get in the captain's seat for combat.

He took a flyer from a glass box that touted Cemetery Reef as a great snorkeling site, *only fifty yards out*. Man, that's all he needed, to think about someone dumping a body out at sea at a place called Cemetery Reef.

Trying to blend in with the locals and tourists, he chained and padlocked his bike to a palm tree and slouched between two buildings to wait for Nick and Claire's arrival. On his phone, he shot a few pictures of the entrances to the club and the beach. The sand was wide, blinding white and crowded. Maybe he could rent a beach umbrella to hide behind. He figured he'd beat them here by about two hours, but he was content to wait. Content at least for that, because he'd like to kill Lexi's kidnapper right now.

Claire's skin crawled as they checked into the Sand and Sea Club. It wasn't the humidity, because there was a nice sea breeze that also kept the bugs pretty much away. It was the prickly feeling they were being watched. Yet she hesitated to scan the people waiting for some sort of snorkeling tour with fins and masks in hand. She didn't want to stare back at anyone in a challenging way. Patience. They had to be patient and wait to be contacted.

She went with Nick to their suite down a hall with breezeways throughout. Two double beds, thank heavens, instead of one. A sitting area and decent-sized bathroom. Fantastic view, of course, through sliding glass doors that led to a private lanai set off from the rooms next to it by flowered trellises. Bright beach umbrellas stuck in the sand provided some shade for patrons in the glare of the sun. Too much of that and Claire's skin would freckle and turn as red as her hair, but what did any of that matter now—matter ever again if they didn't get Lexi back and soon?

Nick put her small bag on the bed farthest from the door. “Don’t unpack too much,” he said. “I’m sure things will work out and you and Lexi, at least, will be leaving soon, and I’ll do whatever our friend wants.”

Dialogue prepared in case there were mics or cameras in the room, of course. That gave her the creeps too: Did Clayton Ames hope for some sort of reading on Nick’s relationship with her? Were they being watched to see if they were affectionate? Made love? More than once, she would have liked to but she’d thought they barely knew each other and circumstances were bad then—ha! How could they even pretend more than clinging to each other when things were so dangerous and desperate? Ames obviously knew enough of what they meant to each other to be sure that threatening Lexi’s well-being would turn the screws on Nick.

She made some small talk about the hotel and the view, unpacked a change of clothes and went into the bathroom. She propped her hands on the seashell-shaped pink sink and stared at herself in the mirror. Grayish bags under her eyes like half-moons. Windblown hair. A bruised bottom lip she’d chewed too hard. Exhaustion. Terror she was trying to control. She hadn’t eaten a thing and she could throw up in this basin right now.

She set to work washing up and changing, then twisted her hair into a topknot. Or, since she didn’t wear it like that much, would that set Lexi off when they were reunited? She took her hair down and brushed it loose again, refreshed her makeup and went out.

Nick was stretched out on his bed, using his laptop. Wi-Fi was included here. She wondered if the dangerous, ubiquitous lackeys who reported to Ames had a way to snag whatever Nick was sending or reading online. Probably. But surely he knew that.

"Lie down and take a nap," Nick said. "I'll be here, waiting."

"Yes, all right. But I'd rather pace. I'm praying we will have Lexi back safe and sound as soon as possible," she said in a loud voice. *Let the eavesdroppers and spies report that to Clayton Ames*, she thought.

She leaned against the open sliding glass door and watched the sunbathers in various sizes of bathing suits or near undress. Could their contact be out there? Was Jace out there?

She jolted when a knock sounded on their hallway door. Had Nick ordered anything while she was in the bathroom? He got up from the bed, but she beat him to the door, slid the bolt and pulled it open.

CHAPTER THREE

The plump, chatty British woman they'd sat next to on the plane stood there, dressed the same as before with a little smile on her lips and a beige envelope in her hand. Claire gasped as Nick appeared beside her. "We meet again," he said to the woman.

"Indeed. A friend has sent you this," she said, extending the envelope to him. "I wasn't to give it to you earlier. If I were you, I'd follow those directions straightaway. That is all I know, so don't inquire more. Ta-ta, then." She turned away and scurried down the hall.

Claire tugged Nick out into the now empty hallway and whispered, "What does it say?"

They bent close as he pulled a card from the stiff vellum envelope. "It's a handwritten invitation," he muttered so quietly that she could hardly hear him. "Our presence is requested, and so on—smart-aleck wording. But here's his address. I'd love to let the FBI have this, but Lexi comes first."

As he started to go back into their room, she grabbed his arm and mouthed, "The FBI? Are they in on this?"

"No," he whispered so quietly she had to read his lips. "But an agent questioned me—grilled me—a couple of years ago over what I knew about the man I used to call 'Uncle Clay.' They're not interested in my father's death but looking into IRS taxation questions about Ames's global companies that are under the umbrella of a massive conglomerate called Ames High. I could only tell them I'd tried to track him but he kept moving and lives mostly as an expat now. Let's get a cab and go see him before he disappears again."

"With Lexi," she muttered as they went back into the room to grab their things. She was annoyed he had not told her about the FBI earlier. What else was he hiding? She'd barely glimpsed the so-called printed invitation, but she would read it on the way.

Before they grabbed their gear, they fell into each other's arms, holding hard. It terrified her to think this might be the last time—if, just maybe, things went wrong. He suddenly held her at arm's length, almost as if he was thrusting her away. He stared into her teary eyes.

"You will leave here with Lexi, no matter what else happens. I said it before and I mean it now—more than ever."

Jace had to move fast when he saw Claire and Nick emerge from the front of the club. His hands shook as he unlocked the chain around his bike. He saw Nick scanning the area, frowning, but he didn't react as if he recognized him. Was he looking for him or a spy or stalker? It didn't matter since they waited barely a minute before a brightly colored cab pulled up and they got in. He had to keep up with his motorbike, but at least the cab had to stop a lot, heading back into George Town.

Jace thought Claire looked pale and nervous, but why wouldn't she? He pictured Lexi, green-eyed like Claire, though she was more blonde than red-haired. Well, strawberry blonde. And she loved strawberry ice cream and her so-called Frozen doll—what a name for a doll. She loved her cousin Jilly, the same age. Yeah, she was as close to Jilly as Claire was to her sister, Jilly's mom, Darcy. That and his international traveling were reasons he'd never so much as considered trying to take "Princess Alexandra," alias Lexi, from Claire when they divorced. But if Claire ever married Nick or anyone else, he'd sure sue for equal time with his daughter. But first, they had to get her back.

He swore under his breath as the cab got through an intersection when the light changed but he didn't. Too many tourists loose in town, taking too long to cross the street, rushing back to their ships. A policeman with a pointed white cap was still holding up his line of traffic.

He revved the bike and stretched as tall as he could, trying to pick out the cab they were in from vehicles one block ahead now. He should have memorized the number on its back, 4-4 something. If they got much farther ahead, he'd have to just guess which private mansion along the area called South Sound they'd gone to, since that's where it looked like they were headed. He prayed he hadn't already ruined his chance to help them and save Lexi.

Claire gazed at the mansions along the South Sound. Some of them reminded her of the massive ones in the Port Royal area of Naples. Even behind privacy walls, they loomed vast, beige-and-white concrete and stucco, some with wood pillars or pastel trim. Their fronts bordered on the canal with boat access. "More like yachts, nuh," their driver said—you might know, the same driver they'd had before, no doubt someone else on Ames's payroll. She could see tall masts or an occasional yacht through the spaces between the buildings. The houses' rears, where she glimpsed an occasional gardener working or a maid putting out the trash or a service or repair truck, faced the road with the South Sound, a lagoon that merged with the blue-green sea. She read on scripted signs lovely names of these huge homes like Golden Pond, Lazy Lagoon, Happy Days, Sea and Sky—and, the one they pulled into through ornate, open wrought iron gates, Nightshade.

Claire squinted, scanning the back garden area within tall walls for any sign of Lexi. A burly man, who wasn't dressed like a gardener, stood on the other side of a shaded fountain, watching them. Could that be Clayton Ames? No, because Nick glared at the man but didn't react.

As they got out—the driver said he'd already been paid—Claire noted the well-kept grass and flowers. The fountain in the shape of a huge, fluted clamshell dominated the area and the wind blew spray onto the surrounding plants.

As the cabbie drove away, Claire tugged on Nick's arm. "See those tall, purplish, trumpetlike flowers around the fountain where that man is standing? They're called deadly nightshade, and their berries are poison."

"Not now, Claire."

"I did a report on poison plants in college. That can cause hallucinations and seizures if you eat it, so watch it if he offers food here."

"I don't think he brought us here to poison us—not that way anyhow."

Her heart pounded so hard that she feared she'd collapse from the cataplexy she controlled through her meds. That debilitating disease was linked to the narcolepsy she'd struggled with for years. She had to be ever vigilant in highly charged, emotional situations, and she couldn't think of anything much worse than this. Her knees went weak when she had to stay strong.

"Well then, what part of it is poison?" he asked quietly when she'd thought he didn't want to hear more.

"Roots, leaves, berries—everything. There's an old legend that the plant belongs to the devil who trims and tends it. Its Latin name comes from one of the three Fates in mythology—can't recall her name—the one who cuts the cord of each person's life to bring death at the time and manner of her choosing."

"Well, isn't this the perfect place for Clayton Ames then?" he muttered, putting his arm around her waist.

"I'm all right," she said, pulling slightly back from him. She couldn't go in to face Ames leaning on Nick.

As he raised his hand to knock on the back door, it opened as if by magic, but of course they had been watched again. A short, handsome, white-haired man with pale blue eyes stood there. He was nattily dressed in white slacks and a navy golf shirt. He wore an expensive-looking gold watch. She couldn't guess his age; he could be anywhere from fifty to eighty. His tanned facial skin was tight and unwrinkled but for the crinkled corners of his narrow eyes. He radiated friendliness, so this could not be Clayton Ames.

Claire was expecting at least a butler, but the man broke into a white-toothed smile and said, "Nicky, welcome. It's been so long, my boy. And, of course, Claire, Lexi's mother. Nicky and I go way back, but I've so wanted to meet you. Please step in, and let's have a chat before we get down to business."

So this man was Ames after all. Of course it was, because Nick had described him as deceptive and slick. And the man's comment about he and "Nicky" going way back was no doubt a veiled reference to those horrible days when Ames murdered—so Nick believed—Nick's father. Yes, Nick was right: this man was dangerous and demented.

Neither man extended his hand. Nick looked carved from stone. Ames clapped him on his shoulder and reached for Claire's hand. She was expecting his touch to be cold, but he felt very warm.

"Welcome to Nightshade," Clayton Ames said, "my home away from home."

★ ★ ★

Jace was furious. He'd lost them, screwed everything up. A row of mansions stretched out here. He saw traffic on this so-called South Sound Road but no cabs. Ordinarily, he'd just call Nick or Claire on his cell, but they'd decided it would be too risky to use phones here. Besides, Nick and Claire could be with Ames now and no way they could take a call. If someone tracked it, that would give his backup presence away.

Then he saw a cab pulling out onto the road from down the way. Yes. Yes! When it passed him as it headed back toward town, he saw part of its ID number was 4-4. Thank God! It had evidently dropped Claire and Nick off and was leaving.

But when he got to the property labeled Nightshade, he didn't see any way to go in without being spotted. Besides, a burly man was looking his way from the other side of wrought iron gates as they automatically closed. As Jace buzzed by, that man was joined by yet another. He'd have to circle back to the For Sale property he'd seen, go through there to the canal and walk back to Nightshade, or at least close enough to case it. Nightshade seemed a strange name, he thought, but the moon could throw some shade at night.

He went a little farther down the road, then circled back. Near the For Sale house, he pretended his motorbike had quit in case anyone was watching. He rolled it up to the wooden gate, but that was locked, so he pushed the bike between the security fence and the neighbor's white concrete wall, then chained it to another grate over a first-floor window.

Since most of the living areas of these big homes faced the canal rather than the expanse of water across the road, he strolled out to the canal and ambled along it, counting the houses until he reached the fifth. He saw some serious boat flesh, as he called luxury watercraft. He stopped before he could be spotted from Nightshade two properties down—

or he hoped so, because he didn't want to tangle with those beefy guards. At least there appeared to be no fences back here.

Until it was dark tonight—and he was doomed if these places had watchdogs—he'd better retrace his steps to the beach just across the road and watch from there. At least he'd be able to tell if Ames moved Claire, Lexi or Nick. That strip of sand and some rocks had other people around so he could blend in, even if there weren't the big numbers like on Seven Mile Beach.

Leaving his bike locked where it was hidden between the two houses, he crossed the road and strolled down the beach, back toward Nightshade. A couple of families sat on the sand or waded in the water; it reminded him of better times when he and Claire had taken Lexi to the beach by the Naples pier. Kids screeched and ran free. Pretty far down the beach, one kid in a straw hat was flying a kite with two women who might be mothers or nannies. But he turned his eyes back to the row of mansions, scanning Nightshade for any sign of Claire or Nick or even Lexi.

Claire gazed aghast at the interior of the mansion. Nothing graced the longest wall in the high-beamed great room but a row of large, lighted fish tanks at eye level. She wondered if Lexi was imprisoned somewhere in this house. It made her want to rip the ceilings, floors and walls apart.

As if they'd come to see his aquariums, Clayton Ames was talking in a maddeningly calm voice about "his babies," the tropical fish, evidently captured from Caribbean waters. If he could talk about his "babies," couldn't she ask about hers? But she followed Nick's lead to merely look interested—watchful, at least—while waiting to see what Ames's next move would be. This all had to mean something, to lead somewhere, but it was pure torture.

"The world may be dog-eat-dog," Ames said as he peered

into a tank and rapped on the glass with his well-manicured fingernails, "but in here it's fish-eat-fish." His nails were fairly long for a man's—devil's claws, she thought, feeling sick to her stomach. "You know, people make a big mistake when they think fish are unintelligent and unresponsive pets. They are capable of learning, and I like to study their behavior—which, of course, is key in your career, Claire."

She started to say something—she wasn't sure what—when Nick said, "I imagine you look at people in the same way, Clayton. Aren't all these tanks difficult to take with you when you move about, or do 'your babies' stay here?"

"Like my immediate staff, they go where I go. The fish may seem antisocial or destructive but from their point of view, they are being constructive," he added, pointing to another tank where a large, lovely specimen was hiding behind a coral rock, evidently lying in wait for its prey. But when it lunged and snatched, at least, it was not at another fish but a piece of floating food.

Usually, Claire was mesmerized by aquarium fish, but it was hardly calming this time. If she wasn't so strung out, waiting for a mention of Lexi—to see Lexi—she would have tried to psych this maniac out. What made him tick besides control of others and his ruthless pursuit of wealth and power? What made that ticking bomb explode?

But she could not stand it one moment more. "Fish doing what comes naturally is one thing, but doing what comes naturally to a mother is worrying about her child," she said, steeling herself to look directly into the man's pale blue eyes.

"I understand, of course, and we will get to that directly. She is being well taken care of. She has some kindly companions with her and is having a fine time, I assure you."

"But how—" Claire started before he held up a palm toward her as if stopping traffic.

"You will see and soon," Ames said.

Nick said, "I'm surprised you don't have piranhas here."

"Very clever, Nicky. But a bit heavy-handed, don't you think? I prefer a more subtle approach. See that fish flaring its gills?" he said, gazing at the glassed-in fish again. His reflection made it look like a twin stared out at them from a watery mirror. "Watch as it opens its mouth wide, making what is termed a 'frontal threat display.' But that can be misinterpreted. In some species that aggressive posture is actually a courtship display. So please, let's sit on the second-floor lanai, have a drink and talk business without any misunderstandings or antagonism. You see, you have both challenged me cleverly and carefully just now, and I appreciate your spirit."

This man was delusional, Claire thought. Did he believe he could control others like this? And yet, wasn't she being delusional to think they had a chance to defy him? She would do almost anything this man asked right now to get Lexi back.

Nick spoke again. "We would appreciate no frontal threats."

Ames chuckled, and Claire shivered. What sort of business deal was this horrible man going to propose? Surely, not that Nick give up his life for Lexi's. The handwritten summons here to Nightshade had been worded so formally, almost like a wedding or reception invitation would have been. She'd kept it to perhaps analyze his handwriting later—if there was to be a later. But whatever this man's game, she had to keep calm and go along. Nick was right that he loved to torment people. He was poison, washed down with sips and gulps of his pseudo kindly presence.

He led them up a curving staircase to a large second-floor deck with a stunning view of the emerald South Sound lagoon that seemed to merge with the glittering sea. They sat in woven wicker chairs around a glass-topped table in the shade of a white umbrella. From this broad balcony, Claire could see people on the beach. A few were swimming or walking in the waves. A girl in a pretty yellow dress and flopping straw hat flew a red kite while her companions cheered and clapped.

A tray of what appeared to be tall glasses of iced tea and pink lemonade awaited them. Ames took an iced tea and raised it to them as if giving a toast.

"To your happiness, both of you and Lexi in the future," he told them.

Neither of them reached for a drink, but Ames ignored that and went on, "And, Nicky, I commend you on managing your frustration and temper, and to have chosen such a great woman as your fiancée, who doesn't demand her daughter back at once."

"Fiancée? Claire and I are not engaged."

"Really? If you want Lexi back, I rather thought you'd both agree to be more than engaged—that is if you wish to live happily ever after. Lexi's excited about your wedding, and I am too."

Claire, who had sat frozen at the mention of marriage, gasped, but Nick choked out, "Wedding?"

"Here, this evening. With Lexi as flower girl. She's been so excited to hear you sent her down ahead to have a good time and help me make plans for the ceremony tonight. It's quite easy to get a license and a celebrant for tourists here, you know, so I've taken that upon myself. We'll have an intimate reception afterward, and the three of you can be on your way tomorrow, though I'd be honored if you'd spend your wedding night here. Your beach hotel is paid up for a week, if you'd like to stay there. Though children aren't usually part of a honeymoon, I'm sure you'd rather have Lexi with you than with me."

Still in shock, Claire sucked in another sharp breath. Nick just gaped at him. He obviously had not seen that coming—just the opposite. But it all made sense to Claire. Her pulse started to pound, and she flushed prickly hot. Nick had not married so he didn't have to worry about protecting a family from this horrible man. But Ames had discovered that Nick now cared about someone who had an only child who meant the world to her. That meant Nick had a new weak spot, and once Nick had married her, Ames would have three people to torment and control, not just one.

But Ames had just said Lexi was with two women, and she'd seen that girl on the beach, who had actually reminded her of Lexi…

Claire vaulted from her chair and leaned over the edge of the beige concrete balcony. She squinted into the stiff sea breeze. Yes! Yes, so close and yet so far. At a distance, in that dress, with strange women! Claire didn't mean to make a sound, but she heard herself scream, "Lexi! Lexi! Lexi!"

CHAPTER FOUR

"My, aren't you a clever girl, but Lexi can't hear you from here," Ames said as he came to stand beside Claire, and Nick rushed to the balcony to stare outward. "It's too far, and the breeze is in the wrong direction to carry your voice. But I assure you, Lexi, with her companions, will disappear before you can even cross the road if you two don't sign on my dotted line. When you do, of course, we'll get Lexi back so she can prepare—like all of us—for a lovely, private wedding this evening. I've had a cake and the attire ordered. Now, don't disappoint the child, as she's tried her pretty frock on already and practiced carrying the rings on a little pillow. I'm sure you'll like those too."

Nick stood silent. He covered Claire's trembling hand with his where she still gripped the balcony. The red kite had taken a dive into the sand, and her two companions were running after Lexi toward it.

"I just love surprises," Ames said, clapping his hands. "Oh, and Nicky, there's more to it for you than just saying 'I do.' Let's you and I chat about that while I send for Lexi to be brought here for a little future family reunion—or not. What do you say, my boy?"

"I say I'm not your boy and never was. That you and I are not finished over this or—or the other matter between us."

"Finished? I hope not. I have another profitable offer to make, which I'm certain you will take. You see, I need your promise to work for me as well as to wed the lovely Claire. You're a fine attorney, just as your father was, and I have a particular case for you to oversee. Why, your future wife, clever forensic psychologist that she is, may be able to help with it too. Because as long as you win that case for me, there won't be a worry in the world about Lexi or your future. Let's step inside, and I'll explain more. Ah, isn't it a lovely day for a wedding, even an evening one? We'll have it right here in moonlight and candlelight with a view of the lagoon and the sea, so romantic."

For the first time in her life, Claire understood murder as a crime of passion. Her head was spinning. Was this a dream or a nightmare? At least Lexi was alive and ran free and in her sights—for now.

"If you want to talk to Nick," she said to Ames, "can I just stand here and watch Lexi until you send for her?"

"Why, of course. And while I do that, I'll have the housemaid Jemma come out to keep you company." He patted her shoulder. She shuddered at his touch and yet she had to obey him at least until they got Lexi back and got out of here. She prayed Nick would agree to anything and everything this man said—because that's exactly what she was going to do.

"Oh, Claire," Ames said, as he followed a grim Nick to the door to go back inside, "I should assure you that, although Lexi was surprised at first that my man who picked her up at your home was not her daddy, she adapted quite well when my people told her the happy surprise you and your betrothed had planned for her. She understands that you two needed time to plan the wedding. Also, I believe she calls you Mr. Nick, doesn't she, my boy? We told her that her new stepfather would be a big part of her life but that she could still see her daddy. That is, if he doesn't hurt himself flying all over the Caribbean, right?"

He turned away, but Claire glimpsed Nick's expression of shock that Ames must know Jace had come down here too. They were doomed, she thought. But she'd marry Nick, keep it in name only, a partnership until they could stop this devil—someday, somehow.

"Look, Clayton," Nick said the moment they sat down in facing black leather club chairs in his darkly paneled den, "I'll do what you say, but can't you leave Claire and Lexi out of it?"

"I've seen via lovely photographs how much you like Claire and evidently want her. Well, what red-blooded bachelor would not? No, you need to marry Claire, and I need her and your darling new stepdaughter for insurance that you will do as I ask on a particular local matter of great importance to me and my business affairs."

"Local? You want a lawyer to try a case here in Grand Cayman?"

"Hardly. You don't have the credentials or the clout here as you do in Collier County. No, this is a case local to you near Naples I need to have you take and win for me. I believe you'll realize why you'd be the ideal attorney on this. And well-paid, of course, so you and your new family can get a very nice home."

"One with your listening devices and hidden cameras built right in."

Ames ignored that and went on, "Once you hear me out, you'll want to do this not only for me."

"For keeping my new wife and stepdaughter safe, you mean."

“My, you’re paranoid. You don’t have what they call a wire on you, do you, Nicky?”

“I’m not that stupid.”

“You’re not stupid at all, which is why I want you to work for me. I was quite annoyed when I found you’d traced the name of my offshore company, Ames High, which stores my resources here in Grand Cayman as well as in a few other places in Europe and Asia. Now that you are working with me, I absolutely expect you to keep that a secret, especially not to share it with any US agencies that may inquire.”

Nick’s stomach went into free fall. He tried not to show surprise, for why should anything shock him with this man? Could Ames know the FBI had interviewed him and that the IRS was on his tail? He said nothing, but met the older man’s eyes with a steady stare. Those cold, pale blue eyes: Nick was certain he had either pulled the trigger of the gun that killed his father or hired the man who did. He clearly recalled his father telling him that “Uncle Clay” was going to stop by that night.

Ames leaned forward in his chair, elbows propped on his knees. It took all the restraint Nick had not to launch himself at the man, to pound him to pieces.

“Nick,” he said, finally dropping the silly *Nicky*, “I need you to defend your friend Chet Hazelton from Goodland in a Collier County court, a criminal case.”

“A criminal case? He goes by Haze, you know.”

“I do know. I know a lot about him.”

“Then with all your spies, listening devices and drones, you realize I have other cases that need my attention. What’s he done? He’s a longtime friend, and I’d work pro bono for him. But I believe he has money flowing in, thanks to your leasing his Fountain of Youth water supply for your so-called health drink Youth Do, as well as the cosmetic firm Fresh Dew corporations.”

"I'm honored how closely you follow my career and my gifts to mankind through those excellent products. Now, Nick, sadly, my friend and yours, Haze Hazelton, is in dire straits."

"Is he being sued for that phony water you use and promote? You have to know that spring his family has owned for years, though it may be worth megamillions, is bogus."

"Nick, Nick. I'd have to sue you for slander and libel if you ever said that in public, but I need you to say just the opposite. I know you've kept your mouth shut for years since your friend believes in his sparkling waters. Worse, you simply must keep up with current events in your own backyard, so to speak. Our mutual friend Haze has something bigger to face. A dreadful murder occurred in Goodland yesterday, and he is the number one suspect, though the police haven't arrested him yet."

Nick sucked in a breath. "I—I didn't know."

"Quite simply, he'll need you to defend him. I'm sure he's been calling your office. He could be arrested any day now for, as they say on TV, murder one."

"Who's he accused of killing?"

Ames ignored that and went on, "And when you do defend him in the media or the public venue of the court, be sure to extol the virtues and the claim that the Goodland water's curative and youth-giving powers are valid and that my products are not only health-giving but anti-aging. You see, the person he's accused of killing said just the opposite."

Nick snorted. Though he'd let Haze have his pipe dream, he'd always figured the miraculous water was all hype and lies. Scientists were on his side that the $292 billion global industry of turning back time in the human body was mostly smoke and mirrors. Desperate Americans were anti-aging crazy, and that was driving the sales of any new book, supplement, food or drink that held the promise of eternal health and life. And the government only controlled meds and food, so that meant the selling of water or cosmetic products that were mostly water was outside their jurisdiction.

Nick asked, “I repeat, he’s likely to be accused of killing whom?”

“I assume you’re familiar with that mouthy rebel Mark Stirling, owner-editor of the Marco Island newspaper, *The Burrowing Owl*, rag that it is. It’s been attacking Haze’s claim that the spring he owns is indeed Ponce de León’s fountain, instead of that one in St. Augustine. But, you see, that’s the same as attacking my company’s claims and my reputation. Before his sad demise, Stirling had even—let’s say—‘burrowed’ his way into probing my offshore profits from the Dew and Do corporations, just when they are starting to take off big-time with the huge Gen-X and millennial markets as well as the aging baby boomers.”

“Haze wouldn’t kill anyone. I’ve known him for years.”

“Precisely, and you can defend him well and get him to avoid a silly expose-the-false-advertising case. Keep your Markwood, Benton and Chase law firm going, but on this case you and your firm will really be working for me—as a priority. That way you and yours, as they say, won’t be endangered like the poor, vulnerable little fish sometimes eaten in my aquariums.”

Again, Nick had to fight to keep from vaulting out of his chair and pounding Ames. But he knew a guard would rush in, and Claire and Lexi would suffer too.

“So, do we have a deal?” Ames asked. “For the wedding and your loyalty to me in the Goodland case?” He extended his hand.

“Do I have a choice? But that’s how you play the game.”

“Nick, it’s not a game. I’m deadly, deadly serious.”

“Did one of your spies or hit men kill Stirling? I’ve always known you killed my father, but you operate through others now. You had everything to lose if this Stirling probed deeper and turned up your offshore accounts."

"How insulting and outrageous. Although Haze hasn't been arrested yet since Stirling had other enemies, I expect you and your clever little forensic psychologist bride can ferret out enough other suspects to muddy the police investigation waters. Meanwhile, after your nuptials, you might want to read the *Naples Daily News* online for today. I believe they're dubbing Stirling's sad demise the Mangrove Murder, since his battered body was wedged under mangrove roots not far from that precious 'fountain of youth.' Nick, win that case for your friend Haze Hazelton—and for me."

Hating this man, hating himself and the trap he was in, Nick thrust out his hand and they shook on it. No contract, though Ames had earlier mentioned signing on the dotted line. He must have meant the marriage license.

When she heard Ames's voice behind her, Claire finally turned away from gazing at Lexi. Nick followed him out onto the balcony, which another housemaid was already setting up for the wedding with a long, damask-covered buffet table and an arched trellis under which they'd take their vows. Unbelievable. She cared for Nick and he cared for her but not to this degree, at least not yet. They'd have to come to an understanding, to set some rules. How well did she really know the man she was expected to live with, sleep with? A forced marriage, a different sort of shotgun wedding.

"Boring business all concluded," Ames said with a clap of his hands, and a tight smile. "I'm sure your intended will share with you later what we intend, Claire." He chuckled at his play on words again. "And," he went on, "I've just sent someone to bring Lexi over so we can move on to wedding plans."

She noted a man in casual clothes, big-shouldered and tall, walking toward Lexi and the women, though she wasn't sure where he'd emerged from. Not this house while she was standing here. Did Ames have this entire property surrounded by guards?

She squinted through the sinking sun to her right side, still trying to keep an eye on Lexi. At least they hadn't locked her up or, from the looks of it, terrified her. The Disney world of princesses and fairies was still real to her at times, so why not a Cinderella fantasy that her mother would marry Prince Nick in a distant land called Grand Cayman?

"Good," she finally said to Ames. "Nick, is everything decided?"

Ames answered for him. "It is, and he can explain it all to you later. We have only about an hour before the celebrant will be here to have you sign the special visitor's marriage license to make things legal in the British territory. Needless to say, the Caymans are often a destination wedding site, and this lovely event is one of my gifts to you. The dresses and Nick's suit are laid out in bedrooms on this level, and I'll bring Lexi right in to see you, Claire. I'm sure both of you, bride and groom, will say the appropriate vows and answer any questions from the celebrant to his—and my—satisfaction. And that includes calling me Paul Kilcorse this evening, not Clayton Ames."

Nick merely nodded. No wonder, Claire thought, Nick and his tech team hadn't been able to trace or locate him here. In Grand Cayman, Clayton Ames didn't exist.

"Jemma," Ames said, turning to the woman who had silently watched Claire, "please escort the bride to her room. Oh, and I'm pleased to say, Nick, now that things are settled between us after all these years, I will stand as your best man this evening, while Lexi does double duty for Claire. After all, now that you are working for and answer to me, I *am* your best man."

As he turned away, Ames again chuckled at his own lame

joke. Nick shot Claire a quick look she couldn't read. Did it say, *I'm sorry* or *At least we'll all survive this*—or *I do love you, despite everything*?

As Nick followed Ames into the house, Claire turned again to gaze out at the beach. The two women were bringing the kite and Lexi back toward the house, trailed by the man. Lexi was barefoot beneath that yellow, flowered dress. Despite the straw hat, Claire hoped they'd put sunscreen on her. She wanted to throw herself off this balcony, to run to her.

"Miss Claire, come on," Jemma urged from behind her. "We do what he say."

"I'll bet," Claire muttered. She started to turn away, but her eye caught something else besides the people on the sand with Lexi. A grungy-looking guy with a pronounced limp and stooped posture was following them at a distance. Another guard? But no—it looked like Jace's body build despite the slouch and lack of well-cut clothes. Still, she couldn't tell his hair or eye color.

But the closer he got, the clearer the image became and Claire realized, yes, Jace was here! He'd made it and he was close! He'd seen Lexi but at least he knew not to just try to grab her. And he was hanging back, maybe so Lexi wouldn't see him. Or else he finally saw the power and evil of the man who owned Nightshade—and, right now, owned them.

CHAPTER FIVE

Claire burst into tears when Lexi came alone into the bedroom with a stuffed green cloth turtle in her arms. "Mommy, Mommy, Mommy!" she cried and ran to her. Claire knelt to her height and covered her face with kisses.

"Are you all right?" Claire asked. "You weren't hurt, were you?"

"I was scared when I saw the man wasn't Daddy. But I'm going to be in your wedding!" she shouted as Claire held her. "But won't Aunt Darcy and Jilly be mad they can't come? I asked Mr. Kilcorse if they could, but he said not now because they are going to see friends in Sarasota tomorrow. Isn't that something that he knew that? Mommy, why are you crying?"

"Just so happy to see you!" Claire choked out, hugging her harder. But she felt even more distraught to realize Ames's web could extend to her sister and her family.

"I saw the pretty dress I'm going to wear," Lexi chattered on as Claire held her at arm's length to look her over. "Oh, there it is on this bed, next to yours, see?" Claire had hardly looked at the stunning pale silk bridal dress lying next to one in a matching color for a flower girl.

"Yes, I see," was all she managed.

"I like light blue! It fits me good. This turtle is mine too. And Eleanor and Ginger gave me this yellow dress, and Jemma let me eat lots of ice cream."

"So they treated you really well? The ladies and Mr. Kilcorse too?"

"He said he is kind of Mr. Nick's uncle. These people you hired are real nice. I didn't like that man who grabbed me, but he 'splained it all real fast. And guess what? There was a lady named Lucille hiding in the backseat that took good care of me. She talked funny. She said she was from England. We got on an airplane, but not a real big one like Daddy flies. And when we got to the Car-been, and Lucille went back to Florida on another plane, I practiced with your and Mr. Nick's rings on a pillow for the wedding. Yours has a big diamond, Mommy! Tied with a ribbon, so I won't drop them, 'cause it's like a slippery pillow."

"Yes, yes, fine," Claire said, finally letting go of her to wipe away tears. So much said. Thank God, they hadn't hurt her. Ames had someone who resembled Jace. Could that have been him on the beach and not Jace? She bet the woman from England was the one on their plane and at their hotel door. Then there were the two with Lexi on the beach—Eleanor and Ginger. And Jemma. How many guards and spies did Ames have working for him here?

"But did you tell Daddy?" Lexi suddenly demanded, hands on her skinny hips. "I mean about this lope-ment wedding? I like secrets, like Mr. Kilcorse's name is really Mr. Clayton Ames, 'cause I overheard him talking to another man about that. You know, like in that Disney movie, *Mulan*. Daddy told me he wants us to be a family again, but we can't if Mr. Nick is my new daddy, can we? I don't think my first daddy will be happy!"

Claire's rising panic kicked up another notch. What else

had Lexi overheard here? And if she blurted things out, would Ames try to keep her or silence her?

"Lexi, that's too much to talk about right now. Later, okay? We'll talk later."

Claire hugged her daughter to her. She had Lexi back but at what price for her and Nick? And Jace.

As Claire stood with Nick under the trellis on the balcony to take their vows, she had to admit that the setting for the wedding was beautiful. And, at least she and Nick were still alive and she—they—had Lexi back and would be able to leave soon. She glanced at Nick standing so close, holding her hand. He looked stoic but fuming. Trying to control her trembling, she gazed out toward the darkness of the night again. The staff had been assembled except for the property guards she'd seen when they first arrived. The so-called celebrant was reading the marriage vows she and Nick repeated. She tried to calm herself, but thoughts and fears ate at her as she responded.

The celebrant was a midsixties, gray-haired, distinguished-looking judge whom Ames—alias Paul Kilcorse—not only knew but seemed quite tight with. So had he really put a fake name over on him, or was the judge on the take like the staff and guards here?

Worse, earlier Claire had learned the other price Nick must pay to get them out of here. Before they had separated to shower and change prior to the ceremony, Nick had stopped her in the hall near the room where Lexi was waiting. He'd whispered, "You know that friend of mine, Chet Hazelton, I told you about on Goodland—the guy whose family's had that old artesian well that's locally rumored to be the real fountain of youth? The local papers do occasional articles on it."

"You mean that water that's in the Youth Do drink and

some kind of face cream? That new Marco Island paper's been attacking that."

He seized her hands in his. "Haze Hazelton's been accused of murdering Mark Stirling, that Marco journalist who's always stirring things up. Ames wants me to defend Haze—and tout the anti-aging products very publicly because they're part of his conglomerate. I had to swear I would. But despite this all being blackmail and forced on me—on us—I do care for you. I promise, we will work together. Let's remember how we really feel and get through this, get out of here, sift things out between us, even if he still controls—"

"Mommy, why are you whispering in the hall?" a little voice had cried through the cracked door. "We have to get our pretty dresses on!"

Ignoring that outburst, Nick had kissed Claire's cheek, and they'd held tight. When he'd hurried to his room and Claire had gone into hers, Lexi had said, "I can see you love Mr. Nick. Should I call him Daddy too or Daddy number two? Mr. Nick doesn't sound so good anymore, does it?"

Claire bit her lower lip before she answered, "Let's all talk about it later—after the wedding and reception. When we leave here."

Now, here during the wedding ceremony, Claire knew that Ames had one of his lackeys—the one she'd first seen in the yard by the fountain—recording everything on video, and there was an occasional click and flash of a cell phone camera or two. Would Ames give them remembrances of this forced ceremony for posterity?

She tried to concentrate on the lovely surroundings again rather than the service itself. The palm trees in the yard, with their fronds at this level, swayed and sighed. The cup of sky beyond the beach seemed set with pavé diamonds, like the ones in the stunning wedding ring she'd just accepted. It felt heavy on her finger, but you might know, it fit. She'd almost dropped Nick's band when she'd slid it on his hand. They were about halfway through their vows. An Anglican Church ceremony, no less. What did God think of this sham of a service?

The wind had shifted, and she could hear the crash of distant surf on the south shore. She was a bit dizzy, so the full moon seemed to roll along the invisible, watery horizon like a huge, watchful eye. It threw a lighted, trembling path across the tops of the waves. If only she, Nick and Lexi could escape on that to safety.

Here on the balcony, the moon, candle glow and lighted torchères not only illumined the scene but kept the bugs away. She was continually aware of Clayton Ames, standing on Nick's other side. If she shot a glance sideways, it seemed that devil's dark silhouette was etched by fire.

She jolted alert again, forcing herself back to this strange reality. After a prayer, Nick said his vows, and then it was her turn.

"Claire Fowler Britten, will you take Nicholas James Markwood to be your husband? Will you love him, comfort him, honor and protect him, and forsaking all others, be faithful to him as long as you both shall live?"

She hesitated a moment. Nick squeezed her hand. Ames cleared his throat. Nick had readily said his part.

But she wanted to refuse. She cared deeply for Nick, wanted to help him, was grateful to him. Was that enough for ever-after? She glanced down at the single orchid on the now empty pillow Lexi held. Ames had given the child a nosegay to carry too, four nightshade blooms, but Claire had thrown them under the tablecloth and fished an orchid out of the punch bowl for her, and the satin pillow was speckled with pink. Rebellion rose in her.

But fear and caution made her answer, "I will."

She could smell fragrant nightshade blossoms mingled with

the sea air. They seemed to crowd around her from her bouquet and trellis, into which someone had woven the stems of the pale blue blooms. She'd taken all those flowers as a warning. Clayton Ames was poison, and he wanted them to remember that.

The celebrant began reading a prayer from the book he held. The final words in the ceremony that had legally joined her and Nick rang out as he addressed Ames and his staff who stood in a half circle around them. "Will you, friends of Nicholas and Claire, support and uphold them in their marriage now and in the years to come?"

"We will!" everyone—strangers and enemies all—declared. Did this intelligent-looking judge not at least sense this was all a fake? But if he was Ames's puppet, it hardly mattered.

"I therefore proclaim that they are husband and wife till death do them part," he announced with a big smile. "Nicholas, you may kiss your bride."

He kissed her cheek lightly and whispered for her ears only, "Later." People applauded. The deed was done. Now they faced a reception, in a place she'd never seen before a few hours ago here in the devil's lair with his minions. She glanced down at the wedding ring on her finger, a large, emerald-cut diamond with smaller diamonds on the band. It looked more like an engagement ring than a wedding band.

Someone behind her called out, "Happy honeymoon!"

Insane! She was terrified. And she knew there would be no real honeymoon, and certainly no happily-ever-after.

With his motorbike, Jace waited in the darkness of South Sound beach for a car to emerge from Nightshade. Surely, Nick had met Clayton Ames's price by now and Claire and Lexi would be sent home. If he could intercept them safely somewhere, he'd fly them home himself. Jace hoped Nick wasn't hurt by all this, but Claire and Lexi were his first concern. If he could help—yeah, even rescue Nick—he would.

As different as this was, he remembered a night near Ramadi in 2006 when he'd had to bail out of his fighter jet over pitch-black terrain, real die-in-the-desert Iraqi territory. But thank God for his comrades' motto to leave no man behind, because a Black Hawk chopper saw his flare before the enemy did.

He wished he had a sort of flare as backup now. The hair stood up on the nape of his neck, and he shivered. However this tropical place was different from the desert, the odds were great: no way he'd leave Claire and Lexi behind in enemy hands. But just who was the enemy? This cloak-and-dagger Clayton Ames or Nick himself? Had he set this up to scare and seduce Claire?

He jolted when the driveway gates opened and a car came out; its headlights sliced across the sand near him. But it was driven by an older gray-haired man who appeared to be alone. Praying Claire and Lexi weren't hidden in the backseat—or even the trunk—he hunkered down and waited, watching the car's taillights. The vehicle drove only a couple of houses toward George Town, then turned in. Jace toyed with the idea of going after the driver and questioning him. He had to be an ally of Ames's, but Jace figured he'd better just camp out here.

Some sort of party was going on up on the second-floor balcony, but the chatter wasn't loud enough to decipher. The noise seemed stilted—jerky at times, a silence followed by forced conversation. At this angle, he couldn't see people unless they walked right up to the edge of the balcony. He'd seen Nick once, since he was so tall, but he couldn't spot Claire or certainly Lexi, so were they still inside? Not knowing what was happening was driving him nuts. Could that be a celebration for Lexi's reunion with Claire? But who were the guests?

Finally, one of the women who had been with Lexi earlier on the beach emerged from the downstairs driveway gate and started to walk back toward town. She was the older woman of the two, the one with silvery hair in a bouncing braid halfway down her back. If she was just a worker at Nightshade, maybe he could pretend to be a passerby and ask her what the party was for. He couldn't risk alarming her, but he'd love to question her.

He lifted his bike from the sand and, walking it along to keep from making noise, followed her.

CHAPTER SIX

After the ceremony, Nick stuck tight to Claire and Lexi as the guests mingled, enjoying champagne and food. Lexi was already working on a bowl of strawberry ice cream. He stood with a drink in one hand and his arm around Claire's waist. She leaned slightly into him. She looked as shell-shocked as he felt.

Silver trays of hot and cold seafood and a decorated two-layer cake adorned the buffet table. He thought the reception was elegant but as bogus as the anti-aging claims of Fresh Dew and Youth Do. As far as he was concerned, this was a party for Ames's extensive local and permanent staff, mostly, as far as he could tell, bodyguards, accountants and domestics.

He knew none of the guests except Ames. Their celebrant had hit-and-run, so to speak. Just as well, although Nick had been hoping to ferret out from him whether it was easy to live in grand style on Grand Cayman under a phony name. If Ames thought he'd broken Nick's spirit and made him into a robot who would forget his father's murder and how Ames toyed with the lives of others, he was dead wrong.

Nick stuck to wine instead of the martinis Ames was drinking at a steady pace. His brain was already on overdrive. He not only had to protect Claire and Lexi, but he wanted to be part of their lives. He always kept an eye on Ames, so last year he'd researched Ames High, Inc.'s products that used the supposed fountain of youth. He'd also done some work on what reputable doctors—not the ones making millions from phony claims—said about the water from the well on a small piece of Marco Island land that Haze had inherited. The site had actually been mentioned in Ponce de León's sailing log from the sixteenth century. But the water was anti-aging only in that it was fresh and great-tasting from a deep aquifer, and water was good for people. Truth in advertising? No way.

Somehow, some way, he was going to defend Haze, keep his new little family safe, but beat Ames at his own game.

"A toast to the bride and groom," Ames said, lifting his martini glass. Guests raised crystal goblets of champagne and cut-glass tumblers of stiffer stuff. Nick forced a smile while Claire nodded and stooped to whisper something to Lexi. He wished he could whisper to Claire without all these ears and eyes.

When Claire stood, he put his arm around her waist again and steered her over to look at the cake as an excuse to get away from Ames. He wanted to assure her that, from now on, he was making decisions—he was going to change their hotel room, get tickets to fly them home, assert himself with Ames, even though he'd promised to do his bidding. He wanted to tell her that he valued her, that they would make key choices together. But, you might know, Ames was right behind them.

"That's a local wedding cake, so it's a bit different," he told them, pointing. "It's more like the consistency of a fruitcake. Well, we all have to learn to like new things, right? It's called heavy cake here, quite an island delicacy. What's in it again, Ginger?" he asked the beautiful, chocolate-skinned woman overseeing the buffet table.

"Coconut, sugar, breadfruit, spices. No flour or eggs," she told them with a slight smile, "but cassava instead to hold it all together. Mr. Kilcorse," she addressed Ames, "Eleanor felt funny, so she went to her car, at the other house where she works, to get her medicine."

"Felt funny? She's not sick, is she?"

Ginger shrugged. "I can cut the cake instead of her."

"Actually, *Mr. Kilcorse,*" Nick said, "as nice as this all is, I'd like to take Claire and Lexi back to our hotel to get some rest. I have new responsibilities now, as you know, so we're going home tomorrow. I'm sure your staff will enjoy the evening even more than we have."

"Ah, but Lexi's been having such a good time. And haven't we all?"

Nick and Ames stared at each other. Claire, God bless her, stood steady by his side, though she'd been trembling earlier. In the heels she wore, she was slightly taller than Ames, and Nick towered over the man. For one moment, he was sure that bothered the bastard, but what a tiny victory.

"Well," Ames said, as if he'd blinked first in a staring contest, "of course, I understand how hectic this has all been. And it is your wedding night. Nick, I send you out to take no risks, but to do your duty, as they say. I'm pleased I could stand in for your father tonight. He would have been proud of you too and of your lovely wife and stepdaughter."

That was almost the last straw. Nick wanted to deck his father's murderer, the murderer he now worked for and had to find a way to outsmart and stop.

Jace began to whistle, because he didn't want to startle the woman from Ames's mansion who walked ahead of him. When she evidently heard his fast footsteps and turned to look at him in the moonlight, he said, "Hi! Sorry if I startled you. Wow, that's some party goin' on up there, isn't it?

How's a guy going to sleep on the beach with all that noise and those lights?"

"Oh, *ya*," she said, starting to walk again. "Mr. Kilcorse's house."

Her accent made her sound German. But Mr. Kilcorse's house? Could he have been watching the wrong mansion? He thought he'd seen which driveway the cab that delivered Claire and Nick had come out of. No, he'd seen Nick up on the balcony so either Ames was using someone else's house or a different name.

"I thought that was Clayton Ames's place," he told her, pushing the motorbike faster to keep up. "I know a guy who works for him," he added, making things up as he went. "I thought maybe I could get a job too." He could tell she looked confused, nervous. He didn't want a scene here or her running back to the house. What if she screamed and people rushed out?

"And I saw a friend of mine up on the balcony too, from the old days, Nick Markwood, so could you just tell me..."

It all happened so fast. She turned and started to run back toward the mansion. He dropped the motorbike and grabbed her arm. Couldn't let her tell on him but he needed her to tell him what was going on. He was so worried and frustrated, he'd just exploded.

She opened her mouth to scream, but Jace clapped a hard hand over it. He lifted her and pulled her back into the dark space between two buildings about four doors down from the lighted mansion.

"Look, I'm not going to hurt you," he told her. "Nothing like that. I just want to know what's going on at Nightshade."

Her eyes were white and wide in fright. He realized he'd really blown it, but he had to know if Claire and Lexi were all right. If they could leave, he wanted to be waiting back at their hotel to fly them home.

"Mmmph," she said against his hand, which he loosened and lowered. "I tell you, you let me go. I show you pictures on my phone from the party, you let me go now."

"All right," he said. "I didn't mean to hurt you, but I have to know. I—like I said, I have a friend there."

He saw for the first time she had a cell phone in her hand. He was lucky she hadn't called for help. She touched the screen a couple of times, held it up and thrust it at him. The picture was so bright at first it hurt his eyes. He blinked, blinked again.

Claire and Nick stood holding hands under a flowered trellis with Lexi next to Claire. All dressed up. Exchanging rings and vows, it looked like. Till death do us part stuff.

He felt like someone had kicked him in the gut. He had a gun on him. He felt like shooting his way into that balcony party at Nightshade. He might as well be dead. Had they been tricked or had he?

The woman flipped to another picture, another. Same scene. An exchange of rings. Reality. A wedding. Surely, Claire hadn't known, but at least she had Lexi back. Or was Markwood really behind all this? He knew she felt for the guy.

He heard a man's voice, close, call "Eleanor? Where are you?"

Jace turned to run for his motorbike out in the street, but someone big tackled him from the darkness. He hit the grass, got a mouthful of it, went for his gun, but couldn't reach it when another big man stepped on his arm.

"I think he's a spy," the woman's voice said. "*Danke*, you got my distress call. He was watching the party from the beach, says he knows Nick Markwood, *ya*."

The two burly men hauled Jace to his feet. One punched him in the stomach so hard he doubled over and retched. They dragged him to his feet, holding one arm bent painfully up behind his back, and walked him down the street between them.

"Bring his bike," one man called to the woman. "And don't go off alone like that. You know the rules and consequences."

Jace had wanted desperately to get into Ames's Nightshade, but not this way. Damn, but he was probably going to be the one to suffer consequences for breaking the rules.

Even though one of Ames's guards drove the car, Claire was grateful to get away from Nightshade. She still wore her silk wedding dress and the pair of Manolo high heels, no less, outrageously expensive ones, of course. It spooked her that every item of clothing had been her and Lexi's correct sizes. Had one of Ames's spies who planted listening devices been in their closets and drawers at home?

"Mommy, I'm tired and my tummy hurts."

"You didn't eat anything from the garden with the fountain, did you?"

"No. I don't eat flowers, but I think they were pretty."

Claire shuddered. She was grateful to escape Ames's Nightshade with its weird fish and poison plants. She recalled again the research she had done on deadly nightshade and the mistake she'd made of bringing some in when she presented her paper. She had learned the hard way that merely rubbing against the plant raised pustules on the skin.

"Just too much ice cream and excitement for your tummy then," she told the child, who was cuddled up between her and Nick on the backseat of the car. "You'll sleep tonight, and we'll go home tomorrow."

"Mr. Nick, will you live with us now? I don't want to move too far from Aunt Darcy and Jilly."

"We'll work everything out, Lexi, promise," he told her. "We'll have to explain some things to your family."

Some things, Claire thought. How much? What could they say? What would Jace say and do when he heard? She could hardly explain all about Ames or that could endanger Darcy's family. He'd evidently already been spying on them too.

When they got back to the Sand and Sea Club and Ames's driver left them with a "Best Wishes," as if they hadn't heard that enough from strangers tonight, Nick went up to the desk to see if they could change rooms. Claire wasn't sure what he was going to tell them as they waited for him in the lobby by the Line Up Here for Cemetery Reef Scuba Trip sign. She felt she was underwater right now, looking through a mask, swimming against the current—with Ames's hungry fish surrounding them. No way was she going into their earlier room with Lexi. Who knew what other surprises awaited them?

Nick, looking a bit relieved for the first time in two days, came over and told them, "I got one just down the hall, a smaller room with one bed, but Lexi can sleep between us or I'll sleep on the sofa. Anything to get away from hidden cameras and bugs."

Lexi came alert at that. "Did you have bugs in your room? Ick."

"Not those kind of bugs," Nick assured her as he unlocked their first previous room, flicked the light switch and looked around, then gestured to Claire. "Looks the same," he said.

They scooped up their things and carried the small brown-and-black checkered Vuitton suitcase that carried Lexi's things—which Claire intended to go through thoroughly in case there was a bug planted there—and changed rooms.

She and Lexi took showers first, then joined Nick out in the room. He was on his laptop. "Leaving orders for a couple of junior lawyers," he told her. "Some wedding night, huh?" he added, crossing his arms over his chest as Claire hustled Lexi into bed. The child was still holding on to the green stuffed turtle. "I'll sleep on that couch daybed thing tonight," he said, gesturing at the navy blue folding sofa along the wall.

Although Claire had thought Lexi was almost comatose,

she piped up, "You know when I said Mr. Ames who is really Mr. Kilcorse or something like that was like a Disney movie, Mommy? Then you said tell you later. Is this later?"

"Yes," Claire said, darting a look at Nick, who came over to stand by her at the side of the bed. Somehow Lexi had picked up on both names. Claire needed to question her about other things she could have overheard. She intended to help Nick—her husband—somehow defy and defeat Ames. "I guess this is later," she told Lexi.

"I'd like to hear about that too," Nick said. "Anything you can remember about things you saw or thought when you were at Nightshade, you just tell us."

"Okay. I think Mr. Ames has two names like in that Disney movie. Did you see *Mulan*?"

"No," Nick said. "Sorry I didn't, but tell us both anyway."

"Okay. Mommy saw it. Mulan was just a girl like me, but when men had to go to war and her daddy couldn't fight, she dressed up like a boy and learned to fight. She took his place. She fought the bad people, but she had a little dragon named Mushu to help her. I have this turtle, so he's like my dragon. Mommy, if you and Mr. Nick have to fight bad people, I will help you. I think you are both afraid of something, and I will help you even if I have to change my name and what I look like—even where I live—I will help you."

Claire collapsed to her knees in tears, bending over the bed and hugging her daughter. Nick knelt too and put his arms around them both, and all three of them held tight.

In that double embrace, for the first time since she'd seen the ransom note, Claire felt, not calm or in control, but courageous. She prayed Jace would understand that this was the way things had to be for now. And her heart skipped a beat to think she really was Mrs. Nicholas Markwood, come hell or high water, and she was praying she wouldn't have to face either of those.

CHAPTER SEVEN

When Nick came out of the bathroom after his shower, Lexi was sound asleep, and Claire was standing by the sliding glass doors, looking out at the dark sea. He wore only jockey shorts and had an extra bath towel over one arm. She'd thrown a T-shirt over her knee-length nylon nightgown. She'd been agonizing, not only wishing they had a way to let Jace know they were all right, but about facing Nick on their wedding night.

"Is she a sound sleeper?" he whispered, with a nod toward Lexi.

Her heart thumped harder. "Usually. Almost as much as me."

"Good. Don't want this to wake her."

He dropped his clothes on his carry-on bag and tossed the towel on the sofa bed where he'd said he'd sleep. Then he bent and shoved the sofa about five feet to block the door to the hall.

"I think we're in the clear," he whispered. "But right now I'm trusting no one but you two. And Heck," he added as he came to stand beside her at the glass doors. He was referring to Hector Munez, his tech guru from Naples who had helped them on the St. Augustine case and did a lot of Nick's online research, including the frustrating task of trying to trace Ames and his spider's web of companies. "I've got him searching for Paul Kilcorse's permanent residence as well as Clayton Ames's now.

"Have you taken your night narcolepsy meds yet?" he whispered. "I know you skipped them last night, so you must be really strung out. But, I hope, the worst of this waking nightmare is over."

"Part of it, at least—until we really get out of here. No, I haven't taken the meds yet tonight. You changed the airline tickets from the ones he bought for us?"

"Yes. Midmorning flight out. And we'll call for our own cab for once instead of just waiting for one that's probably waiting for us. But first, soon as the sun's up, the three of us will take a walk on the beach together. We can't leave Grand Cayman without that. He's not going to ruin—or run—everything for us. Want to sit out on the lanai for a few minutes?"

"I know I said she sleeps well, but I don't want her to wake up in a strange place without me in sight."

"Okay. I know you're worried about Jace too. Frankly, so am I, but we can't risk cell phone contact in case that lets them trace him."

"I thought I saw him on the beach, in disguise, looking like a bum when Lexi was coming in from flying the kite. But then when she said the guy who snatched her looked like him, I realized it could just have been another of Ames's gofers. Like, you know, right now your job is to go kidnap a child."

"Listen. Jace is a big boy and insisted on coming. You said he's been in tough spots, in combat."

"Yes, but he's a pilot, not some undercover agent!"

"Okay, okay."

He pulled her to him, maybe a mistake this time. Her breasts through the T-shirt and nightgown pressed flat against his crisp chest hair. Her hips tilted into his thighs. As exhausted as she was, her entire body came alert. Oh, no, but oh, yes. She cared for this man in more ways than one. Thank heavens he set her back fast and kept his hands on her shoulders, as if holding her away.

Some wedding night, she thought. They certainly weren't strangers, but they had not been lovers, and they had to figure out some rules and regs for this forced marriage—didn't they? When they got back and could really hash things out, what would Nick want and expect? They would have to live together for appearance's sake, to keep Ames's spies at bay, to protect themselves and Lexi. She didn't fully grasp what that devil was expecting of Nick and her either. She dreaded facing her family at home, probably having to lie to them, having to move, to uproot Lexi.

"Don't cry. I know things look dark in more ways than one," Nick whispered, raising one hand to lift her chin.

He gently rubbed his thumb along her sensitive lower lip she chewed too much when she was upset or scared. Her lips parted. He skimmed the slick part of her lower, inner lip. His hand smelled of pine-scented soap and his breath of mint. She felt prickly hot all over from his merest touch.

"You know—like I said, we can work things out," he went on, suddenly seeming to stumble for words. His gaze devoured her. "We'll work together. I promise to take good care of both of you. I—we'll take things slow between us," he promised, his voice not only quiet now but rough.

She began to tremble as she whispered, "We need to talk about what our marriage means. I won't hold you to it once we do what he says, once you can get him arrested or whatever it takes to stop him. But that means we have to be so careful now."

"If I'm too careful, you will drive me crazy. Good night,

wife. Let's both get some sleep, so I don't do something out of my mind right now."

He kissed her hastily but hard on her mouth, reached down to pat her bottom and headed to the sofa bed in front of the door. He yanked the single throw pillow there under his head and flapped the big bath towel over himself, waist to feet.

Claire hurried to the bed and downed the dose of her bitter-tasting sedative on the bedside table. Surely her narcolepsy, the medicine and her physical and emotional exhaustion would knock her out.

She carefully tugged the sheet Lexi had pulled away over both of them. The room had seemed cool before but not now.

For once she didn't sleep right away. She was worried about Jace, but it was Nick's tossing and turning and heavy breathing that made her thoughts and heart race.

Jace's captors half dragged, half marched him through the wrought iron gates of Nightshade, into the service entrance of the house. In what was obviously a laundry room, they turned on the overhead light and tied his arms and legs to a wooden chair with a couple of clotheslines from a plastic basket. The small, windowless room held a washer, dryer, sorting table and one chair beside his.

"Go tell the boss," one goon said to the other.

"I have others who know I'm here," Jace told the man who stayed with him.

"Yeah, well, I do too and I'm betting on them," he said, going through Jace's pockets. Luckily, he'd taken his ID info out. His passport was still in the plane parked in a rented hangar. Man, he'd really blown this but when he'd seen those pictures of Claire and Markwood—with Lexi—getting married he'd lost his mind, lost control.

The man pulled out the key to the motorbike, the one to his room, American dollars and his cell phone. "We know who you are and where you're from," he said. "But I'll let the boss decide where you're going."

Jace's insides did a nosedive. What if this Clayton Kilcorse-Ames was not only a kidnapper but a killer? Blinded by his passion to save Lexi and help Claire, he had not realized it could come to this. Could they still be on the premises? He figured not or he would have been gagged as well as tied in case he shouted for help.

His guard turned on his cell phone and started to skim through something on it. He stopped a moment to lay the keys and cash on the washing machine and sat down in the other chair to glare at the phone.

"Nice pics you got of the outside of Nightshade from across the street," the guy said. "Looking to buy multimillion-dollar property here? Coupla good ones of the balcony with the party."

"Were you at the wedding?" Jace dared to ask.

"Part of the reception. Great coconut shrimp and lobster with hot sauce," the guy replied as if they were just buddies shooting the breeze. But when he'd been hustled in here, pressed between the two goons, he'd felt both carried pistols under their jackets.

Jace tried to get more out of him, but the guy clammed up. He wasn't sure how long he waited. He had no idea what time of night it was and couldn't see his watch. Finally, he heard footsteps in the hall. The door opened. A short, white-haired man stood there in a white terry cloth robe over what looked like black silk pajamas. He motioned for the man guarding Jace to step out in the hall, where he also glimpsed the other man. They closed the door, and Jace faced the man he assumed was Clayton Ames alone.

"Well, the third leg of the triumvirate," the man—the boss—said. "That is, if we don't count your little girl, Lexi."

"Is she all right? Did you let her and Claire go home?"

"And your nemesis Nick Markwood, Claire's new husband. You see, he's my nemesis too, so I think you and I might be able to do business, Jason—Jace—Britten. Frankly, I can use a man of your skills and connections. You can call me Mr. Kilcorse as I'm known around here."

"Yeah, well, Mr. Kilcorse-Ames, I'm previously employed. I'm an international airline pilot, but I suppose you know all that. You're the one who sent me the photos of Claire and Markwood together when they were in St. Augustine."

"Brilliant deduction. I see we have your cell phone, so I'll be sure to send you a few of the wedding pictures."

"I've seen some and that was enough."

"I'm sure you'd like a few reminders of why you'll want to work for me. But to answer your first question, Lexi is fine, a little charmer. She will be going back to Naples soon, with her mother and new stepfather. And I need you to leave that alone, for now, at least."

"Meaning what? And why would I work for you?"

"Ah, let me count the reasons. One, because you like to fly and are a skilled pilot and are likely to be asked to take a leave from your assignment flying to Singapore, which you like so much. By the way, Singapore's getting to be quite a tax haven, and I'd like to have a man on my payroll who knows his way around there. I might have you fly me there yourself. Much better than those crowded public planes, even in first class."

"I'm not on that run anymore. I've asked for assignments closer to home, so if you don't know that, you're slipping."

"Actually, I think the airline has pegged you as unstable in general."

Jace just gaped at him. This guy thought he was God, with his all-knowing information—or just the opposite of God, Satan himself.

His captor went on, "You'd be best off flying a second new Learjet I just bought. It seats eight, and for long flights you'd have a copilot, not be one. I'd pay you about four times the salary you've been making now with a big bonus up front. You can keep the Lear in Naples until I need it somewhere, keep an eye on your little girl and ex-and-future wife if you play your cards right."

"Future wife? What the hell are you talking about?"

"By your dangerous presence here, you've proved you love your daughter and would risk anything for her, and I believe, despite your frustration and anger, you feel that way about your ex too. You'll never get Lexi away from Claire or really be a part of their lives unless by eventually marrying her again. Oh, let me tell you, Nick Markwood is a take-charge guy in every way. But who would Claire and Lexi run to if it doesn't work out with Nick or if something happened to him?"

"You're not—not thinking I'd kill him for you?"

"Of course not. You'd be the first one they'd look at. But I am thinking that the third reason you'll work secretly for me is that if you don't agree, I'll have the two gentlemen who brought you here take you out in a boat to Cemetery Reef and feed you to the fish. Now let's talk business."

"I wish my daddy was flying this plane," Lexi told Nick as their flight took off from Grand Cayman the next morning.

Claire silently wished he was too, that she knew he was all right, at least.

"I'm sure he's a very good pilot," Nick said.

Lexi was in the seat between them with Claire next to the window. They had made a few hasty plans during their beach walk earlier this morning and agreed again not to talk about serious strategies until they were home. They'd learned to put nothing past Clayton Ames, including trusting no one on the plane, even if Nick had arranged the tickets.

Claire was grateful he was handling Lexi so well. She sighed and pressed her forehead to the window and watched below as the plane circled to head north. In a stretch of blue-green water, she glimpsed the outline of what might be one of the many wrecked ships that had run aground on the rocks or reefs here over the years.

"Lots of sailboats out today, and new cruise ships are putting in," she observed.

"I like boats," Lexi said. "Ones with sails like big wings, lots bigger than Tinker Bell's wings in Peter Pan."

"So you like boats?" Nick asked her. "You know, that gives me an idea about where we could live for a while. And it would be lots of fun."

Claire's head snapped around. If he meant on a boat, at least that might keep Ames's lackeys and their eyes and ears away from them.

"But your boat isn't big," she said.

"No, but I know someone whose boat is."

"Mr. Kilcorse doesn't like boats," Lexi said, still holding her green stuffed turtle they had checked again for listening devices, though Nick intended to have it x-rayed too. "Just like Daddy, he likes airplanes. I heard him talking on his cell phone, walking back and forth. He was telling someone he had to pay a lot of money to fly into Cubes."

"Cubes?" Nick asked. "Could he mean Cuba?"

"Maybe. They locked me in a bedroom and said to sleep but I was too scared and peeked and listened under the door. And then he said—"

"Okay, enough for now," Nick said with a pointed look at Claire. "You and Mommy and I will talk about this later."

Claire nodded. It was going to be interesting to use her forensic psychologist training to depose her own daughter as a witness. She'd vowed she was all in to help Nick solve his two cases. One, what was Ames up to and how could they expose and stop him? They had to get something on Ames so the FBI or IRS could step in.

And two, she'd told Nick she'd question witnesses or people of interest in the so-called Mangrove Murder case he'd promised to take to defend his friend. So much for her promise to herself that, after surviving the St. Augustine murder/suicide case, her next Clear Path assignment would be for a local department store that wanted her to question office workers about possible embezzlement.

While Lexi had skipped shells into the water this morning, Claire had told him that she'd help. This trip to Grand Cayman had been bad enough but communist, Castro-held Cuba? That sounded more risky than any other offshore hideout Ames could have holed up in.

Since Nick had said that Ames just disappeared sometimes, could it be to Cuba? The place was off-limits for American businesses and visitors, but Claire knew Cuba had tourists from Canada, so an American could surely sneak in, especially one with money and clout. She'd ask Nick if people had to do big business with the Castro brothers to get a foothold there. No one was going to play with people's lives—forcing them to marry, kidnapping children—not if she could help it. She knew Nick was dedicated to that devil's demise, and surely Jace was too.

As if Nick had read her thoughts, he leaned over Lexi and said in a quiet voice, "I'll get Heck on it, since he has Cuban heritage, but I've learned to put nothing past 'Uncle Clay.'"

"I see that now. I understand."

"Do we have to whisper?" Lexi asked. "I can't hear good with the sound the jet engines make. And I know we're not there yet, 'cause Daddy says you can always tell when you're going down to land. Mr. Nick—I mean, Nick—sometimes Mommy says, don't keep asking this, but are we there yet?"

"Mommy is absolutely right," Nick said with a laser beam look at Claire. "We are definitely not there yet but we're going to be soon, in more ways than one."

CHAPTER EIGHT

"You did what?" Claire's sister, Darcy, cried. She jumped up to close the kitchen door to the living room where their daughters were playing.

"It's no secret. Lexi knows, and she's happy with it," Claire insisted, crossing her arms over her chest. "We just got back last night, and I didn't want to tell you over the phone. I'm surprised Lexi didn't blurt it out. It was all rather rushed, but—yes, Nick and I got married in Grand Cayman at the house of a—a friend of his."

Her blue eyes wide in her freckled face, Darcy collapsed in her seat across the kitchen table and raked her fingers through her spiky blond hair. "Claire, you eloped once before but you were young and crazy. And look what happened to you and Jace—"

"That's way in the past. I wanted you to know about this."

"How thoughtful, after the fact, after all we've been through together. So you won't be an almost neighbor to us anymore. How can I watch Lexi for you, how can the girls stick together—how can we?" Her voice rose to a shrill pitch and tears clumped her eyelashes together.

"I'm so sorry I let you down—all of you, Steve and Drew

too. But it was—it happened and it was necessary, and you'll just have to trust me on th—"

"Necessary! You're pregnant?" she gasped. Finally, Darcy leaned across the table and reached for Claire's clenched hands when her body language before had been stern and standoffish. One of Claire's skills was reading body language and Darcy was hurt as well as mad.

"No, not that kind of necessary," Claire assured her.

"I guess not, now that I think of it." Darcy sat back again. "You've barely known the man three weeks. You could be pregnant, but you wouldn't know this fast. Don't tell me you married him for his money. For financial security? You said you were going to build your consulting company. But it looks to me like you can't even walk a straight line right now, let alone a clear path. You've been bound and determined to be self-sufficient. I get it that the guy is Nick Markwood, eligible bachelor, great-looking, well-off and all that but—I—I just wish I'd been there."

Blinking back her own tears, Claire got up and went around the table. She was almost afraid to touch Darcy at first, but she leaned close and put a hand on her shoulder. She'd always leaned on Darcy. Right now Claire hadn't exactly lied, but she could hardly tell her the truth. She prayed she wasn't endangering Darcy, her husband, Steve, and two kids by sharing even this much. But word would get out, and her family—what was left of it—had to know.

Worse, wait until Jace heard. Once he'd arrived back in US airspace, he texted her from the plane that he'd heard they were headed home with Lexi so he was coming back too. But he'd go absolutely ballistic when he heard his daughter had a new stepfather. He'd feel so betrayed if she couldn't explain it to him—and could she?

"M-m-maybe," Darcy said through sniffles, "I'm more like

our mother than I wanted to admit—like, I mean, maybe I've had my head in the sand, like she always had hers in a book."

"No, it isn't that. I—I just didn't level with you about Nick. This is all on me."

"And here, I was psyching you out that you still cared for Jace and vice versa, but then you're the psych major, not me."

"Don't beat yourself up. Please don't cry. You've been so great to me, always. As the older sister, I should have been the strong one, but it's been you, and I'm trying to catch up on that."

"Stop talking in the past tense, like we're over! Like we won't see each other, or someone's dead. But I guess things have changed."

"Not my feelings for you, for Jilly, Steve and Drew. Darcy, I know I've made a mess of things, and my narcolepsy and cataplexy have been a burden, but—"

The kitchen door banged open, and Darcy's daughter, blonde Jilly, Lexi's age, rushed in sobbing, sucking in huge breaths. "Mom!" she cried and circled around Claire to cling to Darcy on her other side. "Aunt Claire got married, and Lexi was a flower girl, and we weren't invited!"

Darcy shrugged off Claire's touch and held Jilly tight. Lexi came in, hands on hips and tears on her cheeks. "She's not happy for us, Mommy! She's mad at me and you too!"

All four of them sat at the table and cried. Claire hated Clayton Ames even more right now. She made her vow to herself again: she'd do everything she could to help Nick ruin Clayton Ames, if they could find a way—and a way to stay alive.

Jace was glad to see his flying bud, Alex "Ace" Rutherford waiting for him when he taxied Ace's Cirrus SR22 into a back lot hanger at the Naples Municipal Airport. Ace had married money and also had a cabin cruiser and a house in

Grey Oaks, a ritzy, gated clubhouse community in Naples. He worked in stocks and bonds for his father-in-law, though he always said he'd rather be fishing.

"Hey, my man," Ace called out as soon as Jace popped the door, "at least you brought my baby back in one piece."

At least, Jace's thoughts echoed, *Claire and Nick had brought my baby back in one piece.* Ames had assured him they had taken off from Grand Cayman just this morning. When he'd texted Claire, she'd texted back to say they were okay and not much else except to say thanks for the backup help and stay safe. *That's a joke*, he thought. He'd nearly gotten himself killed.

"Hope you didn't doubt me," Jace told his friend, but he doubted himself. Not that he'd had a choice, but he'd agreed to work for the man who had ordered his daughter abducted, who had evidently set it up for Nick and Claire to get hitched. And if Lexi hadn't been kidnapped, he wouldn't be so sure that they weren't in on that.

"Doubt you? No way," Ace said. "Not after we were such a success with 'The Ace and Jace Show' that bombed the hell out of the Taliban. No problems down or back?" he asked, clapping him on the shoulder after Jace climbed down onto the concrete hangar floor. "You look like you haven't slept. You okay, guy?"

"Sure, sure. Your new toy handled great. Hey, I got a new gig from a high roller I met down in the Caymans. Going to fly his new Learjet that will be delivered here in a couple of days. The damn thing's worth about sixty-five million."

"Sweet! He got a company here? Would I or 'Daddy Dear-est' know him?"

"He's an expat, lives down there but needs people flown around from here sometimes."

Ace cocked his head and squinted at him. "No lie? Thought

you loved the international airline gigs and were set on making pilot's chair."

"I'll be more my own boss this way," he told Ace as they watched the mechanic who oversaw private planes walk in to check out the Cirrus.

But, Jace thought, as Ace went over to talk to the guy, that *was* a lie. He'd put himself under Kilcorse-Ames's very tight thumb to save himself. There were perks to the job, but sky-high risk too with very little leeway about taking orders from the top. He'd be flying Ames High, Inc.'s staff here and there on call as well as keeping a close eye on the murder case Ames said Nick would be taking. And he'd sworn to keep an eye on Claire and Nick—which galled him to no end, especially since that's exactly what he wanted to do.

Though he had the perfect excuse to drop in on them to see Lexi, he hated being another of K-A's spies. Still, Claire had betrayed him, maybe not to marry Markwood if she was forced to in order to save Lexi, but to get involved in the first place with that too-clever criminal lawyer. Jace wasn't even sure he'd take Claire back if Markwood dumped her, or, as K-A had hinted, if something bad happened to him. The fact that Markwood took on the man's murder case provided at least temporary life insurance for him.

But what K-A didn't figure on was that Jace was big on paybacks.

"Your eyes are red," Nick observed when he picked Claire up at Darcy's in yet another rented car, this time a Jeep Cherokee. "Did your sister take it hard?"

"Very. Her little girl, just Lexi's age, did too."

"But she said she'd keep Lexi for a little while?"

"We all cried, then made a tenuous truce. Nick," she said as she closed the car door, "I knew it would really hurt her that I more or less eloped. But what Ames is planning to do is dangerous to know, so I couldn't tell her any of that. So where are we going that Lexi couldn't come along? To meet with your endangered species friend Haze?"

"I'll take you to meet him as soon as I can figure out a battle plan. Time's a-wasting since the police may arrest him soon. But first, I wanted you to see a place I think we can live. I didn't want Lexi falling in love with it first, so you can hear me out and decide. You said Jace borrowed his wealthy friend's jet to come down to Grand Cayman. Well, this is a yacht that belongs to a friend of mine who has been after me to return a favor I did for him. That, and Lexi saying she loves boats, made me think of it."

"A yacht? He must owe you a big favor."

"I saved his life—or life without parole—by proving he didn't murder a woman on this boat. A woman who wasn't his wife. I established she was trying to shake him down, that he wasn't having an affair with her and that someone else came on board and killed her before he even got there."

"I remember that in the papers, and on Nancy Grace's TV show too. She always digs up sensational stuff like that—screwed-up lifestyles of the rich and famous. So you're going to show me a yacht where a murder took place?"

"True, but once you see it, you'll forget about that. He hasn't used it much since. He and his wife are still barely speaking. It's a beautiful boat with six cabins and a small back deck pool, no less. It's been just sitting at a marina in Naples Bay."

"It would give us freedom to move around and keep strangers out, at least until you—we—work on this so-called Mangrove Murder. Lexi doesn't start preschool until the New Year. Maybe she'd see it as a vacation."

"We'll tell her it's an extended honeymoon. However hard we have to buckle down," he said, reaching out to take her hand from her lap, "maybe it can be that."

★ ★ ★

As Claire stood on the dock, she thought the *Sylph* looked like a floating palace. Sleek lines, pale gray-and-white hull. It had a Jacuzzi as well as a small pool. She could see that much from where they stood on the dock, so what must it be like inside? She could tell that its owner Dylan Carnahan was excited to have Nick use it for a while, at least. But it had stunned her to hear the man call the yacht his "twenty-million-dollar baby."

Dylan was about Nick's age and almost as tall. He had much lighter hair and seemed to have a—well, a jumpy, nervous persona.

"I owe you everything, pal," Dylan told Nick after they were all introduced where he greeted them on the dock. The man was very talkative. Sometimes that meant a person was hiding something, but this man actually seemed lonely. "I'm happy to hear you have a ready-made family, and the *Sylph*'s all yours for a while," he went on. "I'm gonna probably sell it, but not yet. Despite everything, it's hard to let her go. I'll get you a crew too, as it only has a captain and cook right now. I'd love to have her go out again. She doesn't deserve her bum rap. You know what a 'sylph' is, Claire?"

"Some kind of water nymph?"

"It's a slender, graceful woman. In short, Nick," he said, bumping Nick's upper arm with his fist, "an appropriate ship for your new bride and first mate."

"Fated to be mated—Claire and me and the ship?" Nick countered.

"You got that right. Sorry, Claire," Dylan said, "about the bad publicity here, but Nick saved my hide—not that I was guilty. I know you'll do the same for that guy on Goodland too, pal."

Nick's head snapped around. "How do you know about that?"

"In the paper this morning, made you sound like the attorney from heaven. Don't ask me how they got the word you're defending Hazelton if you didn't tell them. You know, the victim got let go from the staff of the Naples newspaper, but now they sound like they're really into this story, fellow journalist and all that. I saw something on CNN's *Headline News* about it too. I sympathize with the guy, 'cause I know how it feels to have the media mavens on your tail, even if you're innocent."

Nick and Claire looked at each other. The master in distant Grand Cayman was pulling strings again, using the fact Nick was well-known and respected here to set this all up. Local newspaper articles were one thing, but a national TV cable network?

"So, hey, let me show you newlyweds around," Dylan said with a sweep of his arm toward the gangway. Claire almost felt she was boarding one of those Grand Cayman cruise ships.

She tried not to gawk at the opulence of the *Sylph*'s layout and decor. Lexi would absolutely flip out. The wall and fabric color scheme was stark black-and-white with touches of gold throughout. Chrome gleamed everywhere she looked, except in the stainless steel galley, where, Dylan said, the cook would be happy to not just be cooking for himself and the captain.

Everything was so modern, sharp and clean. Two suites and four bedrooms—though Dylan corrected her to use words like *staterooms* and *cabins*; to say *heads* for the four stunning bathrooms; and *passageways* for hallways. It was another world but it would provide privacy and safety.

While the two men huddled at the dining room table over details, Claire stood at the point of the prow, remembering Leonardo DiCaprio's character in the movie *Titanic* shouting, "I'm the king of the world!" What a love story but a tragic one.

She had not been able to say yes, she'd marry Nick, because he hadn't asked, and it had been out of her control. But she'd said yes to living here, despite the fact the lounge had been the scene of a murder. At least this would work until Lexi started school and for the time it took them to clear Hazelton and tout Ames's Youth products.

But what if Hazelton wasn't innocent? She'd have to help Nick find out the truth. As for keeping Lexi safe, they planned to hire an au pair, a sort of nanny, a Hispanic woman related to Heck Munez. They would be docked here, but possibly move to different island ports, or maybe even go to sea.

She went back in and wandered to the master suite again. She'd insist that Nick take this stateroom, and she'd stay in the slightly smaller one next door. They could put Lexi next to hers and each have a cabin to use as an office, when they were here and not onshore at Goodland and beyond, working on the murder case. There would still be a guest bedroom here for Darcy and her family—if they would visit.

As much as Claire feared and hated Clayton Ames, this part of their new situation was working out well. He wouldn't know exactly where they were, and if they saw his drones hovering, Nick had joked, they could shoot them down with the setup for skeet shooting at the back—the aft—of the boat. They could move about at will without cameras and listening devices.

She glanced at the king-size bed decked out in stark black-and-white with gold lightning strikes jagging across the pattern. She couldn't recall much about the murder of the woman that had happened on this ship, so maybe she should try to find that episode of *Nancy Grace* on YouTube again. No, she wouldn't think about all that. She had a lot to do, to get ready for.

She stopped at the doorway to look back once again at the big bed. For the first time she noted there was a mirror on the ceiling over it.

Her insides cartwheeled. She hurried out, closing the door behind her.

CHAPTER NINE

It was almost 5:00 p.m. when Nick drove them around to the back entrance of his law office. Claire had noticed that the discreet sign in front read merely Markwood, Benton & Chase without any mention of attorneys-at-law, but then Nick was already well-known for some big cases in Southwest Florida. Seeing those other names hit Claire hard. She didn't know any of Nick's senior or junior law partners, and only one man who worked with him on his covert company South Shores. Her stomach cramped. Here she was married to Nick, but did she really know him?

"We will have to tell people we're married, won't we?" she asked.

"I've laid the groundwork for that with my assistants. Heck ferreted it out for himself by finding Paul Kilcorse's link to our Grand Cayman marriage license. There's not much my tech expert can't find—except where Ames makes his permanent base."

"If he has one. It's ironic Heck has a Cuban heritage, and that's where Ames might hide out."

Nick just frowned at that. "I told Heck to come in the back

way and meet us in my office. Although he mostly works for me more or less undercover for South Shores, my partners here know he's a consultant. And about announcing our marriage, I'd like for us to have a reception later for friends and family. Right now, this case and protecting you and Lexi come first."

"And protecting yourself."

After they walked to the building, he unlocked the back entrance door, and they went up a concrete staircase, a far cry from the glass-and-carpeted front entry she'd glimpsed with a chandelier and live tropical foliage inside. Although the office building faced the busy Tamiami Trail, it seemed so silent here, even with most of the other lawyers and their staff still at work in offices above. Nick said he'd sent his secretary home early and told the colleagues he intended to use on the Mangrove Murder case not to come to his office right now. Clayton Ames might reek of power, she thought, but in his own realm, criminal attorney Nicholas Markwood did too.

"Nick," she said, turning back to put her hand on his shoulder. Since he was a step below her on the stairs, they faced each other eye to eye. "I thank you for being so good with Lexi. I realize the five o'clock Happy Meal just now at McDonald's is not your usual time and place for dinner, and you were great with Darcy's family when we took Lexi back there for a little longer stay tonight. She's very excited about living on a big boat."

His smile lifted the corners of his mouth and erased the worry line on his forehead. "The good news is I do care for her—and, especially, for you. The bad news is, that's exactly what Ames is banking on to keep me in line with unspoken threats to all of us. But I also want to be good not only with Lexi but with you."

He leaned against the banister and pulled her to him. She put one hand on the back of his neck and the other on his cheek. His beard stubble, so unusual for him, rasped against her damp palm. They both kept their eyes open as they kissed, carefully, gently. But suddenly, he anchored her to him with both hands hard on her waist. They breathed together, moved together, deepened the kiss and their embrace.

A door slammed above them, and the sound echoed in the stairwell. "Boss, you okay?" came Heck's voice with its Hispanic lilt. "Saw you drive up and walk in."

"Yeah, okay. Just a sec."

"Wanted to be sure. After everything, you might need a bodyguard as well as a cyber genius—ha!"

Nick finally moved away from Claire and looked up the stairwell. "You're my man! We were just talking. Be right up!"

With a metallic echo, the door above them closed. As Claire fanned her flushed cheeks and went up ahead of Nick again, he patted her bottom. "You're the one who needs a bodyguard, sweetheart," he whispered up to her, "and I'm it."

"Don't you know redheads tend to flush when they get excited?" she whispered back at him.

"I'm counting on it."

But, despite his teasing, which absolutely rattled her poise, as they walked out onto the third floor and headed toward his office, she could sense that Nick became all business, just as the surroundings seemed to. This hall had dark green carpet with two, tall-backed, upholstered chairs and a large Oriental vase of purple orchids on a dark wood library table. Inside the first door where Heck waited was a secretary's or receptionist's desk, vacant now.

"Best wishes to the newlyweds, *que bueno*!" Heck told them with a grin as he shook Nick's hand and then hers. "If it wasn't out of the frying pan and into the fire with this new mess, we'd celebrate, yes?"

"We still will," Nick promised.

"The little Lexi—she is all right?" Heck asked Claire. "My

cousin Juanita, she's very happy and hopes to work for you, kind of like a *duenna* to your daughter."

"More like a nanny," Nick said. "Claire will be glad to meet her tomorrow. Just so she doesn't get seasick, because we're going to stay on Dylan Carnahan's yacht until we get our own place. Remember it?"

"Oh, sure. Big and beautiful. Hope it's not haunted like the Shadowlawn mansion, yes? I mean—somebody did get murdered there..."

"Shake off that last case," Nick interrupted him, "because we've got a big one here. So give us what you've come up with on the so-called Mangrove Murder. I'll decide who to use here on the staff and get you going on things too, besides trying to track King Kong Clayton Ames-Paul Kilcorse. And of course, Claire's going to help as she did in the St. Augustine case."

"That other Kilcorse name may help but it may be another dead end too," Heck said.

Nick clicked on the conference room lights and sat near the two of them at the corner of the big, dark wood table. This was obviously a conference room for twelve, with extra chairs along the wall under the oil paintings of the Everglades and Ten Thousand Islands. Claire could see in the room beyond a huge desk and bound leather sets of law books lining tall shelves on a stunning Persian-style carpet in rich blues and golds.

She should have known Nick's offices would be expensive and impressive, and she hadn't even seen his house yet. He said he usually ran his South Shores covert operations out of his home and could easily move his office there onto the yacht. Through that private enterprise, he dealt with cases in which he could help someone who had lost a loved one, cases in which it was uncertain whether the death was a murder, suicide or an accident.

She realized that was the same trauma he and his now deceased mother had gone through. How Claire wished she'd known his father, since his loss had inspired Nick to found South Shores and perhaps to become an attorney. She felt honored to be entrusted with helping on this murder investigation, which fit both Nick's public and private endeavors. Thank God Nick recognized her strengths. He was not treating her like the little woman who should be locked up and kept home for protection.

Heck pulled a sheaf of papers—some newspaper articles, some computer printouts—from his well-worn leather satchel. Despite the fact he had helped her and Nick with their last case, she felt she didn't really know him very well, but she was going to be sure she checked out and trusted his cousin Juanita when she interviewed her.

"Boss," Heck said, his stack of papers slid only halfway across the big table, "got to level with you 'bout something first."

Claire held her breath, but Nick seemed calm. "Shoot, *amigo*."

"It's okay to talk free here?"

"I have it swept for bugs twice a week, and I've had it locked."

Claire put in, "He means without me here, don't you, Heck?"

"She's totally on the team," Nick said. "Tell us."

"An FBI agent come snooping 'round me—made me an offer for a job."

Nick's hand also froze partway to the documents. "Was he asking about Ames?"

"Not 'xactly. Even though my not having none of those fancy university credentials like computational math, computer info systems—all that—he offered me a job, cyber agent, starting at about $60,000. They want skilled hackers to work for them in Quantico, Virginia. You believe that?"

"I believe that. You mind telling me the agent's name?"

"It was kind of quiet—hush, I mean. He made me promise not to say, even to my family. That is, till I think it over."

"Tell me this then. Was he tall, really blond? A space between his front teeth?" Nick asked, recalling the look of the FBI agent who grilled him about Ames a couple of years ago.

Heck nodded and hit his fist on the table. "You think it's a setup? Like from Ames to buy me off?"

"I don't think so, but I put nothing past him. Did the agent have an official badge? I'm sure you checked what one looks like. And what did you say?"

"He had a legit badge. I said I'd get back to him."

"I need you, Heck, especially on this case—and tracking Ames to find his home base. I know you're trying to save up to get your grandfather's hacienda back in Havana someday. I repeat, I need you, and I'll top that government salary.

"Listen, please, both of you," Nick went on, looking from one of them to the other and leaning forward over the corner of the table. "I'm really in a bind on this case for more than one reason. We need to fly under the radar on our investigation into this murder of the journalist. I have to make it look like I'm getting ready to defend my friend Haze to appease Ames, but Haze hasn't been formally indicted. So if we're too obvious questioning witnesses—or other suspects—or preparing a case, it will look to the local authorities like we know he'll be arrested, and we don't want that. Ames does, but it would not be fair to a friend or a client and Haze is both."

Claire put in, "You're right. But Ames expects and demands a show trial so you can tout his Fountain of Youth products."

"Exactly. Or else—for all of us."

"I'll be careful," Claire promised, "and we'll try to avoid any public press or media coverage."

"Truth is, I'm not going anywhere, not now anyway," Heck said, extending his hand to Nick, who shook it. "'Cept maybe out in the Ten Thousand Islands with you to a clump of mangroves where Mark Stirling's body was found wedged in the roots. I got you the police report right here, as well as the newspaper articles. Even got one by the guy who took over Stirling's little *The Burrowing Owl* newspaper on Marco Island. He says he's proud to carry on the paper and its causes."

"That was fast," Claire said. "So that man profits from Mark Stirling's death. I'm going to try to learn if others did too."

Frowning, Heck said, "Dead guy, I bet, had others didn't like him. 'Cording to people he worked with at the *Naples Daily News*, he stepped on a lot of feet. You gonna have your arms full psyching out persons of interest who wanted him hurt or gone, Claire."

She and Nick exchanged a quick look. With the FBI snooping around Heck, did that mean they were being watched by them as well as by Ames's people? Surely that was not just because the FBI was interested in Heck. Especially not if it was the same guy who had questioned Nick about Ames years ago.

On the yacht that night, Nick and Claire tucked Lexi in together. She hadn't slept at first, chattering away, all wound up to be on this big boat, *better'n Captain Hook's and not so scary with pirates*. And Nick felt wound up just to be near Claire alone at night.

They had put Lexi in Claire's cabin for the first night, until they brought the child's clothes and toys here when they moved a few of their things in too. When Lexi finally fell asleep, Claire had left the light on low. Lexi had her plush turtle in her arms, though Nick hated the idea of where it had come from. At least he'd checked it three times for listening devices, and he was used to spotting those now.

As they worked together side by side on the sofa in the cabin he'd claimed for an office, Nick told Claire, "I can't wait any longer to go see Haze. How about you go along tomorrow morning, but while I talk to him, see if you can set up interviews with some of the Goodland locals Heck had in his report, beginning with Haze's wife, Maggie?"

"If the interview with Juanita goes well first thing tomorrow morning, so I can leave Lexi with her here, that sounds good. I agree, it might be better if you meet with him alone at first, since you know him. I sure want a crack at him later—word patterns, tone of voice, body language—though I'd just tighten him up and be a distraction right now."

"I can grasp that," he said. He put his hand on her knee. She was even getting to him in her jeans and sweatshirt. He'd tried to focus on planning his approach for the case, but he kept shifting to his approach to Claire. He didn't want to push her, but he wanted her.

"Good idea that I talk to his wife," Claire said, rustling through the papers they had strewed between them. "This article on her that Heck found online from a Sarasota paper makes her sound—well, opinionated and talented. I quote, 'A rabid, local environmentalist, Maggie Hazelton is obsessed with protecting the local burrowing owls. She seems to know more about them than anyone else in the area, which seems apropos since owls used to be considered symbols of secret wisdom.'"

Nick said, "I don't think that breed is on the endangered and protected list yet but Maggie wants them there."

"I've seen pictures of some burrowing owls on Marco, and they are cute. She sounds like a strong, dedicated person. She may have some insights I can pick up on about Haze and his Youth product associates."

"She's always been stridently opinionated, just like Mark

Stirling. I think she was at loggerheads with him on the owl protection too."

"In other words," Claire said, "I think I'm about to become an expert on reading back issues of his *The Burrowing Owl* rabble-rousing weekly newspaper, as well as the current issues by the guy who so quickly took over from Mark. Oh, here's his name and the I'm-in-charge-now-and-I-won't-let-up article Heck mentioned. His name is Wes Ringold. Listen, I can do this background reading and still spend time with Lexi. Performing forensic autopsies often means studying what the dead person wrote in public and in private. It may sound boring but it often points a finger—or flushes someone out of hiding—instead of their burrowing."

"Keep close contact with me, even when we're not together, understand?" he said, frowning at her. He kept from saying, *And that's an order.*

"Aye, aye, Captain," she threw back, still sifting through Heck's reports. Nick could see her sharp mind was working overtime already as she went on, "If I can't meet with his wife, or even set up an appointment, I'll go looking for their neighbor, Ada Cypress. As far as I can tell, she's lived on Goodland near the supposed fountain of youth for years, so maybe she can help. What I suspect is it wasn't an accident that Mark Stirling went out alone into the jigsaw puzzle of those small mangrove islands and just happened to shoot himself in the head, when this report says he didn't own a gun. I don't care if it's still under discussion by the authorities that he might have committed suicide. More importantly, he certainly didn't wedge his body between mangrove roots while the gun washed away somehow."

"And so," Nick told her, moving his bare foot to rub against hers, "as Perry Mason used to say, 'The game's afoot.'"

She laughed and shook her head. "Sherlock Holmes. My

mother must have read Darcy and me every book Arthur Conan Doyle wrote."

"Oh, yeah, him too."

Nick grasped her hand and tugged her gently around to face him more fully. He intended to pull her onto his lap, but just then Lexi's shrill scream jolted them both to their feet.

Claire jumped up and beat Nick to her cabin, shoved the door that was ajar even farther open. Lexi was sitting up in bed with the covers pulled around her, eyes wide open, staring into space in the dim room, still screaming.

Claire tore to the bed, grateful it must just be a nightmare and not someone else in the room with her. After her kidnapping, the child seemed to have adjusted well and yet—

"Lexi, Lexi, sweetheart, it's Mommy." She sat on the bed, pulled the child onto her lap, held her hard, rocked her. "It was just a bad dream."

Claire knew all about bad dreams. Her disease had drowned her with them, at least until her meds were calibrated and she understood the horrors of the night were not her fault. Horrid dreams, dark nightmares, strangers clawing at her, taking her away when she felt paralyzed. The memory of them leaped at her now as she held Lexi. But Lexi had never, thank the Lord, suffered from bad dreams—until now.

"Mommy, Mommy, they took me away. It wasn't really Daddy. The place had big water all around it. I din't know the house and got locked in a room, a pretty one like this. I was afraid without you and Daddy!"

Claire turned her own teary face to Nick. Poor man, standing there, wanting to help but helpless. What an awful first night here on this lovely yacht. He held up both hands and nodded, though she'd said nothing, then backed out of the room slowly.

The screams had slid to sniffles. They held tight to each

other. Claire stretched out beside her daughter on the bed. Finally, Lexi sighed, and her little body began to relax against Claire's.

"He was nice to me, Mommy, but I think he was scary too."

Claire knew she meant Ames. "I think you're right, but he's far away now, and you are safe with Nick and me on a pretty boat, not at all scary like that one in the *Peter Pan* movie."

"But he wants to hurt Nick later, because he was cross with him, maybe like crossing your heart, hope to die. Captain Hook wanted to hurt Peter Pan, and I think I dreamed Mr. Kilcorse wants to hurt Mr. Nick—I mean, Nick."

Now Claire went stiff. "Was that one of the things you heard him say when you were listening under the door?"

Lexi's tousled head rubbed up and down against Claire's throat as she nodded. "I like this boat, Mommy, but in the dream I fell in the water and couldn't breathe—got dead. He said that too, about some man in the water, dead."

Claire drew in a sudden breath. Could Lexi have overheard something about Mark Stirling's death? Nick thought Ames might have set up that murder to promote Haze's so-called fountain of youth, and his own huge investment in the water. Mark Stirling had been attacking not only Haze but the credibility of the water in his small newspaper, and other media outlets had picked up on it.

Yes, she had to interview her own daughter soon and be sure no one else but she and Nick knew what the child had overheard. No way would she ever let Lexi testify in court, even to help Nick. That would make the child an even more obvious target for Ames and his lackeys. So maybe she'd best not tell even Nick everything Lexi had just said, including, *Cross my heart and hope to die.*

CHAPTER TEN

By the time Juanita Munez came aboard the *Sylph* to meet Claire and Lexi, Claire had received two texts from Heck about his cousin. One said that Juanita had lost her husband in an accident when he was working as a roofer. The other said, I know J can help you—and you can help her. J loves kids, has none of her own yet in big family.

Heck arrived with the pretty, twenty-two-year-old woman and, after introductions all around, he disappeared with Nick. Lexi was watching a video in the lounge, so the two women sat around the table on the back deck of the boat still moored at the very end of the Crayton Cove dock.

Juanita defied all the ideas of what Claire thought she might look like—a good lesson for a forensic psychologist. Her dark hair was only collar-length and curled; she was quite thin and a bit taller than Heck. She tried to read the woman's body language in light of what she knew of Juanita's tragedy. But she held her head erect, which suggested self-confidence, and she smiled easily. Her eyes were bright, though they darted about at first, perhaps in awe of the luxurious surroundings or in hopes of spotting Lexi. But Juanita's foot bounced, and she gripped her fingers together tightly in her lap. She was nervous, of course, but then so was Claire. They both wanted this to work.

Claire began, "Though we haven't moved everything in that we need yet, we plan to live on this boat for at least several months and may move about in it, in this general southwest Florida area. You don't get seasick, do you?"

"Oh, no. My family has fishing boats from way back to Cuba days, salt water in the blood. Did Hector tell you our grandfather in Cuba, he have a whole lot of boats? Sad, I never knew him but knew—know—all about him."

"Yes, the Munez family patriarch means a lot to Hector. I think he'd like to reclaim what was lost to your family when Castro took power."

Juanita shook her head so hard her hair bounced. "Very bad, dangerous man. People living there still scared."

Claire thought that summed up how she and Nick were living now—scared because of a bad, dangerous man. Not only had Lexi suffered that nightmare last night, but Claire had also had a narcoleptic dream that had terrified her. As soon as she could, she hoped to get off her powerful doses of meds and try some herbal sleep remedies. But having someone like Juanita—someone Clayton Ames could not have already turned into a spy—would help her cope and sleep better.

She explained to Juanita what her duties would be, her salary and that she hoped she could teach Lexi some Spanish. She showed her Lexi's room and the small cabin nearby, which would be her own. It was still only early October, so the term of employment would probably be until Lexi started preschool in the New Year, hopefully with her cousin who was just her age, or it might be longer, she explained.

"Cousins, the best, besides brothers and sisters," Juanita told her as they walked to sit on the deck again. "I got nineteen cousins, also four sisters, two brothers. I'm the oldest, so I did help care for them—I have experience. Right now, myself, I—I *viuda*...means...means..."

"A widow?"

"Yes, that's it. Widow with no kids of my own."

"Hector told me about your husband. What a terrible loss for you. I'm very sorry."

Her dark eyes grew luminous with unshed tears. "You so blessed to have a husband—second husband, yes, but yours, still living. And your little girl, I promise I take good care of her for you, like she was my own."

"One more thing, Juanita. Since my—my husband," she faltered, struggling for how to say this. "Since he is a well-known attorney who has sent people to prison, he does have some enemies. So we need to be very watchful that strangers don't get near Lexi or this boat. He even plans to hire a bodyguard-driver for when you or I take Lexi ashore, just to be extra careful. Can you deal with that?"

"I dealed with much more than that, Mrs. Claire. Got to be safe—a man on a rooftop or a child on a boat—and I can help you and little Lexi."

So that was that. Claire extended her hand and Juanita took it. "I'm sure you will be great with Lexi. So let's call her in because I told her someone special was coming to meet her. She insisted on watching *Bambi* on TV until we were ready for her."

Claire had tried to talk her out of watching that movie because the young deer's mother dies, and who needed that right now?

About an hour after they left Juanita with Lexi on the yacht, Nick drove them south on the Tamiami Trail and turned onto San Marco Road. It headed through a maze of mangrove islands where they caught occasional glimpses of people fishing from small boats. Here began what locals called the Ten Thousand Islands, some small, some large, but who could ever count them? They were heading toward the little town—permanent population somewhere around three hundred—called Goodland.

Nick loved Goodland, where his longtime friend and new client Haze Hazelton lived in the house several generations of his family had occupied, though it had been rebuilt after the hurricane of 1992. The place was night and day to the groomed, glitzy Florida he usually dealt with. Haze's dad had owned a small motorboat that Nick and his dad had gone out fishing in years ago with the Hazeltons.

Goodland was like a throwback to the 1950s, the locals claimed, and they were proud of it. The attitude there was "We ain't changin'," and they called their bigger neighbor, modern Marco Island, "Mark-up Island" as they saluted it with a raised bottles of beer or their middle fingers. Redneck all the way, a taste of old Florida before all its "petting and prettifying," as Haze's dad, now long dead, used to call it.

Instead of condos and golf courses, Goodland boasted a rec center and houses on stilts or double-wide trailers. Flags flying could be the Confederate Stars and Bars, the skull-and-crossbones pirate flag, or a banner for pro football teams from the Midwest snowbirds.

Goodland had begun as a fishing village, and it still had plenty of that feel with rowboats or motorboats moored on the canals that ran along most backyards. Haze, a friend and fellow basketball team member from Nick's high school years, had later taken him to most of the Goodland bars, especially the best-known one, Stan's Idle Hour, which hosted the Buzzard Lope Festival every year the week before the Super Bowl: outlandish costumes, an imitate-a-buzzard dance contest, great fried mullet and drinks, drinks, drinks.

Nick smiled as they turned toward the town. As comedian Steve Martin would say, this was "a wild and crazy" place, a quirky escape from modern Florida. But, Nick realized, not an escape for Haze, who could soon be accused of and arrested for murder. Not for Claire, who was already knee-deep, like him, in this murder case.

"You smiled and then frowned," Claire told him.

"And how's the rest of my body language and tone of voice, Ms. Forensic Psychologist?"

"Handsome and sexy."

"Hey, say something like that tonight, if Lexi doesn't interrupt us with another nightmare."

"I don't want to think about that. So what should I really know about the Hazeltons that you haven't told me already? And why would anyone believe they have Ponce de León's fabled fountain in their backyard? I mean, I read the place was named and clearly drawn on a Spanish map from 1523 as a spot for galleons to find fresh water, and that Ponce and crew put it here, but fresh or good water doesn't mean it has youth or health properties."

"I'll let Haze do a show-and-tell on all that. We're almost there."

She looked back out the window, as they approached downtown with its several bars and city buildings. There was no police department as Marco Island officials did that duty here. Haze's house and an RV park were just a short drive beyond.

Hard to believe, Nick thought, that he had a beautiful new partner and associate—and a wife. He wanted to not only protect her but win her heart.

"You know," she said, "the roots of the mangroves look like claws grabbing the water and the bottom of the bay. I still don't see how a body could be wedged into them, like they say Stirling's body was. I'm glad we're going out to look at the place his corpse was discovered. Someone had to more or less stick him there—and they must have wanted him to be found."

"Unless," he said, "they expected the sharks that breed in this Ten Thousand Island area to make the body disappear."

"Sharks! Do we really want to go out there? But then, I guess you and I are used to sharks of another kind lately."

"Here we are," he said, turning in under a large house on stilts that had two new-looking pickup trucks parked there. "Get ready to go to work, sweetheart. We'll try divide and conquer—me with Haze and you with Maggie, if she's not out marching for the endangered owls on Marco."

But as if they'd been watching for their arrival, Nick saw the Hazeltons, both in black jeans and boots, thud down the wooden stairs to greet them.

Jace absolutely loved the private jet he'd be flying for Paul Kilcorse. It was as good as laying eyes and hands on a gorgeous woman. He'd take orders about where to fly this big baby, but he had no intention of doing anything illegal. If Kilcorse-Ames, on his own, could get Nick Markwood out of Claire's and Lexi's lives without really hurting him, he could go for that. Not that he couldn't get Claire back on his own, of course, but that would take time and he didn't want her starting a family with Markwood. Jace owed the lawyer for helping to save Lexi, but he didn't owe him Lexi. He had to toe the line with Kilcorse-Ames for now, but he had no intention of hurting even Markwood, if it came to that—just maybe getting him out of his former family's life.

He sat and spun in one of the high-backed white leather swivel seats in the jet's cabin. Eight of these chairs could be locked in place to surround a mahogany conference table. Carpet, a fancy galley, a great private bathroom and a double bed in back. The flight deck equipment was not only first-class but cutting-edge. He'd have to do his homework on a couple of features. He hadn't met the pilot who had flown it here. It was almost as if the jet had brought itself in.

He went forward to sit in the pilot's seat again and stared out the curved, tinted window into the dimly lighted hangar. He hadn't expected the plane to be delivered so quickly, hadn't envisioned it would be so beautiful. But he'd have to get used to the fact he was dealing with the devil. And the devil knew just what to tempt people with. In his case, a generous salary, a career in the pilot's seat and his family back—well, maybe in the future.

That reminded him he was going to find out where the new family was living. He'd asked Claire but she'd fudged about it, said they would be moving around for safety. But he had a right to see his daughter, and Markwood—a lawyer, no less—had to know about visitation rights. It worried him that Darcy claimed she didn't even know for sure where they were, because Darcy and Claire used to know everything about each other. Still, he had figured out that Darcy knew very little about what Nick and Claire were facing on this local murder case too—and who was pulling the strings behind it all.

Jace jumped when someone knocked on the plane's metal exterior behind him. He went out into the cabin and saw a tall blond guy in a gray suit and striped tie had stuck his head through the door to the stairs. It sure wasn't the mechanic who had been looking it over.

"Can I help you?" Jace asked, going to the open door and wondering if the pilot who'd flown it in had come back.

"If you're Jason Britten. I'm a reporter and just noticed this plane. Can I ask if it's private or commercial? The airport office won't say."

"Corporate. That's all I can tell you. But how did you know my name?"

"The office manager said to ask you. Gave your name as the pilot."

"You're a reporter for what—for whom?"

"Actually," he said smiling and extending his hand, which Jace shook reluctantly, "for Uncle Sam. The government keeps an eye on new, long-range planes in South Florida, and the skilled pilots who fly them."

"Because?"

"Because a lot of illegal drugs flow in from South America through here. Because Cuban airspace is still tricky. Just precautions. It's always smart to prepare for trouble before it crashes in."

Jace frowned at this guy's word choice. Bad luck to so much as think the word *crash*. "You're saying you're a reporter for the US government?"

"I report to the US government. FBI Agent Rod Patterson," he said, taking a leather wallet out of his coat pocket and flipping it open to show his badge.

Jace studied it overlong, his mind racing. Despite the authentic-looking ID, was what this guy said legit, or was he tracking Kilcorse-Ames somehow—or was he sent by him to keep an eye on things? There were as many gaps in what he'd said so far as that space between his two front teeth.

"Well," Jace said, handing his badge back, "it's good to know Uncle Sam is on the ball. Can I contact you if I see something suspicious?"

"Please," he said and extended his card to Jace as if he'd produced it from the palm of his hand like a rabbit from a hat. "Anything strange at all you see or hear. That's how we operate, anything strange at all."

He turned and looked down to the right and left, then peered under the stairs. With his hand on the railing and carefully looking down on the steps as he went, he descended and disappeared under the belly of the plane toward the hangar door.

Man, Jace thought, fingering the card that just referred to Patterson as an aviation magazine reporter, he'd also have to learn to hang on and watch his step.

CHAPTER ELEVEN

Claire and Haze's wife, Maggie, stood back a bit as Nick and Haze shook hands, then Haze grabbed Nick's shoulders in a bear hug. Claire read it as more desperate than friendly, but he quickly loosed Nick and stood back.

"Nick, so glad you're here. This thing is way out of hand, big-time media showing up, the police ready to swoop in after they hauled me in and grilled both of us for hours already. Thanks for coming back to represent me, maybe defend me if it gets to that. And really sorry to break up your getaway honeymoon..."

Haze looked over Nick's shoulder and nodded at Claire. Maggie hugged Nick too, then walked around the men to give Claire a welcoming hug before Claire shook hands with Haze.

"The mixed blessing and curse of wrong place, wrong time strikes again," Maggie said, with her hands on her hips in an almost defiant pose. "Protecting something precious like our well water, like the owls—something's going to get in the way. Mark Stirling and his stupid newspaper did, but Haze didn't hurt him. How dare he call it *The Burrowing Owl* when he didn't defend even my little critters like he should!

But sorry to start in like this. Come on up, you two. Coffee and doughnuts await."

Claire quick-studied this couple. They were both fairly tall and lithe. Haze was actually sinewy, very tanned, and it was hard to tell his age, except she knew he'd been a high school classmate of Nick's, so he must be about thirty-nine. The bangs of his sandy-colored hair brushed the top of his round glasses, which were evidently the kind that tinted darker in even the wan sunlight under their house. He reminded her of the folk singer John Denver—and who could believe he was a murderer?

Maggie was also very tanned but with sharp blue eyes and flyaway, shoulder-length hair that looked bleached more by the sun than dyed by a salon. The T-shirt she wore demanded Save Our Owls! and sported a picture of a darling little bird guarding a hole in the ground from which its mate and two babies peeked out. Claire had read about the burrowing owl species but had never seen the colonies in this area.

"Before we go in," Nick said, glancing out toward the backyard along the canal, "Claire's interested in the well. I tried to tell her it's not a babbling brook kind of thing anymore."

"Oh, yeah, sure," Haze said, pointing at a whitish outbuilding. "We'll head over to the old tabby cistern house that covers the well. I have the only key to it. When the Ames High scientists want more seed water, they have to come to me. I keep the key in a safe place, so be right back."

"Seed water?" Claire asked Maggie as Haze dashed up the stairs above their heads.

"That's what the Fresh Dew and Youth Do reps call it. Their scientists mix it with other ingredients, of course, but it's the major component in each product—the magic elixir."

"Do you believe it has youth-giving properties?" Claire questioned.

"Looking at me, you mean? Ha! I'm out in the sun or getting reflection off the water, organizing protests or keeping an eye on the owls. Wait till you see them—the best colony nearby is, unfortunately, over on Marco. Though I'm not a good advertisement for Youth products, sure, I believe in our water. Wait till you get a load of the models hired for the TV and print ad campaigns."

"I've seen them on social media ads," Claire said. "I swear, they're probably all in their twenties, tops, so no wonder they look young."

Maggie rushed on, "See that massive, flourishing old rubber tree over there, next to the shed? The ancient artesian well runs under there, and that's it—the so-called fountain. That tree's hundreds of years old. The 1992 hurricane stripped it down and knocked it flat, but it picked itself up and regrew to look like that with its roots in the well water. Oh, yeah, you keep your skin out of the sun and drink and wash in that water, you'll be looking great for years. You just ask old Ada Cypress, lives over there, wears big palmetto hats all the time outside, but she washes in the diluted well water that spills out onto her grass when it rains. I swear, she's ageless."

She pointed out Ada's house on stilts not far away, but Haze came back with the key and they all walked to the shed. Claire definitely had Ada on her list to interview, though the old woman had evidently refused to talk to the newspaper or TV reporters. Claire had seen her mentioned but not quoted in the articles she'd scanned. She made a mental note of the jerky flow of information Maggie kept throwing at them. Too much? Camouflage for guilt or just nervousness over her husband's plight?

Haze unlocked a brass lock that needed one of those old skeleton-type keys. As he opened the door, cool, clammy air wafted at them. "This old place is built of a conglomerate of rock and shell," he said. "See shells sticking in the walls? It's old-fashioned, Florida concrete called tabby. We got to go down a spiral staircase that leads to the lower level where the water is these days. Early white settlers, Seminole and ancient Calusa Indians before that, drank the water here, even before the Spaniards found it. Word is that kept the Native Americans healthy for years, 'fore something got them, living on the frontier like that, though the Calusa got wiped out by the diseases the Spaniards brought here. This water's not medicine, not if you're sick from something else other than old age."

Claire noted that Haze seemed to think aging was a disease, which surely was not the case. Or was that some of his marketing psychology? She'd have to look into that.

As if she'd read Claire's mind, Maggie said, "Mark Stirling claimed the power of the water was all hype and marketing—a scam. Sure, there's a huge industry today in hang-on-to or get-back-your-youth products, but he should have given our water a chance. He should have tested it over time."

Gripping the top handrail and blocking their way, Haze added, "Wish something could have cured or stopped the bullet someone put in his brain. Sure, neither of us like—liked—him, and I admitted that to the police, Nick. But the guy had a lot of enemies, 'cause he was the slash-and-burn, take-no-prisoners type. But I didn't shoot him and don't know who did."

Nick said, "If you only had a stronger alibi for where you were then, it would nip all this in the bud—not that Maggie's saying you were at home counts for nothing. But we'll find a way to prove you're innocent and that this water has some health properties."

"Some health properties?" Haze challenged. "Especially if there's a trial, it needs to come out loud and clear that our water has strong health and youth-giving properties. I know it's not good to speak ill of the dead, but we have to discredit

Mark Stirling because he tried to discredit us! I'm sure you understand that."

In the dim light, Nick flashed a look at Claire, then turned away. Not only was Nick's friend's attitude a motive for murder, but his demands dovetailed with Clayton Ames's orders to Nick. So had Ames threatened Haze too, or had Haze figured that tactic out for himself?

"Watch your step going down," Maggie told them and gestured for Haze to quiet down and lead the way.

As they descended, the metal steps clattered. The place had only two louvered windows high up, like a barn, so it was dim in here, but Haze had taken an electric lantern hooked over the top handrail and switched it on.

Some rust from the handrail came off in Claire's hand. The metal under their feet swayed a bit, but neither Haze nor Maggie so much as flinched.

"The PR guys from Ames High said to keep it like this, no repairs or modernization," Haze explained. "But we had debts and found plenty of use for the money that didn't include this. They filmed here to show their investors how authentic this fountain is. Sure, it wasn't underground like this when old Ponce de León found it, and it's partly diluted now from groundwater and canal seepage, but it still has the power."

The ragged rock cistern echoed with light and shadows as well as with their voices. As they reached the lower level and shuffled sideways onto a four-foot-wide rock ledge, Nick put his arm around Claire, and they stared into the shifting water several feet below. When Haze cast the light beam down, the water seemed to glow from within like a sunlit gem. Something mesmerizing about the water, its apparently endless depth, its gold to emerald hues, its subtle, beckoning motion, lured Claire, and she leaned slightly forward until Nick pulled her back.

"I can see why people believe it's special," she whispered.

Haze barely breathed the words. "Not just special. Eternal."

While the women went out in the screened Florida room facing the canal, Nick and Haze sat at the kitchen table, drinking coffee and going over a list of possible deposition targets and strategies. Nick could hear Claire's calm voice asking questions and Maggie's more strident tones with her long, meandering answers, though he couldn't make out what they were saying.

"So, have you met Clayton Ames personally?" Nick slid the question in when he and Haze were nearly finished.

"Lately, and years ago. I sure remember him when he was friends with your dad, when you used to call him Uncle Clay. But childhood memories can really skew stuff, right? Lately, I mostly deal with his reps. But know what, friend of mine?" Haze asked, scooting his chair back and slouching down in it to stretch. "I'm betting you or your dad are the ones who first mentioned the artesian well to him and he remembered it, decided to use it. He's done amazing things with it, and with everything he touches, so I hear."

Nick set his jaw hard. He wasn't sure how much to confide in this friend who so obviously was on Ames's side. Besides, this place was probably bristling with hidden mics just the way other houses had been. He'd had to keep himself from blurting out that Claire thought Ames had a Napoleon complex—some short men lusted for power and control.

So he chose, for now, to say nothing. Haze needed to trust him, not argue with him.

"Like, I mean," Haze went on, "the guy has the Midas touch. I know you thought he let your father down on bad investments at the—at the end, but he and his people have been nothing but great to us. That's one reason I insist on paying your regular fee, and I know you don't come cheap, buddy boy. If I didn't value my family inheritance of this place, Mags and I could move almost anywhere and live well, not that she'd leave her owl crusade. Maybe if we'd had kids, it would be different, but she's sure passionate about her cause."

"It's good to have a purpose in life. So the burrowing owl colony is not on endangered status, but protected, right?" Nick asked, glad to be off the subject of Ames, though he had to admit he'd started it. But he needed to know the lay of the land with his client.

"Right. Absolutely," Haze said. "They're protected under the Birds of Prey and The Migratory Bird Acts. The owls are a so-called Species of Special Concern, though she's determined to have them declared endangered."

Nick nodded as he scraped his strewed papers together. Funny, but that's the way he thought of Claire and little Lexi right now. He was passionate about protecting them, and he prayed they would never be endangered again.

Claire gave up counting the numbers of owl artifacts, even out here in the Hazeltons' screened sunroom. Place mats, mugs, a big carving and framed photos galore of burrowing owls. Would Maggie have mentioned the disparaging article Mark Stirling had written about the owls so fast if Maggie herself had had any part in getting rid of Mark? But she did have an airtight alibi that she was in Naples most of the day he died, giving a talk to the Wildlife Conservancy there. She could never have driven back and forth and gotten a boat to dump his body in time—but, the thought hit Claire—could she have made it back and forth all the way by boat? Could she have *not* spent *all* that time at the conservancy in Naples?

"You realize that Mark Stirling had a host of enemies?" Maggie asked for the second time.

"He seems to have been a real rabble-rouser on the page,"

Claire said, tapping the article on the table between them. "Was he that way in person?"

"Always took the anti position. He was fired from the *Naples Daily News*, you know, for being too aggressive, too confrontational—and that's saying something for a reporter these days. Look, Claire, I get it that you're working with Nick to kind of psych people out, so please look into the man's past. Several folks may have seen Haze arguing with him in Stan's Idle Hour, but he ticked other folks off in there too, making fun of the Buzzard Lope Festival, saying Goodland was a great place for condo-building, which no one wants here. 'Goodland, like the rest of Naples, is soon going to be all condos, swimming pools and parking lots,' I believe I quote him word-for-word in an earlier article. Smart aleck. So that ticks off developers in Naples too, not to mention local rednecks or the biker crowd we get in town here."

"Which is probably why the police are taking so long to look at other suspects before they arrest anyone—hopefully, not Haze."

"They told him not to leave the area. The sheriff even said don't leave Goodland, so neither of us should be going out with you to the site where the body was found. But, as I'm sure Haze told Nick, we know two people who could take you right to it in that mess of tiny mangrove islands out there. Ada Cypress, for one, though she's stubborn as a mule. She has an old Seminole dugout canoe she paddles everywhere around here. And Fin Taylor, who takes fishermen out in his charter boat, *Reel Good Time*. His wife's a good friend of mine. Like Ada, Fin—real name Phineas—knows every drop of water around here. I mean out in the bay and islands."

"I'm sure Nick will be looking into all that. Now, you mentioned you had some of the Youth Do drinks and Fresh Dew cosmetics I could sample. I've never bought any, and I'm curious."

"Oh, right," she said, bouncing up. "They sent us a couple of boxes of them. Got them right here, glad you reminded me. And remember, Nick said you'd drive past the owl colony on Marco soon. I'm sure your little girl would love to see those owls. They're only about nine inches tall—the height of this bottle of Dew face wash," she said, plopping down a clear, hard plastic bottle that seemed to shimmer in the light. It reminded Claire of the well water, so they'd done a great job with this packaging. And with the rest, she thought, as Maggie kept pulling bottles and jars from a tissue-paper-lined blue box.

"Here's all of it, I think," she said. "Face cream, moisturizer, body wash, body splash, body lotion. And here's a bottle of the drinkable fountain water, though it comes in berry flavors too."

"The US Food and Drug Administration hasn't yet added safety warnings for energy drinks or these," Claire said.

"Why should they?" Maggie challenged. "It's only fresh springwater from a special aquifer. All the ingredients, in addition to our water, are listed in the print here."

"I'm excited to use some of this."

Maggie gave a little snort and bumped Claire's shoulder lightly with her fist. "You do and you'll start looking like your daughter, I bet. But, Claire, whether or not you believe in this—and I've seen proof it all works—just make sure your new husband believes in Haze and can make everything about my man being guilty of murder go away. Everything, that is, except our precious, magic water."

CHAPTER TWELVE

On the way back to the *Sylph,* talking over all they'd gleaned from the Hazeltons, Nick took a phone call. Claire could hear it was a man's voice. Someone from his office, she thought, as she heard Nick repeat the name of a place where he'd meet the man. *Spanky's?*

At first Nick had looked surprised at the call, though he was hiding it well now. She had thought she was starting to figure Nick out, his body language, tone of voice, at least. He seemed either excited or nervous now. But it was a truism among forensic psychs that it could be hardest to read someone you were first dating or were madly in love with. Hormones or desire got in the way.

Then her belly flip-flopped as she realized she just put Nick in the "first dating" and "madly in love" categories. They were married, for heaven's sake, but again she wasn't sure she knew him at all, or knew how she really felt about him beyond the powerful physical attraction he radiated. And there had to be more than that or all this was a sin and a sham.

"Sounds like a risqué place," she told him when he ended the call but didn't say who it was or what it was about.

"Spanky's? Not really. It's just a down-home restaurant—man food—on Airport Road, named for that 1930s *Our Gang* series. You know," he plunged on, obviously trying to cover something up now, "that old series of reruns on the TV years ago with the so-called Little Rascals."

"The Little Rascals, huh? Never seen it."

"Really wholesome compared to the stuff on TV now. It was before our time. Spanky's is full of old memorabilia and patronized by everyone from truck drivers to the mayor. I need to stop there to see a former client. Can I drop you at your sister's or your place for a little while? You said you had a lot of packing to do of your and Lexi's clothes and stuff like that."

"Stuff like that. Sure. I've got food to make my lunch there if you're going out."

"Claire, I need to see this guy, that's all. Won't take long one way or the other. He's, like they say, 'a blast from the past.'"

"I'll be fine," she told him, realizing she really was not part of his life yet. Hadn't met his friends, his law partners, didn't know his past clients, hadn't so much as been in his house. She was his wife, but in a way, not really.

"Lock the doors," Nick was saying. "I'll go in with you first, though I think we're in the clear while we cooperate with 'Uncle Clay.' Remember, the place is probably still full of listening devices. I'd actually like to hire a bodyguard for you and Lexi to stay on the boat, or drive you around if we're not together."

"So you said. Is this meeting about that?"

He turned off the Trail onto Lakewood Boulevard. "Not sure. If things work out. And, if so, I'll let you have the final say-so, I promise."

"Aye, aye, Captain," she said, trying to sound jaunty and

not annoyed. But in a way, she felt this was their first fight—and even that didn't make her feel like a wife.

Nick spotted the big man at a corner table under an old metal Coca-Cola sign the minute he stopped at the hostess station. He told the girl there that he saw his party waiting and headed over.

Bronco Gates was a man from his and Claire's past, and a man with a past. It was true that he had briefly been a client of Nick's when everything went weird on their last case in St. Augustine. If this worked out, Nick prayed that he could trust the man with the two most precious people in his life. But what would Claire say when she heard who her and Lexi's new bodyguard was?

"Mr. Markwood—sir," Bronco said and stood as if at attention. "Thanks for comin'. Didn't want to bother you at your law office."

Though Nick was tall, the brown-bearded man stood half a head taller. He wore a baseball cap advertising, of all things, Gatorade. His nickname was "Gator Gates," since he hunted alligators annually. His orange Tampa Bay Buccaneers T-shirt stretched over his chest and biceps. His jeans looked like he'd been wrestling on his knees.

Nick extended his hand, and they shook. "Call me Nick, okay? Glad to see you, Bronco, and glad everything worked out okay for you up north."

"Thanks again to you and the lawyer you got me. Thanks to Miss Claire too. How you two doin'?"

"We're off to an interesting start. You might want to call her Mrs. Claire now. We got married in the Caribbean just a couple of days ago."

"Wow. Fast. I mean—good. Wanted to buy you lunch if you'll let me, tell you I 'preciate what you did for me, like I said."

Though Charles, nicknamed Bronco, Gates was not the swiftest guy Nick had ever known, he'd seen he was loyal to his employer. He was emotional for such a burly bruiser, but that was good too, because—with one notable exception—Bronco had a gentle, protective streak. Unfortunately, Claire had had a serious run-in with Bronco back in St. Augustine. Nick didn't know how she'd take it that he thought the guy was a gift from God to protect her and Lexi, which was why he hadn't told her he was meeting with him.

"Are you still hunting snakes in the Glades?" Nick asked. Last he knew, in addition to his hunting alligators, Gates had been working in the Everglades as one of the infamous Swamp Ape Patrol that hunted the escaped, fast-breeding pythons that were becoming a real danger.

"Sure am. Skeeters worse there than in St. Augustine too. Can't use a bangstick to stop a python like you can to get a gator—pow!" he said with a gesture to show how pushing a so-called bangstick against an alligator's head would put a bullet in his small brain.

"Glad you're helping hunt snakes though," Nick told him. "They're breeding out there and then they'll come here."

"Moved my Airstream trailer down here to a RV park near the airport. Got planes goin' overheard day and night, but the price was right. Couldn't stay at Shadowlawn after all that happened—to all of us."

"I know it was hard for you to lose someone you loved, Bronco." Gates's love interest had died tragically, and he was obviously still grieving. The waitress came and took their iced tea orders, chatted and left menus. When she was out of earshot, Nick went on, "I saw how you suffered. I'm going to level with you right away. I have several past enemies—one especially—who I'm scared to death might try to hurt my wife or four-year-old stepdaughter to get at me. I don't know if you're committed to hunting snakes, but my girls need to be protected from a big, human snake. Not that I want you hunting him down. I'm looking for someone to live with us on a big yacht I borrowed from a friend, and be a guard for them on land and sea, even sometimes if I'm with them. I'll top the salary you're making now."

Bronco's brown eyes widened. He hit his chest with his fist. "You mean me? You'd trust me and hire me? Man, I owe you big-time, wouldn't charge you nothing but a place to live and food. I got me a small settlement to leave Shadowlawn, though I hated to do that."

"One thing you did there I need," Nick told him, still ignoring the menus and leaning closer. "Your idea of being a groundskeeper was not being a gardener. You patrolled the grounds at night, and I'd expect you to do the same for us, even though we're on a boat, maybe docked at a marina, or anchored out a ways on the water. I like the fact you have a gun and license to use it—no bangsticks though."

Bronco nodded. Nick hit his index finger on the table to emphasize what he was saying. "And two conditions, Bronco. One, yes, I'm paying you. And two, Claire has to okay it first. I need to make sure she'd be comfortable with you guarding her and her daughter. I hope she'll okay it. I know she spoke out for you when the police came."

"She spoke *to* me too," Bronco said with a big nod. "She calmed me down and made me think about some things. She may not have felt safe with me once before, but you tell her, she gives me this chance, I'll make sure she's safe."

Claire had four boxes packed when Nick backed into her driveway, expecting to load them in the trunk. She'd eaten a peanut butter sandwich and had called Juanita on the *Sylph*. She'd talked to her and Lexi, who seemed to be doing well and informed Claire that she was going to call Juanita by the nickname of Nita and she wanted Nita to call her Lex. So everything seemed to be off to a good start there.

When Claire opened the front door for Nick, he motioned her outside and closed the door after them. He kissed her fast on the lips, a mere peck and said, "Except for the boat, I still don't trust a lot of places for our sharing important news."

"Such as what? How did your business lunch go? I smell corned beef."

"You are good! I had a Reuben and Bronco had roast beef."

"Bronco? You were meeting Bronco Gates, and you couldn't tell me that in the car? Great partnership we have going!"

"I had to see and hear him out first. You ended up on his side, didn't you, saw the good in him?"

"But why is he here? And is he all right?"

"Aha. See. You care," he insisted putting his hands gently on her fists, which she had propped on her hips, then stroking her waist with his thumbs. "He wanted to thank us for what we did for him at Shadowlawn. He appreciates that you listened to him and talked him down. He wants you to know he'll keep you safe, though you weren't safe with him once before, as he put it.

"Claire, I won't hire him if you don't agree, but we need a bodyguard-driver, and he's unemployed except for hunting the pythons in the Glades. I told him we need help from an even bigger snake, so—sweetheart? You and I absolutely, positively are building a partnership, but this one's up to you."

"I'm thinking. I'm thinking if we can totally trust him, after he lost control and scared me to death. But of all the people I think Ames could have located and bought off already to spy on us, Juanita Munez and Bronco Gates are our best bets to trust. I'm trying to be rational about this, not all emotional. Give me a minute on this, okay, while we load my boxes?" She reached up and grabbed his shoulders. She had to get along with this man, who was used to getting his way, but she had to assert herself too. "Thanks for asking me, even though you didn't tell me it was him on the phone. I'm grateful we can work together."

That night was their last at the Crayton Cove Marina in Naples before Bronco and Juanita moved aboard and they set out to anchor at Goodland. Claire finally got around to what she thought of as "deposing Lexi." The child had obviously overheard some scary and maybe important things when she was eavesdropping on Clayton Ames's phone conversation in Nightshade on Grand Cayman. Yet Claire hesitated to bring up anything to do with Lexi's abduction again because she didn't want the nightmares to return—Lexi's or her own.

So, rather than making her questions seem important, she talked to Lexi while the child was sitting in the bathtub in soap bubbles, one of her "most funnest" and relaxing things to do.

Claire sat on the side of the tub, laughing when Lexi blew clusters of bubbles from her hands. Now she had to set the scene with words before mentioning Ames again.

She picked up on some earlier groundwork she'd laid with the child. "I'm so glad you're safe with Nick and me and your new friend Nita, and I know you are going to like Bronco when he comes to stay on the boat tomorrow. He'll work on the boat and drive us around in a car if we get off."

"Mommy, is that because Nick is rich and likes people to work for him?"

"Nick works hard for his money helping people, but he's busy so he does need to hire some other people to help him."

"And this guy Bronco, Mommy. If he has a horse, could he bring it on the boat?"

"He doesn't have a horse, but he does sound like a cowboy, doesn't he? Where he's from in northern Florida, people used to herd cattle, just like out west. Listen, I was hoping before you forget, I could ask you just two questions about something you said you heard Mr. Kilcorse say. We won't be seeing him again, but I'd just like to know."

Lexi stopped flipping suds and wrapped both arms around herself as if she suddenly was cold—typical self-protective body language. "He said a bunch of things, I guess."

"Okay, but one thing is that he might want to hurt Nick, just the way Captain Hook wanted to hurt Peter Pan—something like that."

"But if we don't see him anymore, he can't hurt Nick, can he?"

"No, but did he say something like that?"

She nodded her head. "Yes. Because Nick was cross with him."

"Or could it be he said Nick crossed him?"

"Well, maybe. I think so. Mommy, this water will get cold if we keep talking."

"Just one more question then, and I don't want you to be a bit scared to tell me. Did Mr. Kilcorse mention something about a man in the water?"

Lexi nodded again. The tub water seemed to shiver with the child, though Claire knew it was still quite warm.

"Lexi, can you tell me what you heard, what you remember, then we won't mention any of that anymore, and there will be no bad dreams. Only good ones."

"Some man in the water who was a problem is dead. Shot. He must have been very bad. Mommy, if he was in the water dead, did he drown too?"

Claire knelt beside the tub and leaned over to put her arms around Lexi, however wet she got. Of course, there was no proof Lexi had overheard Ames talking about Mark Stirling's death, but it could be. The man seemed to know and micromanage everything, despite the fact he had lackeys galore working for him. At least, since the child had apparently not overheard more, Claire didn't feel so bad about not telling Nick all of this—not yet anyway. She did not want Lexi to be questioned by others and would never let her testify in court. But she was sure Nick had thought of Ames pulling the strings—and had, at least, hired someone to pull the trigger on the missing murder weapon—that put a bullet in Mark Stirling's brain.

Claire had no intention of even hinting at all that tonight, or Nick might surmise it came from something Lexi said. As she'd tucked the child in this evening, they'd hooked little fingers and promised they would not talk about scary things again because they were all done with that. When Jace called Claire and asked to speak to his daughter, she let him, going in to pick up the wet towel and sop up water from the bathroom floor while the two of them chatted. Just think—would Juanita now give Lexi her baths? No, not if her own mother was around to do it, Claire decided.

She took the phone from a sleepy Lexi and said a quick goodbye to Jace before he could ask where they were again, then went into the lounge in the middle of the boat where Nick, sitting on the leather couch with his papers spread out on the glass coffee table, had a Miami Dolphins football game on the large wall TV.

"Hey," he said. "She in bed? I can mute this game so you can hear her if she calls."

"Good idea, if you don't mind. So, you want to look at the Fresh Dew cosmetics Maggie gave me?"

"Oh, yeah, sure," he said, muting the game, then leaning back on the couch and throwing both arms along the back of it. "I've seen and tested the Youth Do water, even the fruit-flavored kind, but I'd like a close-up and personal look at the women's line items."

She went to her stateroom and brought Maggie's blue box of cosmetics back in, putting it on a space he made on the coffee table. She liked this area on the boat, except for one thing. It was the room where a woman had been murdered. Claire had meant to view again the *Nancy Grace* show where she had highlighted the murder, but thrust that thought aside for now.

"I haven't tried these products, but I guess I should," she told him. "They smell good and probably are good, though I wouldn't bet the farm on their rejuvenation properties."

"This anti-aging stuff is a global industry worth about $292 billion, according to what I've read," he told her, leaning closer as she opened the bottle of body lotion. The seat cushions were soft; she tilted toward him so their shoulders and thighs touched. Like the other items, this one was beautifully packaged, in a clear plastic bottle with pale blue and green tinting that suggested the supposed youth water in it.

As he leaned closer, Nick said, "Here's another factoid I can use in court if it comes to that—60 percent of Americans ages sixty-five and older are pursuing anti-aging interventions of one kind or the other, externals like this or surgery. I think a jury, even a judge, would lean in favor of the public having access to these products—if they're not one big rip-off. And if they are, Ames has us in a tight position where we'd have to decide risking our necks to say so.

"And, that smells great," he admitted, as his dark eyebrows shot up. "Speaking of necks, put a little on, like maybe on your throat."

She opened the bottle and poured a bit into her palm. The liquid too suggested crystalline water, shimmery and silvery. "They've done a great job with this," she said, and arched her neck to smooth some on.

Nick leaned closer yet. He not only breathed the scent in deeply but nuzzled her hair that spilled loose between them. His breath warmed the shell of her ear.

"Yeah, I could like this," he whispered and dropped his arm behind her to tug her tighter while he inhaled again and gently, slowly trailed two fingertips down her neck toward her fluted collarbone. His big hand circled her throat like a warm necklace, then skimmed lower to rest his palm on the cleft between her breasts.

Every inch of her skin leaped alive.

"You know," he whispered, "that stuff is really seductive. Or something is. Claire, this is really our last night alone here. I was thinking we could negotiate some terms for our precious time together—the two of us—before things get even more crazy and complicated. Terms about not just being partners, but husband and wife."

He lifted her onto his lap and tipped her back in his arms. The scent of the lotion on her warming skin enveloped them. Her mind went absolutely blank but for wanting this man, though she made a grab for sanity. *Nick didn't choose me, court me. He had to marry me, because so much was at stake. Shotgun wedding. Talk to him, Claire. Talk. Reason. Not this rush of drowning feelings or you'll be lost. And you wouldn't belong to yourself anymore because you'll be his.*

CHAPTER THIRTEEN

Nick's touch and kiss smothered any protest, and she kissed him back wildly. Somehow he tilted her and turned her. Though he kept his weight off her, she was under him on the couch as he covered her face and neck with kisses.

"That stuff tastes good on you. Must be an aphrodisiac too," he murmured and took her lips again.

Oh, no. She wanted Nick Markwood, but in her head and heart, this wasn't a real marriage. They'd been forced to wed and by a horrible man. They had not chosen each other. And if he wanted to go his own way or she did, this would make it all too impossible. And if she got pregnant...

"Let's go to my room and figure this all out," he said as his lips plunged lower in the damp cleft between her breasts.

"I want to—I want you, but..."

He turned them again, pushing her into the back cushions of the sofa, skimming his free hand along the bare skin of her waist and ribs under her T-shirt, up and down, pressing, kneading, rubbing his thumb under the bottom of her bra. "But what?" he asked, breathing hard. "We've got to trust each other in this, all the way."

"I know," she said, almost panting as he cupped her bottom through her slacks, "but we—this—was forced on us."

His marauding hands stopped, and he lifted his head. It was a Nick she'd never seen, tousled, starry-eyed, totally turned on. She felt the lure and the power of that, but it scared her too. Did she look that way, somewhere between loving and lustful?

"I don't like that word *forced* between the two of us," he said, frowning. "I want only the best things, shared things."

"Yes, yes, me too, so—"

"So hands off for now at least, Mrs. Markwood?"

"Nick, don't be angry."

"Just crazed and crazy. I didn't mean to push, and yet I'd like to."

"You weren't pushing—exactly. I think we feel the same way about each other, kind of, so far."

"Now there's a ringing approval. Big difference between men and women. I'd think of this—this—" he thrust his hips tighter to hers "—as bonding, not bondage. We don't know where this 'arranged marriage' will take us, do we, my favorite psychologist?"

"No, my favorite counselor, we don't."

"Well," he said, sitting up with a groan and pulling her to an upright position beside him, "we'll see how it goes, but you are my ultimate temptation. Even when we have the rest of our makeshift staff here and get busy with interviews and depositions tomorrow, don't think I'm all business with you. Just say the word—that you care enough to trust me—and I'll prove to you it's not just that devil's bargain we made in Grand Cayman keeping us together. Now, if it's okay," he said, clearing his throat and gripping his hands between his spread knees, "I won't walk you to your bedroom door."

She had more to say, but words wouldn't come. The way he'd handled this made her care for him and want him even more. Her legs were shaking, and she felt his intense look down to the pit of her belly. But she scooped up the cosmetic bottles on the table. She whispered, "Good night, Nick."

"Good and lonely," he said with an almost cute pout that nearly swamped her senses. "Beat it, sweetheart," he added and reached out to pat her bottom.

She did, before he could see her tears of relief and regret.

As if to roil Claire's emotions even more, Jace showed up on the dock the next morning and came aboard like a storm trooper. The gangway was down because Juanita had just arrived and they were waiting for Bronco.

"Jace, what are you doing here?" Claire called to him and put down the duffel bag she was carrying for Juanita.

He came right up to Claire and tugged her closer to the rail. "You or your better half should have told me where you were! After all we've been through, I had to figure out where you two were hiding from talking to Lexi. Last night on the phone she said you were near that restaurant we used to like called The Dock, on a boat called *Silver.* Well, she was off on this big yacht's name, but I figured it out."

"Would you please keep your voice down? Why tell you we were here when we're setting out? You could have come here, and we'd be gone."

"Exactly. An extended honeymoon?"

"We need to be on the move and closer to Goodland, and you know why. We'll certainly let you know where we are so you can visit Lexi."

"Claire," he said, grasping her upper arms, "I get it that you and Markwood need to deal with this murder case and keep Lexi safe from, shall we say, the powers that be, but it's only fair that I know where she is—therefore, where you are—and that I can visit her or have time with her."

"She's still sleeping."

"Okay, not right now, but—"

Claire gasped as a man behind Jace yanked him away from her. It wasn't Nick but—

Bronco Gates! He shoved Jace against the glass windows of the salon before he could even fight back. "This guy shouldn't be here, Mrs. Claire?" Bronco bellowed. "He hurting you?"

"No, Bronco! It's okay!" she shouted just as Nick appeared on deck. "It's a man who works for Nick, for us."

Bronco stood back from Jace, who looked like he wanted to slug Bronco. "Oh, sorry," Bronco began, "but Nick said..."

"Said to keep her ex away?" Jace demanded, rounding on Nick.

"Said we needed protection from strangers," Nick put in, stepping in to separate the two men, although Bronco, at least, was obviously standing down.

"It's just a misunderstanding," Claire put in and came closer. "Jace, this is a friend of ours who'll be working aboard, Bronco Gates from St. Augustine. And I think you have all scared off Juanita, Lexi's nanny, who just went below."

"Lexi has a nanny now?" Jace bellowed. "Oh, that new friend she told me about. I thought she meant a girlfriend."

"Jace," Claire said, "we will be in touch."

"Yeah? What if your cell phone or mine doesn't work when you lovebirds are out on the briny?"

"You know how all this happened!" she said. "All of us were blessed to get away in one piece."

"Enough," Nick said. "Save it and we'll all talk later. We need to head out now."

As they used to say, *if looks could kill.* Jace's stare felt like hurled daggers at her and Nick before he stalked down the gangway and down the dock. It scared her how she wanted to run after him, to explain more, to say she was sorry it had to be like this right now. No matter what had happened between them, he didn't deserve to be in the dark like this, thinking she'd *chosen* to move so quickly into marriage with

Nick. At least he was still on his daughter's side, but evidently he wasn't on hers and Nick's.

After their captain docked the *Sylph* at the Mar-Good Marina on Goodland, Claire was on her own while Nick went to spend more time with Haze. Actually, he said he wanted to get some time with Maggie, after what Claire had told him about the woman's intense dislike of Mark Stirling. So Claire walked toward the house of the Hazeltons' neighbor, Ada Cypress.

Claire had researched the woman a bit and not found much except that Cypress was a common Seminole last name and Ada was a longtime widow. Her married last name had been Corby, but she evidently kept her tribal name to market her handiwork of weaving Spanish moss. She must have been named for her grandmother, because Claire found an old *Miami Herald* photograph from the 1930s online, showing a woman named Ada Cypress who had also kept alive the old art of spinning Spanish moss into yarn and weaving beautiful blankets, shawls and saddle pads that were collectors' items and very expensive. It was a lost art now, the article said, but so much of the past seemed that way in South Florida lately. The good thing about Ada Cypress was that her grandmother had lived in the same house on Goodland, so surely this Ada knew the area and the people. Claire thought she would be a great resource for her investigation of possible suspects and motives for the murder.

But to her disappointment, the woman was apparently not at home in her small, framed house on stilts. It had once been a bright blue but was now greatly faded. Standing on the second-floor deck, Claire knocked yet again to give Ada time to answer if she was sleeping. Her last rap on the door made it bounce open. Here on Goodland, maybe people kept to the old way of not locking up.

Claire called in, "Ms. Cypress, are you here? I'm a friend of your neighbors and just wanted to meet you!"

Claire glimpsed the inside of the front room: a wooden floor cluttered with big baskets heaped with the silvery Spanish moss. Draped over long pegs on the wooden walls, spills of shawls or blankets seemed to catch the dim, dancing bars of light through the louvered windows.

She sighed, closed the door and stepped onto the deck that overlooked the canal below, and from that, beyond, the green puzzle pieces of the Ten Thousand Islands. Clumps and trails of the moss hung on the railings or racks out here too, drying in the autumn breeze. A single rocking chair and a ladder-back chair were the only deck furnishings, and the rocker moved in the breeze as if someone unseen sat there.

Claire fingered the fine, spongy texture of a piece of moss. It reminded her of the live oaks at Shadowlawn Manor in St. Augustine where she and Nick had worked together just last month.

Well, she'd better get to work now. Another person they'd decided to interview was Fin Taylor, who had a charter fishing boat down by the marina and knew everyone around here, but Nick had suggested they first see him together. Apparently the man had a raucous reputation, but surely his boat, *Reel Good Time*, would be easy to spot and she could at least pick up one of his brochures if he was out with clients fishing.

But as she started down the steps, she noticed a woman in a woven palmetto hat, poling a dugout canoe down the canal. Yes, standing up in it and poling! She wore the long, distinctive bright geometric patterned skirt typical of Seminole style.

Claire hurried down the stairs and went to where the woman put the canoe perfectly in its place. But she saw that this was not the woman she was looking for, the one who had been obviously named for her ancestor in the old photo Claire had seen. Ada must be at least seventy. This woman looked strong and middle-aged, maybe in her forties, though Claire couldn't see her face well in the shade of the wide hat brim.

"Excuse me, but I'm looking for Ada Cypress, and I wonder

if you know where she is," Claire called out to the woman who really did resemble the older Ada from the newspaper.

"I know where she is, all right. Right here, and I bid you *che-hun-ta-mo,* hello. You want to buy a moss shawl or blanket? Shouldn't be called Spanish moss, you know, here long before that, like the land and water. Better called Seminole moss, eh?" she said with a closemouthed smile at her joke. Claire could hardly hear her. She had to strain to listen to the soft words, almost like listening to a breath of air.

"Oh, I see," Claire said, though she really didn't. She didn't know any Seminoles, so maybe the sun preserved their facial skin instead of aging it. Sometimes First Nation Americans did seem ageless. "I'm a friend of your neighbors, the Hazeltons, and I wanted to meet you, to talk to you," she explained, carefully modulating her voice too so she didn't sound as if she was shouting.

"Not a reporter, come to hurt them?"

"No. Someone come to help them."

The woman climbed out easily with barely a tip to the canoe. It looked handmade, carved out on the inside but with the patina of age outside. Placing the pole in the canoe, she came close to Claire. Strangely, she did not look Claire in the eyes, but stared slightly beyond her as if someone stood behind.

Wow, she really did look like the woman in the old photograph, but then Claire resembled both her paternal grandmother and great-grandmother too. She tried not to show surprise or disbelief.

"We can talk," she said. "I am Ada Cypress. No newspaper writing though, no notes. Just talk."

No notes suited Claire. For sure she had more questions than answers. But here was someone besides the Hazeltons who might resent Mark Stirling's "newspaper writing," so she'd have to be more than intrigued and amazed. She'd have to be careful.

CHAPTER FOURTEEN

Nick could see Claire sitting on the open deck of the nearby house with a woman, evidently Ada Cypress, so he walked the other way after spending time with Haze and Maggie, and headed for the marina where they'd moored the *Sylph*.

Compared to the dock at Crayton Cove where they'd first seen their yacht, the boats here looked smaller and vintage, to put it nicely, especially compared to the yacht that was tied up at the end of the long T-shaped dock. Here were a few old cabin cruisers; a well-used sailboat or two. A couple of the larger slips were empty, since they belonged to charter fishermen who must be out with guests. Most of the private Goodland fishing boats were tied up behind trailers or houses along the canals here, like Haze's, though he was talking about buying a much bigger one with money flowing in "like the well water flowed."

Haze had even quit his job managing The Home Depot store in Naples, saying he was needed here to oversee the fountain and be available when the Ames High rep visited for seed water. Nick hated to admit he had to be wary of his old friend. He cared for him, really did want to defend him if it came to that, but could he totally trust him? Not that he thought he was a murderer, but he was obviously another devotee of Clayton Ames. He had dollar signs in his eyes, and Nick figured it would be crazy to try to make him see Ames's real self. But what if Haze *had* knocked Mark Stirling off on Ames's orders? Lately nothing was what it seemed to be from the outside, including his and Claire's marriage. If Jace Britten knew they weren't sleeping together, maybe he wouldn't be such a jerk.

Nick saw the charter fishing boat, *Reel Good Time*, was not in its slip. Above it was a sign with Fin Taylor's name, phone number and brochures displayed in a plastic-covered holder attached to a mooring post. He took one and scanned it for information.

Phineas "Fin" Taylor was a third-generation charter fishing boat captain here in Goodland, but he could pick up fishermen on Marco Island or in Naples. Half day and full day excursions available. His forty-foot boat, pictured here, could take singles or parties up to six for offshore and inshore fishing—out sixty miles into the Gulf of Mexico or into the Ten Thousand Islands.

No doubt Fin Taylor knew the area where Mark Stirling had probably been shot before his body fell into or was wedged in among the mangroves. But, even though the bullet had been from a pistol pressed tight to his forehead, like many a suicide, where was the boat that had brought him there? According to the reports Heck had given him, the Marco Island Marine Unit had scoured the area looking for a watercraft that had drifted away.

Sure, Mark's kayak was missing from his place, but where was it? Had someone seen it drifting and just taken it? But even with a plea for information in the Naples paper and on local TV, nothing had turned up and no one had come forward with the kayak. Neither had the police been able to trace who had called in about finding Mark's body—a quick call on a cell phone from a woman was all the detective Nick had talked to would say.

He half hoped Claire could turn up a theory on suicide because Mark shooting himself would mean Haze didn't have to stand trial in criminal court. Then there would be no stage for the dog and pony show Ames was demanding to legitimatize and advertise his Youth products. Yet, Nick knew he was trapped. All that *had* to happen or Ames would turn on him—on them—again.

Nick read on in the brochure. The last line, under a photo of a man posing in front of a huge sailfish hanging from a wooden cross post boasted: I Can Help You Land A Monster Fish! Nick snorted. He'd like help landing a monster, and his name was Clayton Ames.

He looked up as a neat-looking white boat with fishing chairs on both the top deck and stern rounded the end of the dock and headed in. Good luck! The craft matched the brochure photo of *Reel Good Time*. Should Nick pretend to be a possible fisherman at first or just level with Taylor from the get-go? He wished Claire was here, because she was so good at this. He'd try playing it by ear.

"Yo!" Captain Fin, who also matched a photo in the brochure, called out to him with a wave. He had two guys with him, both with looming sunburns, so they had to be his fishermen for the day—or half the day since it was just after noon. "Interested in an afternoon catching snapper and tarpon for dinner and bragging rights with some photos?"

"Not this afternoon, but I'm interested in talking to you!" Nick shouted back over the engine noise as the boat backed into its slip. Captain Fin killed the motor, climbed out of the wheelhouse and opened the big ice tank at the back of the boat.

"Got us a mess of good eating here, eh, boys?" he asked

his charters. "I'll get out the knives and have these babies filleted in a flash."

While the two fishermen gathered up some items—they'd obviously used Taylor's fishing gear, which protruded like slender saplings along the sides of the boat—Taylor took out two mean-looking knives, pulled the catch up onto a board and went to work. Gulls soon swooped in to sit on the water and noisily demand the innards. Taylor kept up a steady stream of talk to his charters and Nick as he worked. "Yeah, red snapper and tarpon out there in droves…dolphins followed the boat…saw a bald eagle I whistle for and he comes… I leave other charters in my wake," he boasted.

Nick studied the big-shouldered man. Obviously a guy this glib and local would be a good person to question about the murder/suicide. Captain Fin wore Banana Republic khaki shorts and a T-shirt that advertised *Reel Good Time.* His ball cap was one Nick recognized from pro golfer Greg "Shark" Norman's line of clothes, beige with the outline of a multicolored shark embroidered above the brim. Fin was blond, very tanned with a leaping tarpon tattooed on one forearm with the words, *I'm the catch of the day.*

The guy worked fast. Nick leaned against the post with the brochure still in his hands and his backpack—in lieu of a briefcase around here—over one shoulder, watching and listening. His two customers went off with their catch wrapped in butcher paper, happy as—well, clams.

"Mind if I hose down the boat first?" Fin asked. "Like to do things thorough and proper."

"No, fine. I like watching you work."

"You a doctor or a lawyer? I'm good at nailing where folks come from and what they do," he said as he squirted the slimy work surface and immaculate-looking deck with a hose he took from dockside.

"You are good," Nick said, realizing he'd have to level with him. "I'm a friend of Haze Hazelton from way back and plan to defend him if it comes to that."

"Yeah? A lawyer," he said, squinting up at Nick in the sun. "Saw you in the paper, I think, right? That insurance case, that guy that faked his drowning but his family was getting big money."

"Right. The Sorrento case."

"And then there was a shooting outside the court. I do get off the water and the boat once in a while, see, not an ignoramus."

"Good memory."

"Don't mind if I say so. So, you're really fishing for some info. You just here about Haze or you really want to relax a little? Like that brochure there says, out in the Gulf or inshore fishing."

"I'm considering it. Maybe we can take Haze. He could use some distraction."

"No kidding, with the law breathing down his neck. Who the hell needs that? You believe in that health water stuff?"

"More importantly, do you? Do others around here?"

Fin stepped from his boat onto the dock. "You know," he said, shoving his cap back on his head, "at least now we can make up our own mind about that and everything else. I mean, since Mark Stirling's gone, though I hear he's got an heir apparent. The guy, name of Wes Ringold, couldn't wait to jump right into running the *Owl* paper to stir the waters. Get it? Stir-ling? Anyhow, yeah, folks round here do believe in the ancient waters, you just ask Ada Cypress if you can get her to talk. You know, the silent Seminoles and all that."

If Ada was the silent type, Nick thought, Claire had seemed to be doing okay with her. And this talker had just said a couple of things that were valuable too. Fin Taylor didn't seem to especially like Mark Stirling either, and the new journalist guy, Wes Ringold, who had evidently inherited *The Burrowing Owl*, like Claire had said, could have a motive for murder too.

Claire and Nick ate together on the prow of the yacht, legs stretched out, backs against a slanted window, while Juanita—Nita—and Lexi ate at the table out back by the stern. Bronco was fishing off the dock close by. Claire had a salad and Nick a roast beef sandwich prepared by the chef, no less, who Nick's friend and owner had rehired along with the captain, first mate and a maid. Claire had never felt so rich, but it wasn't what mattered to her: Lexi was safe and having fun. And they were here with Nick. Just being around him, helping him, being his partner in this case, had to be enough for now. And she was happy not to be in the lounge below for once, because the idea of a woman's unsolved murder there still creeped her out.

"So, even though Fin Taylor suggested Ada was close-mouthed, you got along great," Nick prompted. They were both barefoot, and he occasionally stroked her toes with his. She had to admit she'd gotten some good information from Ada, as much as the woman puzzled her. Oh, darn, every time Nick's foot touched her he was messing up her thoughts when she had some important things to say.

"I learned the most when I mentioned—when I was leaving—that I was going to look for you at the marina where we were docked, because you wanted to talk to Captain Taylor. I did not say we were on a huge yacht. She's very basic, very shy and yet she speaks with knowledge and conviction. But, Nick, she's really strange—almost scary."

His head snapped around and he stared at her. "Which means what?"

"She looks just like her grandmother and knows a lot from way back."

"So? What are you saying?"

"I don't know. This fountain of youth stuff is giving me the heebie-jeebies."

He annoyed her when he laughed. "Meaning Ada Cypress knows about it, maybe believes in it?"

"Maggie said Ada washes in it when there's rain runoff. Who knows she doesn't drink it? Maybe has for years?"

"Sweetheart, you think that stuff works? Works to preserve people for years? I can have Heck check out her birth certificate. You know some people, maybe especially Native Americans, carry their age well. I mean, I have no doubt the water could be healthy, good for people, the cosmetics too, because they looked great on you, but—"

"Just never mind. Of course I don't believe Ames's lies, however slick the advertising and presentation. It's mostly marketing, not medicine. But here's what Ada said I think we can use."

"I like that 'we.' Go ahead. I'm listening and I need your help. I trust you and I didn't mean to kid or upset you."

"Okay, here it is. As you can imagine, Ada's heritage as a Seminole is to value and preserve the land and water. She married a white man years ago but doesn't use his last name. Neither will she go back to the tribe, which she claims turned against her for marrying white."

"Really? In this day and age?"

"Aren't you listening? She's very traditional. Nick," she said, putting her plate down and turning toward him, pulling her legs up under herself and putting her hands on his arms, "Motives for murdering mouthy Mark are growing on trees around here. Ada said there are rumors—which *The Burrowing Owl* was pursuing—that Captain Phineas Taylor secretly takes wealthy charters out to catch endangered sharks, which is, of course, against the law."

"What?"

"Maggie may champion those owls, but Ada mentioned

protecting sharks. There used to be five species vulnerable to extinction, she said, but now there are twenty-some. Of course, most Floridians—everyone—see sharks as the enemy, but they are still in danger of being endangered, mostly through overfishing. I'm going to research it more, but if Mark Stirling was investigating that and was ready to accuse your new captain friend you want to go out fishing with someday—well, just like Maggie, Captain Taylor could have a motive for murder."

"Wealthy men—he takes wealthy men fishing," Nick muttered. "Even if 'Uncle Clay' hasn't been around here for years, maybe some of his lackeys have. If they were found out fishing for endangered trophies—just like rich guys blast the heck out of African lions and elephants—that could blow their cover, make them look bad, sully their name or their boss's. Okay, we'll both look into that. Maybe I'll go fishing and chat up Fin more. And he obviously knows the inland waterways where Mark died. Anything we can find to fight back against Ames and his crew is crucial."

"And Ada. I need to find more about Ada."

He seemed to ignore that which annoyed her again. "Meanwhile," he said, "I'm going to call the Marco Island Marine Unit again and see if I can get permission for us to go out into the mangrove islands to look over the scene where Mark's body was found."

"You know what we forensic types always say about a murder scene?"

"Tell me," he said, helping her up and putting an arm around her waist to steady them both on the slightly slanted prow of the yacht.

"The scene is the silent witness. Nick, I'll bet that's true, even if it's way out in the islands with nothing but mangroves, water and sky around."

"And maybe sharks—the real or human kind."

CHAPTER FIFTEEN

"Who says there aren't huge perks working for me—and being married to me?" Nick asked Claire as they walked from the yacht to a canalside restaurant on Goodland late the next morning. "Just look at this fancy place I'm taking you for lunch."

"Pretty impressive," she said, smiling as they approached the Goodland restaurant called Stan's Idle Hour. They had an hour planned for here, but it was hardly going to be idle. This was the place where people had overheard the argument between Haze and Mark Stirling that made Haze the number one suspect for the murder that had happened later that day.

This morning Nick had driven into his office for a few hours while Claire had researched the Seminoles and read articles Heck had found about the Goodland fountain of youth. She'd Googled Fin Taylor and learned his wife, Colleen, ran a small shop and mail order business called Irish Gifts and Goodies out of their Goodland home. She hoped to stop there soon to shop and get an intimate look at the man's house and wife.

"Of course," Nick went on, "you haven't yet taken advantage of one of the best perks, sharing my bed so the maid doesn't have to make up two every day."

Claire just laughed and put her elbow in his ribs. He threw his arm around her waist and hugged her sideways as they walked onto the grounds of the famous—perhaps infamous—seafood restaurant. Its ambiance, if you could call it that, shouted Goodland! It was known for Southern seafood but sometimes questionable people.

Claire had never been here, though she'd sure heard about the place. Stan's was comprised of a two-story building and random sprawl of palmetto-thatched chickee huts. It was famous for its in-season Mullet Festival with its Buzzard Lope Queen Contest. The seafood, booze and crazy goings-on drew around five thousand curious or rowdy folk from Naples, Fort Myers, Miami and who knew where else. Jace had been here more than once. Nick had said he and Haze used to love the place but he hadn't been here for quite a while. Yet today, still pretty much off-season for tourists and snowbirds, the place seemed almost sedate.

Looking at the restaurant and its grounds with a critical eye, Claire evaluated its drawing power as a combination of location, location, location and charming clutter. The area fronted on a dock and canal, as did most of Goodland's buildings. Boats brought many of the patrons who were enjoying drinks and lunch even now. A few trucks with shotgun racks, several with the Confederate flag and a few motorcycles were parked haphazardly in what must pass for the parking area.

The open, wooden Buzzard Lope stage had seen better days with its American flag hanging from the rafters and numerous banners and signs. Nick had said that people ate either inside the two-story pink building or outside at the weathered gray picnic tables. Above it all, wings outspread, loomed a large, gray metal statue of a buzzard in flight.

"Don't look up in case it takes off," Nick kidded her. "I'd

rather eat out here but let's go inside, sit near the bar and ask our questions."

Inside, two female servers hustled from table to table—the place was about a third full—and one of them pointed to a table near the bar. They ordered seafood chowder, conch fritters and coconut shrimp, planning to share everything.

"I'll just order drinks from the bar," Nick told the server.

"Be just a sec with the fritters," the plump, bleached blonde told them and disappeared.

Claire watched as Nick ambled up to the bar where a weathered-looking, middle-aged man was pulling beers. With the buzz of noise in here, she couldn't tell what they were saying. Nick came back with a beer for himself and a shandy for her. "You might know he missed most of the Haze-Mark brouhaha, when he went to the john. But our waitress Betty saw it all."

"Bingo. Are you going to tell her up front who you are?"

"More or less. And hope she's on Haze's side instead of Mark's. Everyone else—except the police—around here is. The bartender also said the loner guy in the corner in the plaid flannel shirt is always here. I'll try him, and you chat up Betty if she comes back before I do."

Again, his trust in her warmed Claire. Despite Clayton Ames's version of a shotgun wedding and the fact "the two shall become one" had not happened yet—because of her—she knew she was falling fast and further in love with Nick Markwood.

Their server came back with their appetizers before Nick returned. Claire saw now her lopsided, foggy, plastic name-tag read Betty.

"My husband and I are friends of Haze Hazelton," Claire told the woman. "We're hoping to prepare a defense for him if he's arrested for Mark Stirling's murder."

Her dark eyebrows lifted, but her face didn't change expression. "You prob'ly heard I was here for the fight got Haze in hot water and maybe got Mark dead," she said. "I been questioned before—by the cops."

She put the conch fritters and dip down, then two glasses of ice water. Balancing her plastic tray on its end on the tabletop and leaning slightly on it, she hovered.

"Do you believe Haze is guilty?" Claire asked.

She shrugged. "Like to steer clear of the cops and court, if it comes to that. You a lawyer?"

"My husband is. And, as I said, on Haze's side. Would you mind telling me what Haze and Mark said to each other that day?"

"It was how they said it, much as what. No secret Stirling's newspaper riled lots of folks. He attacked the youth fountain water in print and with his big mouth in here that day. Haze was saying he was too rash to be a journalist, in too much of a rush to be rich and famous. And Haze was spouting stuff about the fact there's a sacred fountain in lots of places on the planet—in India, Hindu legends, Far East, some spring in France cures people. That's a good one, right? No way a spring of water around here is sacred! Ha!"

"You have an excellent memory."

"Like I said, they yelled pretty loud. Yeah, I got a good memory for good tippers."

"Which my husband is," Claire said, hoping that didn't mean she was offering a bribe. She wished Nick would come back, but she also sensed this woman might clam up with a lawyer here. Betty might not like cops or a court appearance, but she'd probably be called to testify, hearsay or not if all this went to trial.

"Well, the thing is," the woman said, keeping her voice low and leaning closer, "Stirling told Haze he was not only going to debunk his family fountain but the scam of youth water and that face lotion stuff nationwide. Haze gave me some of that, and it felt okay—not real fast results," she admitted, stroking her leathery cheek. She glanced around the room again, then whispered, "That's when Fin jumped in, cussed out Stirling, said he didn't care if he gave his wife discount ad rates, he was a damn liar."

"Okay. Slow down. So Fin Taylor was here too and got in on Haze's side?" Claire asked.

"Well, maybe not on Haze's side but anti-Stirling anyway," Betty admitted. "Geez, I could of told Stirling off too. So Fin just stormed out, and it ended with Haze yelling, 'Just shut your stupid mouth or someone will shut it for you.' Said it twice, threw his drink. That's what the cops are hanging on to."

"Haze shouted that at Stirling, not Fin?"

"You got that right."

"Haze said 'someone'? Not 'I' will shut it for you?"

"Right. And you know what? When Haze said that, couple of folks in here clapped, including me. Didn't wish the man dead, but Mark Stirling was a big mouth, small tipper."

No wonder the police were taking a while to arrest Haze. Maybe they were looking at Fin Taylor too—or others who were here that day and applauded. Claire wondered if they were going to find anyone at all in Southwest Florida who liked Mark Stirling.

Jace loved flying the new jet. Smooth. Sweet. After his passenger left and the plane was safely in its hangar, he walked through it again, cockpit to the cabin. He'd always wanted to fly north and he'd just been to a small airport outside Toronto and flown back by early afternoon. And to pick up just one passenger, a guy who went by the name of Thom Van Cleve. Not plain old Tom, and that last name sounded like the guy should be a duke or an earl. Kind of acted like it too, salesman smooth, fake friendly, but actually aloof. Didn't matter really. It was only business.

Funny thing was, Thom, Duke of Van Cleve, was really tan like he'd been south instead of points north.

"In short," Jace said to the empty cabin, "he probably works for Kilcorse-Ames."

He instantly regretted saying that aloud, because he knew Nick was paranoid about Ames spying and listening in on everything. He wished he was going home to Claire and Lexi instead of heading for an empty condo, even a nice new one Ames's money provided. He hoped he'd only be working for the bastard until he found a way to get himself—and Lexi and Claire—out from under Ames's thumb. But that promise from Ames that he'd help him get Claire and Lexi back someday was terrible but tempting. He missed his daughter and hoped Claire would let him have some time with her soon.

He slumped into the comfortable seat where his passenger had been sitting, reading some papers en route from Toronto to Naples. He noticed a section of a folded newspaper stuffed—or just forgotten—between the seat and the armrest and pulled it out.

Dang, but it was in Spanish. *Granma*, a newspaper evidently put out by the Communist party of Cuba. He could make out that much. It had a photo of his passenger, all smiles, standing next to Raul Castro, Fidel's brother who ran the island now. Jace flipped it open. Yeah, on the second page under the masthead it listed First Secretary of the paper as Raul and the paper's founder as Fidel.

Jace threw himself back into the seat and crumpled the paper in his fists. Cuba? But he was flying out of Toronto. Jace knew the Canadians were permitted access to Cuba, when Americans were not. But surely Ames's expensive health water and cosmetics were not sold in Cuba. No, something else fishy was going on here, and this was just another piece of a big jigsaw puzzle. And whoever managed to put the pieces together might not like the picture that emerged—or even be around long enough to figure it out.

That afternoon, Claire and Nick finally managed to get one of the officers of the Marco Island Marine Unit to lead them out to the site where Mark Stirling's body had been found, the assumed site of his death. Officer Sean Armstrong was a young guy, polite and businesslike, but, Nick thought, with the same closemouthed demeanor he'd come up against before from the local police. He had accepted it since Haze had not been charged and a list of admissible evidence need not be handed over yet, and he didn't want to rock the boat.

He smiled at that thought. He and Claire were in the yacht's small dinghy with an outboard motor, which was usually lowered just to go ashore where it was too shallow to anchor. Rock the boat—yeah, the wind had suddenly come up to make it a little choppy today. The wake from the larger police boat even tilted them when they tied up near the mangrove island with the crazy name of No Name Key. At least they were inshore and somewhat sheltered by randomly shaped large and small mangrove islands. Boat traffic was next to nil out here—the perfect place for a murder or a suicide.

"Right there, Mr. Markwood," Sean called out to them, pointing to a slight indentation in the clawlike roots of the mangrove island while he idled his larger boat next to theirs. "His body was wedged right there. Blood washed off the single stellate wound on his forehead. Corpse snagged underwater but one arm bobbed loose, which is what tipped off the guy going by on the personal watercraft. Some call it a Jet Ski or a WaveRunner. Makes huge noise and waves."

"I was told a woman called in who found the body."

"That came first, then the second call, the personal watercraft guy, at least that's how he described himself. Both on cell phones, both anonymous. Obviously, didn't want to get involved."

"And no gun was found despite scuba divers searching? And no other signs of bullets in these mangroves?" Nick pursued.

"That's right, sir. It's no longer a scene we're controlling, so have a look around if you want. I've got a call coming in, so have to head out. You do know your way back out of here?"

"Yes. Thanks, Officer. We have a map. We'll stay a little longer."

"I didn't hear him get a call," Claire observed when the inboard boat sped away, rocking them again.

"It may have been on his screen. You know, the Marco police and people in general may not feel real warm toward Goodland folks like Haze since the feeling's mutual. Let's tie up here and look around."

"You did hear him give one thing away, didn't you?" she asked as Nick motored them into the little cove in the ragged island. Farther in, sand and silt as well as floating debris had caught to make some solid land among the webs of roots. It was how most islands were born out here.

He killed the motor and tied the boat to a big, crooked branch. He turned to face her where she sat in the prow of the small craft. "You're priceless. What did you hear, partner?" he asked.

"You hadn't mentioned a stellate wound in Stirling's head. Star-shaped. That means it's a contact wound, doesn't it, even more than just close range?"

"Yeah, which is one reason possible suicide is still on the table, like he pressed the gun against his forehead and pulled the trigger. It was in the autopsy report, and I forgot to mention it. I'll let you see it. Or," he added, frowning, "whoever killed him pressed the gun there, but you'd think someone else firing a weapon wouldn't do it so close-up."

Claire shuddered. That would make it a crime of passion, wouldn't it, or a lot of hatred, to put the muzzle right up against someone's skull, maybe look him in the eyes and shoot? And then to wedge the body in the water where sharks could get at it… If Ames had hired a hit man to shut Mark's journalist mouth, would he have had him shot at such close range? Surely, if Clayton Ames was behind it, he didn't want it to look like a suicide, because that wouldn't go to trial and Nick could not publicly praise the fountain that fed the Ames High water and cosmetic products fortune.

"Nick, it has to be murder, doesn't it? Mark could hardly wedge his own dead body under the roots."

"Police report says the tide was going out and, if he fell in the water, his body could have been caught there."

"But would a heavy gun fall to the bottom, tide or not?"

"I hear you, counselor. You told me that the scene is always the silent witness, but this one is really silent—except for its remote location. Listen, the wind and waves are picking up some, so let's head back."

"Nick," she said, reaching out to grip his wrist, "even though they had divers search here, the tide could have moved the gun along the bottom until it snagged on one of these roots."

"Sweetheart, they searched both the roots and the sand underneath. The report I got said they even looked at the mangrove branches and leaves to see if other shots fired could have winged them or embedded. Nothing."

"All right, I hate to agree with Clayton Ames, but I say it's a murder and the killer took the evidence with him. Let's go back. You know, someone was very familiar with the area if they brought him out here to kill him—or meet him here to talk, whatever, then more or less ambushed him. There are enough twists and turns in these so-called Ten Thousand Islands that his murderer wanted privacy, and, as I said, knew the area."

"Haze has known this area all his life, but so have plenty of others."

"They should have found Mark's kayak. He had to come out here in it, didn't he, since it's missing?"

"The police theory is someone found the kayak, took it, then was scared to come forward when they heard or read whose it was. Who knows, maybe the two found-a-body callers wanting to remain anonymous means they stole the kayak. Look, Claire, we're heading back," he said again and loosened her grip to untie the boat. Holding on to branches, he rotated them prow out and leaned back over the stern to start the motor.

They heard a muted roar that, at first, sounded like the surf, but grew louder. An airplane overhead? Sean Armstrong coming back? Must be a boat racing nearby, Nick thought and waited to start the motor. He stayed put in the alcove, and they both craned their necks to look out.

A noisy, one-person silver WaveRunner rushed into view, not going past but coming straight at them. The driver was bent down behind the small windshield. Nick noted a blur of the pale color, the typical rooster plume of water out its rear. Was it out of control, going to hit them? And Claire was in the prow.

She screamed as the edge of the runner glanced sideways off them, jarring their boat. The huge wall of water slammed into them as the craft veered away. Nick grabbed for her, but their small boat tipped sideways, tilted and swamped.

Claire screamed again. Nick smacked backward into the water, surfaced, spitting, sucking air, and grabbed for a branch. Their boat was upside down with the motor propeller sticking straight up.

Where was Claire?

"Claire! Claire!"

He'd have to dive for her. But thank God, she popped up outside the boat, gasping for air.

"You all right?" he shouted, dragging her to him. One arm on the branch, one around her, they rode the rest of the ebbing wake.

"Yes. Just scared. Went—under—the—boat," she gasped out, holding on to him with one arm and paddling with the other. "A man—or boy. Wore a hoodie. Couldn't see—his face."

"Damn idiot! Probably drunk or—"

"Or we're onto something—someone."

He was out of breath but had to say this. "Or," he began again, his voice bitter, "'Uncle Clay' thinks we're getting too many possible perps, looking at others when he wants Haze arrested and in court. I'm thinking he even wants him found guilty. Wants his hands on the eternal spring—buy Haze out—if I lose the case. He's good at double crosses like that."

"Look. The part of the motor in the water—a gasoline slick. It won't work, will it?"

"No way. Let's see if we can right the boat, bail out and row. I hope that bastard's long gone. Someone just raised the stakes, but we're trapped in this, at least until I can find and stop Clayton Ames."

"Nick, look—a life ring! I didn't see that before. Maybe the guy threw it out, not wanting to drown us, just warn us."

The orange ring bobbed toward them as they held to each other and their boat. Nick reached for it.

Next to the small print, Throw This If Someone Is In Distress, were words that didn't make sense as a calling card from Clayton Ames. Large, crudely painted black letters read GET OUT. STAY OUT.

CHAPTER SIXTEEN

"I didn't even think about our cell phones being lost at first," Claire told Nick as they finally got back to the *Sylph*.

They had tried rowing but had been towed by two tourists with their three kids in a rental boat. It was a good thing, Claire thought, because being soaked and in the breeze had really chilled her. At least their hot showers and change of clothes had helped, but they were both still shaken from the attack and the life preserver they felt wasn't meant to really save them at all. It was a definite warning and threat. But from whom?

"At least *we* weren't lost, but, then, I don't think that was the plan," Nick told her as they sat in the yacht's lounge, drinking hot coffee. Even with the late afternoon sunlight streaming in here, Claire felt chilled and uneasy in this room. On their way out of the restaurant earlier today, she'd overheard two men talking about the *Sylph* being haunted because of an unsolved murder here. She knew it was in this very room, and now here they were with an unsolved murder of their own. She'd feel relieved when this Mangrove Murder case was over and they could just go home—wherever home was now.

"Yeah, whose plan, that's the question," Nick was saying.

His voice jolted her back to reality. "Hey, I see someone on the dock, staring at the yacht, looking in," he said, ducking down to look up. He started away, tucking in his shirt. "I don't recognize him so sit tight," he said over his shoulder. "It's not Jace. Lexi and Nita went ashore, right?"

"They said they wouldn't go far. They're feeding seagulls along the shore, and Bronco's with them. I've checked on them twice, once just a few minutes ago."

Claire had the urge to have him dry his wet hair, but that sounded—well, too wifely, and she wasn't ready to really be a wife yet. Was she? And did they have to be on edge every time someone stared at their big boat? If so, maybe they should anchor out a ways, but then, they'd just lost the motor for the dinghy they would need to get to the dock.

She pulled on a Windbreaker and followed Nick partway out to see who the pair of designer jean legs and spotless white, designer running shoes belonged to. She could hear their voices from here.

"Can I help you?" Nick asked the man.

"If you are Nicholas Markwood, yes. I'm Thom Van Cleve, the Ames High rep for the fountain water here. I've been trying to phone you, but all I get is your voice mail."

"And you knew to find me here?"

"Haze Hazelton told me. I'm his liaison, so to speak. I wanted to ask you and your wife to meet me at the Snook Inn on Marco, but now that I'm here, is there someplace we can eat in the area? I'm only here for a short time, as usual."

"Sure. My phone isn't working right now. Come aboard down there at the gangway, and we can eat here. I appreciate getting to meet one of the Ames High reps."

Claire kept herself from making the gag-me-with-a-spoon gesture when Nick walked back toward her.

"So," she said, keeping her voice down, "if he was trying to phone you, maybe he's not behind our being dunked or he'd figure we might have lost our phones. Nick, we need cell replacements pronto. I told Nita and Bronco they could always reach me at my number, anytime and for anything at all."

"Let's feed this guy and hear him out. How about you walk down to get Lexi, Nita and Bronco back on board, then email Heck on your laptop and tell him we need cell replacements fast with the same phone numbers. Then join me and this Van Cleve guy. And I'm counting on you to listen to and psych out every word he says."

Jace was frustrated. Claire was not answering her phone when he thought she'd understood he wanted to pick up Lexi soon for some private time with his daughter. If Claire thought not answering her phone was going to delay his request, that really upset him.

He drove to the Crayton Cove dock in Naples where the *Sylph* had been moored. Nothing at all in its spot. Gone. What if Claire and Lexi were in danger again?

He'd been told by Thom Van Cleve that he could phone him if there was any problem or change of schedule. He was supposed to fly him over to Miami this evening, evidently to meet a tanker truck of the so-called youth water that was being shipped over. But if he phoned him now, he could call in a favor. Since the guy worked for Ames, he probably knew exactly where Markwood had moved the big boat with his daughter on it. He didn't want to have to tangle with attorney Markwood about visitation rights, but he would if he had to. He loved Lexi. Damn it, he might even still love Claire.

He scanned his phone for Van Cleve's number and punched it in.

"Thom Van Cleve here."

"It's Jace, your pilot. Look, I need to know where Nick and Claire Markwood are now because they have my daughter. I mean, I—"

"Just a moment."

Jace could hear muted words while he said to someone, "Excuse me, please, but I need to take this call."

A moment more. "Yes, Jace. If I tell you, you will put off a visit until tomorrow. Understood?"

"Yeah, sure."

"We all follow orders, you know."

"I hear you."

"And you will not divulge your source for that information. You can say you just checked area marinas."

"Agreed."

"They're docked on Goodland at the south marina, not the one with the charter fishing boats. Keep calm. Actually, Markwood told me their phones fell in the water and are out of order right now. Not until tomorrow, Jace, and I'll see you promptly at eight tonight for the Miami flight."

"Roger that. All of that."

Jace punched off. It made him feel better that Claire, Nick too, had lost their phones, so it wasn't that they were just avoiding him, keeping him away. He knew they were under pressure to work for Ames to keep themselves and Lexi safe, but he was also in danger. He had to hang on and pretend to play along until he could find a way to stop that monster too, but, above all else, he wanted to see Lexi.

"Quite frankly," Van Cleve told them over crab po'boy sandwiches and lemonade in the dining room of the yacht, "our mutual friend wants to know if you need any assistance on setting up the case to defend Hazelton or prepare promotion for the fountain water."

Claire thought this man spoke with a Boston accent. Besides, his word choice and allusions suggested an East Coast education. Then too, only she and Darcy would pick up on the Charles Dickens allusion, since "our mutual friend" was the title of a Dickens novel. Funny, Claire thought, but that book was all about money and what it could do for and to people. And it opened with a body being found in the Thames.

But this stranger couldn't mean any of that. Here their mother had read to them all the time, and Claire realized she hadn't read Lexi a book since they'd been on board. But she and Nick were going to take her to see the burrowing owl colony on Marco tomorrow and then to Tigertail Beach for a swim. She just had to get her mind back on this visitor and off worrying about Lexi. But the child had suffered another bad dream last night, one in which she was taken in a boat and was drowning. Now that Lexi had heard about a boat almost hitting theirs and that they had gone in the water, would that produce more shrieking nightmares tonight? Claire tried to force her mind off her fears, but her own childhood with dreadful dreams haunted her yet.

"We are laying the groundwork for a trial if it comes to that," Nick told Van Cleve.

Their guest was, Claire thought, elegant-looking, too well-dressed for around here, and his manners, even eating a sandwich with chunks of crab, were impeccable. Ames managed to find people, anyone he needed, she thought. But why send this man as Haze's contact instead of some good old boy or "Bubba" who would fit right in around here? This guy stood out like a manicured sore thumb.

"And it should, it must, come to a trial, one you will win," Van Cleve said, wiping his mouth with his napkin. "Of course, I can see why you'd investigate other locals who hated Mark Stirling, as it may help you defend Haze. But this information will give you a platform we can expand through the media. Since I'm sure you are also preparing your very public defense of the Youth products, I've brought you some statistics and strategies that may help when you have the floor in the trial."

From the inner pocket of his sport coat, he removed a thin

packet of papers and slid them across the table to Nick. "Of course, any testimonials you have at the time will be invaluable also. Take a close look at that Seminole woman who has, perhaps unwittingly, used the water for years."

Claire gave a little gasp, but Van Cleve kept up his staring match with Nick and didn't seem to notice.

"You know," their guest said, with a quick glance at Claire too, "that Las Vegas and TV magician David Copperfield claims to have discovered the fountain of youth in a cluster of four islands in the Bahamas that he recently purchased for fifty million dollars. He insists dead leaves become full of life again when they come in contact with the water. He says bugs or insects that are nearly dead will fly away. Now, if someone like a performer, an entertainer and illusionist can tout his phony fountain, I'm sure a clever lawyer can promote our real one here.

"And I do owe you two dinner on Marco or in Naples next time I'm here," he said, laying his folded napkin next to his plate and rising. "Maybe something with French or Italian ambiance instead of South Shores, eh?"

Claire sensed Nick bristle, but he hid it well. Was this man alluding to Nick's private endeavor to help those who might be accused of suicide but had actually met an accident or been murdered? If Thom Van Cleve was lying, she couldn't pick up on verbal or body language signs. She only sensed his superior attitude and subtle do-it-or-else demeanor that reeked of Clayton Ames himself.

Nick drove into the office again the next morning, while Claire worked on the yacht. She'd read Lexi a bedtime story last night, and the girl had slept well, though Claire had tossed and turned. Why hadn't her narcolepsy med knocked her out so she could sleep? Her mind had been working overtime… Nick was right down the hall and she could go to him… Someone had tried to make them leave the area… Van Cleve with ice water in his veins had tried to imply something that had certainly crossed her mind: Wasn't Ada Cypress a lot older than she looked? Claire would have to revisit her soon.

But this morning, though loggy and drowsy, Claire had managed to do some work on the new cell phone Heck had brought and programmed for her so it matched her other. She had phoned the Conservancy of Southwest Florida in Naples, an institution that protected and rehabilitated injured wildlife, to ask about Maggie Hazelton's visit with them the day Mark Stirling died. It was a simple piece to the puzzle she hoped to find: Had Maggie, who obviously hated Stirling as much as her husband did, had time to slip away from her talk there? Could she have driven back to Goodland or at least partway, got her hands on a boat and had time to confront and maybe kill Mark? But how had she lured him out into the remote Ten Thousand Islands?

"Oh, no, Maggie Hazelton didn't drive away for any length of time on that afternoon she spent with us," the lady from the conservancy told her over the phone.

Well, there went that theory, Claire thought, until the woman added, "She didn't drive at all, you see, but came by boat and left by boat—had someone pick her up in the Gordon River to leave us, rather in a rush too, something about someone bothering the owl colony on Marco, the very one she showed us photos of."

So Maggie *was* a possible suspect! Or maybe she'd worked with Haze to get rid of Mark.

Claire couldn't wait to tell Nick. And here Lexi was so excited to see those very owls and go swimming at Tigertail Beach. But Claire didn't want to dump that on him the moment he came back to the yacht, which should be any minute now. Claire decided she would just keep the new perp possibility ready to share with Nick tonight when she told him she also intended to revisit Ada Cypress.

★ ★ ★

As soon as Nick returned, Nita, as everyone aboard called her now, was going to have some time off, but Lexi was with her nanny right now, learning some Spanish words. So Claire, ready to head out with a sundress on over her bathing suit, sat up on the deck by the gangway, waiting for Nick. But it was another tall man, a good-looking African American, who came walking up the marina dock.

"Knock, knock," the stranger called out to her. "Mrs. Nick Markwood, I presume?"

Claire stood and looked over the rail to where the man waited on the dock several feet below her. For one moment she hesitated to say who she was. Neither she nor Nick had managed a decent look at the person who had nearly hit them with the WaveRunner yesterday.

But before she could answer, he said, "I'm Wes Ringold, the new editor of *The Burrowing Owl*. Of dire, sad necessity, I took over for Mark Stirling. I would have asked for an interview sooner, but I had a death in the family—my father out in Colorado—and just got back. I'm writing a memorial article about my dad as well as one about Mark." His voice broke and he made what seemed a sincere effort to get his emotions back in check.

She gave him a moment to compose himself. Before she could speak, he went on, "You are one half of the team on the Mangrove Murder investigation, aren't you? You look like your photos from the courthouse tragedy a few weeks ago."

"Yes, I'm Claire Markwood, but my husband's not here right now, and I'm sure you'd rather talk to him." She felt instantly grieved for the man's losing his father as well as Mark Stirling. Wes seemed clever and friendly. He was loose-limbed and lanky with close-cut hair and sharp eyes once he whipped his sunglasses off to look up at her.

"I'd love to interview him also," he told her, "but, in my book—well, now in my paper—a forensic psychologist interview would make for a better read than one with a lawyer. I mean, are you here to do what they call psychological autopsies on Mark or interviews on those of us who knew him? You see, I do my homework."

"I'm sorry you lost your boss and, no doubt, mentor—and your father."

He sighed. "Yes. Thanks. Too many losses of men I looked up to in too short a time. So how about an interview?"

"I'm leaving for the afternoon soon. Perhaps at a later time?"

"Name it. And you're not the only one around here no doubt looking for answers, so I'll trade you a half-hour interview tomorrow for a piece of advice where to look."

"Where to look? You do know how to bait a hook."

"You're a poet and don't know it."

He was clever and somehow instantly likable, so different from Thom Van Cleve. And he offered a hint about where to look? To look for a murderer?

"Well, then," she told him, "I'll drop by your office on Bald Eagle tomorrow morning, over on Marco. I do my research too, you see."

"I'm honored. The hint—follow the path to the pot of gold and remember the luck of the Irish."

"What?" she asked, wondering why he'd mention the Irish, of all things.

"I'll explain it tomorrow when you drop by. See you then," he said with a grin and went off whistling a tune she thought was "It's A Great Day For The Irish."

She stood there, leaning on the railing, racking her brain. The only Irish connection she could think of around here was Fin Taylor's wife's shop, so had Mark Stirling attacked that too? But someone had mentioned that the woman got discount ads in their paper.

Then she saw Nick coming with a huge bouquet of roses in his hands and forgot everything but being relieved and glad he was home—and that they were going out with Lexi for the afternoon, like a family.

CHAPTER SEVENTEEN

"Oh, look at those little owls, Mommy and Nick!" Lexi's high-pitched voice rang out. Claire put her finger to her lips to quiet the child.

They stood outside the ropes looking at a burrowing owl colony on Marco, one of many small ones scattered through the island. Two other families and a man with binoculars around his neck were already standing nearby as well as a woman speaking, who had introduced herself as a volunteer wildlife docent.

She was here, she said, to answer questions, but she seemed to talk all the time in a deep, scratchy voice. No doubt, she also guarded the site from trespass. She stood just inside the short wire fence, giving facts about the owls. Even as he listened, Nick's mind wandered.

He supposed that Maggie Hazelton had assigned volunteers at many of the sites, especially those near high-traffic areas like this one. Though Maggie seemed admirable and altruistic, and Claire had said she didn't want to ruin their day, she'd blurted out the fact that Maggie could have had time to meet and murder Mark. And that Wes Ringold, who'd inherited Mark Stirling's newspaper, had dropped by. She was going to follow up on that by giving him an interview that, she promised, would also be an interview of him, whether he realized it or not. Really, what a deal, Nick told himself, glancing at her sideways. A wife he loved and desired, and a forensic psychologist he needed, all in one beautiful package.

And he'd been amazed at how excited Lexi had been to be going to see birds and a beach. He'd forgotten the simple joys of childhood—except when he thought about the early days with his dad.

He rededicated himself again to somehow stopping Clayton Ames and bringing him to justice. Not only would his dad never have killed himself, but Nick was convinced Ames had killed him personally since he'd been with just him that night. Dad had died, like Mark Stirling, with a close-contact bullet to the brain, though not one in the middle of his forehead. Ames had hardly pulled the trigger on Stirling, because he had the best alibi in the world—he was in Grand Cayman, and Nick could vouch for that. But just like the most evil mafia godfather, he could so easily have ordered it done.

The docent's voice jerked him back to reality. "The average adult bird is nine inches tall and, unlike most owls, they are active both day and night. As you may know, the owl used to be the symbol of wisdom with their wide, all-seeing eyes and rotating necks. Sadly, the number of burrowing owls is declining."

"They sure are cute," Claire whispered to Lexi. "Maybe we can find you a stuffed owl instead of that turtle from Grand Cayman."

"But I like him too! Look! I see little babies peeking out. Can we go closer?"

Nick said, "The fence is here to protect them. Only the lady talking can go inside. As a matter of fact, they are called protected animals since people keep moving closer to their homes and they have to move to find safety."

"Kind of like us, right?" Lexi asked, looking up at him.

Nick squatted and put an arm around the child's shoulders and whispered, "We'll get us a real home, honey, a house as soon as we can. But right now, with your mom and me, Nita and Bronco too, we are safe. Now, those babies peeking out of the burrows are called chicks."

"Are they girl owl babies, 'cause chicks are girls?"

"No," Nick said, trying to stem a smile, "boys or girls."

The volunteer guide shot Nick a narrow-eyed look as if to say she was the only one with owl wisdom. She cleared her throat and went on, "And of all the owls in the world, these are the only ones who nest—live—under the ground."

"Pretty cool, but it would make it hard to keep clean," Lexi told Nick in a whisper, taking his hand as he stood, even as she grabbed Claire's. He blinked back tears at that little gesture.

The three of them started away, heading for their car. Nick looked at Claire and grinned. "You have a very bright child here, Mrs. Markwood."

They all jumped when the guard owl, no doubt the father of the brood, gave a scream and beat his wings. They turned back to watch.

"Oh, dear," the volunteer was saying, her hand fluttering to her chest. "Perhaps he thinks I'm talking too loud, but I want everyone to hear, even those who are leaving before I'm finished. Just one more thing about the tunnels they build underground that go to their nest chamber. There is no back door or escape route for young or old if an enemy enters. Sad to think, these darling creatures have made a dead end for themselves."

Nick's gaze locked with Claire's. "Let's go swimming," he said.

"Yes, let's go."

★ ★ ★

At Tigertail Beach on the island, they played in the surf and picked up shells and sand dollars. For a mid-October day, the beach was crowded with walkers, sunbathers and six young men down the way playing volleyball without a net. Claire tried to cherish the time since Lexi was safe and happy. And to cherish Nick, sweet and sexy without even trying—or was he trying? His hands had wandered on more than her waist as they'd all played in the water.

"Wish we could spend these sand dollars," Lexi said, holding her little stack of them as they headed up the beach toward their umbrella and chairs. "I want to take another ride in a plane, this time one Daddy's flying and that's 'spensive. Me and him are going to take an airboat ride soon, and he said that's like flying on the water."

Claire and Nick exchanged glances, then she looked away. She didn't like and wouldn't accept what he must be thinking. "Oh, you didn't tell me that," she said as they sat back down. "Those do go very fast."

Lexi's little chair was between theirs. Huddled close, they sat in the shade under the large umbrella with its flapping fringe.

"Oh, I forgot, Mommy. Forgot he said not to tell you 'cause you'd worry, but I said you worry all the time anyway."

"Well, let's not worry about anything now and just have a good time. Who wants PB&J sandwiches, potato chips and Lexi's favorite Oreo cookies?"

After they ate, Nick suggested making a hole in the wet sand and making some little sand owls next to it. "Yes! Great idea!" Lexi declared and bounced up.

"Nick, I know I have Ada Cypress on the brain, but doesn't that look like her down the way?" she asked, pointing. "Who else would dress like that and paddle in here in a canoe? Isn't that her dugout beached on the sand farther down? And whatever is she doing?"

Despite his sunglasses, Nick shaded his eyes. "Got me. You want to say hi to her?"

"And see what she seems to be burying in a public place."

Lexi piped up, "She might be making a burrowing hole if she knows about the owls."

While Nick and Lexi stayed behind to work on their sculpture, Claire walked down the packed, wet sand with waves washing her feet. It was Ada, all right, oblivious to others, though she was at a distance from most people.

As Claire approached Ada, who was still looking down, intent on her work, she walked slower. She didn't want to startle her but hoped to see what she was burying. Papers? A newspaper?

Ada looked up suddenly, as if she'd sensed Claire.

"I didn't mean to surprise you," Claire said. "Remember me, Claire Markwood?"

"I saw you coming. This is a special place."

"Yes, the sea is beautiful."

"This beach name honors Tiger Tail, a great Seminole warrior chief who fought against the white soldiers. He fought Andrew Jackson, the man made president of this country, a man who had killed the Seminole and Cherokee," she said with a loud snort.

"Oh, ah—yes. I wondered where the name Tigertail came from. Do you mind if I watch you?"

"If you do not laugh at a foolish old woman past her time."

So how old *was* Ada? Of course, someone in their fifties could call themselves old or even look old from being out in the sun.

"You are burying a stack of newspapers in the sand," Claire said the obvious. She kneeled to get to the same height as Ada so she didn't seem to tower over her.

"Very bad writing. About Seminole casinos getting back at whites for taking their land by cheating them at the gambling tables like they cheated on the land. Best it all be buried with the man who wrote it!" She made a sound, something like *phaaa*!

Claire took off her sunglasses and squinted to make out what the folded newspapers were, but she knew now. The top issue wasn't thick, wasn't the Naples paper. The woman's vehemence at the paper—and at Mark Stirling, both buried now, stunned Claire.

"That newspaper—it's *The Burrowing Owl*, isn't it, Ada?"

"I have many copies, bought them in Goodland so others would not. Maybe this new man, Ringold, be better. I will give you one if you swear to burn it. I bury, you burn. I know other papers are coming and I can't stop them. This is only my ritual, but that is powerful, especially here."

At last, Ada looked up to stare at Claire. Their gazes met and held. Then she pulled the top paper off the pile of them and thrust it at Claire. It was sandy and damp, but Claire took it.

"Read it first," Ada said, shoveling sand with both hands into the hole even as water from a strong wave filled it and washed against their legs. "Then you might understand."

She pointed twice, hard, with finger jabs at the lower, left side of the paper. Her skin looked young without prominent veins or big knuckles. Claire almost asked her what she was pointing at, since it wasn't the top article with the photo of a Seminole Coconut Creek Casino. Ada rose and covered the rest of the hole by shoving in sand with her bare feet, then stomping on it as yet another wave smoothed out her work. Soon, like Mark, it would be completely gone. Yet Claire was unwilling to believe—yet—that this woman would have killed him.

Without another word, Ada turned and walked away, then pushed her canoe out into the surf.

The woman—an old woman, Claire was suddenly convinced, who looked young yet—poled where it was shallow, then paddled out to sea. The path of the sun on the water blinded Claire for a moment, and then Ada seemed to disappear.

Late afternoon that day, Claire was on the phone with Nick. She was on the yacht and he was heading for the marina. He was walking back to Fin Taylor's mooring spot to talk to him again, maybe to charter an inshore fishing trip for him, Haze, Heck and Bronco. He figured he'd learn more about him if they weren't in an interview situation. For once, he seemed reluctant to have Claire take one of the suspects on and seemed to be keeping Fin all to himself.

Talking to Nick, she paced the deck of the *Sylph*. She'd again discussed with him the fact that Maggie Hazelton had had not only motive but the opportunity to murder Mark. But now she was trying to convince him of something she could not quite believe she was saying. Since they'd had Lexi with them, she hadn't told him all about her conversation with Ada yet, though she'd showed him what she'd been burying.

"Nick, I'm telling you, Ada is an old woman, but doesn't look like it. She keeps her face fairly covered, but her skin, even her hands look young."

"You're usually more rational that that. Some people have good skin. Not having one of your off-the-meds hallucinations, are you?"

"Not funny. She's seems to have stepped in from the past and doesn't like living in the present. She is steeped in tribal lore but hasn't lived among them for years, according to the bio info I can find on her. I keep thinking about what Van Cleve said about that magician's claims of a fountain of youth in the Bahamas—leaves rejuvenated, dying insects brought back to life—so why not people too? Remember Maggie's comments about the rubber tree here near their cistern that rejuvenated itself after the hurricane—and that Ada washes in, maybe drinks the runoff cistern water?"

"Let's get real, Claire. Don't let your psychologist knowledge or your woman's intuition get confused. Did you get that paper she gave you laid out to dry?"

"Yes, despite getting sand all over the dining table. That's another thing. What she pointed to is an ad for Fin's wife's Irish Gifts and Goodies Shop, which I intend to visit. And that ties to what Wes Ringold mentioned about the Irish, though I don't know how Colleen Taylor could fit into all this. But, Nick, honestly, what if Van Cleve and Ames are right, that the cistern water here has some youth-preservation qualities?"

"If you're believing anything Ames says now, we're really in trouble."

"I know. I know. But Haze and Maggie believe in it too."

"He's swayed by his family myths and money."

"It's supposedly been tested by chemists and could have some mineral content that works. Things aren't what they seem here, the people or the place."

"Yeah, tested by chemists who are probably on Ames's payroll."

"As are we."

"Claire, we had no choice, and I don't want to argue. Later, then. I'm on the marina dock. Fin's boat's not here but should be in soon. I'll chat him up and call you back or just come back. See you and Lexi for supper."

Before she could say anything else, he was gone. If he trusted her to help him in this Mangrove Murder investigation, why didn't he accept her findings and advice? After she talked to Fin's wife, she'd just call on Ada again and nail down more about her past and how much she hated and wanted to silence Stirling.

And speaking of the past—to her surprise, Jace appeared on the bottom of the gangway. Bronco materialized almost immediately and stood at the top of it as if to block his access to the boat.

"It's okay, Bronco," she called to him before there could be another confrontation.

The big man gave her a nod and walked to the aft, but leaned his elbows on the railing as if to keep an eye on them.

"You should have called," Claire said as Jace came up the gangway. "Or maybe you did, since my phone was lost, but how did you find us anyway?"

"I just checked marinas large enough to take this monster," he told her. He came close and put his hand on the railing close to hers.

He looked good, she thought, maybe a little tired. Though he wore a Florida Gators baseball cap, he seemed to be sporting the same military haircut, the same close shave as usual. His eyes were laser blue and burned her in their intensity.

"So how's married life, Claire?"

"New. Busy."

"I'll bet."

She regretted sounding so abrupt. Sad that, since she'd once eloped with Jace, he had to believe she had run off to marry Nick so fast when she'd known him a much shorter time than she had Jace. But she couldn't go into all that right now. He'd just have to feel hostile until she and Nick got out from under Ames's thumb and could really explain. Besides, though she'd kept knowledge of her disease from Jace, he's the one who had wanted out of their marriage, and that still hurt.

"Claire, I'm here to see Lexi, to set up my scheduled time with her," he interrupted her agonizing. "An airboat ride, maybe miniature golf, just some good dad-daughter fun and talk time so she doesn't get confused about who Daddy really is."

"I wouldn't let her do that, Jace. She loves you and always will."

"Now why do I think I heard that line before in reference to you and me?"

Claire fought to ignore his tense tone. She steadied herself and said only, "The thing is she's exhausted and sleeping right now."

"If she's slept for a while, can you wake her up?"

"I suppose so. Her nanny's with her."

"You've got that lifeguard gorilla on board *and* a nanny? Not to mention a captain and crew? What the hell is this, the lifestyles of the rich and famous? Is Nick Markwood that loaded, or are you two living off King Midas Ames, and just pretending you hate him? Well, can't say I blame you—get it while you can. But I'd hate to think you are on the gravy train, despite these really nice perks, because it just isn't like you."

She could tell that Jace was not only angry but hurt. He even blinked back tears. She was getting upset too, but she still felt for him.

"That's right. And you too hated the man enough to go to Grand Cayman to help find Lexi, and I—we—do appreciate that," she insisted.

"How about tomorrow at ten, then? I'll have her back here before dark, scout's honor. Claire, it's one thing to see you, but I want to see her too."

Behind Jace's back, Claire could see Bronco coming closer, and she didn't want any sort of misunderstanding or confrontation. She fought to control her emotions. "Jace, I'm sorry if I sound unfair or stubborn. It's just that, after her abduction, she needs close watching. She's still having bad dreams about it all. I just wanted you to be double aware of that—to be very watchful when you're with her."

"You think after all that I wouldn't?"

"Ten o'clock tomorrow then, here. See you then."

"For sure. See you."

CHAPTER EIGHTEEN

Nick paced the dock of the marina where Fin Taylor kept his boat. It wasn't the same one where the yacht was moored, but not far. He was fuming over the fact that he and Claire seemed to be arguing without really arguing. Worse, he was furious that she had evidently kept back some key information from him, even if some of it had to be nonsense about Ada.

But not just that. Without Claire hearing, Lexi had mentioned that she'd talked to Mommy about things she overheard Ames saying on the phone about a dead body. The child had only blurted it out when he'd explained to her that it was all right to take the grayish sand dollars washed up on the sand but not the white ones in the water. The grayish ones, he'd told her, were no longer living animals but dead bodies.

"I heard Mr. Kilcorse talk about a dead body in the water. I told Mommy about it," the child had said, before Claire came closer in the surf, so he hadn't asked Lexi more. But if Claire didn't explain, he'd have to question Lexi. So what else was his wife and partner keeping to herself, besides her beautiful body?

Of course, they'd been forced to marry and hadn't outright

chosen to be with each other that way, but was it more than that? Could Ames have privately threatened her about Lexi?

Ames's reach to buy off and control others had always scared Nick. Could it be that years ago Ames had told Nick's father he had to kill himself or he'd hurt his wife and his son? That was a worse thought than if Ames had shot him to stage a suicide.

Didn't Claire realize Lexi could link Ames and his spies and enforcers to Mark Stirling's murder? He needed to know that. Nailing Ames for hiring a hit man, even if he didn't pull the trigger, could be one way to get him on trial. Then Nick would be more than happy to expose in open court and the national media the fact that Ames High's youth water was a con—if it was, and Claire was fighting him on that too.

He threw himself down on the wooden bench to wait for Fin to put in. He also had to wait to confront the woman—in person, in private—who not only turned him on, but, he hoped, had not secretly turned on him.

As soon as Claire settled down from Jace's sudden appearance, she went back inside and reread the Irish imports ad on the bottom right corner of the first page of the newspaper Ada had been burying. It was hard to read the damp, sandy paper. It tore easily, and the print on the back of the page bled through.

She had previously read several of the sample issues archived on the paper's website to get a flavor for Stirling's articles. She would describe the style of his big, front-page articles as brilliant but brutal. No wonder he had a lot of enemies, which gave her and Nick a lot of suspects. To defend Haze on trial if he was charged, they had to have laid the groundwork for someone else as a likely killer.

But this advertisement was so different. A scalloped edge around the ad as well as a cluster of shamrocks tied by a bow made it look impressive and expensive, yet somehow delicate and feminine. The Irish Gifts and Goodies Shop hours were eight to eight. She'd researched it online too and learned it was a small place, attached to the Taylor home. The shop did a lot of mail orders, but people were welcome to drop in.

So Claire decided to go there now instead of putting it off until tomorrow, the day she'd promised to stop by *The Burrowing Owl* newspaper office. She was dying to know if Wes Ringold's off-kilter Irish allusions somehow pointed to Colleen Taylor's shop.

She told Nita and Bronco where she was going and, like Nick on this small island, decided to walk, though Bronco had driven both their cars to the parking lot. He'd also brought his truck, with his trailer still attached, which fit right in around here. The Taylors' house wasn't far; she'd seen that street listed on the local map they'd picked up at Stan's Idle Hour.

Among the island's double-wide and single trailers and houses on stilts, the Taylor home and Colleen's small shop stood out as high-class. The house was two stories, light green with a slanted tin roof. A white picket fence circled a yard of cut grass and well-tended flower beds of bright crotons, begonias and ever-blooming rosebushes. The shop, with its hand-painted sign, must be just a first-floor front room with large windows in which hung stained glass pieces of shamrocks, leprechauns, harps and Celtic crosses.

The storm door was open but the screen door was locked so she knocked.

Silence at first. Then, "Com-ing straight-aw-ay!" sang a voice from the depths of the house.

The woman's appearance supported her Irish name. Colleen Taylor was, like Claire, a natural redhead with green eyes. Claire's first crazy thought was that Colleen could have been her sister. She was short but very shapely and pretty.

"Come in then, and I know who you are, Mrs. Markwood.

Not many a stranger living in big boats round these parts. And I hope we won't be strangers for long, then."

"I must say, you are the perfect advertisement for this place," Claire said as Colleen unlocked the screen door with a key on a long chain full of them, and she stepped inside. They exchanged greetings and a bit of small talk about the weather and the shop. Another surprise—the woman seemed to have a lilt to her normal speaking voice. Perhaps she really *was* Irish, but here in little Goodland?

"Yes," she told Claire when she inquired, "I really am from the old sod. Met Fin when he was in the navy and stationed briefly in Ireland, that he was. He courted me from afar, and then later came to woo and wed me. Well, to be a fisherman's wife—an Irish lass thought she could handle that."

The bio check Claire had done on Fin had mentioned they had two grown sons, one in the navy and one living in Michigan. Colleen, she recalled, was forty-two, so she must have married young. She didn't look her age as her complexion resembled porcelain tinged with pink and a dusting of golden freckles, more like Darcy's skin.

"You have some lovely things here," Claire complimented her, looking around. The first case held silk scarves, most in green and white, some with harps, some with a shamrock border. "I saw the nice ad for your shop in *The Burrowing Owl* and just had to see it for myself."

"Yes, it was a lovely ad." She sighed hard, then cleared her throat.

Claire noticed Colleen's eyes were bloodshot. Surely she hadn't been crying. Or drinking? Claire smelled nothing but flower fragrances in here. Perhaps she had allergies.

"Oh, and I must admit this shop ties me down a bit," she rushed on, "but I love it. I spend a lot of time filling mail orders too, and, of course, Fin is gone a lot, very busy with his charters."

Claire noted Colleen's face had gone sad and her bouncy tone had drooped. It must be hard to have her children away and her husband so busy. Claire admired her for creating a career and pastime in a place so far away and different from her homeland.

"So, look around a bit, and I'll answer any questions," Colleen prompted. "I keep the cases locked but I will open them all for you."

"I have a four-year-old daughter who would love everything in here," Claire said, trying to keep things light. Though it hadn't seemed so at first, Colleen looked nervous. Maybe she'd been lying down and was just suddenly exerted, but Claire's psychologist radar went up. Perhaps, like Claire herself with Jace before their separation and divorce, this woman had had an argument with her husband, maybe about spending so much time away while she was stuck here—but no. She had to watch jumping to conclusions and identifying with someone so quickly.

"A little girl would love these fairy figurines!" Colleen told her, gesturing her over to a glassed-in case in which she flipped the lights on, then unlocked it with another key on the chain. "And, over here, many a man favors these Guinness goods, shot glasses, mugs, bottle openers. This last case of jewelry that I sell so much of—over here—has harps, St. Bridget's Cross and tricolored claddagh rings. Oh, and some lovely neck scarves, the latest fashion statement instead of necklaces, you know."

Despite her flitting from place to place in this small room with its bright green soffit and carpet, Colleen's posture had seemed to stiffen and her shoulders had rolled forward in an almost protective stance. But then, she was hunched over the cases, pointing things out. Sudden posture changes when nothing disturbing or threatening had been discussed was still an instinctive way of protecting oneself. On the other hand, this woman had no clue Claire was here to psych her out. It could just be she was having a bad day.

And then Claire noticed Colleen did not wear a wedding ring, though there was a pale white mark where one had been recently. She was surprised the woman had been out in the sun, since she claimed she stayed inside here a lot and hardly had the skin for a tan.

"So," Claire asked, "do you ever go out on your husband's boat?"

"Oh, I have, of course," she said, rearranging some of the lovely rings in their slits on a green velvet board. "We Irish are seafarers from way back, from before the times of St. Brendan, of course."

Why did she keep saying *of course*? Claire wished she knew her basal, usual voice, posture and behavior. Again, she scolded herself for instinctively identifying with this woman.

"You know," Claire said, "I think my little girl would love that claddagh ring with the two hands holding the heart. I recently remarried, and it could assure her that both I and her stepfather care for her—as well as her own father."

"Oh, that's lovely," Colleen said, "and I have it in small sizes." Her voice was outright shaky now. Maybe she was going through menopause, though it might be a bit early for that. Such a situation had thrown off a report of Claire's once before.

"I'd love to have you come to the *Sylph* for lunch soon," Claire said. "Someone from a seafaring land with a husband who is often at sea ought to enjoy a big ship."

"Oh, thanks awfully, but I'm pretty tied up here. And I'm sure the both of you are busy, working to defend Haze, if it comes to that. Here, let me show you the child's ring. We have a grandchild coming soon up north and I intend to see she gets one too, when she's old enough—the ultrasound says a girl. Oh, how I'd love to go up when she's born, stay there a bit, but I just found out my daughter-in-law's mother will do that."

So maybe *that* had caused the nervousness or sadness. It sounded as if Colleen had found out some things about Claire too, why she was here on Goodland, what Nick planned to do for Haze. A frown seemed to press down on Colleen's face, and she kept blinking, maybe blinking back tears? But that was sometimes the body language sign that someone was lying. Claire had not asked one pointed question, so lying about what?

"I think we have unfinished business," Nick told Claire after she had tucked Lexi in and joined him. They stood on the deck of the yacht, staring out into the deep darkness of the sea. Clouds cloaked the stars and moon.

"A lot. I've got to tell you about my visit with Colleen Taylor today, and we didn't finish discussing Ada."

"I don't mean that. Or my talk with Fin today where I booked *Reel Good Time* for a fishing trip with Heck and Bronco too. I mean you and me."

"You mean the state of our marriage?" She leaned on the rail, facing him. She looked beautiful even in muted light from a curtained stateroom.

"More like the foundation of it, which I know was forced and shaky. Claire, don't blame Lexi but when we were talking about sand dollars and shells being the remains of animals today—bodies—she said she told you she'd overheard Ames mention a dead body in water on his phone. So what else did she hear, and I can't believe you didn't tell me about that."

"Yes, I—she said some things."

"That's key information. You know that."

She narrowed her eyes and met his. She thrust her chin out but her lower lip trembled. "I have to protect her above all, Nick. I can't have her interrogated, dragged into court or—"

He moved closer, still not touching her. "As if I'd do that!"

"Not that I blame you, but you are on a crusade to stop and destroy Clayton Ames!"

"Keep your voice down, even out here. You bet I am. But you think I'd sacrifice Lexi—or you—to do that? Then you don't know me very damn well at all, so it's a good thing not to trust a stranger."

"That's ridiculous. And you keep things back from me too, don't you?"

"Like what?"

"I don't know—that's the point."

"Talk about ridiculous!"

"Like I haven't met your partners at the firm yet. Like you didn't tell me it was Bronco who was on the phone the other day. You had to meet with him first before you mentioned hiring him to me."

"That's nothing like this. Small potatoes next to a full steak dinner."

"It isn't. You think it's easy to be uprooted, to alienate my sister, lie to her? I realized today how much I miss her when I was with Colleen Taylor. I had a kind of natural affinity to her."

"Well, too bad you and I don't seem to have that."

"That's not true. You know it isn't," she insisted, hitting her fist on the railing.

He took her by the shoulders and turned her toward him. "Claire. Just tell me what else Lexi said she overheard. There was more, right?"

"Yes, counselor. Do I need to swear on a Bible I'll tell you the whole truth, nothing but the truth?"

"It would be nice to be trusted. Not only as a lawyer by a partner but as a husband by a wife."

He felt bad when tears trickled down her cheeks, but he

didn't let her go. Damn right, he was on a crusade to stop Ames, though surely not at any cost.

"She got the idea," Claire went on, "that 'Mr. Kilcorse' might want to hurt you—like, she said, Captain Hook wanted to hurt Peter Pan. But, Nick, you know that. I wasn't holding back key information there."

"Is there more? Is there?"

"Lexi said that might be because you were cross with him. I asked her if Mr. Kilcorse could have said Nick crossed him, and she said maybe. Just telling me that really shook her up, brought back traumatic memories, and she had nightmares after. Please don't hash this out with her again."

He swore under his breath, sighed and dropped his hold on her. He leaned his elbows on the railing again.

"You should have told me, Claire. You should have trusted me not to question her more, believed I'd protect her. It's just another sign you don't trust me or you don't love me, even if I can accept that she comes first."

"That's not true—that I don't love you," she insisted. "That's what amazes and scares me. I do, and if Lexi and I lose you in this—this battle you are in with Ames—it would kill me too."

Head held high, crying hard now, she turned and hurried away.

CHAPTER NINETEEN

Claire rushed to her bedroom, closed the door and smothered her sobs in her pillow. She flopped over to lie on her back, staring at the dark ceiling, half fearing, half wishing Nick would knock on her door.

Claire knew she'd been clutching at straws to accuse Nick of keeping things back from her. He'd soon told her about seeing Bronco, and let her make the decision to hire him or not. But she had kept important information from him. Would he call her "partner" and mean it? Would he even trust her anymore?

Her tears ran down into her hair and ears, so she sat up and reached for a tissue from the bedside table. She wiped her eyes and blew her nose. No use being so stuffed up tonight she couldn't sleep. This agonizing wasn't doing any good. She needed her rest, and even her narcolepsy meds had not helped her conk out last night. She'd just take a shower and see if she could relax before she took the potent stuff tonight.

She took a lukewarm shower and pulled on her nightgown, brushed her teeth and looked at herself in the mirror. "Claire Fowler, formerly Britten, now Markwood," she whispered.

"Who are you? You love Lexi, Darcy and her family. And now Nick Markwood, don't you?"

She nodded at the woman in the mirror, then reached for her hairbrush and pulled it hard through her hair. She padded barefoot back into the bedroom, grabbed the silk robe that matched this favorite nightgown—a bride with nothing new to wear, she thought.

She headed for the door. She had to apologize to Nick. She'd blurted out that she loved him but had to assure him she meant it.

Trembling, she opened her door and went out into the hall. And ran right into Nick, standing with his fist raised.

"Oh!" she cried and jumped back as if he'd been a stranger intent on assault.

"I was going to knock on your door."

"Sorry to let you down."

"You were going to check on Lexi or what?"

"Coming to see you."

"Dressed—undressed like that?"

"Obviously. Definitely."

His eyes went thoroughly over her. "To argue again—more?"

She shook her head and whispered, "No. I meant what I said, that I love you. It can happen fast, you know, even when other people try to force everything."

He nodded once, then picked her up so easily. Her arms went around his neck. He walked the few steps to his stateroom and shoved the partly open door wider with his foot. It was dim inside, only a lamp on his desk threw light. He put her down and closed the door, then took a step back, not touching her, but his eyes burned her. He wore jockey shorts and a T-shirt and smelled of pine soap.

"I want to make love to you, Claire. I want us to share a bed now and in the future. But if you say 'no,' okay. So either sit on the other side of my worktable to talk or walk to our bed with me."

"I think lawyers and forensic psychologists talk too much."

A hint of a smile softened his intent expression. "Me too."

They held hands and walked to his big bed. They tumbled into it together. No words needed then, just touching, holding, kissing. Despite a forced marriage, everything was mutual now.

And then, on her back as his mouth and hands erased her sanity, she glanced up. Oh, right! A huge mirror on the ceiling. Now she knew who the wanton woman in the reflection was. It was her and she belonged to Nick Markwood.

They kissed endlessly, explored, even smiled, giggled. She welcomed his powerful touch, was lost in it. Yet she gave as good as she got, glancing up at the huge ceiling mirror now and then to assure herself this was real. No dream but brash and beautiful, the things they did.

The only rational move he made in his barely leashed passion was reaching for something in the bedside table drawer when he had her out of her mind with need.

"I want a family," he spoke at last, his voice raspy. "Someone for Lexi, but not yet. Not till we get through this—and, together, we will."

"Till death do us part."

He lifted his tousled head. "Don't say it that way, sweetheart. We're going to survive—to live for a long, long time. And this is a new beginning, our real wedding night. Claire, I love you and always will," he whispered.

It was the union of two bodies, two lives, two lovers finally wed.

"Mommy said to be careful in the airboat," Lexi told Jace as they got on board the large watercraft with four other people already seated and their pilot sitting just behind. "I think she had a ride in one and saw gators or something like that."

"We will see gators and lots of birds," Jace promised, putting his arm around her. "This is going to be a fun ride and a fun day. So how are you and Mommy getting along on that big boat?"

"Good. There's lots of room. Everybody has their own rooms."

"No kidding? Mommy and Nick too?"

She nodded. "But they were in one bed last night. I got scared when she wasn't in hers, 'cause I peek sometimes, just to be sure. Me and her have bad dreams, and I don't want her to be scared."

"Okay, I see," Jace said with a nod. What to make of all that? He hated to admit it, but in his gut he still yearned to protect Claire as well as Lexi. He still wanted Claire, wanted to make amends. Could it be a child's skewed view of things, or could Claire not have been sleeping with Markwood—until now? If it took a while, maybe she was still uncertain about who she loved. He blamed himself. He'd screwed up things so badly with her, but—

The big, upright propeller behind them roared to life. Jace leaned close to Lexi and said, "There's no motor under the boat so we can go on real shallow water. We're moving by air. That's like a big fan back there. Hold on to me now."

As they moved slowly out, then surged away from the dock down a waterway, Lexi shouted, "But I feel hot air in my face. Not cool, like a fan blows. And if it has a propeller, is it like an airplane?"

"Not exactly. Planes have motors."

"Bronco says python snakes are out here. I don't want to see one of those. They have lots of babies and get really big."

"Bronco said that, huh? What else did he say?" Jace asked, despite the fact they were going faster and the whir of the propeller was louder.

"That he likes keeping an eye on me and Nita better than hunting snakes."

"Sounds like a smart guy to me."

"I can tell he likes Nita. I do too."

"And Nick and Mommy like each other?" he asked, though he hated himself for circling back to that. Their relationship tormented and hurt him.

"Oh, yeah, but I heard them argue last night, so I went back to bed 'stead of tell them. That was before she wasn't in her room. 'Specially, I didn't tell them I heard them, 'cause it was about a dead body Mr. Kilcorse said something about on the phone."

"Kilcorse, huh? What else did he say?"

"He doesn't like Nick but I do."

"Yeah, okay. We'd better quit talking until we stop. Pretty noisy and we don't want to yell."

"So won't that scare the animals away?"

"We'll slow down or stop to see them."

As Lexi nodded and finally kept still to look around at the passing Everglades scenery, Jace's last words stuck in his throat and his brain. He had to stop agonizing over Claire and Markwood. And, whatever benefits fell his way, he had to stop trusting a dangerous man like Clayton Ames to run his life, because that could cost his life—and theirs too.

The Burrowing Owl newspaper had a small space above a dentist's office on Bald Eagle Drive not far from San Marco, the main road with the bridge onto Marco Island. How Claire wished, as she parked her car, that she'd be interviewing Mark Stirling today instead of his protégé Wes Ringold.

Are you suicidal? she'd ask. *If not, who has threatened you besides Haze and Fin Taylor? Has Maggie Hazelton confronted you? Have you ever been warned to lay off attacking the Fountain of Youth products like Fresh Dew and Youth Do?*

Though she'd hardly slept at all last night in Nick's—now their—bed, she felt alive and alert, so she took the stairs instead of the elevator and knocked on the door. It had frosted glass and a simple sign, The Burrowing Owl, Founded 2013, Ed. Mark Stirling.

It said something, didn't it, she thought, that Wes had not been in a big hurry to put his own name in place of Mark's? She'd Googled Wes and found he was quite young—twenty-five, a two-year graduate in journalism from Ohio University in Athens, Ohio. He was a Fort Myers, Florida, native and had interned briefly at the Fort Myers *News-Press*. His parents were divorced, mother in Fort Myers, father in Conifer, Colorado, grandparents in Ohio. He was a young man on the rise, so she needed to watch for signs he was in too much of a hurry and, perhaps had taken a shortcut by dispatching his aggressive, ambitious boss, Mark Stirling. But in the brief meeting they'd had yesterday, she hadn't sensed the slightest hint of that.

She also wanted to hear his so-called hint about something Irish, because, if he was alluding to Colleen's shop, he'd have to really explain himself. She had liked the woman, had even felt sorry for her evidently unhappy state.

She knocked on the door. A shadow loomed on the other side of the glass, and Wes opened the door, smiling.

"Welcome and thanks," he said and motioned her in. "I didn't want to go out on my rounds, hoping you would drop by. Have a seat, as limited as they are."

She sat in one of the two leather-upholstered chairs on this side of the messy, big desk, which sported two laptops. Nick had said the police had Mark's so who knew why Wes needed two. He sat in the facing chair, sitting slightly forward, as if in anticipation.

"I hope," he said, "you didn't come today just because I offered you a hint with an Irish flavor."

"That did intrigue me, but, frankly, so does anyone who knew Mark Stirling up close and personal. My husband and I are intent on finding the cause of his death, and I don't mean a bullet in the forehead. I mean the motive behind it. Wes, could he have been suicidal? You knew him well."

"Suicidal, no. Hell-on-wheels ambitious, yes. I saw no sign of self-destructiveness in Mark Stirling. It's pretty obvious he had people who resented his—our—investigative journalism though."

"Enough that someone would have killed him for that—enough that you fear for your life if you continue that cause?"

"I don't write with the edge he did, and I triple-check facts and cite all sources."

"And he didn't?"

"He couldn't or some people would not have talked to give him the slants he wanted and needed. Take the illegal shark fishing issue, for example, not to mention the Fountain of Youth water. That's a whole other shark tank, if you know what I mean. Listen, Claire. I'm holding you to your promise to do an interview—not one focused on Mark's death, but about how forensic psychologists work. But I see it like this. First of all, I'm aware the police looked at me briefly—briefly—to see if Mark and I got along, if I lusted for his position, this paper, so to speak. Second, because I'm black—yes, I'm going to say this, the three-hundred-pound gorilla in the room—people think I won't turn over as many beehives as he did. Maybe they think I'm not up to it, not as smart, more careful, I don't know. Maybe they expect my only cause to be black rights. This is still the Deep South, and, yeah, I'm ambitious, but I'm not brutal, and Mark could be brutal—in print, I mean."

He sat back and took a deep breath, then went on, "I see that one thing about forensic psychologists is they are good listeners. I had to get that off my chest, clear the air—and I don't usually use clichés."

He smiled at her. "Tell you what," he said, "just to show I bargain in good faith, here's the Irish clue— Mark spent a lot of time, and free advertising, in and on Colleen Taylor's shop in town. Enough said, at least by me. You look surprised, though you're pretty good at keeping a poker face—oops, another cliché."

"I am surprised. I just met her yesterday and liked her."

"You two resemble each other—go figure. The point is, Mark liked her too. I'll let you take it from there without citing your source. So what made you decide to get into the psychology major of forensics?" he asked, reaching back to his desk to pull one of the laptops onto his lap. "And, yes, I realize you don't do actual autopsies, just ones on people's lives—dead people. You know, here's the headline I'm going to use for this interview—The Dead Still Speak, If You Know How To Listen. And I think you know how to hear the living too, Claire Markwood, so I appreciate your listening to me just now, like I was on a psychiatrist's couch. I know the difference between psychologist and psychiatrist, believe me."

"I appreciate your calm demeanor and up-front honesty," she told him, though she'd seen liars, guilty ones, come off as helpful and apparently generous—and overly talkative and ingratiating. "And thanks for your Irish clue, even though I doubt—I hope—it won't lead anywhere but to a marriage problem with a woman whose husband is gone a lot."

He gave a huge shrug, but his expression was intent, not dismissive. "Probably not," he told her.

Even as she began to answer his interview questions—blessedly, as he'd promised, not focusing on the Mangrove Murder case—she remembered something else she'd done recently and not shared with Nick. Trying to lessen her unease about the woman who was strangled on the *Sylph* in the lounge, more than once she'd Googled newspaper articles on that trial with the accused Dylan Carnahan, who had loaned them the yacht. And she'd become almost as obsessed with that murder as she was with this case.

CHAPTER TWENTY

Nick said he had several surprises for Claire when she got back—though for the first time, she thought of it as *when she got home.*

"But you didn't have to get me anything," she told him. "Last night was enough."

"Not for me, it wasn't," he said with a devilish grin. "Here, sit down." He tugged her down next to him on the couch in the lounge. Maybe, she thought, their growing, mutual happiness could dispel the feelings she always got in this room in which she knew what had happened.

"First of all," Nick told her, seeming as excited as Lexi for once, "I've invited your sister and family to come take a cruise with us on Saturday."

"Oh, that's great!" she cried and threw her arms around him. "I know Lexi's been missing Jilly, and I still need to patch things up with Darcy. You'll like Steve. Hardworking, salt-of-the-earth kind of guy."

"We can take a little jaunt out past the Naples pier or to Fort Myers. I hate to use the crew and fuel on this big baby for pure pleasure, but I'll insist on reimbursing Dylan for the day. I was going to surprise you when your family arrived, but I thought I'd better tell you and Lexi ahead of time."

"Nick, that's a wonderful gift!"

"Okay, so far, definitely, so good," he said. "That's for Saturday. Monday afternoon, 4:30 p.m., you are invited to a post-wedding reception to meet the others at the firm. I can't wait to show you off, but we were so busy when we got back. After all, here I am using you not on a South Shores assignment this time, but as full-firm consultant, so you're one of the adjunct staff now."

"Oh, that's lovely too. I can't wait to meet them."

"Lastly..." He cleared his throat, suddenly looking nervous and intent. "Claire, if you'd like us to take out a United States wedding license and get married here too, we can do that, though the Grand Cayman document and service were completely legal. I checked."

"You know, I would like that, and my family would appreciate it too. But let's do it when we have the time—and peace of mind—to really enjoy it, when all this is over."

She could tell he was thinking about Clayton Ames's hold on them again. Funny, but once she'd shared her body with him, did that mean she also shared his thoughts? It was more than just her skills as a psychologist kicking in. Was she more mentally in tune with Nick than she had been with Jace?

"So, like some kid, I couldn't wait to spring all that on you," he said, smiling again. "How did it go with Wes Ringold? Did he stick to a straight interview, or was he actually fishing for inside info on this case? Did he look guilty at all?"

"Negative on any guilt vibes, at least for now, and he did stick to a straight interview. But I'm going to have to go back to visit Colleen Taylor again, as well as Ada. Wes implied Colleen was having an affair with Mark Stirling—another red alert for a possible motive if something blew up between them—or if Fin found out and wanted revenge. If Mark and

Colleen were involved, maybe that would explain the distant meeting spot where he was killed. But, Nick, every instinct I have tells me Colleen didn't do it," she said with a sigh that seemed to deflate her earlier joy.

"I'm sorry. I know you like her, but I'm glad you're willing to check it out. Since 'us fellas' are going out fishing with Fin this afternoon, it would be the perfect time for you to see her again, but be careful. You said she gave hints of being unstable."

"No, of being upset, and aren't we all at times? You're starting to sound like a forensic psychologist, looking at all the angles, Mr. Defense Attorney. But you're right. Who knows, especially sitting here in this room, where a person was murdered? You cleared Dylan Carnahan, so the killer of the woman on this boat is still out there too."

Nick had to admit it was a beautiful day for offshore fishing. At least they weren't going way out to deep sea, though he felt he was adrift in his own deep seas half the time now. He'd thought at first to ask for an inshore trip, but what good would it do to try to get Fin close to the murder site? If he was at all guilty—and now, with his wife's possible relationship to the victim—Nick would only tip the guy off if he asked to fish near No Name Key.

Nick had thought of bringing Haze today, but decided he didn't want him spending time with another "suspect" so he'd only brought Bronco and Heck. Nick could tell Heck was the most excited of them all, much more than he was, as fishing wasn't really his thing, and Bronco preferred airboats and shallow water to the Gulf of Mexico.

As they got aboard, Heck said, "My grandfather, he went fishing with Hemingway in Cuba, knew him."

"Cool. Hemingway was a real macho man and great fisherman, I heard," Fin said and went back to the wheelhouse to pilot them away from the dock.

"Was he an old-time actor?" Bronco asked, sitting already in the stern of the boat. Maybe, Nick thought, he shouldn't have brought Bronco, but he'd dropped Nita and Lexi at the library on the East Trail for story time so they didn't need him watching over them. Darcy and Jilly were there too.

"He means Ernest Hemingway, the great American writer," Heck told Bronco. "He lived in Florida, but also in Cuba for about twenty years. You ever read *The Old Man and the Sea*, Nick?" he said, turning away from Bronco.

"Back in high school. That's interesting about your grandfather, Heck. I know he was like a father to you after yours died young. I'll bet you'd love to visit there, see your family's hacienda."

"Not only see it. Get it back. Castro good as stole it. Anyway, my grandfather, he used to drink daiquiris with him—Hemingway, not Castro—in his favorite bar La Floridita in Havana. Love to see that place too, and someday, I will. I'll go in from Canada, get there somehow."

Nick squeezed his friend's shoulder. "Let's have a few drinks on the yacht, and you can reminisce about his stories. Claire would love to hear them too."

Heck nodded and wiped his eyes behind his sunglasses. It was the one thing Nick had seen that could get his tech guru emotional.

"So, all right," Fin called from the wheelhouse. "Here we go to look for 'thar she blows!'"

He started the motor, let it idle, then came back to cast off the ropes. He'd already showed Nick his so-called 'plotter's screen,' which looked like a video monitor. Their boat on it was a blinking dot, but Fin said he did things his own way and never looked at it. He'd claimed he had the real nautical depth charts in his head.

For sure, Nick observed, the guy prided himself in doing things his own way. If Claire was here, she'd jump right in with more questions, but he didn't want to tip him off. Yet had their captain not only eliminated a man who was threatening to expose an illegal shark fishing business, but one who also was sleeping with his wife?

Once they got several miles out into the Gulf from Goodland, Nick tried to keep his mind on Fin's explanation of what to do if a fish hit one of their three lines. Bronco was still sitting on a cushion in the stern while Nick and Heck sat in the fighting chairs on the deck. But Nick reminded himself again that he wasn't just here to fish—at least not *for* fish.

"You often see sharks out here?" he asked Fin when the guy finally took a breath from explaining how to land a fish.

Fin frowned at him then looked away. "Oh, sure. They'll come to the chum I use to entice other fish. That chum hides the human scent, works like a charm. They love the squid parts I mix with canned cat food to draw fish, a secret recipe."

"Ick," Bronco said.

Speaking of fish, Nick thought, the big guy was looking a little green around the gills as the waves picked up a bit. Here was a man who caught gators and pythons but got squeamish over waves. It said a lot that he'd readily agreed to come along anyway.

"In that Hemingway story I mentioned," Heck put in, "sharks ate a huge marlin carcass strapped to a small boat and—"

"Hang on, Heck! Oh, boy, look at that!" Fin shouted when something hit hard on Heck's line. "Let it run before you reel in! A sword! I swear that's a swordfish, and they usually lie deep this time of day."

Fin was right. A swordfish! Even Bronco got excited to see the huge fish clear the water in a spray-flinging arch, then tear away. The fish shimmered in purple, blue and silver colors. Nick could hear Heck's line spooling out fast.

"That baby's over nine feet if he's an inch!" Fin shouted, now back at the helm to maneuver the boat. "And his sword's a good three feet long! They don't stab with it but slice at their pray. I've seen sharks come to that blood in the water. Swordfish make good eating at restaurants—pricey—tastes better if you caught it. Maybe that stupid *Owl* paper can take a pic of that and give *me* some *good* publicity for once. Yowsa! Hang on, Heck! He's gonna run again."

"They endangered?" Bronco asked.

"Threatened!" Fin yelled over the noise of the motor and their voices. "Their stock's been rebuilt in the Atlantic, so don't worry none about that. Don't worry about nothing—that's my motto," he added with a scowl Nick's way.

After an hour battle, when the big fish finally managed to break the line by swimming under the boat, Nick did not feel one bit bad for a deflated Fin, only for Heck. And he realized without even tipping Fin off about suspecting him of possible illegal shark hunting for rich charters—friends of Ames, like Thom Van Cleve?—the man had shown his antagonism for the *The Burrowing Owl*. He'd just wait and see if Claire turned up the other motive for murder.

"I'm back again," Claire greeted Colleen when she opened the shop door. "I thought I'd buy myself a ring like my daughter's and see if I could get you to reconsider lunch with me on the *Sylph* today."

"Oh, you're so kind. And I don't want you to think I'm not grateful."

She led Claire over to the counter with the claddagh rings and unlocked the glass case. "Listen," Colleen said in a rush, "why don't we have some tea first? I was just going to fill the pot straightaway."

"All right. That sounds lovely."

"I can ice yours if you'd rather. South Florida and not Ireland, I know. I realize you Americans like your coffee. That's one thing I've not adapted to."

"I'll take tea the way you do."

"With a spot of milk then. I'd love to show you my new Royal Tara bone china I just got in. The plates have the Irish blessing right on them. You know, the one that starts 'May the road rise up to meet you,' and ends 'Until we meet again, may God hold you in the hollow of his hands.'"

Her voice quavered on that last line. Claire followed Colleen out of the shop and into her house, but, even walking behind her, she could tell the woman had started to cry. She tried to stifle a sob, and her shoulders shook. Colleen swiped at her eyes before she turned around.

"I can see you're distressed," Claire said. "Let's sit down. I can fix the tea if you show me where it is."

"I'm all right. Just—on edge lately. Fin's so busy, of course. So much local upheaval for such a little place."

"You mean with Mark Stirling's death?"

Colleen startled, and Claire feared at first she'd overstepped—or had learned what she didn't want to know. Standing in the doorway to her kitchen, Colleen nodded and wiped her eyes with an already damp handkerchief she pulled from the pocket of her slacks. "He was a very nice person. Scottish heritage but loved the Irish gifts here, bought some for friends."

Friends, Claire thought. Mark Stirling had friends? But it was Colleen's words, *He was a very nice person*, that really floored her. No one else had said that about the man. But it was spoken so sincerely that Claire couldn't believe Colleen could have been angry with Mark. But shouldn't she have been, since Mark was harassing her husband with articles on illegal shark fishing?

"Oh, that's right, I did see an ad in his paper for your shop," Claire said in the awkward silence.

"Yes. Nice ads. Smashing, really. He insisted on paying me for the items he bought and charged me a nominal fee for the ads."

Would she admit that, Claire wondered, if there had been something illicit going on?

"I'll get the tea," Colleen said, suddenly seeming to pull herself together. Her expression changed, went from soft and vulnerable to hard and determined. Almost steely eyed.

An interesting transformation: Which persona was this woman, really?

"Come on in with me then. There's a nice little nook in the kitchen or we can take ourselves out back, and I haven't forgotten the ring. Lovely to have the company, really."

The kitchen was immaculate with lace curtains, and the copper kettle boiled all too quickly. Just when Claire was going to try to get Colleen to expand on her opinion of Mark Stirling, the woman said, "Don't be miffed now that I've turned down your kind offer of lunch on the yacht. I hate to bring this up as I'm sure you and your husband must concentrate on this current murder case. But I read that Nick Markwood and his firm defended another accused man. You see, I'd rather not visit the *Sylph*, because I knew the woman who was strangled there and, since your husband defended that man who owns the yacht and he walked free, Sondra's case has never been solved."

Claire stared at her, wordless for once.

"And," Colleen added, as she poured the boiling water in the pot, "that's so sad, so very sad, when a murderer walks free, and no one even knows who he—or she—is."

"Who—how did you know Sondra McMillan?" Claire asked. Her heart was beating hard. Her hand shook so that it rattled her teacup in the saucer, so she put her other hand on it to keep it quiet.

"She shopped here. Her Irish roots ran deep. Her problem was she was beautiful and newly divorced. Emotionally needy, I dare say."

"But being beautiful—most wouldn't see that as a problem. But I must admit I read about the trial and saw her picture."

"The yacht was on Marco Island then, not here, as I'm sure you read—or your husband told you," she said. "Her ex-husband had an ironclad alibi. He was living out West and was at work." She poured a bit of milk in her tea. And stirred. And stirred.

Claire recalled Nick had told her that Fin had made a joke about Mark Stirling's name and the fact he always stirred up trouble. She suddenly feared she'd stepped into a spider's web and she wasn't sure who was spinning it.

CHAPTER TWENTY-ONE

Waiting for Nick to get back from his fishing trip, Claire hunkered down in her stateroom office to research more about the Sondra McMillan murder. She told herself not to feel guilty that she wasn't working on their Mangrove Murder case again. Hadn't she exhausted herself over it, both online and off? And Heck had—well, researched the heck out of it too. She couldn't fight her interest in the shipboard murder any more than she could help her fascination with Colleen.

The words *Breaking News* streaked across Claire's laptop screen as she got to the website and page she wanted. Hunched over her laptop, she watched an archived *Nancy Grace* show on YouTube about the Unsolved Yacht Murder. One segment had interviews, and one was called Verdict Watch while the jury was sequestered.

Nick was featured on one segment. She watched it carefully. After the trial, he explained why his client, Dylan Carnahan, was acquitted and should have been. She supposed Nick could convince anyone of anything. Another later segment had the headline Carnahan Should Be Retried: Is There A Mystery Murderer Or Did He Get Off Scot-Free?

"Mystery murderer—that's a good one," Claire muttered as she took notes on a legal pad by hand. "Maybe Nancy Grace can send a reporter down here to find Mark Stirling's mystery murderer."

She looked up a moment to rest her eyes and saw the back of Bronco's head outside the cabin window as he bent over something on deck. Lexi was taking a nap so he wasn't helping to watch her. The child was really getting too old for long daily naps, but she ran herself ragged—like her mother. And she was always physically and emotionally exhausted after Jace brought her back. Nita had some time to herself right now, but Claire didn't know where she was.

Until, that is, she stood to stretch and glance out through the window. Nita was in Bronco's arms, the two madly kissing one another.

"Breaking news, indeed," Claire whispered. Isn't that all they needed? Yet, hadn't she herself fallen in love with someone she was working with? Her first instinct was to phone Nick to confer, but she didn't want him lecturing Nita or Bronco. What if they quit? Poor Bronco not long ago had lost a woman he loved, which had caused a volatile reaction. As big as he was, he had a real problem with self-esteem and controlling his emotions. She felt sorry for him, and she and Lexi valued Nita, but this wasn't good, was it?

She saw the two of them parting with a fond backward glance, so she sat down and returned to Nancy Grace's next segment. Claire knew she should be spending her time getting more background on Fin and Colleen Taylor as well as Ada Cypress, but this Sondra McMillan murder haunted her. Now Nita and Bronco had upset her too, making it hard to concentrate.

This six-minute segment had the title *Carnahan Should Be Retried*. In it Nancy Grace was admitting, in her usual dramatic style—she probably would have loved the Mark Stirling brand of journalism—that Sondra McMillan might have been up to something underhanded, since "just maybe" she hadn't been invited onto the yacht. "But she didn't deserve to die!" Nancy insisted. "So what if she'd dated a series of men? There might be no direct proof one of them was Carnahan, or that any of them hurt her, but she didn't deserve to die!"

Forget having Colleen Taylor to lunch here, Claire thought, and forget Nancy Grace's sensational subjects and style. She'd get Nick to invite Dylan Carnahan here, so she could chat him up.

This short video, which looked as if it had been taken in the courtroom, showed a blown-up poster of the lounge of the *Sylph*. Claire gasped. The long couch was the same one she and Nick used. The position of the dead woman's body was outlined on the floor, though the corpse was gone in the photo. The blood on the area rug—it was bare tile now—made a terrible stain, like a Rorschach inkblot test, as if demanding, "What do you see here?"

"What indeed? But if she was strangled," Claire asked aloud, "why the blood?"

She went back to reading local newspaper articles on the murder from various media websites. Amazing! Mark Stirling had a byline for the Naples paper from which he'd been let go shortly after. So he had covered the Carnahan trial.

She read the article. Nick must have hated this coverage, if he'd seen it. Mark Stirling's article was slanted to make Sondra sound absolutely guileless and helpless, and he intimated Dylan had invited her on board, despite what Dylan had testified. Stirling made Sondra sound as if some of the loose woman reports were lies.

And, oh, it was Dylan Carnahan's blood on the floor. He'd claimed, when he'd found her there, that he'd cut himself trying to slice off the ligature someone had put around her neck. He had no idea who she was, but he'd pressed his mouth to hers, so, yes, he had traces of her lipstick on his mouth from trying to breathe life back into her. Finally, he'd called 9-1-1.

Next on this segment came a video of people leaving the courtroom in Naples after the trial. Nick, with Carnahan, and, evidently, two of his team, were in the background.

But also walking out of the courtroom was a middle-aged Seminole man with—it had to be!—Ada Cypress.

After the fishing trip, Nick had gone back onshore to talk to Haze and Maggie again. Both of them were scared that an arrest was imminent. When he returned to the yacht, he and Claire sat on deck with goblets of wine before an early dinner. The sun was still fairly high, but they were exhausted. Claire told him about her research on Sondra McMillan's murder, including that Mark had covered the trial. Nick said he tried not to read the papers, because they just distracted him.

Then she broke it to him about Bronco and Nita. No more keeping things to herself, she vowed. They were a real team now.

"Oh, no," he said. "Bronco and Nita? Isn't that all we need? I think I should talk to him and you talk to her. Not to say we don't approve, but just to keep it quiet and controlled. I think we know how instant attractions work. I just hope Heck wouldn't object, since he's the one who brought Nita to us. Because she's his cousin and with his protective macho ethic, I don't want him to get involved, but I'll have to mention it—tell him it's okay with us—within reason."

"Reason? If people are madly in love? But all right. We need both of them, and they're good people, good with Lexi."

"And things have been working out so well, at least with them watching Lexi and the yacht. The worst thing Bronco's done since he's been here is hang a picture of him standing over a dead gator on the wall in his cabin next to the one of a fourteen-foot python he killed, but maybe that will act as a deterrent to keep Nita out of his room." His grin was really a grimace, and he shook his head. Claire reached out to lightly grasp the nape of his neck and stroked his skin with her thumb.

With a sigh, Nick went on, "How he sleeps with that stuff on the wall is beyond me, and—I just thought of something. He uses a bangstick to dispense gators, and that always leaves a stellate—star-shaped wound."

"Like the one in Mark's forehead? But there can't be a connection. The autopsy stated it was a bullet wound."

"I know. Entry and exit wounds, but a bangstick could too. Just a coincidence, but..."

They recited together, "In crime investigation, there are no coincidences not worth looking into."

Nick said, "I hate for us to have to be so paranoid about everyone and everything. Knowing Clayton Ames does that to you. And your seeing Ada Cypress leaving the courtroom is one thing you can pursue, but a Bronco and Mark Stirling connection? No way. Bronco's been out chasing snakes in the Glades, not the human ones around here. I'll go talk to him, though, just about being discreet with Nita," he said, draining the rest of his wine. "You can mention it to her later. Be right back."

But he wasn't right back and when he rejoined her, Nick was upset. Even more upset than he'd been about her obsession with the old Carnahan-McMillan murder case, though he'd agreed to have Dylan invited to his own yacht soon.

"What happened?" she asked, getting up from her deck chair to join him at the ship's rail.

"He took it bad. Thought I didn't trust him. Also, Heck had already told him to keep his hands off Nita—then he didn't."

"Oh, no. Since Bronco lost his last love and exploded..."

"Yeah. He's really shook up, so I better go talk to him again. You want to come along, back me up?"

"Yes, I'll go too. That's all we need, either of them upset and quitting. Ah, the problems of the bosses of the world."

"Except for Clayton Ames who just eliminates his problems—literally. Let's go talk to Bronco then to Nita."

But as they headed down the deck, Nita came running at them, crying.

"He's gone! He said goodbye, that he was a curse."

"Gone where?" Nick asked, hitting his fist on the railing.

"Grabbed some of his stuff. Back to working alone in the Glades, he said, where he can't hurt no one, where he be trusted."

With Claire and Nita after him, Nick ran around to the dockside of the ship just in time to see Bronco's truck roar out of the parking lot, despite the fact he was pulling his small Airstream trailer.

Nick swore. "I'm going after him. If he gets all the way to his Everglades snake station, he told me where it is, not far off the highway, I'm afraid he'll do something crazy—again."

"Nita," Claire said, "take care of Lexi. Feed her if we're gone too long. I'm going too. I've calmed him down before when he was upset. We'll bring him back, and all four of us will talk this over."

"I'm very scared he will hurt himself!" Nita shouted after them as Nick dug out his car keys and they ran for the gangway. "You be careful driving fast so you not hurt too!"

"I can't believe he got out of here so fast," Claire told Nick as they drove out of Goodland and didn't see the Airstream ahead on the road. "We'll just have to hope he told Nita where he was really going. He'd have to drive this way. We'll catch up with him on the Trail. So where is this so-called snake station?"

"Just off Loop Road at the edge of Big Cypress National Preserve. I guess there's an old picnic table there and a place to put his trailer. The Burmese pythons some idiot let loose are breeding. Those snakes lay up to one hundred eggs at a time. The US Fish and Wildlife Commission had assigned him that area, and I guess he'll want that job back now. Some Florida animals are endangered, but the pythons will end up endangering humans down here if they're not controlled. That includes the areas right at their back door, like the Miccosukee Seminole reservation to the northeast."

"Yeah, well, I almost always feel endangered out there," she admitted. "The Glades have everything from snakes, bears, panthers and gators—not to mention voracious mosquitoes. I heard someone say if the Everglades aren't saved, they could become the Neverglades."

He gave a little snort. "Don't worry. I know this area fairly well from when Dad and I used to camp. We'll spot Bronco before we get that far in."

But they didn't see him or catch up to him. He must have been driving like a maniac, Claire thought. Or had he pulled off for gas or food and they'd passed him, so he was behind them? The red sun sank slowly behind them like a bloodshot eye in their rearview mirror. Nick went just slightly over the speed limit.

They turned off Route 41 and drove even deeper into the Everglades on a one-lane dirt road. On both sides, cattails nodded in the wind, and tea-colored water ran through the sloughs and stood in the saw grass prairies as far as the eye could see. Pine island hammocks rose from the saw grass, and strangler figs gripped palmettos up to their blue-green fronds of spiky fans. Clumps of gray, ghostly looking slash pines looked absolutely dead. It was impossible to tell if Bronco was behind them since a cloud of their own dust pursued them.

"Nick, we have to turn back."

"As soon as we get to his off-road place, if he's not there," Nick promised. "According to what he told me, it's only two more miles in. He parks the trailer there, goes out on foot with poles and nets."

"What if he's irrational or violent? We'll have to let him go—from the yacht."

"Claire, don't you see? You of all people, so good at psyching people out?" Nick demanded, leaning forward and gripping the steering wheel harder.

She was shocked at his tone and the tears in his eyes. And then her scrambled thoughts and fears collided.

"You mean he might be suicidal?"

"He didn't strike out at anyone, did he? Not like before. He's turned his losses, his frustrations and fears inward. Even if we don't take him back on board, we have to bring him back, get him some help if it comes to that. If only someone had done that for my dad. Okay, I'm going to slow down because his pull-off place has to be near here, on the left, barely off this road."

She glanced back again instead of straining to look ahead. The dust cloud still trailed them up the road. Her stomach went into free fall: Where could they even turn around here? She shouldn't have come, but she couldn't let Nick go alone, and she wanted to help Bronco—again.

She heard Nick, whom she'd never seen cry, sniff hard. She reached over to squeeze his shoulder. "I—Nick, I'm sorry. I didn't get all that at first, and I understand about your dad. Bronco's been so stable, so kind and dedicated on the yacht, and I don't think Nita would be taken in by someone she didn't trust. She seems level-headed, really, but she did lose her young husband not long ago, which could make anyone vulnerable."

Crazy, but she thought of her salesman father being gone so much and how her mother retreated into other people's fictional lives and loves by burying herself in books. She thought of Sondra McMillan's divorce and the implications she'd become promiscuous. She remembered how Jace used to be gone so much, flying the Pacific and Asia routes he loved, her own divorce and how she'd buried herself in work to set up her small consulting business Clear Path. And she thought of the woman she considered her new friend, Colleen Taylor, whose husband was busy all the time, and who might have loved Mark Stirling. Desperate women who had lost their men and fought back in their own ways…

"Claire! There it is! I think we just passed it. I'm going to back up, but I didn't see the trailer. Maybe we beat him here."

Thank heavens, they had the windows up. The dust cloud behind them caught up in the wind and cloaked their view, swallowing the car and the ghostly slash pines that lined this section of the road. For a moment, Nick didn't move the car. The dust seemed slightly pink as the sun sank lower in the west behind them. When the cloud settled a bit, he began to back up.

Crack! Boom!

The car shuddered. They heard a strange flopping sound.

"Flat tire?" he muttered.

"Out here? I hope not!"

Another blast. Closer. Louder.

"Gun. Gun! Get down!" he shouted. He undid their seat belts so they could hunch lower. "Sounds like a rifle. What the hell? Got to get us out of here!"

In that awkward position, he held hard to the steering wheel and tried to back the car away. At least one flopping, flat tire made him lose control and sent them off the road. More dust. They banged backward into something. Claire braced herself as they were jolted without their seat belts.

The car jerked to a stop. Nick tried to drive forward, but their wheels spun. As other cracking sounds came closer, they hunkered down, each in their own footwell. The next blast shattered the driver's side back window, spewing shards of glass and drowning out Claire's scream.

CHAPTER TWENTY-TWO

Nick had no intention of making a break for the trees. Maybe that was the shooter's intent. Talk about a terrorist. Clayton Ames was that—but was he behind this attack or was someone else?

Nick wanted to hold Claire, comfort her, but the console between them was a barrier. He was scared to so much as lift his head, in case the shooter wanted to blow it off, though he didn't think he would. Fear and control was the name of this game.

When it was silent again, Nick counted to fifty. Then, reaching across to hold Claire down, he slowly raised his head and looked around. Through the slowly settling dust, he saw no one unless someone was hunkered down behind the trees. There was no sign of Bronco's trailer on the road or in the pull-off.

"Anyone?" Claire asked, but when she started to raise her head, he pushed her back down.

"Don't see a soul," he whispered. "But that doesn't mean he's not out there. I have a gun locked in my desk at the office and one hidden on the yacht, but not in the car."

"Maybe he left. Just wanted to scare us." Her voice was a trembling whisper.

"And to threaten or warn us. I don't think it's some random potshot this deep in the Glades."

"Like the guy on the WaveRunner at the mangrove death scene. Either sent by Ames, or we're being followed by someone whose cage we've rattled. Maybe the person who killed Stirling and wants us to stop sniffing around—just to let Haze take the blame for it. Hopefully, like the WaveRunner guy, he's taken off now. It's pretty obvious we didn't heed the message on that life ring—*Get out! Stay out!*"

"But we're stuck here—at least one tire is blown and the rest are stuck. And we are not getting out of this car. The backseat is probably covered with glass since there's even some up here. You aren't cut, are you?"

"No. I think the high seatbacks and headrests saved us from that, let alone taking a bullet. I'm okay, really. Except I don't like the vultures I can see circling in the sky over us as the sun sets," she said, looking up. "I think we have human ones circling too. But you mean we're going to stay in the car all night? Wait him out? Nick, no one—that is, no one we can trust—knows exactly where we are except—"

"Except Bronco. I'm going to crawl into the backseat and brush the glass off in case we're stuck for the night. Here," he said, taking his cell phone from the console pocket and handing it to her. "Try 9-1-1. You don't have yours with you, do you?"

"I didn't have time to grab it and I knew you had yours."

"I'm not holding out hope. Huge stretches out here have no cell towers. We need to be able to huddle, and all we can do here is hold hands."

"You mean 'cuddle'? How romantic under a darkening sky marooned in the 'Neverglades,'" she said, but her voice quavered.

"Not the way I'd prefer for us to spend our second night

sleeping together, but I love you for your courage as well as for your other qualities."

"To know you love me almost makes crazy things like this okay," she said with a sniff. "But what if he, or she, sneaks up on us?"

"Gone with the wind, I think. We're better off in here. I was thinking of waiting until it got pitch-dark, but the minute we open a car door to get out, the lights will pop on and—"

"And we'd be sitting ducks just waiting for a bullet, not to mention wild animals out here at night—like Bronco's gators or pythons."

"I still don't think he's behind this," he said as she tried his phone. He squirmed his way into the backseat, kneeling on broken glass on the floor and brushing it off the seat.

"Your phone only says Roaming. Oh, now No Network Available. Lexi's going to be scared without us. I don't want her to have another nightmare alone."

"Nita's there but shook up too. And we don't have your meds."

"That could be more bad news. I don't need a narcoleptic nightmare on top of all this," she said with a huge sigh. "I should have grabbed my purse, because I have extra pills there, but we were in such a hurry..."

Her voice trailed off.

"Nick," she said with a sob she'd obviously been trying to hold back, "we've been in a hurry since we met, haven't we? Trouble and danger. Now this."

"Don't be scared. Ames wants us alive to do his bidding."

"Unless, like we said, it's someone else with a gun who thinks we're asking too many questions and trailed us when we drove away from Goodland. Maybe Fin? Even Thom Van Cleve?"

"Is Jace good with guns?"

"Jace? He wouldn't! How can you say that?"

"Because he hates my guts, and we have Lexi—and I have you. I know you still care about him but—"

"He's her father, that's all."

"But I can see it in his eyes. And do we know who he flies for now? Nail him on it sometime, or I will. Actually, I asked Heck to find out and he couldn't—and that's trouble. It's like there's some phony company he's working for."

"Nick, after everything we—and Lexi—went through on Grand Cayman, I can't imagine he'd knowingly work for Ames, though Ames could have a company fronting for him. I know he can twist the truth and people's arms, but Jace told me that when he saw us leave Nightshade with Lexi, he got off the island as fast as he could."

"Let's not argue. You agreed we're in this together, and tonight we are. Before you join me on our bed for the night," he said, trying to calm himself too, "reach under your seat and pull out my spare briefcase. It's empty. Maybe I can jam it in this shattered window to keep the skeeters out, as Bronco calls them."

"And snakes."

"Claire, snakes aren't going to slither in here."

"Pythons are huge, and they sense warm bodies, even in the dark! I read about that. They coil around them and suffocate them."

"Yeah, well you're really helping here with talk like that. Should we worry about the so-called Swamp Ape too?"

"What's that?"

"A phony, local giant, kind of like the Abominable Snowman, a yeti or whatever. Some locals have taken bogus pictures of it, but let's be reasonable here."

"Reasonable? Like you suspecting Jace of shooting at us? Like believing in and promoting a fountain of youth?" she cried, her voice rising on another sob. "Like I'm starting to think Ada Cypress might be an old, old woman who looks fifty? Like there's someone so terrible and powerful he can threaten us from far away and hire anyone to do his bidding?"

"Sweetheart, hand me the briefcase and come back here. If no one comes looking for us by morning, we'll walk down the road to get help. Just keep low, crawl back here and let me hold you."

She did, thrusting the briefcase at him first. With one hand, reaching over his head, he wedged it in the jagged frame of broken glass. He lay with his back to the rear of the seat and pulled her into his arms in front of him.

She pressed back against him as if she was sitting in his lap. "Nick, if I have a bad dream, or hallucinate, just talk me down, okay? I'm scared, not only being out here in the dark like this with—things—around, but about how things are going."

"They're going well for you and me personally, intimately," he insisted, kissing the nape of her neck through her tousled hair. "Lexi's adapting, maybe even thriving."

"I mean this Mangrove Murder mess. Trying to sift through things and keep ahead of Ames in case we have to cross him by telling the police someone else murdered Mark. That would ruin your day in court when you're blackmailed into promoting Ames's youth products."

"I know. That goes against everything I believe, every oath I ever took. I keep praying somehow we'll find a way to stop Ames and stay safe."

"Yeah, like right now," she said, but he was fighting not to laugh at the way she'd worded that. They hadn't stayed *safe* since they'd met.

Damn, but he did love her, needed her. They quieted, holding tight, straining to listen for footfalls, for anything, as the sounds of the wilderness night crept in: tree frogs and bullfrogs drumming, then a *who, who.* "Who indeed," he said, giving her a little squeeze, "but that's only an owl."

"Maybe a burrowing one?"

"Doubt it out here. Try to sleep."

"No way. Without my meds, I fear my dreams, though reality is pretty scary too. Nick, it's darker than dark out here! I'm trying to be upbeat, but what are we going to do?"

"Hold on. Hold on like this and just—hold on."

Jace left the clubhouse bar at the Royal Poinciana Golf Club he'd just joined for a fat fee. He'd played eighteen holes today and tonight had passed up a chance to pick up a clingy, tipsy redhead, but she wasn't the redhead he wanted—probably, stupid sot that he was, still loved.

Feeling a bit woozy, he headed for his new Lexus. It wasn't far to his condo. No more living in the Lakewood area. He was moving up in the world.

But the truth was, he didn't give a damn. He'd rather not be spending Ames's money. He'd rather be going home to Claire and Lexi, at least the old Claire and Lexi. How had it happened he'd lost them? Couldn't blame Markwood for that, though he'd like to. Claire was on her own by the time she'd met Nick. But the years she was married to him, how had he been so blind, so stupid not to know she was on powerful meds for her narcolepsy and cataplexy, ones that could turn her into a kind of freaked-out zombie? And she'd managed to hide that from him. But it was his fault too, not to recognize the signs. Oh, yeah, Attorney Nicholas Markwood was welcome to her.

He fumbled to get his keys out and saw a guy standing by his car, maybe having a smoke. No—no cigarette. Did he know him?

"Oh, Mr. Van Cleve. I thought, if you came back, I'd be flying you in," Jace told him, hoping he wasn't slurring his words.

"Not flying me or anyone else in, if you're, as they used to say, 'in your cups.' You've got to stay sober all the time in case you get a sudden call to fly."

"I don't drink much, really. Things got a bit out of hand this evening, so—just this once."

"Once is too many. I saw your pricey fee for this club on your company credit account and tracked you down to be sure you can fly in a couple of chemists—water experts, to be exact—soon so they can help lay the groundwork for the trial, working with Nick Markwood. They're in LA, but I believe you used to fly into there a lot."

"I like cross-country flights, the views, the clouds."

"Just heed my warning because there are views, then there are views," he said and whipped out his cell phone, which lit up brightly with a flick of his thumb across its face.

Suddenly, Jace was staring at a picture of Lexi. Lexi sitting with that Mexican, or whatever she was, nanny of hers in—it looked like kiddie library time. And, yeah, there was Claire's sister, Darcy, and her little girl, Jilly, too.

Jace felt sick to his stomach, but not so sick he didn't want to pound this bastard through the pavement.

"Nice picture, cute kids," Van Cleve said as the screen went dark. "Story time at the East Naples library. So here's a moral from a story for you. Flyboy signs on to help tycoon. But flyboy still cares about ex-wifey and offspring."

Jace just gaped at him. Had this man read his mind? No, more likely, Clayton Ames had.

"But," Van Cleve went on in a monotone voice, "flyboy needs to do exactly what he signed on to do for the tycoon. Know whose side he's on and why. Or else happily-ever-after story time could have a sad ending, and we don't want that." His voice sharpened. "Shape up, Jace. Sober up and shut up. Drinks and bars with babes don't make for discreet assignments. See you around."

The man stalked away, crossed the parking lot, then lights popped on in a distant car and he drove into the darkness. Jace thought he might throw up, not from whiskey and beer but raw fear.

CHAPTER TWENTY-THREE

Fearing deep sleep where a narcoleptic nightmare might occur, Claire slept only fitfully off and on. She knew Nick struggled to stay awake. The slightest sound set them off. Despite the comfort of his arms around her, she was so nervous that twice she'd had to relieve herself, though he'd barely opened the car door for her to go right there. The brief overhead door light nearly blinded them.

As light and a faint fog sifted in at dawn, they heard a muted roar.

They both jerked alert. "A search airplane overhead?" she asked and tried to sit up.

"A vehicle on the road behind us. Stay down! It looks like Bronco's truck, but wait until I see it's him, and he's okay."

Nick got out, but she peeked over the backseat. Yes, Bronco. Apparently alone. She hated to think this way, but she was glad she could see both of his hands were empty.

To her relief Bronco gave Nick a one-armed hug. She couldn't hear what they were saying, so she got out and went closer. When they saw her, they walked toward her. Bronco was obviously anxious to explain. For a guy who didn't say a lot, he called out, "Mrs. Claire, I drove around, then parked by the beach all night. Didn't come out here like I told Nita. Ashamed. Nick said there was a shooter, but it wasn't me. Hate guns. You guys been good to me. First thing this morning I went back to 'pologize, and Nita told me 'bout what you did. Man, she was shook but just told Lexi you went out. I said, let me check 'fore you call the police. Thank God the reason you didn't come back was just 'cause of a flat tire and a spin off the road! All my fault."

"And mine for rushing out here," Nick admitted as the three of them stood between their vehicles. Claire noticed that Nick kept glancing around. "But I knew you needed a friend. As for the flat tire and the shattered back window you haven't seen..."

"Man, sorry! No, didn't see the window!" he said, walking closer to the car. "Someone shot at you? Maybe stalked you?"

With an exaggerated shrug, Nick said, "So see, we need you to watch over things. And we don't mind your seeing—dating, ah, romancing—Nita, as long she's okay with it and it doesn't interfere with either of your jobs."

Claire smiled at Nick as Bronco beamed at them. After locking the car and leaving a note in the window in case someone found it, they squeezed Claire between them in Bronco's truck and headed back to town. Claire was convinced that this, at least, was a temporary happy ending.

Claire was glad to hear Darcy's voice on the phone the next morning, but she had no plans to tell her she'd spent the night in the Glades after being shot at.

"I'm starting to really like your husband," Darcy said. "He invited Steve and me to the meet-the-law-firm reception Monday."

"And the Saturday cruise tomorrow. I can't wait to show—"

"Claire, hold on a sec. That's one reason I called. Jilly's

come down with the chicken pox, and I bet Drew catches them from her too, so we'll have to postpone that. I'm so sorry—really I am. But that means that Lexi might get them too since they were at the library story hour, not to mention other kids there. I'm going to call the librarian and warn her."

"Oh, Darcy, no. I'm so sorry too, but things like that are not anyone's fault. You didn't know she was coming down with anything. Give Jilly a hug for me."

"About those other kids—I counted nine of them from the photo one of the fathers took and, I guess, sent everyone a copy, though I'm not sure how he knew our address. Did you get one? Lexi's in it, center stage with Jilly."

"No, but we still have our mail going to Nick's office. I'll watch her for a breakout. But you and Steve will be there Monday? Glad to hear that, as I've met almost no one in Nick's professional world except his tech advisor."

"Claire, listen, are you happy?"

"I have Lexi and Nick and the career I always wanted, helping people who need help, working on the truth."

"You didn't answer my question, honey. Kiss Lexi for me and be safe and happy, however busy you are."

After they ended the call, Claire thought that was kind of a strange thing to say. Darcy didn't know they weren't safe. And why would Darcy think she wasn't happy? Good things were happening. Nick had arranged for Bronco to get counseling for his anger management and self-image. And Heck had promised to get her the verbatim court records of the Dylan Carnahan trial.

Claire was exhausted. She intended to walk over to Ada Cypress's place after lunch, but she lay down for a few minutes. Her body was limp, but her mind was spinning.

Lexi showed no sign of the chicken pox—yet—but Claire had put her down for a nap and left Bronco and Nita chatting in deck chairs. Just a quick nap for herself…ten minutes…then to Ada's. She was grateful she had not had a terrible nightmare in the car last night. Nick had seen that only once when she went off her meds, that is, someone took her off them. But she'd taken a pill when they got back to the yacht, though not the liquid dosage of powerful stuff she still used at night.

Just a few minutes of sleep to make up for last night, she told herself. She was as tired as she'd been in high school before she was diagnosed, when people teased and mocked her for always falling asleep…

Falling for Nick. Yes, she had fallen for him. But she still felt for Jace, maybe felt sorry for him, wanted him to do well, wanted him to accept the way things were now…at least he was still flying…

Flying… Claire was flying but she landed on the Goodland dock and walked up the gangway to the yacht. Someone she knew owned it, but why was thick saw grass growing on the deck? That stuff could cut you. And palmetto with strangler figs hung over the windows. Strangest of all, bushes of nightshade with its purplish flowers and poison berries crowded against the ship's railings.

But what a beautiful, big boat! As it set out to sea, she went inside to look around. The lounge was lovely, but something was very, very wrong. She expected Darcy to visit, but it wasn't her sister who stood at the door, gesturing for her to enter. No, it was that other red-haired woman, the Irish one who knew dead people.

The woman pointed to the lounge and said, "I know you. I know what you are here for."

As Claire went into the lounge, she saw a bloom of blood stained the carpet, and a woman was lying dead inside the outline of her body. Did what the woman at the door said mean the dead woman was still talking? Yes, her lips were moving. She was whispering, but Claire could not hear what she said and she needed to know. She went one step closer and gasped. The dead woman whispering was herself, as if she gazed down into a mirror!

Claire awoke with such a jolt that she nearly threw herself off the bed. A dreadful dream! What did it all mean? she wondered, as if her nightmares ever made sense.

She felt still so caught up in it, so petrified that she could not move for a moment. She stared at the ceiling, thinking she was in Nick's—their—bed, and would see her own reflection, not herself dead like in the dream. But this ceiling was blank, white and told her nothing.

Groaning, she rolled to her side and pulled her knees up nearly to her chest. When she went off her meds, things always got deep and dark, like that buried eternal fountain of fathomless water.

Reality slowly seeped back in. She wanted to talk to Ada Cypress, but what did this dream mean? "Can't figure out my narc dreams, never could," she told herself and sat up unsteadily.

But she was determined, she told herself as she slowly stood, to figure out what Ada knew about the woman who had been murdered on this yacht. Why had Ada been at the Carnahan trial? And she was desperate to learn if Ada was middle-aged or ageless.

After spending more time with Lexi, Claire walked to Ada Cypress's house. Trying to shut out the clinging remnants of the nightmare in which her own lips were trying to tell her—warn her—about something, instead she forced herself to recall things she'd learned about Ada's people.

Claire was intrigued by the fact that the Seminoles were traditionally matriarchal so that the men left their families to become part of their wives' kin, pretty much the opposite of most cultures. The Seminoles were proud that they were the only Native Americans who "never surrendered." Other tribes were vanquished or forced off their lands by the white man, but the Seminoles flourished in the Glades by finding their "final hiding place" there. Was Ada hiding something that would help her and Nick?

It had annoyed Claire that he had never quite seemed to recognize Ada's potential importance in this investigation. Nor did he pay attention each time Claire tried to hint that there was something weird about her. Maybe he was afraid that he'd look silly in court if he claimed Ada's use of the fountain water kept her young. And Claire didn't want the private, maybe secretive, old—how old?—woman to be dragged into court against her will. Ada had earlier made clear she wanted nothing to do with publicity. But why then was she at the sensational murder trial where Nick defended and exonerated Dylan Carnahan?

Ada's canoe was pulled up on the bank, so Claire assumed she was home. She probably didn't own a car. Maggie had mentioned she took her to get groceries sometimes, and Claire had never seen a vehicle here. As she climbed the steps, she smelled some strange aroma. Smoke? None came from the chimney. Maybe Ada was cooking inside.

The heady, earthy smell got stronger as Claire walked the elevated deck that led to the front door. Was there a back door? She hadn't noticed.

This door was ajar. She was going to knock, but glimpsed Ada inside, sitting cross-legged on the floor, inhaling smoke through what looked like a hollowed-out piece of sugarcane. Surely, she wasn't using marijuana. What was that alluring scent? Something was burning low in a clay dish from which she drew the smoke. Just a small pile of leaves?

As Claire stared and lifted her hand to knock, Ada slowly turned her head and expelled a plume of green-gray smoke.

"I thought you would come back," the woman said. "This is just bay leaves, good for protection. The 'old ones' had chants to go with it. The legends say drink it or smoke it to stop bad dreams if you see a ghost."

Claire stepped inside but went no farther. Yet the smoke seemed to envelop her. She felt afraid but somehow soothed too, despite the uncanny coincidence of Ada mentioning bad dreams.

"And have you seen a ghost?" Claire asked, her voice shaky.

"We all have. You also. Yes?"

"Yes," Claire admitted as goose bumps skimmed her skin. The hair on the nape of her neck prickled. Seeing herself again in that dream…dead…whispering… Did this woman read minds? Claire told herself that she had to question her, keep things grounded in reality, in the murder trial, the youth fountain.

"Then sit," Ada said. "I see in your eyes you know some things, and I do too."

As if stepping into a cloud and another dream, Claire sat.

CHAPTER TWENTY-FOUR

For a southwest Florida guy, snow this time of year always amazed Jace, but this was mid-October, and those were the Rocky Mountains. Jace gazed down at the jagged peaks as he flew the Learjet toward LA to pick up the two water experts.

Jace wondered just how much control Nick Markwood had over the case he was probably going to present in court to defend not only Haze Hazelton—if he was indicted—but the supposed magic water. He kind of liked the idea of the mastermind of Grand Cayman pulling Markwood's strings, but he hated the idea of someone pulling his.

One thing he'd always loved about flying, even when he was a copilot with lots of rules and regs, was freedom. He felt like his own man thousands of feet in the air heading cross-country or over the Pacific. But with a guy like Van Cleve dogging him, spying on him, he might have made a mistake to sign on that rich bastard's dotted line.

Except he'd had no choice that desperate night on Grand Cayman. He would have just disappeared as Kilcorse-Ames had threatened, "I'll have these two gentlemen who brought you here take you out in a boat to Cemetery Reef and feed you to the fish." And worse now—that photo Van Cleve showed him of Lexi, Jilly and Darcy was sheer threat. So, until he could figure out how to make Ames leave them all alone, he had to play his game.

"Phew!" Jace said, expelling a rush of air. That horrible night was all too real, like a bad movie spooling back through his brain. Despite the diversion of spending his big salary, he wasn't on this side of evil, and Kilcorse-Ames was that. But how to escape him? How to protect Lexi, to keep Claire safe to care for her?

Should he warn Markwood and come clean about being forced to work for Ames too? Or was Markwood, with that big yacht and Claire for prizes, actually on Kilcorse-Ames's side? He didn't trust Markwood as far as he could throw him.

Sometimes, the way things had gone lately, he felt it would be easier to just bring this jet down into one of those snow-white mountain peaks, especially when he was flying alone like this and wouldn't kill anyone else. He'd get back at K-A that way too, obliterating this expensive jet. Maybe someday if he had that devil himself as a passenger...

He shook his head, trying to throw off that ridiculous, terrible thought. He'd never wanted to kill anyone but the enemy in Iraq. He'd never been suicidal, ever. There had to be a decent way to get out from under the devil's thumb, to win Claire back, to have Lexi in his home again.

He rechecked the altimeter and speedometer screens and thought of Lexi after their "real fast" airboat ride. The little sweetheart had thought he'd named his new Lexus after her.

"You know what?" he'd asked her.

"What?" she said, bouncing along beside him with her hand in his.

"Next time we go out for a special day, we're going to ride on what's called a Jet Ski, a WaveRunner, instead of an airboat. I went on one not long ago, and it was really fun. It goes fast over the water, but you'll have to wear a life preserver."

"To preserve my life? And you better wear one too."

"Yeah, my Lexi-Lexus. I'd better wear one too."

He gazed down at the ground again, at the pointed peaks, rotating slowly under him, far, far below.

Claire didn't mind the bay leaf smoke. It didn't make her cough; it kind of soothed her. She had to concentrate on the questions she'd rehearsed for Ada.

"No, thanks, I'm fine," she lied to Ada when the woman offered her the pipe. "So, I'll just be honest, because I know you will be honest with me." Her voice sounded a bit strange. Maybe because she was breathing the smoke or was just nervous. This woman not only intrigued her, she scared her.

"If I can," Ada said. "Ask then."

"When I was doing some research lately on another case my husband worked on, I saw a photo of you outside the court building in Naples. I'll bet that was unusual for you."

Ada nodded and sucked in another breath of the smoke.

Claire hoped she wasn't babbling. Usually, she was calm in interviews, even with possible hostile suspects. "I don't mean to imply a connection between that case and the one we're preparing for now," she told Ada. "But do you mind if I ask you why you were at that trial?"

Ada put the pipe down on the floor. "Yes, I mind. My people are private in their hearts despite having public alligator wrestling shows and the casinos. But you honor me by asking me and not others, so I will say, it was about the casinos—and about a friend of my gr—my son."

"But how was that trial about the casinos?"

"It is like this. My son—he lives with the tribe deep in the Glades—helped to oversee one of the casinos. There, he—and isn't this a good way to say it?—*fell* for a deceitful woman, a white woman, Sondra McMillan, the murdered woman that trial was for."

Claire realized that Ada was hesitating as she spoke, as if afraid to say too much. And speaking in longer sentences than usual. But with such a unique person, did that mean she was lying? Claire had the feeling Ada always spoke the truth, however she cloaked it, or said nothing at all. She was so hard to read. And Claire's own hardly brilliant forensic psychologist response was, "Oh."

"He did not harm the woman who died. Someone else did, one of the other men she caught in her net of beauty, maybe even the one accused."

"My husband proved Dylan Carnahan innocent."

Ada gave a little snort. "I saw your husband take people's words apart in court. I suppose he could make a tree seem guilty. It is his way to show others have their reasons for a murder. It is why poor Haze should not come to trial. Others will suffer, be pulled in."

Including you? Claire wanted to ask. "But my husband, Haze's defense lawyer, will defend him. That's what he's pledged to do," Claire insisted, feeling she had to rush to Nick's defense.

"That Sondra could have ruined him—my son, Jimmie Cypress, I mean. Too often my people stand accused because they are not understood or trusted."

"But that didn't happen with your son, did it? He was not accused."

"Your husband questioned him before the trial. He could have called him to testify, but did not."

"There, you see. Nick is always after the truth, not just to defend his clients. And he obviously trusted your son."

Ada's stare seemed to bore into Claire's brain. Claire too had not only sat through but testified in a trial where Nick was the opposing lawyer. He'd cross-examined her thoroughly and been tough but fair. Of course, any good lawyer had enemies, but she hoped Ada Cypress was not one of them.

"Ada—I just—thank you for explaining about your son Jimmie. I'm glad there was no problem for him at that trial, that Nick believed in him, didn't question him publicly."

"And, I hope for the same for myself in this coming trial about the fountain water, if Haze is arrested. That your husband will not question me there."

Claire's pulse pounded. "But why would you be called to testify? Just as a neighbor of the accused? As a character witness, as they say?"

"Because I believe in the water. But I don't want to say that in court with all the TV and the paper reporters there. Mark Stirling's attacks were bad enough, about the water, about my people. But a hundred of him?"

Claire startled as the woman spit into the dish of burned bay leaves. So did Ada have something to do with Mark's death? And could—should—Nick use her as a possible suspect, a person of interest, for she surely was?

"I know you believe in the water," Claire repeated the woman's words. "Maggie said you have used it…over time. It seems to have done wonders for you, however old you are."

Again Ada narrowed her eyes at Claire. "You try the water and you go into court and say it. But you are already young and healthy."

Confession time, Claire thought. Build more of a bond with this woman. And she did not want to leave here without knowing if the fountain waters really worked for Ada.

"I'm not that young and I have a serious health problem I have to medicate with pills and some vile stuff I drink at night," Claire told her, fighting to blink back tears that suddenly threatened. "It definitely does not taste like good water."

"I am sorry. We all have our sadnesses, yes?"

Ada rose by simply standing, without getting on her knees or putting a hand to the floor. "The water must be protected at any cost," she went on. "And already Haze has sold his soul when he sells it for profit. Best you go now, for I have said enough for one day."

Claire scrambled to her feet. "I thank you for your honesty and kindness. It is good of Haze and Maggie to let you use the water."

"It is not really theirs and not for those who buy and sell it. It has belonged to the earth and to my people for years."

Claire followed Ada out onto the raised deck. The woman pointed down over the railing away from the canal toward the back of her house. "It runs off there, especially if it rains," Ada said. Claire hurried to stand beside her at the rickety railing draped with drying moss and looked down.

She saw a spot where the grass was greener, where the speckled croton plants were brighter and a firecracker bush taller than anything around. Claire gasped. Even in the midst of lush plants and green grass, it was like a tiny Garden of Eden. Behind those plants, she could just glimpse what seemed to be a series of small stepping stones near a place where the grass looked bent down by water flow.

"Here," Ada said, stooping to a large earthenware glazed pot that sat on the deck, "take some home. Wash in it, drink it, not that diluted, fake stuff they sell from it. Ask Haze for more. Here," she repeated and effortlessly poured some water from the heavy-looking pot into an empty but clean plastic jar that still bore its peanut butter label.

"You ask questions and you listen," Ada said. "I like that. But beware of where you love, for that can bring the ghosts. That is what my gr—I mean, my son Jimmie learned. So I have learned. Go now for you have tired an old woman."

Claire stood her ground. "How old are you really, Ada?"

"Haven't you heard never to ask a woman that? I just feel

old, that is all. Do all you can to protect the water. I will never be questioned again because that would not protect the water. You and your husband must do that."

Holding the peanut butter jar of supposed youth-preserving water, Claire just stared as Ada Cypress cut off her next question, went inside and closed the door.

"Nick, can't you just have this water tested, peanut butter jar or not?" Claire asked. "See, it looks clean, the jar and the water. You said two water experts are flying in." She was not backing down from their argument in the lounge of the *Sylph,* which was not her favorite place right now.

"Look, Claire, Ada can't be much over fifty. So what if Heck can't locate her birth certificate? Not uncommon in the tribe. Quit obsessing about the eternal water part of this. It's marketing for Ames, not reality."

"I'm sure she could have had her son when she was young, but—"

"Didn't Heck tell you? She doesn't have a son, just a daughter, so if she told you different, she's lying, and you're supposed to be good at psyching that out."

"No, her son, Jimmie Cypress, oversees the casino nearest to Miami. The man in the picture with her at the trial."

"I had Heck look into her past even though you were questioning her. That Jimmie Cypress she was with can't be her son. Maybe in tribal talk, a great-grandson is a son. Or a 'son' might be someone she's taken under her wing, I don't know."

"Nick, it's my job to listen carefully." But even as she insisted, her knees went weak and she sank onto the couch. Hadn't Ada stumbled over saying Jimmie was her son? Maybe she'd started to say grandson—or maybe great-grandson—twice.

"Look, Claire. We don't understand all the tribal customs. Maybe Seminole women marry young and she still doesn't look her age, that's all. Even if I argue in court that the water is the real deal—and this is eating at me—I don't believe it. It's killing me not only to have to work for Ames, but to lie for him and in court where I always strive to bring out the truth. But with what you said about Ada hating Mark Stirling for more than one reason, I think we should bring her in to testify."

"I'd feel like a traitor if she was summoned to court. She doesn't want that, above all. I'm not implying she's one of our suspects, though she does want to protect the fountain waters at any cost."

"See there. A motive, not to mention the other one of her being angry about Mark Stirling's attacks on the Seminoles rigging the games—cheating—at their casinos to get back at the whites for taking their land. You just said this so-called 'son' worked at one of them."

"She's afraid of the way you take witnesses apart."

"Didn't work with you in the insurance fraud case, did it, because you were telling the truth when you testified? But, sweetheart, listen," he said, taking her shoulders in a hard grip and turning her toward him on the couch, "I think you're getting too involved with some of the people in this case. Wait—wait—I understand, because so much is at stake here for you, me and Lexi, but you're too protective of Ada and even Colleen Taylor. Both of those women, as well as Fin, have motives we need to probe further and maybe bring out in court."

She pulled away from him. "I have been up close and personal with them, in a way you haven't! I feel like their friend, not their inquisitor."

"Big mistake. I'm just warning you—"

"Nick, we have to stick together, believe in each other on this!"

"We are. We are. It's just that I'm a wreck over this case.

I've always been scared for myself, taking Ames on, but with you and Lexi, it's worse. Damn, I'd like to send you both away where you'd be safe while I take this on alone. I hate doing that bastard's bidding! I hate going against my good instincts by promoting his products in a show trial to help and please him."

"And I hate that we're arguing, that you don't trust the way I'm handling possible witnesses."

"Or possible suspects."

"I'd bet on Fin first, even though you found out he was with clients on his boat when that WaveRunner almost swamped us. He could have hired someone. He obviously knows lots of guys around here."

"Stay away from Fin. And another thing that's eating at me—can we trust Haze? He's on Ames's side because of the money flowing to him like—like springwater. And much as I've defended him in the past, that's a reason I don't trust him, or maybe Maggie, either. I can't believe she's so bitter, even vindictive, over preserving owls, however cute they are. But when Mark Stirling questioned the power of the water, she turned against him for that too. Like Ada, a double motive."

"Mommy," came a high voice from the doorway. "Are you guys fighting over the owls? I told Daddy him and me—"

"He and I," Claire corrected automatically.

"Right. We should go see them after the WaveRunning ride."

Claire turned away from Nick and went to hug Lexi. She picked her up, which was getting difficult now.

"You and Daddy are going on a WaveRunner?"

"Right. He likes them."

Claire met Nick's stern stare. She felt a rush of anger again, that Nick might have been right about Jace being untrustworthy. And she hated to admit it, but she probably *was* getting too subjective over Colleen and Ada. Maybe she should talk to Haze's wife, Maggie, more.

Clutching Lexi to her, she could sense Nick's thoughts again and they scared her: Could Jace be hoping to sabotage their efforts? To get Lexi all to himself? Or something more dire than that?

CHAPTER TWENTY-FIVE

Despite their argument that night, Claire and Nick were still so exhausted from their night in the Glades that they slept in the same bed, barely touching. Back on her meds, Claire's sleep was sound, but the first thing she thought of in the morning was Lexi's overhearing the mention of owls last night.

Claire didn't believe in omens, but they'd heard that owl cry in the Glades, and that reminded her she needed to talk to the all-time owl champion, Maggie. Claire not only wanted to know how she was coping but to carefully learn if she knew much about Colleen and Mark. Nick was right that Claire wanted to help Maggie, Haze and Colleen too.

She hurried out to breakfast to tell Nick what she had planned, but he was already gone. Feeling deflated, she spent some time with Lexi, then left her talking to her chicken-poxed cousin Jilly on the phone with Nita nearby. She wondered how she and Bronco were doing, but didn't ask as she left in a rush for the Hazelton home that guarded their fountain of youth.

Today, she could use at least a swig of that youth water,

she thought, as she headed down the gangway of the yacht. She ached all over and felt older than her thirty-two years.

But there was another legacy of their terrifying night in the Glades: she was now even more afraid than ever. Someone was watching, stalking them. Her skin prickled all over when she was out in the open like this. Of course, they knew that spying was Ames's standard method of operation. But to think, in this retro, strangely charming little place that seemed so quiet and laid-back, someone could be watching, someone who had perhaps nearly drowned them and shot at them. It made her feel naked and exposed.

She quickened her steps, avoiding her usual path through the thick copse of cypress trees. Several delivery trucks were rumbling in to provision Stan's Idle Hour and the other restaurants and bars. Taking a wider path around Ada's home, she stayed on the main road, if you could call it that. Though she would rather have surprised Maggie, she'd phoned to be sure she was home.

"Hey, great to see you again!" Maggie called from the top of the house stairs and motioned for her to come up. When Claire joined her, she said in a rush, "I've been waiting for you. Haze had to get away for a while, pressure and all. The sheriff told him not to go far, and we're scared to death an arrest is coming. He's out fishing with a friend on the canal just along the highway, not far. Come on in. I've got coffee and Danishes."

Though Claire had eaten a decent breakfast to try to stoke her energy for the day, she followed Maggie into the screened Florida room that overlooked the canal and accepted a mug of coffee. Maybe misery did love company, for Maggie looked more edgy than before. Dark circles hung under her blue eyes like half-moons. She wore no makeup, and her white-blond hair looked as if it had been combed by her fingers.

They talked at first about the owls Claire and Nick had

taken Lexi to see. She didn't share about their night ordeal in the Glades.

"So, other than working this case, how are the newlyweds?" Maggie asked. "Haze says you're going to have a reception at the law office."

"Yes, on Monday. We've been so busy that I haven't met most of his colleagues yet."

"Hopefully they're all busy getting ready to help Haze if it comes to that. I'm afraid it will. Claire," she said, leaning forward in her chair, "you two have to turn up other suspects for Mark Stirling's murder to get Haze off, even though Nick is here to defend the youth waters too. You know darn well—and so does the sheriff's office, which is why he's taking his time—that a lot of people hated Mark Stirling."

Claire put her mug down on the coffee table and took a small notebook and pen from her purse. Usually, she liked to seem to only be listening, not recording, but she wanted Maggie to expand on what she'd just said. "Can you list them for me, so we leave no stone unturned?"

"Look, I love Ada Cypress, partly because she minds her own business and believes in the water. But even she hated Stirling's guts for attacking the Seminole casinos as well as our fountain of youth. Then there's Fin Taylor, because Stirling kept harping on the sharks and was going to accuse Fin of illegal takes on them—and Fin is one to fight back, believe me. Just how ambitious was Wes Ringold to get his hands on that newspaper? And, okay, I was upset Mark didn't think the owls were endangered or worth a damn, but I had nothing to do with harming him, though, obviously, I was upset he called our youth water bogus."

Claire actually thought it was a good sign that Maggie had included herself in the possible suspect list, but maybe she'd thought she dare not leave herself out. Before Claire could speak, a motorboat buzzed past on the canal, making so much noise for a moment that she had to repeat her next question. Time to go fishing, that is for whether Maggie knew about a possible affair between Colleen and Mark. But she hesitated to ask.

"Do you think Colleen Taylor was angry over Mark's treatment of Fin? I never asked you if you know her well."

Maggie smacked both palms on her knees. "Of course, I know her well! I love Colleen. After all we're both married to Goodland year-round—ha! But she's the turn the other cheek kind," Maggie insisted. "You know the old saying, 'Don't knock over the beehive, if you want to gather honey'? That's her motto in general, including with Mark Stirling."

"How did that work for her? Was she able to get him to back off from her husband by being friendly with him or what?"

"More or less, I guess," Maggie said, frowning now and almost drawling those words. If Maggie knew anything of a Colleen-Mark affair, she obviously wasn't saying so. She raked her finger through her hair, making some strands stand even more on end. "Look, you should ask her all that. I don't think it really worked with bulldog Stirling, but she didn't give up. She even advertised in that rag. You know, he dared to take the name of that paper from our little owls, then did nothing for them!"

Had Maggie just changed the subject? Or, as claustrophobic a place as Goodland was, didn't she know at least that Colleen might have done more than turn the other cheek to Mark Stirling? Were the two women friends, and Maggie was covering for her? Doubtful, with Haze's future at stake.

Claire jolted when an obviously masculine cry of "Who? Who?" sounded through the screens of this elevated room.

Maggie jolted alert. "Oh. Oh, no. Sorry. Not an owl, for sure. Just one of my owl-watch volunteers. We owl fanatics always imitate their cry, kind of as a joke, even on phone calls, silly to outsiders I'm sure. I need to give him some money to pay for supplies—ropes to keep people away from the burrows, a portable microphone for a large, open area. I'll have to—I have his money. Be right back." She jumped up and hurried out.

Claire took the moment to look closer at the cluster of photos on the corner table and on the one unscreened wall. Close-ups of owls. A wedding photo of the much younger Hazeltons taken on the shore with huge waves rolling in behind. One picture of them with Fin on his fishing boat. Colleen wasn't in it, but maybe she'd taken the picture.

She gasped. One with Clayton Ames! Had Nick ever seen that? It sat behind the larger wedding picture, or she might have seen it herself before. Smiling, the three of them in the photo stood in the underground grotto with the spring behind. It had obviously been taken with a flash camera for the rough walls were etched in shadows and all their eyes glowed red. And scribbled in the lower left-hand corner, *Water, water everywhere and plenty to drink and sell. Let's Aim High!*

Ames had been here in person! Ames knew Goodland. Her hands shaking, Claire picked the frame up and slid the photo out to see if there was a date or anything written on the back of it. Nothing. As she put it back, she had to keep herself from shattering it against the wall.

Glancing out through the screen, she saw a young man not only talking but gesturing to Maggie as she gave him the envelope she'd mentioned. Although his owl cry had been close by, they were at quite a distance from the house, down along the canal. His body language suggested anger; hers, wariness, nervousness. It looked as if she was telling him to leave, get going.

Claire squinted into the morning sun to see better, then shaded her eyes. He was maybe twenty, had a scruffy beard but wore a baseball cap so she couldn't see much of his face.

Cutoffs, T-shirt, sandals despite the cool mid-October wind today. He didn't look like a happy camper.

Finally the young man walked away, stuffing the envelope in a back pocket. He went farther down the canal, then shoved something away from a small, distant dock and mounted it.

Claire realized she had not heard a motorboat a few minutes before when he roared away on a WaveRunner. It was the same color as the one that had almost run them down at the site of Mark's murder.

"Sure it's partly the magic of marketing more than medicine or miracles," Dr. Seth Shaw told Nick in his law office where he was meeting with the water men who would help him prepare for trial, and even—Ames was insisting—be called as expert witnesses to testify at it. "But the water works," Dr. Shaw insisted.

"If so, is it because of its youth-preserving and enhancing properties or merely the belief in it, an aging population's passion to stay young?" Nick challenged. He hated Ames controlling his plans for a defense trial almost as much as he hated the man for controlling his life.

"Look," the other guy, Dr. Tom Anderson, older and calmer, picked up their sell-job. "Haven't you heard that people with religious faith do better when they're ill? If people take a useless pill but believe it will help, they get better—the placebo effect. Of course, there's a mental, even spiritual aspect to this, but that's all for the good too. We're here to explain all that to you now and to return to testify later that 'the water works.'"

"Sounds like a new promo line for the water products."

"Just for the drinks, I hear. That motto's too gung ho for the female cosmetic products."

Talk about marketing pasting over or prettying up the truth, Nick thought. Both of these chemists had no doubt been bought off by Ames to parrot the party line. But he should talk, since he and Claire were under Ames's control too.

He thought about Ada Cypress, though he didn't mention her. Claire didn't want Ada dragged into court to help prove the water worked, but she might be a convincing witness. Nick didn't want to lose his soul in all this, nor Claire's love. It was bad enough he might lose his life.

"So, if Hazelton goes to trial," he said, "you two will leave your jobs to come from California again to testify?"

"Exactly. We're key to all this—and understand you are too," the younger man, who was somehow the main spokesman, said. They were both leaning forward in their chairs. They'd brought a packet of facts and figures about their tests of the water, which lay on the polished wood surface of Nick's desk.

Seth Shaw knocked his fist there. "Let's just say a benevolent and interested party thinks enough of us that he sent his private Learjet for us and would again, so let's go over these facts we've brought you."

Damn! Nick thought. Lexi had told Claire that Daddy had to fly to California to get some men who knew all about water but not the kind you swim in. Heck hadn't been able to research who Jace flew for now, and Claire hadn't yet asked him. But Ames had surely sent Jace Britten, his new pilot, to fly these guys here in that Learjet.

Claire felt really rattled when she left Maggie's house. She had not let on she'd seen the man who had come by WaveRunner. It could mean nothing—or everything. If this was the same man who had threatened them, maybe Maggie was paying him off for that as well as for following them into the Glades and shooting at the car. But what motive could Maggie possibly have to try to scare them off this case that could mean her husband's freedom and his life?

The message from the man on the WaveRunner had been Get Out! Stay Out! But wouldn't Maggie want them to stay close, plan Haze's defense? She'd just insisted she did. Unless she wanted Haze to be found guilty and sent away so the youth water fountain was hers alone. Or unless she herself was somehow guilty of Mark's murder and would let her husband take the fall for that. She couldn't wait to tell Nick so they could sort it out together.

Although she hadn't planned to, Claire decided to stop to see Ada on her way back to the yacht. She saw the dugout canoe was here and the door to her place was ajar again, so she was surely home. As scared as Claire was of the woman at times, she was totally intrigued by her too. She would not stay long.

She went up the wooden stairs, noting for the first time the railing had been worn smooth by time or weather—or the touch of ageless hands. "Ada? Ada, it's Claire!"

As she had last time, she peered through the door left ajar, but no Ada in sight. She stuck her head inside the front room. "Ada, are you here?"

On the worn worktable lay three identical shawls of Spanish moss she must have finished recently. Even from here, they looked beautiful, all in a silvery pale green, nearly the color of the underground cistern waters.

"Ada, I don't mean to bother you," Claire called. "I see you've been working."

Even from here, Claire could also see three notes pinned to the shawls, so someone must be coming to pick them up. Her heart beat hard as she stepped inside. Oh, Maggie's name was on one of the shawls. She touched the texture of it, soft but sturdy, and read the note in large, painstaking printing: *Take care. Ada.*

The middle shawl was labeled Colleen Taylor and the note read: *Stay there. Ada.*

Claire gasped aloud to see her own name on the third shawl with the words *Beware. Ada.*

And behind the shawls lay a full-page letter, this one addressed to Jimmie Cypress and written in smaller printing.

Holding her breath, Claire leaned over to read it.

> I should not have let you meet her in this house. I fear you hurt her but won't tell. I bless the sacred tribal waters but won't be here to tell of that either. Not in their public place with all eyes and ears like pointed swords. Bury me on our land and do not be sad for many of my years were good.

Claire staggered back. These read like farewell notes, or worse.

She scrambled to get her cell phone out of her purse. She had to call Nick. When only his voice mail picked up, she glanced out the door at the back of Maggie and Haze's place. She could get help there.

As she ran toward the Hazelton house, she saw the door to the old tabby building over the cistern was open. Maybe Maggie had gone in for some reason, or Haze had come home. They would help her. They would know what to do, for ageless Ada surely meant to kill herself.

CHAPTER TWENTY-SIX

Claire didn't have a light. It would be pitch-black in the cistern without one. Surely, Maggie or Haze were down there, but what if only Ada was? Did she have a key to the cistern all these years the Hazeltons didn't know about? They had thought she'd bathed or drunk the runoff rainwater from the spring, but what if...

Not wanting to take the time to find a flashlight, Claire rushed into the outbuilding over the waters. Yes, the door down to the water was open too!

At the top of the spiral stairs, she saw wan, wavering light reflected from below. Someone was surely down there with a flashlight or lantern.

Gripping the rusty banister, she called down, "Maggie? Haze? Are you there? I need your help to find Ada!"

No sound but the clank of her feet on the metal steps and the whispered shifting of the waters below. As she descended, silvery patterns danced even brighter on the rough rock. She could imagine Ada coming down here to reflect, even to worship the sacred tribal waters. She pictured her sitting in silence, not responding to Claire's shout, saying farewell to the spring that years of myth had called a fountain.

Claire peered over the waters she'd seen only once before. A bright, electric lantern sat on a rocky ledge by the edge of the spring. But no one was in the small grotto area.

Had she been lured down here, set up to be locked in from above? No one would hear her scream from here, nor would her cell work under all this rock. What if Ada or even Maggie was the murderer and needed to get her out of the way?

Terrified anew, she started to go back up the steps, but glanced down once more.

And saw floating just under the surface, drifting slowly away from being hidden on this side of the rocky rim a body, faceup, buoyed by brightly colored skirts looking like a flower.

Claire screamed, and it echoed. She wanted to flee but what if Ada was still alive? She looked so—so peaceful.

Her pulse pounding, Claire went down to the spring level and knelt to peer closely at Ada. Not moving. Drowned. No doubt a suicide.

But she looked alive, only sleeping. How long would these waters preserve her like this? And if it got out that Ames's Youth water had a dead body floating in it, there would be hell to pay. Maybe Ada had done this here to get back at those who profited off the water.

Claire prayed she'd had no part in driving Ada to this. Wide-eyed, stunned, she stared at the old woman. The memory of her nightmare leaped at her where she herself was the dead woman, faceup, on the floor of the yacht.

Ada looked lost, but somehow found, with a little smile on her face, looking younger than ever.

Claire hated to admit it, even to herself, but she suddenly believed in the power of this water, at least for Ada.

Claire sucked in a sob and fled up the stairs to get help.

★ ★ ★

Time became a blur for Claire, but just over an hour later, the tiny grotto was crowded with people. After they had explained they knew nothing of this and had not unlocked the door, Haze and Maggie had been sent upstairs by the sheriff. The Naples-based Collier County medical examiner and an assistant were still here as well as a police photographer and two medics. Claire had only been allowed to stay to reenact for them exactly how she'd found Ada, and Nick had arrived at breakneck speed to be with her, claiming to be Claire's lawyer as well as Haze's. The flash from the photographs exploded in the rough rock grotto and in Claire's brain.

Ada had finally been removed from the water and lay in a body bag that had not yet been zipped up. A puddle had formed around her from her hair and clothes. In the stark police lights, that water and her wet form looked silvery—unearthly.

"All right, then," Sheriff Scott said, "I think we're about done here. None of the media gets in, and I'll make the only statement when this gets out. You boys need help with getting the body bag up out of here on those twisty stairs, let me know. We're gonna go seal off her house, but according to what Ms. Markwood says is there, it's an open-and-shut case of suicide. Ms. Markwood, Counselor, you two want to come along?" he said, pointing at Nick. "I'll need the photographer too," he said over his shoulder, and gestured for Claire to go first up the stairs.

Nick turned back to the sheriff. "No autopsy needed, I hope. It's obvious what happened, and that would be an indignity to her and her people."

"She sure looks calm and peaceful, doesn't she? Untouched. But it's up to the ME there. I've called her closest relative, and he'll be here soon."

The ME, a woman Claire had met before, spoke up. "I concur no autopsy, unless we find some unusual bruise or a wound on her."

"Man," Sheriff Scott said, "that's all we need here, considering an arrest warrant is already in the offing for your client who owns this site, Counselor, and Ms. Markwood here says she found the door unlocked they supposedly had the only key to open. Far as we can tell, there's no key on the body or lying here. Let's go now."

From four steps up, Claire glanced down at the scene once more, but everything had changed from the way she wanted to remember it. The two bright klieg lights, balanced precariously on the narrow rock ledge, soaked the usually silent, dim area with stark colors.

The ME's assistant was finally zipping up the body bag, so Ada disappeared slowly. Her calm, unlined face and the single strand of beads around her smooth neck reminded Claire of something she'd read about Seminole women. Throughout their lives, they wore many strands of bright beads that signified life events and special times, but they took them off over their later years or gave them away until they were buried with just one string—their life beads, the very first strand given to them as a child. Today Ada had worn that single string of beads.

So many questions, ones more important than that. In Ada's note to Jimmie Cypress—whom Claire now believed must be her grandson or even great-grandson—who had Jimmie been meeting in Ada's house? Even in her dazed state, it seemed clear to Claire: Sondra McMillan. But would the police figure that out and question Jimmie again? And would they question Claire or the other two women for whom Ada had left the shawls and the notes? Again, Claire hoped she had not done or said anything to encourage Ada to take her life.

★ ★ ★

"I know you're distraught," Nick said when they were back on the yacht. "That was tough, finding her like that. I realize she fascinated you."

They were eating an early dinner on the stern deck, but Claire hadn't touched her food. She'd sat with Lexi until the child had gone to sleep and Nita took over. The poor child had evidently come down with chicken pox. Nick had phoned a doctor friend who would come here to check on her tomorrow.

"You can't blame yourself for Ada's death," Nick insisted when she didn't answer.

"I just wish the sheriff had let me have that shawl with my name on it right now. I may not see it again, and it's—it's her legacy to me."

"I'm sure you'll get it back. Sheriff Scott needed the other two to question Maggie and Colleen about the cryptic notes too. But, Claire, her legacy to you is the message to beware, and that's not good. It's like some curse from the grave."

"Not from her. She accepted me. We had a kind of understanding." She blew her nose, though she wasn't crying. "But she was afraid you or the prosecution in Haze's trial would drag her into court."

"Did you ever stop to think that she might have been approached by one of Ames's lackeys? They're thick as thieves around here lately. Maybe they insisted she go into court as exhibit A on the power of the youth waters. Maybe that put her over the edge. She didn't want to be the one to commercialize her people's sacred water even more. Or she had a personal fear of having to go public and become a laughingstock or bizarre example. Maybe we're not to blame at all."

Claire smacked her full iced tea glass on the table so hard the tea sloshed out clear toward Nick. "Maybe, maybe, maybe! If so, Ames not only runs but ruins everything again! Of course he'd want to put her on display! As grieved as I am, as afraid of him as I am, I'd do anything to get back at him!"

"Shh. Even though Heck's been teaching Bronco how to sweep the yacht for listening devices, you never know. But are you game to go with me to a place I know Ames's bugs are ready and waiting for us? To help me assure him we're doing what he wants right down the line, even if we aren't?"

"Where?" she whispered, wiping up her tea from the table with her napkin. "Now?"

"I haven't been back to my house in days, but I'm thinking I should go. And that we should plan a little drama for him to overhear. Also, since my house is on a cul-de-sac, we can lie low there and see if we're followed, as we must have been when we went to the murder scene and rushed out into the Glades. What do you say? We can write the script together in the car on the way into Naples. Hey, you haven't eaten your lunch but I understand. I think I have some PB&J in my refrigerator at home and your choice, madam, of either wine or beer."

Her anger ebbed, and she sighed. "Anything to confuse him, stop him. And your mention of us maybe being followed reminds me of something important I have to tell you about Maggie today. Ada's death put it out of my head."

"Shoot. Well, maybe I shouldn't put it that way," he said, reaching over the table to gently grasp her wrist with his big, warm hand.

"I saw Maggie pay off a young man who came to her place on a WaveRunner today, a man she seemed really nervous around. She walked him far away from the house, I think, so I couldn't see him or overhear what they were saying. She said he came for money for the owl cause, Nick. Nick?" she said when he just stared at her and didn't answer.

Finally, he said, "You know that old saying, 'Absolute power corrupts absolutely.' Well, big money does too. It's as far-out of an idea as Jace riding a WaveRunner and stalking us, but—"

"But what if Maggie has something to do with Mark Stirling's death?" Claire finished his thought. "Or wants us to think someone besides Haze did? Should we confront her?"

"Not yet. It could blow everything up, and I'm pretty sure the sheriff is going to arrest Haze soon. Ames will have a fit if we get Maggie under suspicion too. Since they have no children—I'm just thinking out loud now—who would get control of the Youth water fortune if they were in collusion for Mark's death or were set up for it? I'd better ask Haze about a will, if they have named heirs. Because that could open up another whole number of possible suspects. If someone gets rid of Haze and Maggie—voilà, someone's filthy rich if they have the fountain. I can't believe I haven't thought of that before. I don't know what I'd do without you."

He tugged her around the table, shoved his chair out and pulled her onto his lap.

"Without me, you'd still be the playboy of the Western world," she whispered, putting her arms around his shoulders and leaning her forehead against his. "And you'd have to find another forensic psychologist to hire, hopefully one with benefits, as they say these days about bed partners."

"As bad as this all is, I love you, Claire. And as much as I'd like one of your 'benefits' right now, let's buy ourselves some insurance while we sort this out. Let's assure Ames we're on board. You know, let's not even plan the conversation we want him to overhear in the rental car, just in case he's got that bugged. Let's just sit on the end of the dock and talk it out, then improvise from that at the house."

"All right, Counselor. You know, I'll bet I'm the first wife to ever marry a man without being in his house once—or since."

They stood and hugged. He kissed her hard. Claire felt a little stronger, a little better. Still, it haunted her that poor Ada had felt she must escape. No way were she and Nick going to do anything but stay and fight.

CHAPTER TWENTY-SEVEN

As Nick and Claire drove their rental car into Naples, he kept checking in his rearview mirror to see if they were being followed. Traffic on the Trail was so thick he couldn't tell. And all he needed was to have an accident of his own making right now, so he had to be careful.

In the seat beside him, Claire had gone quiet, but not really calm. Still he felt he'd steadied her a bit. He was used to doing that for himself but he was still getting the feel of her.

And he'd like to have the feel of her again, make love to her. He'd almost taken her to bed right before they'd left the yacht. Why did things keep getting in the way of intimacy? If only they could chuck the burden of this case, go off together, have a real honeymoon.

He shifted his weight in the seat, remembering the soft, scented feel of her against him, under him. He cleared his throat and changed positions yet again. It would be private at his house, but if there were mics to pick up sounds—or worse, cameras—he'd have to control himself, go with the phony program they'd planned. That mirror on the ceiling of the yacht's master bedroom, which he'd hated at first, he really liked now, but he didn't need another viewer, especially not Ames and his lackeys.

"You okay, sweetheart?" he asked, with another quick glance in the rearview mirror. Absolutely no way to know if the male driver almost tailgating him—and on his phone—could be following. He didn't look that young, and Claire had said Maggie's friend was around twenty.

"Just thinking," she said.

"Uh-oh!"

"Very funny," she said and punched his arm. "Just missing Ada. Can you believe that? I really didn't know her well and I miss her. I feel that way about Colleen too—close when I've not spent that much time with her. No more lectures about that, please," she insisted, raising both hands. "I've learned my lesson not to let my feelings control my head in this. You were right about that."

"I'm guilty of that too. I feel really let down with Maggie for either meddling at best, lying at worst—and what that might mean."

Claire nodded and sighed, turning away. But he saw she was only turning her head to check who pulled up next to them at stoplights. At least they were almost at the turnoff.

As for trying to bolster Claire's mood, whenever he'd been depressed over his father's death, his mother's grief or his own troubles in life, planning to get even with Ames always got him going again. Just as in his past, there was no time for Claire—for either of them—to mourn their losses. It only sapped their strength.

But he was deeply disturbed by the possibility of Maggie's treachery. If she'd paid some young punk to nearly hit them in the water at the murder scene, she must have known exactly where that place was. It was as upsetting as his earlier suspicion that Jace might have been the guy on the Wave-

Runner. If Jace turned out to be a liar, it would really take a toll on Claire.

Unfortunately, when Nick had asked Lexi yesterday if her daddy had a gun, she'd said, *No. Just a big rifle he hunts with. Like for bears in the Glades. But it's not loaded in the house so it doesn't hurt anyone. 'Specially me, even if we don't have that house anymore.* If Claire knew he'd been quizzing her child, and about Jace, Nick knew he'd be toast.

But she'd been right to mention earlier the screwed-up way Ames had forced them to marry. He felt bad that she had never been inside his home. Even now, he was taking her there to see it for the wrong reason. He didn't really know her family; she would only meet his law team two days from now. And strangest of all in their version of a shotgun marriage, Nick had been forced by Ames to become an instant father to little Lexi despite the fact her own father hovered—and Nick now suspected him even more of working for the enemy since he'd obviously flown those water experts in. He'd find out soon, because he'd made a secret, important phone call to have someone settle things with Jace once and for all. He hated to be back to keeping things from Claire, but on this, he just couldn't share.

He parked the car in his driveway on 21st Avenue South. The front yard grass had a big yellow patch where apparently one of the automatic lawn sprinklers wasn't working. The beige stucco ranch house had its backyard on the waterway called the Egret Channel where he still kept his small motorboat. One glance through the front picture window and the Florida room showed it was still in its place, tied along the breakwall and covered with a well-worn tarp.

"Aqualane Shores is a beautiful area," Claire observed, looking around, up and down the dead-end street from the front porch. At least they'd lost the tailgater he'd been watching, and no car seemed to be following or passing by. "Not one of the newest areas, but classic," she went on. "I read it was a mangrove swamp years ago. Look at all these new mansions here and there, dwarfing some of the original places!"

"Yeah. Like mine—now ours. The huge, Spanish-themed ones have really been sprouting amid the late 1960s and 1970s ranch house structures. Buy a big lot, tear down the old place and build a new, bigger, better one. But even a little older house like this, with its small pool and lot, is worth big bucks because of location, location and location."

"I can imagine," she said, taking his arm.

"Once I could afford this, it was our downsize place from where we lived when Dad was alive. It got my mother out of the little apartment she'd been stuck in after he died. The insurance company reneged on his life insurance since the cause of death was ruled a suicide. More than once I've taken cases to help a family like ours fight the big insurance boys over suicide that really wasn't—or, at least, was a questionable ruling."

"Which means you probably have enemies beyond Ames High, Inc. So this place became your bachelor pad after she died?"

"When I moved back in here from my little apartment, I didn't do a lot of entertaining. After law school, I became a workaholic, building the firm, setting up South Shores on the side. I tried to give my best to each client and my growing staff. I only wish my father could know how it all worked out. Not so much that he'd be proud of me, but so he'd know I'm not giving up on vindicating him and, yeah—getting justice, even revenge against Ames."

Taking her hand in his, he said, "Before we go in, let's go around the back where I can see the street. If we're standing in front like this, someone following might stay way back. If it's someone local, they'd maybe know this is a dead end and wouldn't turn in."

They went to a back corner of the house and stood behind a spray of dwarf palms and watched the street. Only a single car drove by, one Nick recognized as belonging to a neighbor. "A retired couple from New York City," he told Claire. "Let's go in the back way and start the little soap opera we have planned for our audience."

But as he fished out his keys, Claire gripped his arm. "There," she whispered, tugging him back farther into the foliage. "That young man walking the dog on the sidewalk and looking at the house as he goes by. I think that's the guy Maggie paid off. He looked like a beach bum before but a lot better now. Yes, I'm sure that's him. Should we try to talk to him, pretend we don't know who he is?"

"If he was armed with a WaveRunner and a gun before, not yet. And that looks like a pit bull to me. We can find him later since all we have to do is go somewhere off the beaten path and he seems to appear. We'll confront Maggie first, so he doesn't tip her off. Today, it's not only poor Ada, but poor Haze."

Claire's phone went off, and she tried to muffle it, though the man had walked past the house. She fished her phone out of her purse and stared at the caller ID. Oh, Wes Ringold.

"It's the new *The Burrowing Owl* editor," she whispered. She followed Nick as he hurried around the other side of the house to keep an eye on the man. "I'd better take it. Maybe he turned something up. Hello, Wes," she said, speaking quietly. "Claire, here."

"Claire, glad I got you. I'm sure you'd like to make a statement about finding Ada Cypress drowned, set the record straight before everyone else jumps on it about whether it was a suicide or not. So are you on the yacht in Goodland? I can come right over."

"Sorry, Wes, but Sheriff Scott made it very clear that he's the only point person right now for the tragedy."

He blew out a breath. She could tell he was frustrated and annoyed. "Pretty weird," he said. "So she was found on the same property where my sources tell me Hazelton is going to see an indictment for murder real soon."

"The place was right out her back door, and she valued the—" She stopped herself just in time.

"So, can you give me anything else?" he went on as she watched Nick motion that the man with the dog was now walking back the other way. "This will appear in the same issue your interview will, so it will make a great piece," Wes coaxed, his tone soothing now. "I can tell you're still going to stand up for Haze Hazelton. I'd give you and your husband a good platform to do that."

"Thanks, Wes, but not now. Sorry."

"Now, listen to me, bec—"

She punched off as Nick walked over to her, then unlocked the back door. "Of course he wanted a statement," she said. "I upset him. Maybe he's not really the mild-mannered Clark Kent he pretends to be."

"He's not Superman either and bears watching. I've heard TV reporters say about murder cases, 'If it bleeds, it leads.' Really. No doubt, Wes thinks the same way. He's looking for sensational headlines to sell papers, just like Stirling was." He shook his head. "He's on the list, but not at the top. I think our shadow's gone too. Maybe he decided twice by this place is enough, but we'll keep an eye out for him. Let's go in. And once we're inside, it's showtime. You ready?"

She felt she wasn't really ready for anything, but she gave him a quick hug and whispered, "Curtain up."

As Jace jogged along the hard-packed sand of the beach near Doctor's Pass, he tried to keep an ear tuned to the phone in his bathing suit pocket. The California experts were still here in Naples, he assumed, because he hadn't been contacted to fly them back. The watch-the-sunset crowd wasn't too big this early evening. Meanwhile, he was staying sober and more watchful too, especially for Thom Van Cleve. Yet he felt he was living the life of a celibate monk, and that bothered him, especially when he kept thinking of the newlywed Markwoods.

But, evidently he wasn't being watchful enough. Until they were quite close up, he hadn't noticed that the guy running toward him was the tall, blond FBI agent who had boarded the plane in the hangar and given him the song and dance routine about being a reporter before he admitted who he was—if that was the truth. It had been in the back of Jace's mind ever since that he might be another spy working for Nick Markwood's "Uncle Clay" instead of for "Uncle Sam."

Before the guy got to him, Jace slowed his pace, then went up a few steps and sat where the dry sand met the wave-washed shore. He whipped off his aviator-style sunglasses. Yeah, the man also made a turn and flopped down beside him as if they were long-lost running buddies.

"I guess you remember me," he said. He was out of breath too.

"Rod Patterson, but I doubt that's your real name. Here's what you need to remember. I'm sick and tired of being watched."

"Obviously by others too, since I haven't been following you, physically, that is. When you took that one-day flight, I did lose contact though."

Jace was not only angry now but panicked. This must be another of Kilcorse-Ames's spies. "What do you mean, you haven't followed me physically?" he demanded.

"I can track you through this," he said, pulling his cell phone from the pocket of his hoodie sweatshirt. "That is, through yours. See that plane circling up there?" he asked, pointing with his phone.

Jace squinted up at it. "Yeah, a Cessna, largest one they make."

"It has a logo on it for Palm Tree Research, but that's a fake company. Does that sound at all familiar—someone flying for a fake company? It's really a flying electronic tracking device. It can locate criminals of all kinds, kidnappers, killers—even pilots working for such, through their cell phones."

Jace's head snapped around. He'd been agonizing over the fact Van Cleve had flashed a picture of Lexi and her cousin at him on his cell phone, especially since Lexi had been abducted before.

"So," Patterson went on, "are you listening?"

"You gonna make me an offer I can't refuse?"

"One you shouldn't refuse. Our government does very necessary surveillance of criminal activity. All kinds, but we'll leave it at that for now. In this age of terrorism, we have a fleet of planes—not jets—that fly over our country and even other territories when needed, Mexico, Cuba. Through people's cell phones, we can pinpoint the location of—shall we say—problems, which have happened or are about to happen."

"So how do I come in? My background is jets."

"Which makes flying in and overseeing this large operation we call 'Stingray' a cinch for you. Consider this a preliminary career-change interview. Yeah, I know you have a job, but this one has lifesaving perks," he said, emphasizing those last two words.

Jace wondered whose life exactly. His? Lexi's?

"And this program," Patterson went on, "may begin using jets in the future. However, besides your excellent dossier and the fact this would provide you and your daughter with Witness Protection Program assurance, we would need something else from you."

"Wait a sec. You're going way too fast for me."

"I doubt it. Namely, we would need help in locating and nailing the mastermind who has already caused you and your daughter trouble. If I'm reading you right—or my informant is—you'll be willing to help us to protect your daughter."

Jace swore under his breath. "But Witness Protection? Isn't that run by the Justice Department to hide criminals until they can testify?"

"Not only criminals. You and your daughter no doubt could be invaluable noncriminal witnesses. WITSEC, as they call it, yes, is run by the Justice Department, as is the FBI, so I could liaise."

"Liaise exactly what? And how do I know you're not working for the man you're calling the mastermind, and just double-checking on my loyalty to him? I shouldn't even be talking to you, especially out in the open like this."

"Worried about Van Cleve? Or anyone else? Don't, at least right now. I—and that plane overhead—know where they are, and it's not near here. But your mentioning your loyalty to the mastermind makes me realize you *are* flying for him, which could be construed as a criminal act in and of itself. But how do you know this is not a double cross? Because Nick Markwood thinks you and your daughter—as well as his wife—could benefit from the Witness Protection Program. That is, until you and Markwood—with our help—manage to find, arrest and testify against the mastermind. Then, you'd have this important government career waiting for you."

His mind racing, Jace frowned down at his feet. A colony of tiny coquina shells were just upending and reburying themselves to fight the slosh of the next incoming wave.

"I—I need to think about it, of course."

"Not for long. Talk to no one but Markwood. Here's his cell number," he added, handing him a piece of paper, "so you don't have to go through Claire to talk to him, meet with him. I'll be in touch. And, Jace, don't try to change or toss your phone. The antenna under the fuselage of that plane and the camera mounted just above its belly would have your new phone ID fast. By the way, this isn't a secret system, and all the privacy protection fanatics and a lot of media are exposing and fighting it. But our government needs to protect an expensive, essential endeavor. You ever see that Jack Nicholson movie, *A Few Good Men*, Jace?"

"Yeah, I remember it."

"There's a climatic line where he yells at the courtroom, 'You can't handle the truth!' He was talking about everything—tricks, underhanded stuff, expenses too—that our government has to accept to keep us all safe. The suitcase-sized tracking systems in each plane are worth about $400,000 apiece, so that's why we need good pilots—and in your case, the man to not only fly these south shores, but to oversee things—you know, like that old US Marines recruiting motto 'We're Looking for a Few Good Men.' I know you were a great navy pilot, Jace, and your country needs you on this new, important endeavor. Later, then. Don't call me, I'll call you, but talk to Markwood first. Soon."

Patterson pocketed his phone, got up and, without another word or look, jogged back the way he'd come. Jace looked up at the plane still circling with the sinking sun behind it. For sure, not an aircraft the local Realtors used to show or photograph luxury beach property. Not one of the planes that trailed the advertising banners. Imagine that. A spy plane of sorts right here.

And Markwood was working with that guy. Nick had more or less recommended him for this new job. But Jace knew he'd be dead meat if he just cut out on Kilcorse-Ames, so that was why the idea of WITSEC was not a bad one. For him, for Lexi, maybe Claire too. That meant Markwood did love them, care for them, want to protect them. Jace liked him for that, at least.

Still, could he trust that he was not being set up again, by either Patterson or K-A? He had to talk to Markwood about it.

And, without Claire there or Lexi anywhere around, that's exactly what he was going to do.

CHAPTER TWENTY-EIGHT

"So, I'm hoping," Nick launched into his prepared lines in the living room after he gave Claire a tour, "as soon as we win this case for Haze—and for Ames—we can move back in here. Though the yacht's a great plan B, I can't ask Dylan to loan it to us forever. The guy's got to sell it, especially after what happened there. No wonder he's still estranged from his wife."

Claire recalled that Nick didn't want them to mention here that Dylan had accepted their invitation to dinner Sunday evening. She was really nervous about their winging this despite the fact they both knew the main points they wanted to make. Although she could shoot the breeze with anyone, she half hoped this place wasn't bugged now. Lately, she felt she was losing her poise and her patience. What if this sounded too planned or fake? And even the idea of cameras hidden here gave her the creeps. If they did get through this mess, she'd talk to Nick about buying a house somewhere else, though he did seem attached to this one.

Trying to speak in a normal voice and remembering to move around, so it didn't sound staged, Claire played her part. "It's in the wind that Haze is going to be arrested soon. At least we have enough other possible suspects that you can muddy the waters in court—sorry to put it that way—to show someone besides Haze murdered Mark Stirling. But you know," she went on, getting to a point Nick had insisted on, "it's going to look really strange for you to call an expert forensic psychologist to testify if it comes out she not only works for you but is your wife."

"Good point, but I'm hoping it will be such an open-and-shut case with all the evidence I'll have that I won't have to call you to the stand. Like you said, Stirling and his rabble-rousing rag had so many enemies, that—if it wasn't suicide—it should not be pinned on Haze just because they had an argument in a restaurant bar. Especially a place with such a crazy reputation."

"I think things will work out well if—when—Haze gets his day in court," she said.

"And the thrust of the defense will be that he had such strong faith in the power of the water that he was satisfied with only telling Stirling off. Since she died, we can't call Ada Cypress to the stand anymore. I can claim that Haze wasn't worried that a small, local paper could really damage the water's reputation. Look at all the good that Fountain of Youth is doing, both for those who drink the water and those who use the cosmetics. No way Haze needed to kill Stirling, because he knew, even if the waters were tested, their benefits could be proved."

"So that's where the testimonies of those so-called water experts will come in?"

"Right. I gave them a hard time in my office only so I knew they'd hold up under the prosecution's cross-examination. Can't give away all my secrets, even to you, sweetheart."

Claire wasn't sure whether she would burst out laughing or crying at the mention of keeping secrets. That's exactly what they were doing here to be certain Ames stayed away, content and misled. At least, thank heavens, she and Nick weren't keeping secrets from each other anymore.

That night, in their bed, though with all the lights off so it was just them without the wild woman and man in the mirror above them, they made frenzied love to each other. Although Claire was so aware of her body, and his, it was an almost out-of-body experience, since her mind and heart seemed so involved too. They were two people but somehow one, not only when they were locked together, but when they just held tight afterward, awed by the power of it all.

They slept, then woke. She had to take her second dose of meds soon. But his hands were on her again, caressing, moving. "Mmm," she murmured and stretched. "I hope it's not morning yet."

He nuzzled her throat and trailed kisses lower. "I'll be a wreck with all I have to do tomorrow—a happy, happy wreck. We'll both nod off during dinner with Dylan, also at the reception at the firm the next day too."

"Mmm, but that's Monday and today's Sunday."

"No rest for the wicked," he said and cupped her breast with his free hand.

"Yes, you are wicked. But really, do you have to go somewhere today? I'm going to spend the morning with Lexi, poor darling, though at least she'll have one childhood disease behind her."

"How about I read her a book for once, instead of you? And aren't you going with me to talk to Maggie?"

"Right. I guess something's happened to me this night that has erased all rational thought. Yes, I dread it, but I'm going too. Darn reality."

"I texted Heck to get a copy of Haze's and Maggie's Last Will and Testaments so I don't have to ask them for those directly. I don't want them to think I want it because Haze will be found guilty and sent away."

"Or put on death row," she said. "If only he had a more solid alibi than Maggie's say-so for that day Mark died. Nick, I can't think, can't talk when you do that."

"Then just don't think or talk right now," he added and turned her more to face him. "Or at least think and talk about how much you love me."

"I do. And trust you too."

She felt him draw back a bit at that. "Nick?" she said.

"We've been through a lot and aren't done yet, that's all," he said, rather gruffly. "Not done yet here either, my love."

Instead of Nick reading to Lexi on Sunday morning, the three of them watched the old Disney animated *Alice in Wonderland.* They were all in the child's bed, though the two adults were dressed, and Lexi, between them, was the only one under the covers. Claire thought it was so sweet that Lexi had tilted her head against Nick's shoulder instead of her own for once as they watched. Surely, Nick was bored to death, but, even if he was thinking and planning, he kept his eyes open. She knew something was bothering him, but why not? Everything was on the line for them, which made moments like this seem so precious.

Afterward, Lexi, pox marks and all, told them, "I don't know why Alice had to follow that rabbit in the first place. But Daddy said dogs that race on tracks in Florida follow some kind of rabbit. At least the dogs think that's what it is. He said someday we will adopt one of those racing dogs, 'cause people aren't nice to them after they can't race anymore."

Nick's eyes met Claire's over the child's tousled head.

Claire spoke first. "That sounds like a nice thing to do. But if Daddy gets one of those greyhound dogs, you would have to visit him to see it."

"Oh, right. You know the scariest part of that Alice movie?"

Nick said, "I'll bet I know, but tell us."

"When that bad queen said, 'Off with her head!' I know it's just pretend, but that is not right, is it, Nick?"

"Nope. Not good at all, but you know it's all pretend."

"Right. So did you ever be a lawyer to help someone when a bad person wanted to cut off their head?"

"Well, not exactly that. But I do try to help people if a bad person has hurt them, or if people believe someone already hurt a person, but they really didn't. See, the Queen of Hearts thought Alice was bad, but she really wasn't."

"Even if she kept her head, Alice could have used you," Lexi declared. "And I hope you can help that old school friend of yours and Mommy does too, right?"

"Right!" Claire said. "Nick, have you ever heard or given a better explanation of what you do for a living?"

"Never so clearly or succinctly."

"Well, what does a sink have to do with it?" Lexi asked.

"I think I just fell down a rabbit hole," Nick said. He hugged his stepdaughter and got up. "I'll leave you two for a while. I'm going to—ah, clear my head and take a little walk, Claire. Be back soon."

"I wish, like in *Alice,* this case was all just a bad dream," Claire called after him.

"Love you both, and that's real," he said and closed the door behind him.

Actually, Nick thought as he glanced at his watch and hurried off the yacht and down the dock, he'd almost rather fall down a rabbit hole than go with Claire to face Maggie in—he glanced at his watch again—an hour. He just had to clear his head. It was not only having to accuse Maggie of deception and maybe worse that was riling him, but dealing with his own deception. He and Claire had vowed to come clean with everything, but he just couldn't tell her about his latest plan yet. For Jace. For her and Lexi. But it might be the only way to keep her and the child safe.

He walked a ways along the concrete breakwater, then sat down on it, dangling his legs toward the water. He could see the *Sylph* from here. Bronco was on deck, and Nita came out to stand beside him. They didn't even touch, so he hoped he hadn't put the fear of God into them about a relationship. But in broad daylight, when they were both technically working, good for them. He remembered how hard it had been to keep his hands off Claire when they first worked together. Now here they were legal and together, and he was thinking of giving all that up. At least for a while until he survived Ames and stopped him for good.

He jumped when his cell rang. He dug it out of his back jeans pocket. Heck was calling. Good. He hoped he had some info he needed.

"Hey, *amigo*," he answered the phone.

"Got what you need, Boss. Haze didn't blink an eye that you'd asked about their wills, dug them right out for me. They're pretty recent."

"You have them?"

"No, but I read them and took notes. Here's what you want to know. You sitting down?"

"Just tell me."

"Of course, if he dies, most of it goes to her. They both or she passes, some of it goes to Mrs. Hazelton's Burrowing Owl Protection Fund. Ah, 20 percent, if I recall, but that would be a lot of money. No surprise there."

"Go on," Nick prompted, thinking of the young man she'd already given some money to, a guy she'd told Claire was working with owl protection. He sure hoped Maggie hadn't been cheating on Haze the way it looked like Colleen Taylor had on Fin. But he was really starting to question Maggie's part in all this.

"Don't mean to make a joke of this, but that's going to be a bunch of rich owls," Heck said. "Okay, so another 20 percent goes into a trust fund for Maggie's great-niece and great-nephew, but they and their parents can't touch the money 'cept for college. The kids are only ages two and four right now. So that means their parents, her niece and nephew, won't inherit directly, so they wouldn't have a motive to make Haze and Maggie look guilty. Besides they live in Indiana, so they don't know diddly 'bout people here to kill anybody."

"Tell me the bottom line, Heck. I can tell there's a bottom line."

"*Sí*, always. The control of their property, including the water, goes to someone you might know."

Nick almost shouted, "Ames inherits the youth fountain if Haze and Maggie die?"

"Not directly and not only if they die, but if they are incapacitated or unable to protect it. Small print, but pretty big news, right?"

"Then I'll bet Ames really wants me to lose this case! Did he use his real name or Paul Kilcorse? Or the corporation's name?"

"No, the property goes to someone works for Ames. Someone you know and just told me about, a guy from California named Dr. Seth Shaw who's a water expert and—"

"And is on Ames's payroll, as is half of this country at least, damn him!"

Nick covered his eyes with his free hand and hunched over as if he was going to be sick. He clenched his teeth.

"You there, Boss?"

"Unfortunately, though I'd rather be somewhere else."

"*Sí*, a big spider's web, huh? But at least we know who's the spider."

CHAPTER TWENTY-NINE

About an hour later, Claire and Nick headed out to talk to Maggie. Nick had tried to calm down about the new link to Ames in Haze's and Maggie's wills. He didn't want to upset Claire more than she already was. He would use this new info for ammunition when he told her of his plan, because she wasn't going to like it, and he'd need everything he had to convince her.

They met Maggie on a stretch of mangrove beach near the entrance to the island. She'd agreed to the site readily as Nick thought she would. She'd been telling Claire she was really worried about Haze's state of mind and probably thought they were going to talk about that without a chance for him to overhear. So at first, Nick did talk about that.

"He's not so depressed he might be a flight risk or worse?" he asked Maggie as the three of them sat on a tree trunk turned to driftwood. The high tide waves washed nearly at their feet.

"Suicidal, you mean?" she asked. "No, because he has faith in you. And in the youth water and our business associate's strength."

Claire said, "By the way, I saw a photo of Clayton Ames here on Goodland with you two. You hadn't mentioned that."

"It's no secret we're working with him," Maggie said, with a shrug. She sounded so suddenly defensive that Nick frowned at Claire to go slower. "The waters are so important and unique that he flew in to see the spring cistern himself last year, that's all."

Well, what the heck, Nick thought. He'd told Claire she should bring up the young mystery man with the WaveRunner, not Clayton Ames. But Claire had good sense about when to back off and when to pursue. It was what he'd hired her for.

"Actually," Claire was saying, "while I was looking at that photo of the three of you, I glanced out the Florida room window and saw you in the distance with your Save Our Owls volunteer, the one who left on the WaveRunner."

Maggie's head snapped around toward Claire and her fists tightened. "Meaning what? I told you exactly what I was paying him for."

"Maggie," Nick said, leaning forward with his elbows on his knees, "Claire and I are really paranoid about WaveRunners, ones that silver color especially. We didn't want to alarm you and Haze, but when we were out looking at the murder site, a young guy on a personal watercraft just like that one nearly ran us over. He threw a life ring at us that said we should get out and stay out. In other words, someone doesn't want us digging into who might have killed Stirling if it wasn't Haze. At least that's how we read the message."

"Oh, that's terrible. And—and you think my friend was that man?"

"It would help," Nick went on, "if you could give us his name, address and phone number. You see, we figure the WaveRunner rider is the same man who shot at us out in the Glades."

"Whoa!" she said, jumping up and facing them with her

back to the water. "You're going too fast for me. What exactly are—I mean, you think he's trying to make you believe it was someone else who killed Mark? You don't think Haze hired him? Or the man on the WaveRunner was Haze?"

Claire said, "That not what we're saying. The man's build wasn't right for Haze, even though he hid his face with a hoodie and the water spray was big between us. Since you were paying such a man—and acted really nervous about it the day I was with you—we're wondering if *you* were paying your friend to make us think the murderer was someone else besides Haze. Or do you know for sure it wasn't Haze because it was someone else?"

Maggie gasped for air, speechless, so Nick jumped in. "Let's face it, you had a motive or two for getting rid of Mark Stirling too."

"You think I hired someone to scare you off? And—I can see it on your faces—because I'm the one who got rid of Mark Stirling? That's absurd!"

"Great," Nick said, his voice absolutely calm. "So let us have the name and address of your friend, the WaveRunner rider. We'll check it out and that's that, before the sheriff or county prosecutor gets a clue and comes after you too. Then we won't have to worry about it. All three of us need to keep working together to support Haze—and the miraculous water."

He'd tried to keep the sarcasm from his voice. But he was angry too, at Ames, at this entire spider's web as Heck had put it. All he wanted was to protect Claire and Lexi, build the three of them into a family and now, at best, his client's wife was taking things into her own hands. All he needed was to have to defend her, or both of them, in court while praising the youth water.

To his surprise, when he thought Maggie would remain defiant, she burst into tears and covered her face with both hands just as the incoming tide sloshed around her ankles.

Claire jumped up and brought her back to sit between them. She had her arm around Maggie's waist, and Nick put his hand on her shoulder as Maggie bent over her knees and sobbed.

Finally, she quieted enough to talk, wiping her nose and face with her shirttail, until Claire handed her a tissue from her backpack. "It isn't what you think," she gasped out. "I was only trying to help Haze."

"Maggie!" Nick shouted. "How damn noble, but you could have gotten us killed! And screwed up everything! What if your errand boy testifies that you hired him to nearly drown us, shoot at us! You could go to jail for attempted murder and make Haze look not innocent but damn guilty. What a dangerous way to supposedly protect him—and us!"

"I told my friend to be careful, and he obviously was," she gasped out, exploding into sobs again and talking through them. "I *was* thinking of...of helping Haze—and that that would...would help your case too."

Nick saw Claire fight back tears and anger. It wasn't going to help to shout at each other. It was only going to help to get to the bottom of this, keep Haze out of court, keep Ames away for good and forever.

"Tell us your thinking," Claire encouraged her. Nick was grateful again for her presence because he still wanted to shake more out of the distraught woman. "Does Haze know you hired this guy?"

"No. But I—I did hire him. But just so you'd keep looking at others, because, I swear, Haze did not kill that man, and I thought it might help you take the blame off him. He doesn't have an alibi beyond the fact I knew he was at the house the day Mark died. B-but I was just hoping if you told the sheriff about the things happening to you, he would think someone else was involved then. But you didn't even report it to the sheriff, did you?"

"No," Nick said. "We wanted to find who was behind it

first, not make it public record or have the sheriff think we were trying to divert him. Nor did we need it in *The Burrowing Owl*."

"Or, I'll bet," Maggie said as she blew her nose again, "have Mr. Ames find out you weren't handling things, weren't full steam ahead on just defending Haze and promoting the water."

Nick's gaze slammed into Claire's. So Maggie, no doubt Haze too, knew to fear Ames, even though they seemed to be on his side.

"Please don't tell the sheriff," Maggie pleaded. "And do we have to tell Haze?" She sat up straight at last, but her face was still ravaged by tears. "He'll be furious with me. He'll say I should never have tried to help that way."

Still trying to rein in his temper, Nick told her, "Then I agree with Haze. We'll let you explain it to him right away—and the right way, or I'll tell him myself. But tell us something else."

"Yes. Anything to help—really."

"The Dr. Seth Shaw who's in your and Haze's wills as an heir to protect the property and the cistern if anything happens to you two—how did you find him?"

Looking hopeless and scared, she shook her head. "He found us. Part of the lucrative deal for the youth water. Ames High, Inc., through a man named Thom Van Cleve, said that was part of the deal. And it was such a good deal—still is."

"So you didn't realize that made you two—well, sitting ducks, to be eliminated?" Nick asked.

"As long as we were on their side, we figured we were safe. It wasn't just the money," she insisted. "Haze's family has believed in that water for generations, and we didn't want to keep it just for ourselves. It belongs to all mankind, though I'm sorry to say Ada didn't agree," she said as she started to cry again. "I swear to God, I'm telling you the truth. Go ahead and talk to Jesse Winslow, the 'WaveRunner guy,' if you want, but—"

"Maggie," Nick said, "the WaveRunner scare was bad enough, but he's been following us when we leave Goodland, as you probably know. And, I repeat, he could have killed us, shooting at us in the Glades."

"Honestly, I just told him to follow you, especially if you drove out of town, to only shoot around the car, not *at* you, and then to get away... Just wanted you to be sure someone was after you."

Nick and Claire exchanged another hard glance behind Maggie's head. Was she telling the truth now or not?

"Let's the three of us go talk to Haze," Nick said, standing and pulling Maggie to her feet. "Now, before something else hits."

As they walked out past the clawlike mangrove roots that reached into their path, Claire steadied Maggie with her hand on the woman's arm. However composed Nick was acting, he still felt frustrated and furious. This confession, which he didn't need later on the stand, was bad enough. But if his plan using Jace worked out, he didn't know how he was going to get along without Claire.

"Oh, no!" Maggie cried when the three of them approached her house and saw the sheriff's car was parked outside it. "Terrible timing, if this is what I think it is! Oh, no."

"Keep calm," Nick said, "and let me do the talking. If he's arrested, I'll go with him. We've got a bail bond plan set to go, and he won't be gone long."

"It's like Ada left us with a curse!" Maggie insisted.

Claire was practically holding her up as Nick stretched his strides to get to the house ahead of them. He called back over his shoulder, "Both of you, hold it together for Haze and appearances' sake. Claire, get those tears and mascara off her face."

He went up the steps two at a time, just in time to hear

the sheriff's deputy, while Sheriff Scott stood there too, read Haze his Miranda rights.

"Good timing, Counselor," the sheriff said. "Heard Mrs. Hazelton went for a walk with you two. Glad you're back. It took us a while to investigate other people of interest for the murder of Mark Stirling, but timing, motive and proximity points to your client as our probable suspect. Can't see waiting any longer."

"I'll drive my car, but I'll go in with him for the booking."

"And spring him right away, I'm sure. You ever watch that old TV show *The Apprentice*, Attorney Markwood? The theme song was just three words repeated, *'Money, money, money!'* I'd bet my retirement pension on this trial, when we have it, will be real well-oiled with the same."

"You sound like you have your mind made up about guilt and innocence already before a jury of this man's peers is even selected. I'll make a note of that," Nick countered as Claire and Maggie came in.

Maggie rushed to hug her husband. "It will be all right, Haze," she choked out. "Everything will be all right."

Nick's gaze slammed into Claire's. She pressed her lips together and nodded as if to encourage him. Right then and there, he prayed that, sooner or later, everything would be all right between them too, because there was a big storm coming.

Nick had Haze out on bond in two hours, though he had to make a Sunday afternoon call to a bail bondsman he'd worked with before, not that the Hazeltons didn't have the money for it, but the banks were closed today. He drove Haze back to Goodland and into Maggie's waiting arms. Neither of them said a word about her extracurricular hiring of the WaveRunner rider. They were all so shaken that later would be soon enough for that.

Nick sat in his car in the marina parking lot, just thinking.

He guessed he believed Maggie about sending Jesse Winslow after him and Claire only to help Haze. But sometimes he wasn't sure what he believed anymore. He was going to call the private detective the law firm sometimes used to locate and tail Winslow, first thing Monday. The guy could deny everything but not if he was caught in the act of following him or Claire.

You might know, Dylan Carnahan was coming to the yacht for dinner this evening when Nick didn't want to talk to anyone but Claire and Lexi—and Jace. All he needed right now was the "ghost of cases past." He knew Claire was intrigued and annoyed by the fact that he'd gotten Dylan off but never proved who murdered a woman in the salon of the *Sylph*. She'd spent time she didn't have looking into Sondra McMillan's death when, right now, Mark Stirling's was the only one that mattered.

His cell sounded. He expected word of Haze's arrest had reached his law team or Heck, but the caller ID said Jason Britten.

Nick knew he should hustle back to the yacht, but he'd have to take care of this now, and if he didn't, he wouldn't have to explain—to lie—to Claire about where he was going. She'd assume he was still in town at the sheriff's, and she could surely entertain Dylan until he got there. But, if this desperate plan of his came to fruition, would she ever forgive him, ever understand and believe how much she and Lexi mattered to him?

He answered Jace's call. They made plans to meet now at the Snook Inn on Marco. It was a stilted conversation, but Nick was thinking—maybe Jace was too—that surely, in a public place, no one would lose his temper. He put his phone on voice mail only and, watching in his rearview mirror, drove away from quiet little Goodland toward busy, glitzy Marco Island.

CHAPTER THIRTY

Nick saw Jace get out of his car in the parking lot of the waterside Snook Inn at the same time he arrived, but he waited for him at the entrance to the popular restaurant. Others were starting to arrive, and none of what he had to say should be in earshot of anyone else.

"Jace."

"Nick."

They shook hands. Despite the fact there was an outdoor bar and tables, Nick said, "You mind if we sit outside on a bench along the water for a few minutes? The tables are pretty close in there."

"Fine. Lead the way."

They sat on the hardwood bench just as three dolphins swam past in the wide Marco River, heading out toward the Gulf. Lexi had said seeing dolphins was good luck, but Nick didn't share that with Jace. It would sound like rubbing it in, and he needed this to go well.

"Thanks for meeting me. I—Claire and Lexi too—need your help."

"Anything for them. How is Lexi's chicken pox?"

"She got upset when she looked in the mirror, but since her cousin has them too—"

"Jilly."

"Yeah, Jilly. She's okay with it. Look, Jace, I know how much they, especially Lexi, still mean to you."

"That's right. Absence makes the heart grow fonder."

"That's what I'm afraid of," he said, wondering how he'd ever do without them. "Just let me lay this out, okay, before saying yay or nay. I need help to keep them safe, and you're the one to help."

Jace looked around, evidently to make sure they were alone. Only a couple of screeching seagulls and the dolphins circling back were in sight. Suddenly looking nervous, Jace kept his voice low. "Another kidnap threat? Clayton Ames again?"

"I'm scared he could pull something like that. I need to convince Claire to take Lexi and hide out until this Mangrove Murder trial is over. Ames's orders are that I not only get Haze off but promote his products in that public forum. Either way, win or lose for Haze, who's been formally charged with murder today, Ames ends up with control of the Youth water."

"It figures. So, a show trial that will turn into a circus reality TV type show—a big infomercial."

Nick nodded. "But in case something goes wrong, before the trial even starts, I need to get Claire and Lexi out of here. And hidden, which is no small task considering the way Ames operates."

"So I've seen. That's where the Witness Protection Program comes in?"

"Patterson explained that?"

"Mentioned it, more like, along with the Stingray project buy off for me so I would cooperate."

Nick bent one knee on the bench and turned more toward Jace. Their hard gazes met and held. After all the tense times in court he'd been through, he was scared he wouldn't be able to convince him, much more than any judge or jury he'd faced.

He told Jace, "Here's what I've come up with in my desperation. And when you hear this, you'll know I'm desperate, trusting you with this, when you could just give it all away to Ames." Or try to win Claire back, though he didn't say so.

"But I won't," Jace said, "because you're betting it might mean Claire and Lexi would be hurt or worse."

"That's what I'm hoping, believing and trusting. For several years, FBI Agent Rod Patterson has wanted to get his hands on Ames for avoiding huge taxes and generally meddling in US commercial and dangerous foreign interests. Patterson contacted me about five years ago, realizing I held a grudge against Ames too. Patterson and I both know you're flying for Ames, which could be a big problem for you with the FBI and Justice Department if you don't change sides."

"I won't waste time denying it. He threatened my life on Grand Cayman, said he'd have his goons feed me to the fish, and I took the only way out. I resent being under his thumb and I'm listening."

"The Justice Department is willing to give Claire WITSEC protection until this trial is over, and beyond until we can lure Ames back to the US where he can be arrested or extradited if we can find him abroad. He visits here rarely and when he does, he must go incognito. The Hazeltons have a quite recent photo of him on Goodland."

"They should have snagged him then, but he probably had some poor sap like me flying him in and out in a phony company plane."

Nick was surprised that Jace was so easily going along with this, admitting things, but then he was angry at Ames too. Or maybe that was the power of love. But was he agreeing too easily to all this? Nick had no choice but to forge ahead.

"But here's where you would come in," he said. "As soon

as possible, I'd like for you to fly Claire, Lexi, and two of our domestic staff, me and my tech assistant, to a secret destination site where the four of them will assume false identities and stay until this is over. When they're settled, you and I—with my tech guy I can't do without—would fly back."

"We wouldn't fly direct to where they'd go, that's for sure. Something roundabout, a diversion. Wish I could take you all in that bastard's new jet, but I don't know if I could swing that without getting caught. For all I know, he's got hidden trackers on it. And you see that small plane circling over there?" he said, pointing.

"So? Not Ames's spies watching you or me, I hope."

"I'll bet Patterson knows we're meeting. At least he knows our cell phones are. Tell him to explain more about that Stingray project to you. But are you sure you can trust *him*?"

"Can I trust you? I don't want to give Claire up, or Lexi either, Jace. You had them both longer than me, so I think you understand. I have to do this. I have to trust you to get them there, then later, that you'd head back to check on them when you can get away, because I'll be stuck with this trial until we can lure Ames here somehow."

"Where are we taking them?"

"Not a need-to-know for you yet. You'll help?"

"Not for you. For them, for me. I've acted like a jerk sometimes with Claire."

"Yeah, me too."

"You told her, and she's on board with this?"

"Not yet, and that could be the big snag. But she has to agree, for Lexi's sake, at least. Desperate times demand desperate measures, and it's the only way out I can see, whatever happens to me."

"You do love her. By the way, warn her that Ames's man Thom Van Cleve is carrying around a cell phone photo of Lexi at the library story hour—with Darcy and Jilly in the photo too. If we could rent a 747, we could fly everyone Ames has ever threatened to wherever. But you got to tell me where."

"I can't until right before the flight so you fuel up, get maps or whatever. Patterson's rules, not mine."

"At least I know what size plane we'll need."

"And here's the kicker, the way you'll know how much I'm willing to give up. Patterson thinks if Ames learns you're in on this, you'll go to the head of Ames's revised hit list. He—we—think you should disappear quickly too, maybe even return to the site to guard Claire and Lexi while I get through the trial, and give the FBI and Justice more time to track Ames down. Actually, Patterson thinks he might have moved from Grand Cayman to Cuba."

"Cuba? No kidding? Cozy with the Castros, the way he operates. You know, when I flew Ames's guy Van Cleve in here, I found a Havana communist newspaper in his seat on the plane."

"So maybe that's where Ames is holed up now—no doubt, in style, like in some sweet hacienda on par with Nightshade."

"Hell, Nick, they say politics makes strange bedfellows, but so does this, you and me really working together, not separately like we did on Grand Cayman. You know Patterson's taken a page from Ames's book to dangle a government fly-and-spy career in front of me, but I'll tell you this. If I never get a thing out of this caper but my girls safe—yeah, I know Claire loves you and Lexi thinks you're a really neat stepdad—that would be enough."

He thrust out his hand toward Nick. They shook and meant it this time. Nick realized he'd never really known Jace Britten before, but then Claire had fallen in love with him and he was Lexi's father. Now if only Claire would see the wisdom of all this—and if he could not only bear to part with them for a while, but, despite what he'd said, trust this man to care for them and then give them back.

Claire was really ticked at Nick. Not that he was, no doubt, having to spend more time with Haze after he got him out on bail, but that Dylan Carnahan would be here soon for dinner, and Nick was the one who really knew the man, and yet wasn't here to receive him. Each time she tried Nick's cell to remind him Dylan would be here soon, it went to voice mail. Considering she'd wanted their guest here so she could carefully learn more about Sondra's death, she guessed she had only herself to blame for her unease at greeting him alone.

Here he came up the gangway of his own yacht he'd been kind enough to loan them, and Nick was still nowhere in sight. She had planned for the three of them to have cocktails before the crab cakes, grouper and salad dinner she'd planned. At least, she could stall with the cocktails to give Nick time to get back.

"Dylan, welcome to your own beautiful yacht," she told him and offered her hand. He held it too long, and she pulled it back. She smelled liquor on his breath.

"Nick will be back soon," she explained, "but Haze Hazelton was arrested and booked this afternoon, so he's with him and his wife. I imagine he's out on bond by now."

"I can sure sympathize with another of Nick's clients getting arrested. I know exactly how Haze feels, raw panic, especially if, like me, he's innocent. I'm sure Nick believes he is and will prove it."

His frown lifted to a slight smile. When she gestured he should lead the way and assuming he'd walk the outer deck to the stern seating area she'd indicated, she was surprised that he headed inside to the salon, looked around and sat on the long couch. It didn't seem to bother him, but she didn't like the idea of being here where Sondra's body was found.

"Ah, it's great to be back home!" he said, looking around.

"Wine or a cocktail? Or we can wait for Nick for that."

"Jack Daniel's with a splash of water would be fine. Here, let me mix it," he said, popping up and coming over to the bar. "That's right, Nick drinks Glenlivet Scotch." Without looking down, he reached for a glass under the counter. "Oh, sorry for taking over," he said, "and sorrier I didn't ask what you wanted. Is there still Chablis in the little fridge here?"

"Chablis would be fine," she said, noting how adept he was with the drinks, but then this was his bar. "We could go out on the back deck. I'm sure Nick will be here soon," she repeated.

"The October wind's a bit chilly," he said, handing her a goblet of wine, then clinking ice into his glass. "Let's just sit in here. Really—despite what happened here—my fave spot on the *Sylph* except for that mirrored master bedroom, eh?" he said and winked as he mixed his drink. He took a big swig of it, then immediately refilled it.

He carried his glass over to the couch. "Yes, a woman, a stranger, died here," he said quietly, almost as if to himself. "But I like to face my ghosts because I had nothing to do with that, Claire. Nick's a great defense attorney but he had an innocent man to defend—as I'm sure he does with Hazelton too, as I said. So, sit down."

She did, not close, crossing her legs, feeling awkward and—for some reason, slightly scared, maybe just because Nick wasn't here, maybe because, in her mind's eye, she kept seeing the photo of the outline of a body here, which became her own body in that terrible dream.

"So will you sell the *Sylph*?" she asked, copping out when she had meant to steer the conversation toward his ideas of who could have strangled Sondra.

"My wife wants me to. I'm waiting for her to serve me with

divorce papers and then I'd probably have to with big-time alimony. Actually, I think she's afraid of me now."

"Surely, she doesn't think you did it."

He shrugged. "I was having an affair but not with poor Sondra McMillan, though she was evidently going through men like—like I go through Jack Daniel's."

Claire wondered if that list of men included Ada's grandson or great-grandson Jimmie Cypress. Once Nick got past the Mangrove Murder case, maybe she should ask him to look into Jimmie's possible part in Sondra's murder. But she nearly spilled her drink at Dylan's next comment. Had she heard what he just said?

"What?" she asked him.

"I said, Mark Stirling was on Sondra's hook. It didn't come out in my trial, but I found out later when someone told me why he'd been fired from the paper he worked for. Obviously, Nick can't look into her as a possible suspect for eliminating Stirling since she's gone. But I've heard since my trial that Sondra and Stirling were a really hot item."

"He—had he known her long?"

"Long enough," he said and took another big swig of his drink, then stared into the amber liquid as he swirled it in his glass. "It was in covering my trial that he ran afoul of the powers that be and got fired when they found out one of their own reporters had been in lust with the woman who was also sleeping with a Seminole casino insider and then somehow managed to get herself murdered on my yacht. The stupid slut caused me a lot of trouble, considering I didn't touch her, didn't even know her! I just found her here like that—dead on the floor—and tried to help her, and look at the grief it got me.

"And you can tell Nick—who is almost never late," he said, glancing at his expensive watch, "that I wish he could convince my wife I'm innocent like he did the jury." He raised his glass to Claire before draining it. She could tell that he was going to ask her what she thought about it all. He was going to get another drink and keep drinking. She took the first sip of her wine, but it tasted bitter.

She got up to call the cook on the intership phone to tell him not to hold dinner for Nick but to serve it now. She needed to get some hot food in this man, who seemed as tense and edgy as she was.

Not a good idea, Claire, she scolded herself, to dabble in Sondra's murder, nor to have this man here on a day like this, except for the fact that he'd spilled the beans about Mark Stirling's relationship with Sondra. That could have biased Mark's coverage of Dylan's trial. But, offhand, she couldn't fathom any way the two murders could be connected.

"You know something strange?" Dylan asked. Her heartbeat kicked up and her pulse pounded harder as he got up and came after her toward the bar.

Without waiting for her reply, he went on, "A couple of years ago—probably four or five, when I took some friends fishing on Fin Taylor's *Reel Good Time,* Fin introduced me to Haze in Stan's Idle Hour bar. When I heard his claims about the springwater, I asked him if I could bottle some of it and try to sell it in South Florida, for starters. But he said no thanks, that he had a hot prospect for that, and I guess he did! Ironic, huh, now that the water business has gone bonkers internationally, and I'm here still wishing I had it—but not holding a grudge."

Hemmed in behind the bar, Claire knew she had to get hold of herself. For once, she was psyching herself out instead of someone else. She had the strangest vibes around and about this man. Despite Nick's winning Dylan's case, could he have had some part in getting rid of Sondra, maybe so his wife didn't find out, or because Sondra was blackmailing him?

"So what kind of a personal staff are you two lovebirds

keeping here besides my cook and captain?" Dylan asked in a sudden shift of topics. Maybe her growing alarm had showed on her face.

"Speaking of staff," she told him, "I'm going to call for dinner, and I'm sure Nick will join us soon. As for staff here, we have a nanny for my daughter on board—and a bodyguard."

"A bodyguard, no less?" he asked, stopping at the end of the bar, though he still blocked her in. "You know, I actually kept a bartender on board once. I'll just mix another drink," he said, coming closer again while she grabbed the phone.

Thank heavens, Nick walked in the door. Now things would be under control with no more suspicions or surprises.

CHAPTER THIRTY-ONE

With Nick home at last, Claire calmed down. Had she imagined that the vibes from his friend and former client Dylan were menacing? Maybe she was working too hard. She had to stop thinking that Dylan could have killed Sondra. Surely, Nick would have figured that out. He'd told her he never took a client he absolutely knew was guilty, and she was sure he wouldn't have been able to live with himself if he knew he'd helped exonerate a murderer.

She felt somehow disloyal to be using her forensic psychology skills on her own husband, but something else, something new, seemed to be bothering him. Granted, it was eating at him to have to push Youth water products that he thought were fakes. But then, when he'd taken Haze Hazelton's case—or been assigned to it rather—he'd never had his and his family's lives threatened by a powerful enemy either.

When Nick finally steered their dinner conversation back to Sondra's murder, Dylan shared with him the same bombshell he'd told Claire: that Sondra had been involved with Mark Stirling. Nick managed not to show much emotion, but Claire could tell that annoyed him and shook him up.

Even when Dylan mentioned that he'd once asked Haze for a monopoly on the water and been refused, Nick seemed only distracted. Probably, she thought, he was already planning how he was going to handle Haze's murder trial since nothing could stop that now except a guilty plea, which would put both Haze and Nick in Ames's crosshairs.

She noted Nick kept chewing his lower lip while Dylan seemed a lot calmer—as if he'd been to the confession booth and felt forgiven. Was Nick now thinking that Dylan could have known more than he'd testified to in court when Nick had gambled to put him on the stand? But she made a silent vow not to bring any of that up tonight. They needed to be together, to think and talk about good things for once, happy things, just to have some quiet downtime.

Finally, Dylan was gone so things were bound to go smoother. Except for his two bombshells, she was sorry she'd pushed Nick to ask him here tonight. It was a mistake, and she vowed not to make another.

Once they were alone in their bedroom, Nick kissed Claire thoroughly and held her tight. He hoped she couldn't tell that he was really shaken up. He wasn't sure how he'd gotten through dinner conversation with Dylan and then just now visiting Lexi in her room to say good-night. The chicken pox had sapped her strength, and her low-grade fever made her restless. He knew the feeling. And he hated to put the sweet little girl through what was coming, let alone talk her mother into it.

He was tempted to tumble Claire right into bed before he told her what he was dreading, but that wouldn't be fair. Kind of a cheap shot before he lowered the boom. But he tugged her over to the bed and sat her there, both of them fully dressed. He leaned close and took her hands in his.

"What?" she said. "What is it? Something about Haze's

arrest? Has he turned on Maggie for what she did? She said she wouldn't tell him until morning because he'd never sleep, and he'd been a wreck waiting for the arrest. Or Dylan's revelations?"

"No, not any of that."

"You sensed I didn't like or trust him."

"Claire, even though he's more or less our landlord, that is, our 'yachtlord,' I can understand that. Especially since he came clean about once offering Haze a deal for the water and just happened to mention that Stirling was involved with Sondra, which I didn't know. Did he do or say something out of line before I got home?"

"No, just bad vibes. He called Sondra a stupid slut."

"You're not thinking he was guilty of her murder? Just like with this Mangrove Murder case, I looked into every possibility. Haze isn't guilty of killing Mark either."

"Then who is?"

"I don't know! I'm not Perry Mason solving a crime within a sixty-minute TV show, but maybe if I push hard enough it will come out on the stand. I'm going to call Fin Taylor to testify. He's good at flying off the handle and may say something. But, listen, it's you and me I want to talk about, as well as Lexi and Ames, so—"

"Don't put her in the same sentence with that madman."

"I need to talk to you about Jace."

When she winced, he realized he was holding her hand much too tight. She tugged her hands back, and he let her. "I hope you're not going to drag him onto the stand. Nick, Jace didn't even know Mark Stirling. However upset he is about our marriage and the fact he has to ask permission to see Lexi, I think we need to leave well enough alone with him—leave him alone!"

"Wait, just listen. You go ballistic over anything I say about Jace. Just keep calm. I'm not anti-Jace."

"You're not? So what is it? I read that in you all evening, that it isn't just Haze's arrest or Dylan's revelations bothering you. Tell me."

"I—your glib defense attorney husband—I'm making a mess of this. I love you, Claire, you and Lexi, so don't forget that, please."

Jace sat on the dock near the prow of the *Sylph* and dangled his feet over the edge. Despite the ambient lights from the yacht and a few strung down the dock, Goodland didn't have a lot of lights, so the stars stood out real clear, almost like when he used to fly far from cities or over the Pacific. He even watched the space station go overhead on its regular trajectory, like a small, constant light in the darkness. He'd thought once he'd like to be an astronaut, but had changed his mind, that is, loving Claire and having Lexi had changed his mind. Before things went so, so bad.

Frowning, he took his cell phone out of his jacket pocket and flicked his thumb across the screen. He opened the email Van Cleve had recently sent him of photos from Claire and Nick's wedding at Nightshade. Again, he hated being manipulated and used. K-A obviously wanted to keep him wounded and angry at Nick, maybe Claire too.

He darkened the screen fast when he heard footsteps. The guy that guarded the ship came down the gangway and walked the dock toward him. Nick had said he'd tell the big bruiser—named Bronco, no less—that he was coming, but that Jace should wait to board until Nick had told Claire their plan. Jace assumed that Bronco and Lexi's nanny would be the two domestic staff Nick wanted to go on the escape plane, though he'd said he wouldn't mention that to Bronco until things were set. Nor would Jace look for a plane to borrow or rent until close to takeoff—if Claire agreed. He figured he'd need one that seated seven.

"You doing okay?" Bronco asked him as Jace jammed his phone in his back pocket. "Want something to eat?"

"Thanks for the nice welcome this time."

"Just doing my job. And it doesn't hurt what I do to be suspicious."

"Good point. Wish I had a friend like you."

"Nick say I was a friend?"

"I got that idea. Are you?"

"Want to be, though I make my share of mistakes."

"Yeah," Jace said, "me too. No, I don't need anything to eat. I had a solo shrimp dinner at a place on Marco. Don't like to eat by myself, but Nick had to get back here."

"I'd better go back on board. I'll come get you if it's time."

"Okay. Good, Bronco. But that may be a while."

"Claire, I know you've been worried that Jace and I seemed hostile to one another," Nick said, trying to start again in a logical way. "But, even after Grand Cayman, we're really not. As a matter of fact, I've talked to him, and we agree on something we hope you'll—well, you'll get on board with. For your sake and Lexi's too."

"What? Like what?"

He decided not to tell her to keep quiet again. Just plunge ahead, get her to hear him out, then bring Jace in. Hopefully, he hadn't changed his mind and would show up to back him on this.

"Jace and I are still worried about your safety and especially Lexi's. Things are heating up, and we can't trust Ames to keep his hands off either of you if he doesn't like the way the trial goes, if I don't do enough song and dance numbers promoting the Youth water. Anything could set him off, and we know he's got operatives here. I hope you won't say something like he's given us his word. His word is worth nothing."

"You—were you with Jace tonight?"

"Yes, but this is bigger than Jace and me, you or even Lexi. I was contacted by the FBI several years ago and again not long ago. So was Jace recently, when they suspected him of flying for Ames. Our government sees Ames as an enemy too, ruthless, dangerous, powerful."

"They don't plan to take Lexi away for safekeeping, do they? I wouldn't even trust them. She's not going anywhere without me!"

"Exactly. Although it will hurt me to have the two of you leave here for a while, I can't do what I intend when I'm scared to death Ames is going to grab either or both of you. I may decide to cross-examine Ames's water experts in court to get them to give him away. Or I might bring in objective experts to show some of their facts are skewed or fudged."

"Nick, what about your own safety?"

"I know. Especially if it comes out that someone other than Haze killed Stirling. As for my phony courtroom efforts to promote the youth waters—hell, I hope it all goes down the drain. Meanwhile, Jace admits he was captured and threatened by Ames on Grand Cayman, so he's flying that new state-of-the-art jet for him right now and not for some shadowy, fictional corporation."

She sucked in a sharp breath and covered her head with both hands. "Then—then, can you trust Jace?"

"I think he'd die before he'd let anyone hurt Lexi. Is it a gamble? If so, trusting him to help us is one I—we—have to take."

"So, even with Bronco we need more protection, like FBI agents here to guard Lexi and me while you're in court?"

"Not enough. Have you heard of the Witness Protection Program they call WITSEC?"

"But I have no intention of testifying against Ames. You—you didn't plan to call me to the stand, right?"

"I want to avoid that at all costs. But what if the prosecution does, since you've been helping with this investigation? The last thing in the world I want is to send you and Lexi away. But one of Ames's men showed Jace a photo of Lexi and Nita at the library story hour, and Darcy and Jilly were in the photo too."

She sprang from the bed and started to pace. "I never thought of that, that he'd reach out further than just us. So Darcy and Jilly are in danger too? They won't leave here, won't leave Steve!"

"I didn't say that, don't know any of that. But we'll have to tell Darcy more than we have. Here's the deal. You, Lexi, Nita and Bronco will be flown out of here by Jace—Heck and I will go too, just to be sure you're settled—at least until Haze's trial is over."

"But he just got arrested. How long would we be gone? A trial could take months to start and last longer."

"I'll bet it won't. I won't ask for delays, and Ames wants that good Youth water promotion soon."

"But go where? I can't leave Lexi, but I can't leave you either."

Nick couldn't help it, but his eyes prickled with unshed tears. For a moment he was speechless. A wife, a child, a future with them. He realized like a kick to the gut that's all he'd ever really wanted—that and justice for his dad as well as for others who had been hurt or killed.

"I want to say no way," she told him as she came close, sat down again and hugged him hard. He clamped her to him. "I want to be furious you thought all this out without a word to me, met with Jace and are willing to send me—us—away, but it does show you love us. You would miss us too."

"So much," he got out, but his words were muffled in her hair. "Maybe we can find a way to Skype, phone, email—something, but Jace says our own government can trace that, and they have their WITSEC rules. And for safety's sake…

Claire, Jace said he'd wait outside until I talked to you. Let's go sit out on the stern, and I'll have Bronco bring him on board. The government's going to protect him too—even offered him a job flying and overseeing surveillance planes once this is over. And if it works out, he'd visit you, check on you while you and Lexi are away. How much, I don't know yet."

She lifted her head from his shoulder and stared into his eyes. "Then maybe we've finally found something to help us fight and stop Clayton Ames. I don't mean Jace but the most powerful nation on Earth. And it just might take the entire weight of the US government to even things out."

Jace was nervous as he sat with Nick and Claire on the darkened stern of the yacht. He felt really awkward, like he should be arguing with them, not telling them one damn thing about nearly losing his life the night he met Kilcorse-Ames at Nightshade on Grand Cayman. After that, there was no small talk, even about Lexi or her illness; they got right to it.

"The program the FBI wants me to head up and fly for—if, I swear, I live through this," Jace told them, "is not top secret and goes by the name Stingray. Since it threatens people's privacy, it's sometimes exposed by media outlets, big and small."

Nick put in, "Heck, my tech guy, found out it appeared in an article in our favorite publication, *The Burrowing Owl.* Somehow Mark Stirling keeps coming up as if he's speaking from the grave, if we just know how to listen."

Jace said, "You mean he could have been knocked off for that—like by Patterson for blowing the whistle on their project?"

"No, I don't mean that. This madness has to stop somewhere, but I think Stirling's real murderer might be Thom Van Cleve, on Ames's orders, of course."

"Man, I'd believe that," Jace said. "Van Cleve's also as slippery and cold-blooded as a snake."

Nick nodded and said, "But if I tried to bring any of that out, Ames would have my head on a platter. My mission is to clear Haze but promote Ames High, Inc."

Claire appeared not to be crying. "All you'd need to infuriate Ames is to subpoena Van Cleve, as if he'd tell the truth on the stand," he told Nick.

"I've thought about that. At least Claire and Lexi won't be here in the line of fire, if that's my last resort."

Claire said, "Nick, if I have to leave—and for Lexi's sake, I'm agreeing for now, though it makes me sick—I have to see Darcy first. To make her understand, even to warn her to be careful. And I'll be careful setting up a short meeting with her."

"I'm hoping Ames's targets would not stretch beyond you and Lexi to get to me, but you can't tell her much. It would endanger her and you. That's why I'm not telling anyone where you're headed until Jace takes off with us in the plane from Key West, then heads out to the final destination, north instead of south."

"Could you please just say our temporary destination instead of our final one?" Claire asked and blew her nose. Jace noted her eyelids were swollen, and she had cried or wiped her mascara off before she sat down. Gray circles shadowed her beautiful eyes. Her hair was a mess, and she looked exhausted. But she looked beautiful, and he longed to comfort and hold her. Hell, maybe if this crazy plan worked, he'd get that chance.

"Are the three of us agreed then?" Jace asked. "If so, Nick's going to call Patterson in the morning and set things in motion, and I'll line up two rental planes. I think we all need some sleep."

"If Claire gives the final okay, we have a plan," Nick said.

"I didn't mean to keep this back from you, sweetheart, but things had to be in order first."

"I hate this," Claire said. "I hate all of this, but, as I said, I will do it for Lexi—and for both of you. Living in fear and controlled by others, that's no way to bring up a child. Let's pray this nightmare is over soon and that the next person to be arrested, go on trial or worse, is Clayton Ames."

Like a team ready to head into the final, sudden death game, the three of them gripped hands.

CHAPTER THIRTY-TWO

Feeling as if she'd been fighting the undertow of a raging surf all night, Claire rolled over in bed the next morning and reached for Nick. Gone.

Oh, that's right, it was Monday, the day of the office reception, and he'd said he'd head into work early. How ironic the law firm was celebrating the Markwood newlyweds, when they were about to be apart for who knew how long? Nick had said he'd planned to phone Rod Patterson from his car to put things in motion as he drove into Naples.

As a precautionary plan so she wouldn't be driving alone, Heck was scheduled to pick her up this afternoon to take her to the law office. She hadn't seen him for a while. Maybe she'd ask him what he thought about Sondra McMillan's murder, since he'd worked with Nick on background research for Dylan's trial. She just couldn't let that go. If there was something subconscious eating at her about Sondra's murder—and Mark's—she wished she'd remember it. She sometimes wondered if the strong narcolepsy meds she took buried thoughts she should be able to grasp.

Her insides cartwheeled at her next thought. This was probably one of the last few days she and Nick would be together and for how long? Pray God, not forever, if something went really wrong with their desperate plan. And here, she'd overslept and he was already on his way to work.

They'd made such hurried love last night they'd paid no attention to birth control. Wouldn't that be all she—they—needed, for her to conceive a child right now?

She got up, used the bathroom and showered. She'd wait to put on makeup and fix her hair closer to the late afternoon reception. She planned to spend the morning with Lexi, have their breakfast sent in to the child's room. The doctor friend of Nick's who had made a house call—a boat call—had assured them that Lexi's chicken pox would run its course this week, and she was on the upswing. At least the child's fever had never been much. Claire knew Lexi would cry when Nick left them, even with Nita and Bronco there, wherever there was. No way she could make it a game or innocent story when they took their secret flight or even after they were stashed at some safe haven far from here. Lexi and Claire used to miss Jace when he was away on long flights, but this would be worse, a different kind of danger.

But now, she had to meet Darcy at some safe, public place where she could talk to her, to try to explain some of this without putting her in danger. She knew just the place and wouldn't even have to name it over the phone. It was near Darcy's house, in the last place they'd taken their mother before she died. Hopefully, not a bad omen.

Just think, Claire told herself as she hurried down the hall toward Lexi's room, when they'd escaped from Grand Cayman, she'd figured she'd be helping Nick with this case and maybe with South Shores but also have time to spend with Darcy and resurrect her antifraud firm, Clear Path. But there was no safe, clear path left to her and her loved ones anymore.

To Claire's surprise, Nita stood in the hall outside Lexi's

room as if waiting for her. "Oh, good," Nita said. "I was thinking you might have to call Mr. Nick. See, he left his phone. I was looking for Lexi's turtle and found it—the phone—on a chair out back." She waved the stuffed turtle Ames had given the child, but handed over the phone. It wasn't Nick's, but she didn't say so. It must be Jace's. Surely he'd missed it by now and would be back for it soon. Obviously, she couldn't call him on it to tell him she had it.

"Thanks, Nita. Tell Lexi I'll be right in."

Claire did a U-turn back to her room. Jace probably had the phone synced to his laptop, so she could contact him that way if he still had his laptop on him. He might not realize where he'd lost the phone.

She sat on the big bed and turned the phone on. And gasped as the screen lit with a photo she'd never seen of her and Nick's wedding on Grand Cayman. With Ames standing, smiling in the background.

She dropped the phone on the bed as if it had burned her.

She flopped back on the unmade bed and stared up at herself in the ceiling mirror. So was Jace to be trusted? Had he been eating his heart out over her marrying Nick? How deep was he really in with Clayton Ames?

Her first impulse was to call Nick, but what if someone was picking up on their cell phone conversations from here? Nick had warned her to say nothing private when she called, and Jace had explained the FBI's Stingray surveillance, though that was just to locate people, not eavesdrop.

She got up, took her own phone and fought to calm herself as she called Darcy instead. Who knew when they'd have to leave here with the secretive WITSEC protection program? She'd hate to go without clearing some things with Darcy, so now was the time. They had been so close for years—until lately.

Her sister answered right away. "Hey, Darcy, it's Claire.

Listen, we need to compare how our chicken-poxed girls are doing. Can you meet me in about an hour or so at the place we last took Mom—you know, so don't blurt it out."

"Oh. Sure. Just us? Steve and I will be at the reception today. We're looking forward to it and then rescheduling a visit to the yacht."

Claire blinked back tears. "Sure, but it's a lovely day, so I thought we'd just catch up first. There will be a lot of people at the reception I don't know, and not much quiet sister time."

"Okay. Ten thirty?"

"See you then and there. Sounds good."

But the truth was, Claire thought as she ended the call, nothing sounded good right now. She raked her fingers through her hair and decided she'd better put on some eye makeup so Darcy didn't think she was sick. She'd spend some time with Lexi and give Jace's phone to Nita in case he showed up later. She'd get Bronco to take her into town, since she'd promised Nick not to drive off Goodland alone.

And then she'd try to patch things up with Darcy, though without being able to share with her one darn thing about what she was doing or the danger she was facing.

"Nick," his secretary's, Cheryl's, voice came over the intercom, "there's a man at reception who insists on seeing you with no appointment."

"Jace Britten?" he asked, shoving his casework aside on his big desk.

"A Thom Van Cleve. He's most adamant, says it affects the Mangrove Murder case, but I can call security and have him—"

"Alert security, but have whoever responds wait outside my office door once he's here. Escort Van Cleve in."

Nick slid open his top left desk drawer where he kept a loaded Glock. He'd never had to use it, but he was a criminal lawyer, and they tended to make as many enemies as allies. He hadn't been kidding when he'd blurted out to Claire that Van Cleve could be Stirling's killer. He assumed his mission protected him and Ames's operatives had kept him safe for now, but you never knew.

He stood behind his desk when Cheryl brought the man in. She went out and left the door slightly ajar. Nick did not go around to greet him. He'd glimpsed one of the men they kept on staff for strange situations outside in the hall already.

He didn't—just couldn't—shake the man's hand. "Have a seat, Mr. Van Cleve. Dare I think you have a message from the top?"

Van Cleve was thin and had beard stubble, maybe to make up for his balding head. The man shrugged. "And dare I ask if we are being recorded?"

"Isn't everything I say these days?" Nick countered. He sat back in his chair with his elbows on the armrests, steepling his fingers before his face.

"A sense of humor. But I hear good sense too. I'll make this brief. Our mutual friend is pleased with your progress but wants you to stay on task, especially now that Hazelton has been charged with the journalist's murder."

"Our mutual friend is obviously aware that if Hazelton did not kill Stirling, someone else did and that will have to come out. Present company excepted, of course, but I'll have to suggest or even prove another murderer."

Van Cleve's eyes widened, then narrowed again. Nick thought surprise and raw fear flickered there for a moment.

But coldly stoic again, Van Cleve said, "He just wanted you to know you can accuse someone else in court as long as the fountain of youth is not judged guilty in any way. It does what the products claim. That's all—for now."

Nick was amazed when the man rose and started out. But he turned back at the door and leaned against it to close it.

Nick shifted in his chair. He could get to his gun fast. No, he fought to calm himself. Ames needed him, and as long as he played along, he and his girls must be safe. Especially, he prayed, when they were two thousand miles north of here.

"Nick," Van Cleve said, crossing his arms over his chest, "better keep an eye on your wife's ex. He keeps an eye on you, and you never know. After a divorce, fathers have been known to abduct their own children and run off with them."

Nick's stomach twisted. He had the wildest urge to leap around his desk and grab this messenger from hell, to beat his head against the door. But he said in his best calm, commanding courtroom voice, "I'll keep an eye on him, though I've found that so-called uncles do it too, and that would be the last straw for me and 'Uncle Clay' if it ever happens again."

Van Cleve gave a snort and seemed to startle. "I'll pass that threat on. Good morning, lovely day, isn't it," the smart aleck said to the security guard as he left.

Nick slammed his drawer with the gun. He'd be taking that with him when they left. And it better be soon. He hoped Jace—if he could trust him—was working on lining up a plane.

"You want me to tail you two?" Bronco asked Claire when they pulled into the Naples Botanical Gardens parking lot.

"Good idea, but stay way back. If you see someone else following us, keep him in sight but don't confront him."

"Got it. You just be careful though."

Claire was really nervous as she paid for her ticket and walked into the beautiful grounds. It had boardwalks linking several distinct areas with stunning flowers and foliage, but she headed straight for the water garden where she and Darcy had taken their mother on their last outing before her final illness.

The gardens had been new then. *This place looks like a Monet painting of his water lilies from Giverny*, Mother had said and given them a talk on the artist's life from some novel she'd read. She'd never been to France, never really been anywhere, but she was a walking, talking library. Claire and Darcy used to give each other eye rolls at her lecturing them like some professor, but they missed her so much now. And Claire knew she was about to start missing Darcy and her family—for how long and from where?

Claire saw Darcy down by the pond. The water was laced with a pastel palette of white, pink and purple water lilies just like the last time she'd seen it. Such a serene place, but Claire's stomach felt twisted tight.

They hugged, then stood together at the water's edge between the palms. Claire glanced back and around. Just Bronco, keeping his distance. No one else right now on this late Monday morning.

Darcy said, "I can almost see her here. I think it's the last time she was ever outside—and without a book."

Claire pressed her lips together but she couldn't smile. Maybe she shouldn't have picked this place. She felt like crying already. She had to get to this, but how?

"Darcy, as you can imagine, Nick, as a defense attorney, has had a lot of people grateful for his work, but also some who were ticked off."

"No kidding. Like that guy that shot your client—and you."

"Right," she said as they strolled around the grassy edge of the pond. "It looks like it would be best if Lexi and I actually hide out for a while until Nick gets through this trial."

Darcy's head snapped around. "You're kidding. So, not because of a past court case but this one about the youth water and the journalist getting killed?"

"Right," she repeated. But she was afraid to tell her sister anything about Clayton Ames. "It will hopefully only be for a while, and I'll try to contact you through channels."

"Channels? So Nick isn't just stashing you at some safe house near here for a while—like with that big guy up there on duty?"

"It's more complicated than that."

"But when will you be back? Claire, honey—this sounds like something out of *NCIS* or *Law & Order.* Did you find something in a forensic interview that endangers you?"

They turned and clasped elbows, as if holding each other up. Claire stared at Darcy. Anyone could tell they were sisters, though Darcy had a blond, pixie haircut, freckles and blue eyes to Claire's longer red hair, pale skin and green eyes. Darcy was younger but she'd always been the steady one, especially through Claire's divorce. But Darcy was crying now. Tears clumped her lashes and pooled in her eyes.

"Claire, do you love Nick? And is he good to Lexi?" she demanded.

"Yes and yes!"

"Well, then, 'Claire de Looney,'" she said, using her childhood nickname, "I guess you will do what you have to do, and we will all miss you till you're back safe and sound."

"Thanks for understanding, 'Mr. Darcy.'"

"Thank God Mom didn't prefer *Jane Eyre* and I didn't end up named Rochester."

Sucking in simultaneous sobs, they hugged each other.

Claire told her, "I'll try to stay in touch but just didn't want you to think Lexi and I had been abducted by aliens."

Darcy squeezed Claire's shoulders and leaned back to look full in her face. "Are you going to the same place you went before? Were people after Nick then too, and you took Lexi to hide out, then decided to marry him?"

"No. No, it isn't that. Don't worry. I trust Nick."

"Jace isn't hanging on too hard, is he?"

Claire shook her head but she knew that might be a lie. Was Jace in this plan just to protect Lexi and everyone else was expendable?

"Claire," Darcy said and gave her a little shake. "Listen, let's plan to meet back here, and you can tell me everything when you get back this time. We'll make a wish, and I'll keep praying that you'll be safe."

"And you just be careful too," she said, not wanting to panic Darcy, but wanting to warn her. "Take care of Jilly and the rest of the family, in case some idiot believes in guilt by association. Just be more aware, and I'll see you and Steve this afternoon at the reception, all right?"

"Sure. All right," Darcy said, though her voice snagged on a sob again.

"Let's not walk out together until we meet here next time," Claire told her with another glance to see if Bronco was still watching. He was.

"Then you think you're being followed?" Darcy asked, whispering now as if anyone could hear.

"Hopefully just by that man over there who works for us. He and Lexi's nanny will be going too, so I won't be alone taking care of Lexi."

"Claire, whatever happens, you *won't* be alone," Darcy told her as she wiped away tears from under both her eyes. "One for all and all for one."

"Name that book or author—Alexandre Dumas and *The Three Musketeers*."

"You win the Mother-asked-a-question prize! Ta-da! See you tonight, Claire. Love you—always."

"Me too. Thanks for understanding and always being there. Don't know what I'd ever do without you."

CHAPTER THIRTY-THREE

Claire had not worn a dressy dress since her wedding just a little over two weeks ago. She had chosen her sleeveless, pleat-skirted jade green one today because its color went well with her hair and accentuated her eyes. Still thinking of her brief time with Darcy today, she remembered how the same colors had not looked good on them growing up, but they'd shared clothes anyway. Actually, this dress would look great on Colleen Taylor, who had coloring closer to Claire's.

"You lookin' good, Mrs. Claire," Bronco told her as she kissed Lexi goodbye one more time, then went down the gangway to join Heck, who was waiting for her on the dock. Even he had dressed up, really fancy for the brilliant, eccentric techie. He wore a suit coat and buttoned shirt, even a tie. She'd never seen him in anything but jeans and a T-shirt, though, she supposed when he went into the firm he spiffed up a bit.

Once they were in the car, it didn't take Heck long to say, "Nita says she's really liking that Bronco. But Nick says he got a temper problem."

"I hope Nick told you Bronco's working on that. He's a

very protective person, so I'm sure Nita's safe around him, if that's what you mean. We're trusting him to help protect us and Lexi too."

"Nick thought I might get upset. *Sí*, it is my way, my Cuban blood."

"Heck, they both seem happy. She's definitely of age and since she lost her husband, aren't you happy for her too?"

"Oh, sure. Just don't want him going too fast, taking 'vantage of her. She's with him 'cause of me suggesting her to you. I just don't want no broken hearts."

"I don't either. I'll keep an eye on things, so don't you go treating her like she's your daughter instead of your adult cousin. Deal?"

"Sure. You're good for Nick, maybe he be good for her."

After that, they chatted easily as he drove them north into Naples on the Tamiami Trail, but she couldn't wait to steer their conversation to one thing.

"Dylan Carnahan came for dinner last night," she told him.

"So the boss said when he called today to make sure I knew the time to get you. Haven't laid eyes on that hombre since he walked out of court a free man, thanks to Nick."

"I know you must have put in hours helping him prepare for that trial. Was there anything at all to link him to Sondra's murder?"

"Not that we found. *Sí*, he waited too long to call the squad, but he was panicked he was gonna look guilty. And he was having an affair, but not with her. That looked bad, and his wife wouldn't give him no alibi. Word was, Sondra thought she could threaten him, maybe con him out of some money so she went right on board the yacht."

"I can't believe she didn't fight back. She was a really well-built woman."

"That's for sure. Really stacked. Part of how she drew guys in."

"I don't mean that. I mean it's hard to believe she could be strangled to death."

"By a silk scarf, no less. It was evidence. It was twisted, and she was probably grabbed from behind, taken by surprise. Someone must of put it over her head fast. A woman's scarf. It didn't match what she had on that day. It had green-and-white stripes, and her dress had, what you call it—poky dots. Her killer probably had the scarf—another reason Nick got Carnahan off. What guy carries a silk scarf around, see?"

"I guess I do see. Were the stripes bright or pale green?"

"Not sure. Nick tell you I'm color-blind? Everything looks green-yellow to me, but I can tell white. I'll send you a pic of the scarf tomorrow. If I still have it and if we're still here."

"I don't know why I can't let it go—Sondra's murder. Just the fact it happened on the yacht, I guess."

"You not believe in ghosts, no?"

"Not that kind. Only the kind that haunt Nick and me like Ames, and we're working on that. I just wish I knew what kind of things to pack."

"Be prepared, *sí*?"

"Exactly. You know, Heck, when we leave here, I'm going to miss it. Thanks for all your help to Nick and me too."

"Sure. Sure," he repeated, suddenly seeming a bit embarrassed or on edge. "I think the world of Nick, and now, you do too."

Claire was nervous at the law firm reception, and that wasn't like her. Too much happening too fast. She and Nick had stood in an informal reception line at first, but darned if she could recall more than half of the twenty-some names of people she'd been introduced to right now, and she hadn't even had much wine. How insane that they couldn't live a normal life, enjoy this, go out to dinner with friends, take Lexi here and there, just relax.

What had really rattled her was Nick's information that the local private detective he'd hired just today to tail Maggie's spy, Jesse Winslow, was waiting in his office right now to give them a report. Although Maggie had assured them she'd call Jesse off immediately, this detective—whose name Nick didn't give her—wanted to see them, despite this party.

Chatting with people along the way, Nick steered Claire into his office.

Nick's detective was dressed like a tourist heading out to dinner, slacks, golf shirt, ball cap in his hands. Nick still didn't give the man's name, but she was sure there was a reason for that. He'd been introducing her to everyone else this afternoon.

"No, don't hit the lights," the man said when Nick reached for the switch. "I don't want someone looking up or in here."

"Then let's make this quick," Nick told the man. "We can't disappear from our reception, and you need to get back on this, so what's the news? Did you lose him?"

"No way, since he's still tailing you. Take a look out the corner window over there, but don't stand too close. He's not only following you around, but I think he has some sort of cell phone receptor in that big backpack."

Nick swore under his breath as he looked out the window. "Is that the same guy?" Nick asked Claire as she stood slightly behind him and peeked around.

"Looks like the one I saw Maggie talking to and the one that strolled past your house with the dog. But she gave us his name, so she must not have intended to keep him on this. Surely, he wouldn't do it on his own. Maybe someone else spotted him and decided to use him."

"I think we can guess who," Nick muttered.

The detective said, "You want him arrested and questioned, Mr. Markwood?"

"No, I want him followed. He might lead you back to

Maggie, which I doubt, or someone else. But that backpack he has—you think he can pick up cell phone conversations?"

"It's why I didn't phone you to say I'm on to him."

Claire said, "So, even more so now, we need to watch our own conversations," she told Nick, gripping his upper arm.

"Okay," Nick told the man. "Two can play the stalking game. Keep on him."

"Should I come to the yacht rather than phone if I have other info?"

Nick nodded. They shook hands, and the man slipped out.

"But we won't be there long," Claire said, whispering.

"I can't tell even him that." He spoke so low she could barely hear him. "I just hope my calls to Rod Patterson weren't picked up. Plus, Jace called right before you arrived to say he's set everything in motion, but he didn't give details. We absolutely need to get you and Lexi out of here. I'm hoping this shindig assures anyone watching us that it's business as usual."

He leaned forward and kissed her.

"Better watch that lipstick on your mouth," she said. "People will think we've been in here fooling around."

"Don't I wish? Claire, before we go back out, one more thing," he said, putting one hand on her bare shoulder and whispering in a raspy voice. "Ames's messenger boy, Thom Van Cleve, our guest for lunch on the yacht, came here today to reinforce and remind me, now that Haze has been formally accused, to protect and praise the Youth water or else."

"Oh, no! He came here?"

"Jace flew him in a while ago, and he's dogged him too. They're hoping to keep Jace in line and on the payroll, but being ordered around and controlled has infuriated him too. I had this office swept for listening devices after Van Cleve left, that's how obsessed I'm getting, or I wouldn't have let my messenger in here. But it was clean—and now we've got the man on the street to worry about. I'll bet Maggie fired him and Van Cleve hired him."

"We've had nothing but trouble since we've been together. I wish I could say things are getting better."

"They will. When I get you to the safe place out in the wild blue yonder, we'll have some time alone before I leave..." His voice trailed off.

"I'll kidnap you and make you stay."

"I'd like that. Very much," he said and tapped the rim of his wine goblet to hers.

"Well," she rushed on, still whispering, "neither did I have a chance to tell you that Jace left his cell on the yacht, and Nita found it this morning, so that's one phone that wasn't tapped last night, or whatever they call it these days. But get this. The first thing that came up when I turned it on was an email to Jace from Van Cleve with a photo of our wedding ceremony at Nightshade with your favorite 'uncle' gloating in the background. Jace stopped by to pick it up when I was with Darcy. But I'm getting paranoid too. Can we trust even him?"

"You used to go ballistic when I talked like that. We have no choice now. Yes, I think so. He loves Lexi. So how did it go with Darcy?"

"I didn't tell her much, but she supported me. Nick, I'm afraid for her—for them."

"When I get back from Ma—hell, didn't mean to say that. Anyway, I'll be in touch with her."

"We're going to Massachusetts? Manhattan to get lost in the crowds? Marrakech in Morocco? The Mariana Islands? Jace is used to flying over water."

"Very funny. I love you, Claire, down to your smart, sturdy backbone. Later for more—more of everything, okay?"

As they went back out into the buzzing reception room, he lifted his wineglass in a sort of salute as they passed the group of young, eager junior partners they had talked to earlier. They were still hanging around between the bar and the appetizer table, making up their meal for all Claire could tell. The receptionist and secretaries had their own little gathering over by the reception room windows, and she was glad they were included. She liked his secretary, Cheryl, who was the only one she'd really talked to before.

"I think you've all met Claire," he told the last group they hadn't chatted with. Again she observed Nick switch to senior partner, assured, in charge and in control, apparently not worried or scared at all.

The names came too fast for her again, but she'd learn them all. When times were better. When things were safe. Nick was right that they dared not cancel this tonight, or the Ames-spies of the world would smell a rat. Actually, she was starting to agree with Nick that the rat's name was not Haze or Maggie or Fin Taylor, but Thom Van Cleve.

CHAPTER THIRTY-FOUR

"I don't want you to go into work this morning," Claire told Nick as she got out of bed and wrapped a terry cloth robe around her nightgown and watched him get dressed. No way was she sleeping in today. She had so much to do.

"We have to keep up appearances."

"But isn't today the day?"

"Tonight," he said, sitting on the bed to put his socks on. "Have yourself and Lexi packed."

"Packed more for the equator or the North Pole?"

"WITSEC never tells, but it's cool most places, even getting cooler here."

"But I know you know our destination. Ma—what?"

She sat down on the bed next to him, but then crawled behind him and put her arms around his shoulders and neck, pressing her breasts into his back. He had his tie through his shirt collar in a knot, but he hadn't pulled it tight yet. Again, she thought of Sondra, probably approached from behind by someone she knew and then strangled. She remembered that Heck had said he'd send her a picture of that murder weapon this morning. As soon as Nick was on his way, before packing for her and Lexi, she'd check her phone, or better yet, her laptop, to be sure she could see it enlarged. She'd have to let it all go then, take care of herself and her own before their departure tonight.

Nick reached behind and pushed her back on the bed. Though he was fully dressed—well, but for one sock—he pulled her robe open and slid his hand up along her hip and ribs, ruffling her silk nightgown, nearly up to her chin. He lifted one knee between her legs.

"You are so tempting," he murmured as his narrowed gaze heated her. "Always were. Don't forget you're mine, even if we're apart, even if Jace comes for a while—always, always, mine."

"Nick, I love you!"

"Who needs breakfast with a delicious feast like this?" he said as his hands and mouth descended on her.

Claire was still dazed and dazzled when Nick hurried off a half hour late, but she forced herself to shower and dress before checking her laptop. Yes, an email and an attachment from Heck to download. She sat forward, staring at the screen as the picture opened. She gasped. A strange and lovely murder weapon, but that made sense. The scarf had stripes of stark white and kelly green. Claire had seen that very scarf or one like it among the other Irish items just a short walk from here.

Colleen had told her that Sondra had often bought things at her shop, so maybe Sondra had brought it with her to the yacht and had it tied to her purse or something, despite the fact her dress was red polka-dot. Or what if someone else bought it there—the murderer.

She'd ask Nita to pack for Lexi, let Lexi pick out some of her favorite toys—and that darned stuffed turtle Ames gave her. Though she hadn't told Nick, she'd packed for herself last night and her single suitcase was under the bed. He'd promised they could shop or mail order other things when they arrived at their destination.

But now, she was going to ask Colleen if Sondra had bought this scarf at her shop. And, had anyone else bought one like it? She printed out the picture to have a larger version of it, grabbed her purse and went to tell Nita where she was going.

Claire hurried toward the Irish shop and was a bit out of breath when she got there. Colleen's everlasting roses were still in bright bloom. Some people called them knockout roses, but Claire had never liked the double meaning of that. Though they were sturdy, it sounded like some prizefighter had named them, some man, at least.

When she found the screen door locked, she wasn't surprised. Colleen seemed to be careful about that, even on quiet Goodland. She knocked. "Colleen?" she called in. "It's Claire. I need to ask you something. Are you home?"

This reminded her of the day she'd called for Ada and she hadn't been there, but now she heard footsteps coming. Colleen appeared in a burst of energy.

"I keep the screen door locked in these terrible times with people being harmed," she said. She merely unhooked the door, but Claire saw she still wore her dangling chain of keys that opened her display cases. Colleen wore a peasant skirt, a simple white blouse and sandals.

"So sad about Ada Cypress," Colleen went on. "I know I have too much of the gift of gab, but do you think she was as old as the rumors say?" She opened the door and motioned Claire in, so she stepped past Colleen and looked around the shop. It looked just as she'd seen it before except plates and saucers of the Irish bone china Colleen had showed her last time were stacked on one of the glass cases, evidently waiting to be put away or on display.

"She was older than most but didn't look it," Claire said,

not wanting to get off on that tangent. "She would have been a good advertisement for the waters, not that they need a boost, despite what some think."

"Well, faith and begorra, as my grandfather used to say. You know, I dream sometimes of going big with my Irish wares, but I probably won't. Big isn't always better. So what can I do for you?"

"You remember our talk about Sondra McMillan's death?"

"That case isn't being opened again, is it?" she asked, wide-eyed. "Did they find who did it? One of her male conquests, I'll bet, if not Dylan himself. You might know the man has a good Irish name, the cad. It comes from an Irish word meaning *faithful* or *loyal.* And it came out in the trial he was cheating on his wife. Ha!"

"No, I haven't heard the case is being reopened or about another suspect—yet. But I was wondering if you ever saw a picture of the scarf Sondra was strangled with."

"No. Come in, come all the way in. I not only claim the luck of the Irish, but the hospitality of the Irish, and I believe you and I can be friends, if you will only settle down here on Goodland and not stay on that yacht. But what about the scarf? Why do you mention that? Sit right there," she insisted, motioning to the only chair in the room. "Now tell me."

But Claire didn't sit. She went over to the case with the linen handkerchiefs and silk scarves under the stack of china and bent over them, catching her own reflection in the glass.

"I'm hoping you can recall if Sondra got it here, and, more importantly, if anyone else bought one. I have a printed picture of it," she explained, taking the photo from her purse and unfolding it.

Colleen frowned at the picture. "I do recall," she said and stepped away to reach over to open the back of the display case with a key. "Yes, Sondra bought one, but someone else did too—just like it. Ada. She loved the colors, nature's colors, the colors of the holy waters, she said, and bought one just like that."

"Ada called the spring *holy waters*? That doesn't sound like her. It sounds—well, Catholic."

"Why, yes, she said that. Here, look under here, in this stack. I think near the bottom is one like it. Yes, I remember Ada liked this one too, then bought the other."

Claire started to get that prickly feeling that something was wrong. She couldn't reconcile Ada, who wove Spanish moss into shawls, with a silk scarf. She bent closer as Colleen picked through the slippery pile of scarves, many green and white.

"Let's see, where is that identical one?" Colleen muttered and pulled out the entire pile to spill them on the top of the case.

Claire glanced down to search for the very one herself. Nick might not want to open the case again, especially if a dead woman was the strangler, but she had to have the answer. If he had to go to court unsure who really killed Mark, it might help him to know, at least, who killed poor Sondra.

Quick as lightning, Colleen threw her long key chain over Claire's head and yanked it tight around her neck.

CHAPTER THIRTY-FIVE

Claire fought for her life. Shock. Pain. Fear. Blackness closing in, but all clear now. Colleen killed Sondra. Killed Mark too. No time now. Can't breathe, no air.

Her first impulse was to twist to face Colleen to get some slack. The metal key chain burned and cut into her neck. Dizzy. Blackout soon.

She kicked backward at her, hit only air. Going down. Going to die. Lexi! Nick!

She grabbed the only weapon she could see, the top dinner plate, and smashed it on the display case. Glass shattered. Broken plate. Gasping for air, she swung it behind her and hit something. Cut something. Warm blood spurted.

"Nooooo!" Colleen screamed.

Claire shoved the plate back again. Hit nothing, but the chain loosened just a bit. She jammed her right index finger in but that felt cut too. She sucked in a ragged breath and turned to hit out at the woman. The broken plate must have cut her. Blood was pulsing from her inner wrist. The chain loosened around Claire's neck as Colleen tried to stem the blood with her other hand.

Dizzy, horrified, Claire kicked at her, raked her fingernails at Colleen's distorted face. They both went to their knees, fell to the floor. Yanking the key chain from the woman's hands, Claire gasped for air, panting like a dog. Dizzy. Very dizzy. The seawater had turned red. Was she drowning in it and couldn't breathe?

Holding her bleeding wrist, Colleen tried to crawl away on the floor.

"It's not my fault," she screamed. "Mark only used me to get things on Fin. He was going back to Sondra! Didn't mean to hurt him, but he said he knew I'd killed her, followed her onto the yacht and…ah! Had to shoot Mark. Too much blood!"

Claire shook her head, trying to clear it. Still gasping for air, ignoring the fiery ring of pain around her neck, she scrambled for her purse and her phone. Nick had said be careful with phone calls, no calls.

But she had to—had to get help for herself and this murderer she had liked, had trusted. How had she been so stupid, let Nick down? She'd felt a bond with Colleen.

She dialed 9-1-1. Her voice wouldn't work at first, a mere croak. She tried again, whispered for an emergency squad and the sheriff. And then, despite his warning, she called Nick.

The Marco Island EMS came first, screaming their sirens onto quiet Goodland. The medics bandaged the now unconscious Colleen before she could bleed out. They started an IV right away, then carried her out on a stretcher. The second group of medics cleaned, salved and bandaged Claire's neck, bruised and bleeding, like a red necklace, one of them said, turning black-and-blue. They had her on a stretcher too, near where she'd fallen. They told her not to move, that her husband had just arrived and he'd said not to take her to the hospital.

He didn't tell them why, but she knew. They might want to keep her there for observation and that would ruin their escape. She'd be a sitting duck for Van Cleve or Jesse Winslow to pay a visit to her in a public place, and get her for ruining Ames's master plan. Colleen would go to trial now, not Haze, and the public forum to praise and promote Ames's big investment in Youth water was ruined.

Nick rushed in, kneeled by her side and held her hand. She could hardly talk. Her neck and throat still hurt, but she whispered to him, "I'm so sorry. Thought I knew her. Could trust her."

"Shh, it's all right."

"It isn't. I had to use the cell phone to call you."

"I'll take care of things, of you. Just rest, sweetheart. Thank God you're alive. I'll be right back."

She heard his voice outside. He was saying to someone, "No, I told you I'll have a doctor who's a friend of mine come to the ship, so I'll take her with me. Has Mrs. Taylor's husband been notified?"

"He's out with his fishing boat somewhere, but we'll get him soon," a voice she couldn't quite place said. "He's got a ship-to-shore aboard but isn't answering."

Oh, she thought. Sheriff Scott. Sheriff Scott had arrived. He'd want to talk to her, and talking hurt. But it hurt more that the murderer was Colleen.

Nick's voice came again, then yet another one she didn't know. Despite his comforting words, she hoped she hadn't ruined their escape tonight at least. The sheriff would want a statement, tell her not to leave, that she'd have to testify against Colleen.

And how long would it take for Van Cleve or Ames himself to find out there would be no show trial to boost the Youth water products and to humble and control Nick to do his bidding? Would Nick's life be on the line then too?

He came back, kneeling on the bloody floor in his suit and held her hand again. He leaned close over her.

"I'd say 'good job,'" he told her. "You solved Mark's murder and Sondra's too. But we're going to have to change your hands-on technique, if we want to see our first anniversary, sweetheart."

"Don't joke. I just liked Colleen too much. I needed to stay more suspicious of her," she said, coughing. Not only was her voice raw, but she hurt all over. "Now that there won't be the court trial Ames wants, you're in more trouble too."

"So I'll disappear with you and stay there, until the feds find him."

"But the sheriff will make you—us—stay."

"I called Rod Patterson. He just arrived. I think he'll make the sheriff see things our way—that is, the FBI's way. I'm hoping we can be out of here shortly after I can get you home, before word reaches Ames. Wherever he is, I think he's the one calling the shots. Now, I've promised the sheriff he'll receive your signed statement of Colleen's attack on you and her confession, so we'll take care of that and leave it for him. Patterson knows where Van Cleve is right now—in Miami. But I have to get you up and going. Do you think you can walk to my car outside?"

"Just dizzy and exhausted. Nick, I'm fine to go wherever we're going, just as long as we're all together."

"Jace will have a plane at the airport after dark. Bronco will take us there in his trailer. All systems go to Key West, where we'll board another plane for the longer flight. Key West is just to throw off anyone tailing us since it's the gateway to points south."

"But we're going north?"

He nodded. "I'll tell everyone when we're in the air. Jace doesn't even know our destination yet, only the mileage. I'm going to help you get up. If you want me to carry you, I can. We have a long way to go."

★ ★ ★

The next hours passed in a blur. Claire dictated her statement for the sheriff to Nick, though it was still painful to talk. She signed it, and he had Bronco go out to give it to the deputy waiting in his car. Claire wore her only turtleneck top to hide the black-and-blue circle around her neck so Lexi wouldn't see it. As soon as it was dark, Bronco with a backpack, and Nita with her small suitcase met them in the lounge. Nick had told Bronco and Nita this was dangerous, but they were loyal—and, obviously, so happy to be together.

Claire hated waiting in the lounge, for she could envision how Colleen strangled the unsuspecting Sondra here, then planned to bide her time until she could kill Mark too. It was possible Colleen had given Sondra the idea of blackmailing or conning Dylan just to frame him as the murderer. It had come out in his trial that the ship's crew had been given the day off, so, somehow, perhaps Colleen had known that.

In a way, Claire was glad they were leaving this lovely yacht. She still didn't like Dylan Carnahan, though he'd been helpful and generous. She prayed other people in the vast unknown out there would be too.

Nita had dressed Lexi warmly. A Barbie doll's head protruded from her bright pink Cinderella backpack, and she carried her stuffed turtle from Grand Cayman. It always reminded Claire of Clayton Ames.

"Is your headache better, Mommy?" she asked. "I'm glad I finally get to go in a plane Daddy is flying. But can we see out the windows if it's dark?"

Nick, hefting two suitcases for the three of them, told her, "When we get to our surprise vacation, it will be light, and you will like it a lot. In the winter there is snow and sled rides and in the summer lots of horses."

"This isn't really a trip to Disney World where they have the pretend sled rides, is it?" Lexi asked.

Nick chuckled, but Claire cried. She could not shake the weight of her fear. Wiping her eyes quickly so no one would see, she turned around to look behind her. The trauma of Colleen throwing that chain over her head haunted her, especially here.

She saw Nick adjust his belt through his shirt and jacket. He had all of their new IDs, credit cards and money strapped around his waist under his clothes in a sort of pouch. In another pack hung around his neck, but hidden by his zipped-up jacket, he had a pistol and ammunition. Another WITSEC agent would meet them at their destination. Claire had even more money in a smaller pouch strapped around her waist. The quickness and amount of detail involved in all this by the FBI had driven home the fact that Ames was definitely a wanted man, more dangerous to the entire country than they could have imagined.

Instead of marching down the gangway and off the dock, even in the dark, they went down the ladder on the yacht's starboard side in two groups and took the dinghy that had replaced the one ruined when the WaveRunner swamped them. Like refugees fleeing a murderous regime, they gathered again onshore in the parking lot and hurried to Bronco's Airstream trailer. Huddled inside, they sat down, here and there, as he drove them away.

"This is like a game," Lexi said. "Isn't it, Mommy?"

"Yes, sweetheart. More or less."

"I guess it might be like hide-and-seek."

In the dim single light inside the trailer, Claire's gaze slammed into Nick's. Hide-and-seek, indeed. She blinked back tears again. Nick reached for her and they held hands behind Lexi's back as the child sat on Bronco's bed between them.

A half hour later, after Nick had nearly hurt his own neck looking out the back window to see if they were being followed, they turned off Airport Pulling Road toward the Naples Municipal Airport. On its southern border, as a jet roared skyward overhead, Bronco pulled into a trailer court called Rock Creek. He parked the Airstream in the spot he'd rented for the winter, and they piled out with their baggage. Heck was waiting for them there with a tall backpack on. He hugged Nita and nodded stiffly at Bronco. But their tension over Nita was nothing compared to everything else.

"Clothes and my online gear in this pack," Heck said to Nick. "Let's go. I know where the plane's waiting, just a short hike to that first hangar."

"If you can take one suitcase and Bronco the other," Nick told him, "I'll carry Lexi and help Claire."

"Because," Lexi put in, "she has a headache."

In a line, they straggled onto the airport grounds and headed for the first shadowy hangar. Nick had explained that Jace had thought it better that they get on board the first of the two planes out of sight of the small terminal building.

Inside the hangar, Jace was waiting, pacing. Lexi ran to him for a hug, but he quickly passed her to Nick. "Claire," Jace said with a nod. She wondered if he knew that she'd almost been killed, and that they might not be under Ames's protection anymore. Nick hustled her and Lexi up the steps of the jet and told them, "Be right back. I need to talk to Jace."

Claire strapped Lexi in as the others stowed their gear. She saw Heck would sit up front, Bronco and Nita behind them. Bronco had his arm around Nita. There were empty seats, because this plane that she'd seen was called a Hawker H25 seated ten. But the last row of seats had been taken out and now held their baggage and gear. Obviously, Jace had to take whatever plane he could get without drawing attention. And to think they would leave this plane in Key West and take yet another.

Nick came back to them as Jace entered, closed and sealed

the door, then went into the lighted cockpit to continue going through his check off list. She'd seen him walking around the airplane outside, looking it over. He'd always prided himself on safety, and there were even more reasons for that right now.

His hand on the armrests of her seat, Nick leaned close and said, "There's a seat for a copilot, so I'm going up there with him for now."

"But I wanted to see him fly us," Lexi said. "He said one time I could."

"Not now. You stay with Mommy," Nick said. "Maybe when we take the next plane and know we're safe."

"Aren't we safe now?" the child asked.

"Of course, we are," he told them, and bent to kiss Lexi's cheek, then Claire's.

Claire held Lexi's hand as the plane taxied out of the hangar onto the runway and roared off into the darkness.

CHAPTER THIRTY-SIX

Nick never thought he'd be in this situation. Leaving the business he'd built, his property, though Patterson had his directions for what to say, whom to put in charge and what to cover. But here he was, married with a four-year-old child and depending on his wife's ex, literally trusting him with the lives of people he cared deeply about. But Ames had to be stopped at any cost, and if he needed the FBI and WITSEC to help with that, so be it.

Nor did he like flying at night, but they'd figured it was their best bet. He'd flown into Key West before on business. In the daylight, the water was gin clear, and he could usually see every snorkeling reef in the area. Tonight, there was utter blackness over the Gulf of Mexico below and then a spattering of ground lights, but the stars seemed to guide them—and the array of instruments that lit Jace's stoic profile.

Jace spoke, jolting Nick's thoughts. "Key West is the only airport I've been to where the tower controllers demand that you repeat every instruction verbatim or they restate their instructions again, so get ready for some chatter."

"Fine by me. I don't mind everyone being sure."

"It would be nice if we were."

"Yeah."

"And don't panic when it's a bumpy landing because the Key West runway's in bad shape. I didn't tell you, but Rod Patterson arranged for the plane we'll be flying next. He pulled some strings for us just like he did to get Claire out of Florida without having to stay to testify against Colleen Taylor, so I want to take good care of that plane."

"Glad we have Patterson on our side. And thanks, Jace. I appreciate your expertise and kindness too."

They were soon on the ground, and Nick herded everyone into the terminal to use the bathrooms before their longer flight. Jace rushed in to hit the john last while Bronco stood guard over the plane, which was off to the side of the major runway beside a dark field.

The Pilatus PC-12, as Jace called it, was silver with long blue stripes, and seated up to nine passengers. Nick figured he'd sit with Jace for a while on this leg of the journey too, at least until they were over land. Just in case they were being tracked by radar, they were going to make a southwest swing out over the Gulf as if they were heading to South America. Then they would turn due north. South shores had been his home and South Shores his attempt to help others, but it was north shores ahead for now.

Jace thought the takeoff was smooth, considering the runway. He kept a good eye on his computer screens and readouts. Ironic, how many times he'd sat in a cockpit, flying precious human cargo, wishing he was in the pilot's seat and now he was. He'd missed Claire and Lexi on those long, transpacific flights. Now he had them with him but they really weren't his anymore, thanks or no thanks to this man beside him. Here Jace had thought he'd be able to visit his girls outside

Florida without Nick around, but Nick was not only going but was staying too.

"I promised everyone I'd tell them our destination," Nick said, unfastening his seat belt. He'd just explained it to Jace. "Before Lexi falls asleep, be right back. You're going to have to give her a daylight flight some other time. But on our destination island, you won't be able to fly or that might help someone to trace you and us. At least you can put this plane down on a small airstrip on the mainland, and we'll take a ferry over since the water's not frozen yet. Rod said in the winter, some just drive snowmobiles back and forth across the frozen Lake Huron to the island."

Jace squinted at a readout that registered fuel in the tanks and fuel pressure. "Yeah, sure, go ahead, tell them where we're headed. You know, I keep picturing how furious Kilcorse-Ames will be when he figures out you and I are working together on this, when he was banking on just the opposite and that we would only work for him."

"Okay, everybody, here's the word on our final destination," Nick told them and clapped his hands, as if he needed to have their full attention. He'd left the cockpit door open so Jace could hear too, since he only knew their destination but not about the area.

"We're going to be living in a beautiful, old home that overlooks Lake Huron on an island called Mackinac Island in northern Michigan," Nick announced. "We'll have different names there, which I'll explain later."

Lexi piped up. "I still want to be Lexi Britten. Do I have to be Lexi Markwood now?"

"Just listen, honey, okay? We'll land at a county airport in a city called Cheboygan, Michigan, and take a bus, then a ferry—that's a big boat, Lexi—to get to our new house. It will be beautiful living there, but the winter will be cold. When spring comes, lots of people come to visit—"

"Mommy, can Aunt Darcy and Jilly come?" he heard Lexi whisper.

"And Lexi will love the carriage rides," Nick plunged on. "We aren't sure how long we will be there…"

"Nick!" Jace called from the cockpit. "Can you come here a sec? Now!"

Nick went back in.

"Close the door."

"What? Not another plane follow—"

"The fuel pressure's dropping bad."

"Which means what?" Nick asked, sitting back in the co-pilot seat. They seemed to be flying steady, but his insides lurched.

"That there's a problem. I checked the damn thing, the fuel supply line and its fitting before I went into the terminal. But I'm reading fuel starvation. Can't get fuel from the other tanks either."

"We need to turn back? Get it fixed?"

"We're too far out. I'm hoping it's an erroneous readout, but listen to me. If the fuel line is loose, all fuel supply to the turbine will be lost and the engine will shut down."

"What the hell did—"

"Listen to me. I can feather the prop and set up a glide to delay the descent, but if this was sabotage, and the engine quits, we'll descend at, ah—" he said, looking at his altimeter screen, "about seven hundred feet per minute. That gives us about fourteen minutes before we hit dark water and that's hard to gauge. It can be worse than a hard, bumpy runway, and I'll do it with the gear up. But I'll see the waves only a few seconds before we ditch. Damn, there it goes."

"The engine? That can't be. We were so careful not to be followed to Key West. Can't you restart it?"

"Not without a fuel flow. I'll radio Miami air traffic control. They're tracking planes and can hopefully find us at least by morning, but we're actually closer to Cuba. I just hope and pray someone else isn't tracking us and finds us first."

"I can't believe this—and yet I can."

"Go back where we stowed the baggage. There are two orange life rafts aft, behind the last seats. Be sure no one pulls the rip cord for those until we're out the door, though they should inflate their life vests inside. Nick, be certain everyone has a life vest. You do one raft, get your two men on the other. No baggage. You and I guard Claire and Lexi once we're out..."

Nick wanted to scream that they were already out: out of time, out of solutions, out of courage, out of their minds. He tried to concentrate as Jace rattled off other directions, about opening the door, getting out into the rafts if water poured in—when water poured in. Nick's fear for the others, let alone himself, screamed so loud he had to fight to listen to Jace, to remember everything he said.

He could tell they were already descending, though Jace was keeping the plane level and the nose slightly up. He went back out into the cabin. He blinked back tears when Claire smiled at him and Lexi yawned with her head trustingly on her mother's shoulder.

"Now listen to me, everyone," he announced in as steady and stern a voice as he could muster. "We are having a problem with the engine."

Bronco said, "I don't even hear it no more."

Nick ignored that. "We are going to make a water landing. We have rafts, and Jace is going to declare an emergency with Miami air traffic control. They will track us and help us, at least when daylight comes."

Nita gave a little scream and started crying. Bronco put his arm around her, then said, "I'll help, Nick. Just show me what to do." Heck looked like he was going to throw up. And

Claire? What a woman. She twisted her neck to look up at him and nodded, though he knew it pained her every time she moved. Why was he thinking of such trivia now when they all might die? But if this wasn't chance, and Ames was somehow behind it, he had to live, not only to save Lexi and Claire, but to finally stop that damn bastard.

Claire was saying, "Lexi, get your coat back on, then your life vest. Mommy will help you. We are going to take a boat ride for a while, and everything will be all right."

The three men scrambled to get the two uninflated life rafts and drag them near the door. Nick started repeating what Jace yelled out from the cockpit, so he sounded like an echo, "We are all going out the front door into the rafts once they are inflated right next to the plane in the water. The sea is not too rough tonight. I will open the door when Jace gives the okay. If that door jams, Bronco will open the back baggage door. Some water will get in, even though Jace will put the plane down carefully. Do not be afraid if water comes into the plane."

"But won't it sink?" Nita asked. She looked on the edge of hysteria. "I can feel we're going down."

Jace went silent, so Nick was on his own now. "Didn't you all see those pictures of that plane with lots more people than us that landed on the Hudson River in New York?" Nick said, pulling that one out of his hat. "We're going to be all right and we're going to lock our rafts together and just float until someone comes to help us."

He went back to the cockpit door. "Jace, can I do something?"

"Get back in your seat and strap in. Everyone's head down on their knees and braced with their hands. When I say so, we go!"

Claire was terrified, but she didn't let on. For Lexi's sake. To help Nick. So that Nita would stop crying. This could not be happening. Not with all they'd been through and their well-laid plans. Ames had to be behind this.

Nick was in a seat behind them, calmly promising Lexi he'd take her on horse rides. An eternity seemed to tick by.

"I see the water!" Jace shouted from the cockpit. "Brace! Brace!"

Claire braced with one hand and put the other on Lexi's head. The plane seemed to do a big belly flop, rise again, go down. They could hear and feel the smack of water. They coasted, rocked. Jace had them skidding across the waves.

When they came to a rocking stop, Jace shouted "Go! Door, rafts, go!"

Claire unbuckled Lexi, and Nick appeared from behind to pick her up. Despite orders of no baggage, Claire slung her purse over her arm. Her meds...she'd need her meds. Bronco and Heck handled the front side door as Jace stumbled out of the cockpit, trying to keep his balance. They were starting to list. Jace popped the door open before anyone else could get to it. Cold air smacked them. Water sloshed in but only ankle deep.

Nita screamed. The rafts went out, one, the next, one held by a cord to Heck's wrist, one to Bronco's. They hissed as Jace inflated them. Jace shouted, "Nick, get into this raft, and I'll pass Lexi and Claire down. You three get ready for the second one!"

"No, I'm not letting go of Mommy!"

Jace pulled her away from Claire and, on his belly in the door of the plane, getting sopping wet, handed the screaming child to Nick who had dropped into one raft. Jace pulled Claire to the door of the plane. The wind seemed strong, and the plane tilted even more. Salt spray spewed in her face. With his arm tight around her, he said in her ear, "Sorry this went bad. Whatever happens, I still love my girls."

Salt water stung her eyes, or tears, as he handed her down

to Nick as if she was another child. She huddled in the bottom of the raft, wrapped around Lexi who clung so hard she hurt her neck.

Nick held to the wing of the plane until the others dropped into the second raft. The plane was listing toward them now. Would it suck them all under? Claire wished he'd let go of the plane, get them away from the huge, sinking mass, but they had to wait for Jace. Jace, who she knew she loved too, always would.

"Shove off, Nick!" Jace shouted as he helped Heck and Bronco into the other raft last. "Get away now! I'll walk the wing to get in. Go!"

Nick shoved them away with his hands, then one foot. No paddle but Nick paddled with his arm over the side of the raft, under the wing.

Jace, holding some sort of emergency pack, started walking the wing. The plane lurched and he skidded off into the waves, but surfaced, spitting water. Claire could tell Nick didn't know what to do: get them away or go back for Jace.

"I'll help you paddle!" she screamed. Keeping Lexi between her ankles, she leaned over the bubble of the raft's edge and dipped her hand in the water, again, again. Nick did too until he could haul the sopping, heavy man over the side into the raft. The box of whatever he had was tied to his wrist, so they pulled that over too.

Spitting water, Jace said, "Yell at them to get away. It's going down. This five-million-dollar FBI plane is going down."

Nick and Claire paddled, then Jace too. Heck and Bronco moved their raft clear of the plane. They were nearly thirty feet away when the plane tilted again, gave a huge almost human gasp and went under into the darkness.

It was so silent then, but for the wind and water. Bronco and Heck paddled their raft close and they tied them together.

Nita had stopped crying. Claire, leaning against Nick, held the trembling Lexi. At least they were all alive, Claire thought. And, though it took all this, they were together. She prayed the Coast Guard or someone would find them as soon as daylight came. It was so very dark, as dark as one of her narcoleptic nightmares, a black night of the soul.

"Jace," she said, desperate to keep spirits up, "where are we? Could we just drift into the Florida coast?"

"We're closer to Cuba, and with this wind direction..."

"Oh." She held Lexi closer. Nick tightened his arm around her.

Jace said, "I'm sorry, Claire. Everyone. I checked things out, so someone tampered with the plane after that, unless it was screwed up even earlier."

"In the end, you saved us," she told him. Clinging to Lexi, she settled closer to keep Nick warm, since he'd taken off his dry jacket to put over Jace's shaking shoulders. She raised her voice so everyone could hear, however much it hurt her throat.

"Since we're all together," she promised, "we are absolutely going to be all right!"

★ ★ ★ ★ ★

AUTHOR'S NOTE

So ends book two of the SOUTH SHORES series, but the story of Claire, Nick and Jace does not end here. I hope you will look for book #3, *FALLING DARKNESS*, in May.

It has been great fun to use Naples, Florida, as a story setting since my husband and I lived there for thirty winters as snowbirds. I figure that adds up to over nine years, but only several months and weeks at one time. We have visited the locations I use in this novel, including Goodland, which is a place and story unto itself.

In March of 1997, we visited a fascinating person, Elhanon Combs, who owned the then Mar-Good Resort on Goodland and claimed that the cistern water under his property was Ponce de León's actual fountain of youth, rather than the one claimed by St. Augustine, Florida, or other locations. He told us then (and told the local newspaper, *The Islander*, in a January 1997 interview) "I think old Ponce de León found the fountain of youth here… This tree [a rubber tree that kept rejuvenating itself] is living proof." He showed us the underground water source. When I had the idea for this book and we revisited the site eighteen years later, Elhanon had died and the Mar-Good property had become a small park, but I remembered his claims.

As we drove around Goodland in March, 2015, and I took photos for research and my author Facebook page, I made plans for this novel, tying the Goodland fountain of youth to the youth cosmetic industry. People today spend billions worldwide, trying to stay young in various ways.

I love eccentric, historic Florida, small-town ambience and unique settings, so it was fun to write this novel. We have also been to Grand Cayman twice, so revisiting that location was great author fodder too.

Special thanks to Florida pilot and friend, John Hawkins, for his advice on flying into Key West and beyond and on private planes in general. Any mistakes are mine, not his. Thanks to Lee Ann Parsons for the information on the burrowing owls. Of course, special appreciation to my travel companion, proofreader and business manager, my husband, Don. And as ever to my editors, Nicole Brebner and Emily Ohanjanians, and agent, Annelise Robey. "Onward and upward!"

I close with a quote that was at first attributed to the Italian actress Sophia Loren, which she recited on her eightieth birthday in 2014. However, I found this was taken from *Hope Notes: 52 Meditations to Nudge Your World (2004)* by Wayne Willis, "There is a fountain of youth: It is your mind, your talents, the creativity you bring to your life and the lives of the people you love. When you learn to tap this source, you will have truly defeated age."

If you liked DROWNING TIDES, make sure you read the first book in the SOUTH SHORES *series, CHASING SHADOWS!*

And don't miss the next book, FALLING DARKNESS, coming soon from MIRA Books!
Turn the page for a sneak peek…

2014

After their airplane skidded over the water and sank, their two life rafts tied together seemed so small in the vast, dark sea. Claire held her four-year-old daughter Lexi close to keep her warm and calm, though she was neither of those things herself. The child had gone silent, no more screams or sobs. Claire's husband Nick's arm around them felt like a band of iron, a moving one, since he too was shaking from the cold and shock.

Her ex-husband, Jace—Lexi's father—was the fourth person in their raft. He'd been the pilot of the borrowed private plane that had nearly plunged all seven of them beneath the surface to drown. So far, only Lexi's nanny, Nita, in the next raft had been seasick, though they were all sick at heart and scared to death. Nita was praying aloud and, no doubt, the others were doing so silently.

"Where are we, really?" Lexi asked. "Near a beach at home?"

Her teeth chattering, Claire told her, "Not quite, but off the coast of Florida." She didn't add they were in the wide Straits of Florida but much closer to dangerous, forbidden Cuba.

The sea, so rough at first that their little rubber islands had slid from trough to trough, seemed to be calming now. Breaks in the clouds revealed a scattering of stars that looked like they were dancing and a crooked sliver of moon like a sharp, tilted smile.

"Nobody's gonna find us till mornin'," Bronco, their family bodyguard, spoke up from the other raft. The big, bold man was trying to be strong, but his voice quavered too.

Nita, who had been moaning, began to cry again, though she was sheltered in the other raft between her cousin Hector, called Heck, Nick's tech genius, and Bronco, who had his arms around her.

Heck said, "Yeah, well, we're valuable to the FBI, so they'll have their net out for us. Just hope someone else doesn't, and they tampered with the plane. You-know-who has a long arm—and an army of spies."

"That can't be," Nick said. "Before we took off, Jace checked the plane, and Bronco guarded it. It had to be a malfunction, not sabotage."

Bronco said, "But you know, boss, the plane was parked by that dark Key West field. I didn't tell you, but some guy came up and asked me how much it cost. Took my eyes off the plane to get rid of him, head him back to the terminal."

"I did all the checkups," Jace told them, "but that was before I hit the john when all of you were still in the terminal. I still can't believe it. And, since the FBI arranged for that plane, who knows if we can trust them? Maybe you-know-who got to them too, or at least to that contact guy Patterson. I don't trust anyone anymore—except you, Lexi," he added and rubbed the child's back.

"And you trust Mommy and Nick too!" she insisted.

"Listen up, all of you." Nick took over the conversation again, like them raising his voice to be heard over the wind and waves. "So far our adversary's dealt in torment, not total annihilation."

Lexi stirred against Claire. "What's nilation?"

"Don't worry about that, or anything," Claire whispered

to her. Nick was evidently using big words so Lexi wouldn't catch on to the deadly mess they were in whether they were rescued from the water or were on shore.

They had fled Florida with the help of the Federal Witness Protection Program, WITSEC, to stay safe until the US government could locate and extradite Nick's nemesis, a powerful international businessman with a long reach. The FBI wanted their hands on Clayton Ames as badly as Nick did, but Ames made a habit of living abroad and moving around. When it came to catching, extraditing and prosecuting the man who was now among the US government's most wanted, Claire knew Nick wished he was a vigilante or hit man instead of a criminal lawyer who could only accuse and testify.

"Okay, enough about all that for now," Nick said. "Whoever rescues us, the new identification papers I have for all of us in this waterproof pouch are what we will have to go by. Lexi, we are going to have new, pretend names for a while, but it's a secret only the seven of us can share. I was telling you on the plane that we are going to live in a new place for a while, and we need to learn these names and the story of where we came from."

"Is it like a game?"

"Yes, but a very serious, important game."

"Like life," Jace muttered. Then he said louder, "That box I had strapped to me has some drinking water, some medical supplies and a few rations. *Semper paratus, semper fi.* Listen up, everybody. You're with an ex-navy pilot who has never crashed before but has training for it. We're going to be rescued, but meanwhile, we need to keep our heads up and work together. Like Claire said when we first made it into the rafts, we'll be okay."

Tears stung Claire's eyes and not just from the saltwater spray. The only two men she'd ever loved were with her: Jace, her ex, who had claimed he still loved her when he'd helped her out of the sinking plane and into the raft; and Nick, who had taken her life and love by storm. They had been forced by his nemesis Clayton Ames to marry, but she had come to not only desire but love Nick. Thank God, the three of them were getting along in this desperate flight. But to live all together as the WITSEC program had planned? That scared her almost as much as this shifting, sliding, endless sea.

As dawn broke, raising their hopes they would be spotted, Jace passed around the water canteen again so they could each take a drink as a chaser after a tasteless biscuit. Nick saw that Jace had put the dry jacket he had loaned him around Lexi. Jace looked like a Viking at sea, ruddy and blond compared to Nick's dark hair dusted with silver.

The two men's gazes met. They'd been at loggerheads over Claire, so Nick hoped they could work together to be rescued. But their hideout plans for that had been for northern Michigan, not on a rubber raft in the middle of the Straits of Florida.

Nick looked away and hit his fist hard on his knee. He'd left his prosperous Naples, Florida law firm of Markwood, Benton and Chase in the hands of the other partners. He'd used the cover story he was leaving immediately for Belgium to assist an important government figure with legal advice. He'd told them he was taking his family and a small support staff with him and asked them to cover his cases.

True, they were used to his going off to work on his private South Shores project, for which he advised and sometime defended people shattered by suicides that could be murders. But his lies haunted him, since he wasn't allowed to trust anyone but this group with the knowledge of his part in the Witness Protection Program, which was run under the aegis of the FBI.

Hell, he thought, forget the desertion of his friends and his law firm being the worst that could happen. Not only had their plane crashed, but he'd just seen a fin—more than one—slice through a wave near them. Sharks! Who knew how long they'd been so close in the dark. And Jace had fallen into the water getting them off the plane.

A shark—that was the way he'd always thought of the man he was certain had not only ruined his father financially, but murdered him too and made it look like a suicide. Clayton Ames, a deadly, devouring shark.

"Jace!" Nick hissed, and the man's eyes flew open.

What? Jace mouthed. Nick pointed at the circling fins and read Jace's lips as he cursed silently. There were at least three sharks near them.

Nick noted Heck had seen them too. His right-hand man had mentioned these waters were full of them, a threat to Cubans fleeing the island, though it hadn't stopped the influx to the States. The refugees included Heck's and Nita's Cuban parents years ago, looking for a better life for their families. It was what he wanted for his new family. Maybe he should have stuck it out in Naples, though Ames knew they were all there. He had to be stopped, and the US government's help was the best way.

"Time for the name game," Jace whispered. "Let's not focus on new dangers."

"Hard not to," Claire put in. So she'd seen them too.

Nick wondered how she had stayed so calm. Despite her disease of narcolepsy, the woman had guts and stamina. He'd seen that up close and personal in the two murder/suicide cases they'd worked together. He also saw now that, though her eyes were wide on the fins, she quickly shifted Lexi lower between her spread legs rather than on her lap so that the girl could not see the sharks. Now if only everyone else would keep their mouths shut…

"Let's not talk at all about things we see here," Claire called out, "but instead learn our new names and identities. That way, when we get ashore, we can just get some help before we all head to Michigan—to Mackinac Island, with all the horses, remember, Lexi?"

"I'm going to find one I like to ride."

"Right," Nick said, opening the seal on the plastic pouch he wore under his shirt like a wide belt. He'd kept their newly created passports, credit cards and quite a lot of cash in mostly big bills dry. He pulled out what he'd thought of as his cheat sheet with the names he and Rob Patterson, their FBI contact, had come up with for everyone.

"Okay," he said, giving his stepdaughter a one-armed hug, "we will start with Lexi. Our family's new last name—you, Lexi, your mom and me—is Randal. Oh, yeah, Jace's too." He spelled Randal and let her repeat it. He tried to ignore Jace's scowl. As supportive as he was being, since he was on Ames's hit list too, Nick knew Jace was thoroughly teed off that he had to act the part of Nick's brother and Lexi's uncle.

"And your first name, Miss Randal," Nick went on to Lexi, "is Megan, but you can be called Meggie if you want. It's up to you."

For a moment he figured she was going to say she wanted to keep her own name or take her best friend and cousin's name, Jilly, but she said, "Meggie is more like me."

"Good!" he said. "Did everybody hear that? This is Meggie Randal. Her mother's name is Jenna Randal, mine is Jack Randal, and Jace is Seth Randal, my brother and Le—Meggie's uncle."

They all went around and said their new names: Heck was now Roberto, called Berto, Ochoa; Nita was his cousin, Lorena Ochoa; and Bronco Gates was Cody Carson.

Bronco piped up. "Suits me. Nothin' much suits me but glad I'm here to help all you and 'specially Lorena Ochoa here," he said, giving Nita's shoulders a squeeze. "Glad to make your 'quaintance, *Senorita* Lorena."

Heck rolled his eyes and shook his head over that. He knew Bronco had eyes for Nita, and that obviously annoyed him. No, he must be looking at the sharks again, staring off a ways at the horizon.

But was Jace nuts? He was getting to his knees in the raft, rocking it more than the waves did.

"Seth," Nick said. "What?"

"To the south. Is that a boat?" he asked, pointing.

Everyone sat up and craned to look. It was, even though the silhouette was small. It was slow moving but seemed to be coming straight for them.

"We need to make a flag, a banner that shows up against the sea and sky."

"I'm wearing something bright," Nita said. "My skirt." Without a moment's hesitation, she wriggled out of it as Heck twisted around to look at the boat again and Bronco stripped off his jacket to cover her panties and bare legs.

"Everyone sit tight!" Jace ordered. "I'm the only one who stands."

Nick tried to brace Jace's legs as he got up and stood shakily. Using his arm as a flagpole, he waved the bright pink skirt until they were certain the small vessel turned even more their way. Unfortunately, the sharks were still circling, and the ramshackle craft looked like it was coming from the direction of Cuba where it was rumored Ames might be living all cozy with the Castro brothers. So, Nick thought, as desperate as they were, with all the deceit and treachery they'd faced already, would the boat bring friend or foe?